THE TAMMY PIERRE SERIES

Book One: The Lyme Regis Murders

Book Two: The Black Candle Killings

Book Three: The Politician's Wife

THE POLITICIAN'S WIFE

Hare um scare um diddle dum dare um,
The lady knew she'd planned to cheat.
A hare um scare um diddle dum dare um.
But lost her hands and lost her feet,
And then her head, it was far from neat.
With a hare um scare um diddle dum dare um.
The moral of this blood-soaked tale,
Contract to win, though you're bound to fail,
For life is not a holy grail.
So hare um scare um diddle dum dare um.

R.A.

PROLOGUE

THE BODY was that of a woman of indeterminate age. Only partially decomposed, it had lain undiscovered in the undergrowth of the Heath for several days. The clothing was either that of a vagrant, or else the choice of an individual who favoured bohemian dress. Comprising baggy, purple harem pants ill matched with a filthy, once white, balloon-sleeved blouse, the ensemble was already rotting through exposure to the elements.

The pathologist had remarked, that while the removal of the victim's head, hands and feet would render identification problematic, DNA taken from the corpse would no doubt prove conclusive once a missing person had been reported. The pathologist's other observation was that, notwithstanding this being an obvious case of murder, the body showed signs of a sustained attack, post-mortem. It was as though the killer had spent time venting an almost insane rage against the victim, whose slaughter had not been enough in itself to satisfy the lust for, what? Revenge? Perverse sexual gratification? Cause of death had not yet been determined.

*   *   *   *   *

The little man settled wire spectacles on the end of his nose, undid the buttons of his leather jacket for comfort and ease of movement, then peered through the telescopic sights of his semi-automatic, Accuracy International AW50 rifle. Weighing four times that of a typical assault weapon, it's the snipers' choice. Boasting a thousand yards range, firing five rounds every 1.6 seconds and matched with a Dual 50 suppressor, the man, cradling the rifle on the open fanlight of the empty property, experienced an overwhelming urge to engage the trigger to watch his prey blown apart.

Dressed in a grey track suit and white trainers, with an athlete's loping stride she was showing several months' pregnant. He reckoned she must be at least six feet tall, her curly, cropped hair and coffee, cream complexion marking her out as mixed race.

She was making for the small modern block of flats dead ahead of him and would soon be out of view. He had her head in his sights. It gave him a high like nothing else. Just one little squeeze. His heart laboured heavy with regret, like a lead ball in his chest. It was agony. The urge to shoot was almost irresistible. It was irresistible.

As she turned into the block he loosed off a silenced burst. The lightest touch on the trigger. Two seconds, six rounds. They thudded off the front wall of one of the Victorian terraced houses that sidled up to her property. Brick chippings flew off in a random shower. Curtains were disturbed. A pair of curious eyes peering to left and right, seeing nothing retreated from the window.

Dream on, he decided. Unlikely he'd get a chance to use the gun on this assignment. Not impossible, but whatever, there'd be another opportunity in time and another. There always was.

CHAPTER 1 DAY 1

PRESENT DAY

LIKE A BOMB going off, the unexpected backfire of a car rattled the bedroom window, leaving her shocked, the immediate consequence of which was unplanned.

The baby moved inside her, the tiniest stirring. An imagined hand or foot pressing against her belly. Exploring. Enquiring. Of course, it was too early. Her imagination, then. Maybe in another month? But certainly not yet. It troubled her. This renewed feeling of femininity. With her height, her strength and her skills, she could take on any man, and prevail. Had done. Frequently.

But with a soul now growing within her she was aware, perhaps for the first time in her life, of her own comparative vulnerability. That passing car. A jolt. And a revelation. As though she were being reminded, against her will, that she was, after all, a woman. And yet, she pondered, What is it with me? I am female, yet not one of them, unless they fancy me. I identify more easily with men, but wouldn't want to be one of them either. I love Dov, I admit, more than he realises, but I won't marry him.

She'd not felt like this the last time. So confused. That is, the last time she'd been pregnant. For then it had been a time of joy. Joy in the knowledge she was carrying antique dealer Dov's child. Dov, her sometime Israeli boyfriend and martial arts coach upon whom she could always rely for moral support. But then it was also a time of sadness, with the loss of live-in girlfriend and PA, the flame-haired, effervescent Ginny Jones, whom she'd injudiciously chosen over Dov, only to find that he too had moved on.

She was alone now, apart from the burgeoning life she carried. But, after all, she'd lost that earlier baby anyway. To her astonishment, it had left her devastated. Physically ill at the time. Too much strenuous physical activity the doctor had announced, furious with her. Her own pig-headed obstinacy in refusing to admit to any possible failure in her own indestructibility.

She had high levels of testosterone, suffered bouts of agonising endometriosis and an irregular monthly cycle. But, against all odds, she was pregnant again. An unimagined second time. And she wanted this baby. Wanted it more than anything she'd ever wanted in her life. Whosever baby it was.

Because that was her dilemma. She simply didn't know and wasn't sure whether she wished to know if the child she was carrying was her lover, Dov's. Or whether the life inside her was there, care of the leader of a band of Free Syrian Army rebels, a man called Nabil. A man she'd witnessed being blown apart by a assassin's rifle, but not before he'd saved her life. Even now the recollection made her weep. Ginny, her erstwhile business and life-partner, would have been understanding. Dov, appalled. And it was his approval and respect she craved most.

The apartment was quiet as an empty church, the silence only broken by a tap dripping in the bathroom. She couldn't shake off the sense of isolation. Wondered what Dov was doing, reluctantly accepting how much she missed him. Couldn't wait to see him again. The twin rarities of a man who would gladly commit, chasing after a woman who would not.

Of course there'd been others before Dov. Dozens. Maybe more, if she were honest with herself. Restlessly searching for something that was always just out of reach. What was it she craved? Did she even know? Variety?

Excitement? A father to offspring she never realised she'd crave? At least until this second pregnancy had changed everything again. Stupid, stupid, stupid. Too late now for regrets.

But this time, it was a time of fear too. If she miscarried, at thirty-eight years of age, there'd unlikely be another chance. It would have to be now, or not at all. Turning sideways to the full-length mirror on the wall of her bedroom, she examined her reflection critically, and mused inconsequentially, For the first time in my life, I'm developing a bosom. Dov will be pleased. The silly prospect thrilled her more than she'd have cared to admit.

The pregnancy would slow her down, of course, particularly in the latter stages. She'd be confined to deskwork, forensic accounting and business consultations in her office or via Zoom. Strenuous activity was too dicey. The outlook was disheartening. She'd have to get used to being static. Not what she'd signed up to when she opened her detective agency.

But still, the prospect of a baby? She was overwhelmed.

This time all would be well, no doubts. So exciting. She smiled fleetingly as a familiar tightening in her abdomen and stab in the gut were chased by a soporific sense of heaviness, followed by a flush of fluid, and the helpless realisation that despite all her hopes and fears, she was losing this baby too.

Then her landline rang out, a discordant wail splintering the silence, jangling her nerves; but before she could reach it, it stopped.

CHAPTER 2

SIX WEEKS AGO

"YOU USE THIS to kill him, Filipek." He was a neat little man, the sort you'd pass by in crowded streets or mainline stations without a second glance. Brown leather jacket pressed blue jeans, open-neck white shirt. Wire-rim spectacles the only distinguishing feature. That, and perhaps the accent which might have been Czech, or possibly Russian. A youthful, if pale complexion, with short black hair, apparently greying prematurely at the temples. Hard to put an age to the man. But forty? Forty-five?

They were seated opposite each other in a crowded, back-street coffee bar in Soho. The place was mainly bare brickwork and framed photographs of famous authors, journalists and film stars. All typical of the area. Modern jazz in the shape of Thelonious Monk over the speakers mingled with the tumult of conversation, making it difficult to hear anyone talking other than the one you were sitting closest to.

She'd got there earlier while the place was still comparatively empty and bagged a table, restlessly drinking coffee after coffee as she waited for him to arrive. About the same age as the man, she looked nervous, kept primping the side of her cropped blond hair, as though it might make a difference to her appearance, which was the sartorial opposite of his. The coat she wore was a shabby, belted wool blend in navy blue. A Peter Pan collared blouse in red with a white motif peeped out from under the coat which she pulled closer about her neck, despite the enveloping heat in the place.

"It wasn't part of the deal, Nicolai." She sounded nervous, laced her fingers together. It was just a ploy.

"There is no deal, Filipek. There never was. And don't calling me Nicolai," he hissed. "You calling me Nick."

"Why? Do you think calling you Nick is going to help disguise your likely origins? I mean, the accent isn't too hard to recognise. Nick," she added, sounding bolder.

"You don't argue with me. You defy me, you are defy our controllers. And no-one, that is no-one, argue with them. Certainly not some unimportant, working-class shit traitor." His accent grew more pronounced as he became angrier.

"Traitor?" she said, astonished. "Isn't this supposed to be all about the working classes? And it's traitors like me working for the cause that keep you supplied with information. Anyway, I am not killing anyone." She sounded defiant. "I've been providing intel for more than twenty years," she asserted. "I've never been asked to kill anyone. Why now? What's changed?"

He ran his fingers through his hair, increasingly frustrated. "Keeping your voice down," he muttered, looking over his shoulder as though someone might overhear. "Are you mad?"

"This was your choice of venue, Nick. Not mine."

"You do not question instruction receive. Not unless you want to join some of the comrades who choose to stray."

"They were the traitors," she insisted. "Not me. They knew what to expect." She was resolute now, more assertive, wondered how she'd ever got to this place. Recruited twenty-five years ago while at the LSE, it had all been so glamorous at the time. All so relevant.

Her grandparents had come to the UK in the post-war period, seventy years ago, and imbued her mother with the essence of Communism. Her father, who'd met her mother at a Ukrainian social group in South London, was a discreet Communist, but didn't object to his wife giving their daughter a Russian name and a grounding in the philosophy. After that they left their daughter to her own political devices. None of this had initially been picked up by MI5 or MI6. Later the position became more confused.

She, Larissa Filipek, and others in the LSE Socialist Society, all quietly committed Marxists, were going to make a utopian society, one where there was total equality. All planning to be for the workers, for which read, State controlled, of course. Central planning, without the need or acceptance of private enterprise.

The leader of the Soc-Soc was tall and debonair, he made it all sound like an adventure, a move towards that visionary dream. He insisted she leave the Socialist Society and start to make overtures to the Conservative Society. She'd claim she'd changed her views. Had come home at last. Grown up. She survived the opprobrium of her deserted comrades and made new friends. Friends who had no idea her views on Marxism had remained entirely unaltered.

At first it was minor things she passed along. Reports on members of the Conservative Society who might themselves be fodder one day for the security services, MI5 and MI6. She formed relationships, had affairs, in some cases with men she found revolting. But then, it was all in a good cause, her recruiter told her. The cause. It had helped she was bright. Very bright, gaining a First in Politics and Economics. It was then easy to get a job in the Ministry of Defence. Her credentials, including her brief membership of the Soc-Soc, easily justified as youthful folly.

Much later, she got to learn of the sordidness of traitors like Burgess and Maclean, of Anthony Blunt, the Queen Mother's personal friend, and worst of all, the activities of that most suave of English spies, Kim Philby. He, a respected member of the Establishment who was responsible for the deaths of thousands, before defecting to Russia where he was faced with the traumas of living a champagne lifestyle in his own chosen utopia.

But by then it was too late for her to get out. And anyway, she still wanted her vision of the Marxist dream. And so she didn't get out. She stayed on, gaining promotion and with that, trust, so that she was delivered of ever more classified information. But killing wasn't part of her job description, she insisted to Nick. And she wasn't about to add it to her CV, any more than was absolutely necessary. She turned away from Nick, irritated.

He pushed a paperback towards her. "I said, you use this to kill him."

Turning back to Nick, she said, "A paperback?" She was incredulous. It was a novel titled *Ticket to Ride*. It reminded her of an old Beatles number.

"Tape inside page 100 you find Left Luggage ticket for the office in Kings Cross station. Go there with ticket and you will collect an envelope in which you find key to safety deposit box in Access Self Storage. Box 100, from which you extract telescopic umbrella."

"Let me guess," she said, "with ricin in the tip?" She glanced ceilingward as though seeking inspiration. "So, why bother with Left Luggage? Why not just give me the bloody key to Box 100 in the first place?"

"Why do you argue?" He threw up his hands in frustration. "Just do as you are told."

She had a moment of inspiration. "You're new to this, aren't you? That's why all this stupid nonsense. Why did they send you instead of my usual contact? What's happened to Anatoly?"

"Anthony on holiday."

"Anthony, is it? And, holiday? What holiday? This isn't a nine-to-five job."

Then, revelation. "Anatoly slipped up somewhere, didn't he? So now he's been discarded, right? Eliminated. No room for errors in this game. The State demands absolute loyalty but gives none in return. Sorry, I. I won't do it."

"You will do it. So prissy miss. You have do it plenty times before, I think," he muttered. "Now is no different. No tell me you not done it before."

"I'm supposed to provide intel. That's all. I'm not a killer. I agreed to spy, not murder." Let the idiot squirm, she decided. The man was an amateur.

"You will do as you told. Or else we take back your Russian passport. Maybe tell your bourgeois husband. You get pay good money."

"Tell him, if you want," she snarled. "And anyway, I don't do it for the money; which, incidentally is total crap. You couldn't feed a gerbil on it."

"What is gerbil?" he muttered. "You have friend, yes?"

"What do you mean, I have friend, yes?" She frowned, not wanting to guess what was coming next. "Of course I have friends."

"Make things difficult for friends. Maybe eliminate."

The woman, Filipek, grew chill. "You bastard," she mouthed. But he was right, of course. What he didn't know was that killing for her was addictive, though she wasn't about to enlighten him in that respect. In fact, she wanted to break the habit. Trouble was, she was good at it. Really good. Got a high from it like nothing else on earth. Yes, she'd done it before. For the Party. Many times before.

It seemed no-one had told Nick. If any of her lovers knew they'd be horrified. If her husband knew? Well, what if he did know? She couldn't be sure, but she reckoned Oscar wasn't exactly pristine. Late-night calls he took in his study. Conversations abruptly ended when she came into the room.

"Take book, Filipek. Ticket on page 100. Instruction on page 200. Two persons. Will be easy for you." He thought about things for a moment, then sneered, "Is good book to read? *Ticket to Ride?*"

The press next day reported the deaths of two Russian dissident ex-journalists, a married couple, on a street in Hornsey. Poison, thought to be ricin, administered through the tip of an umbrella, the likely weapon.

The only witness, a teenage scooter rider, had mentioned a middle-aged lady with close-cropped blond hair, wearing a belted blue coat, hurrying from the area.

CHAPTER 3 DAY 1

PRESENT DAY

SHE LAY BACK on the bed, her pulse gradually slowing. Calm returning. False alarm. "Dieu merci," she murmured, in a passing nod to her semi-French roots. The baby wasn't about to be aborted after all. The notion that she'd have to disappoint Papa for a second time, averted.

Her father, retired Trinidadian architect Matthew Pierre, a Parkinson's sufferer, would be overjoyed when Tammy, an only child, eventually broke the news of her fresh pregnancy, but that wouldn't be until she was much further along with it. Safer in the knowledge she would likely proceed to term.

Recalling Maman, her vivacious Parisian mother who'd died of breast cancer ten years ago, she envisaged the general advice and support on matters of upbringing that would have been forthcoming from that source. All of it with a tangled excess of love and abandon. Maman would have insisted Tammy give up work in her present state, probably provoking a heated debate. She'd only ever seen Maman cry once; that was when one of Tammy's school classmates, in a fit of spite, had called her 'un cochon brun', a brown pig. Tammy had dealt with the matter in her own way, a firm hand ensuring there'd be no repetition.

Towering over the others in her year, with a tendency to arrogance, she was brought down to earth when Maman revealed her identical twin sister had been still-born. Tamsin means twin, Maman's choice. The revelation disturbed her, accounting for the ever-present sense of something missing in her life.

It had been a happy childhood, the early years in Paris, which she loved. Later, removing to London after the devastation of Maman's untimely death.

Regarded as exotic and unpredictable, Tammy was, like her father, given to introspection, though subject to her mother's occasional bouts of volatility. Everybody's anchor, everybody's rock, Maman would have made a matchless grand-mère. Tammy felt a twist of love at the memory.

A plaintive 'mew' got her attention as Risky, the hitherto unclaimed stray black Siamese she'd found one night struggling on her windowsill, leapt onto the bed and cosied up to her. As she stroked the pet behind the ears and under the chin, the Siamese turned and licked Tammy's palm and fingers, as though seeking out the scars sustained when her mistress had struggled free of the plastic bonds of a multiple murderer, cutting herself savagely in the process.

Rosemary Sharpe, a DCI with whom Tammy had worked on what was described in the press as 'The Black Candle Killings', had once remarked how beautiful Tammy's hands were. Sadly, they were beautiful no longer. The surgeon had said they might heal completely in time. The emphasis here on 'might'. But for now she could hardly bear to look at them. What, she wondered, would Dov make of the jagged red and pink tracks across her palms and the insides of her fingers.

And Ginny Jones? Would she be appalled if she ever got to see the damage? She'd planned to put Ginny out of her mind after the break-up of their relationship. But then there'd been their brief reunion at the time of the Black Candles affair. Ginny had broken off her own current relationship to be with Tammy, an affair Tammy had protested was lunatic. The man involved had all but raped Ginny during her time at university, and Ginny's protests that she'd unwittingly encouraged it, did nothing to convince Tammy.

It was Ginny's earlier ultimatum, effectively, 'Him or me,' referring to Dov, that had Tammy choose Ginny, only to find that Ginny, realising the child Tammy was carrying was Dov's, made the choice for her. Tammy had arrived home excitedly expecting to find her lover waiting for her, only to discover Ginny had departed, leaving her without either lover in her life.

A depressing start to the day, and she'd all but decided to do a line that morning when she was worried she'd lost the baby. A line, plus a panatella, her favoured smoke, together with a generous slug of Bison Grass vodka to compensate her disappointment. Still, none of that now. Nothing to put the pregnancy at risk. A brief moment to be relished. All was well. Then her mobile sang out.

"Tammy Pierre," she announced, before noticing the caller ID showed Detective Chief Superintendent Bob Walker, the former boss from her days in the Met, where she'd been fast-tracked to Detective Inspector, before leaving to open her own private investigator's agency, Pierre Search and Security. With, in smaller letters underneath, the legend 'Discreet investigations. Forensic accounting. Personal security.'

"Bob!" she enthused, shifting to a more comfortable position. "How nice. To what do I owe, et cetera, et cetera? And anyway, how are you?"

"More to the point, Tammy, how are you?" A deep fatherly voice. "And how are the hands? You dealt with a monster, but at what cost, I keep asking myself."

"The hands are fine," she responded, with a confidence she didn't feel. She wasn't going to disappoint Bob with any signs of self-doubt; the affair of the Black Candles had been a success, even if it came close to being her comeuppance. But she'd been scared badly by the event which had tested her to the limit, a lesson she could have done without. If this were to be her first real test since that time, it was a test she couldn't afford to fail.

"I truly hope so," said Bob. "He had to be stopped, but frankly, you were amazing. You know, if you ever want to re-join the force…?"

Bob was interrupted by a peal of laughter from Tammy. "I'll give it some thought, Bob." She paused for a microsecond, then went on, "Well now, I've thought about it at length..."

This time it was Bob Walker's turn to laugh. "Okay, okay. Point taken."

"So, is this a social call," she asked, reaching for a glass of water from the bedside table. "Or is there the possibility of work?"

"It's work." He was his usual business self.

"You know, Bob, you're becoming one of my most lucrative sources of revenue."

"Glad to hear it. You know full well, there's no-one I'd rather employ."

"Merci, monsieur. So, what's the deal?" she asked, her curiosity piqued, her spirits in the ascendancy after the morning's near shock.

"Do you know of the MP Oscar Mountford?" Bob asked.

"Of course. He's shone in a number of minor ministerial posts, now tipped as a likely candidate for Chancellor in the imminent reshuffle." Gulping back some of the water, Tammy replaced the cup on the bedside table.

"That's the man. Well, it seems his wife has gone missing. Just disappeared into thin air. No note. No warning. Clearly totally out of character." He hesitated for a moment as though reconsidering. "Well, maybe not totally out of character. But certainly not an expected or explicable absence. He's understandably concerned. Perhaps, worried might be closer to the way he's feeling right now."

"You want me to find her?"

"Exactly," he announced, with emphasis.

"But isn't this a matter for the police? Shouldn't you have a team on this already, Bob?"

"No, not in this case. As we're batting in the dark, we need absolute discretion. Obviously, the last thing

Mountford wants is for anything to happen to his wife, or equally, if there's a rational explanation for what's happened, anything to impact his career."

"Understood. Though I must say, if everything I've read about the man is accurate he's probably more concerned for his career than his wife. Still, is there nothing at all to go on? No leads? No guesses?"

"Her car, an Audi SUV, was tracked, using ANPR, to London Heathrow a month and a half ago. It's still in one of the long-stay car parks where she left it."

"A month and a half, you say. Why's it taken so long for this to be followed up? I mean, whatever the trail might have been, is likely to have gone cold by now."

"Exactly what I told Mountford when he contacted us. Me that is. Only two weeks ago."

"By which time she'd been missing for six weeks," she offered. "To which he responded?"

"Well, he said she'd often gone AWOL. It seems they've lived an open marriage for years, and he stopped trying to have her account for her absences a long time ago."

"Hmm! So, which long-stay did she leave her car in?"

"Terminal 3."

"Possibly aiming for the US?" Tammy suggested. "And? Was she tracked into the airport? CCTV?"

"She was, but it was particularly crowded. She's seen entering one of the ladies' toilets, but we couldn't find her coming out. No back windows to escape from, so the only likely explanation is that she changed her appearance."

"From which it follows, she wasn't kidnapped."

"Exactly."

"So the question is, why would she run away?" She was sitting up in bed now, gazing at a tree on the opposite side of the road as it swayed gently in the breeze. It was easier to focus her thoughts if she wasn't distracted by anything in her immediate vicinity. Possibly, apart from the cat. "Because that's what it looks like, doesn't it," she continued. "Escape? From what, then? An abusive husband? Absconding to be with a lover? But then you said the marriage was an open one. Escape from pursuers? If she's committed some sort of crime, or criminal activity?"

"You've just about covered it, Tammy. Unless the obvious, which is not so obvious."

This should, with luck, prove a straightforward investigation. No physical strain involved. No need to risk the pregnancy, or the wrath of her Doctor Aziz. Later she would question the wisdom of her judgement.

"I know," she offered. "Something we've not thought of. Something to be found out once we start looking."

"Where will you start?"

"With the husband, I guess. Maybe, our boys in Wapping too. Those're the first things that come to mind."

"I'll help all I can, but even my department isn't aware of what's going on here. That's why I've brought you in."

"I'll get onto it immediately. What can you tell me about Mountford that you think I should know?"

In the moments before Bob responded Tammy could almost hear the thoughts going through his head. A meticulous man, Bob Walker had made his way up the career ladder through persistence, vision, integrity and a refusal to accept that a solution couldn't be found to an apparently insoluble problem. He'd been Tammy's tutor, mentor and, eventually, almost her nemesis when she'd vastly overstepped the mark, totalling the car of a driver who'd cut her up, then given her the finger. Bob had made it clear her career hung by a thread. An ignominious dismissal would have crushed her prospects in the force for good and she shuddered at the recollection. But he'd had enough faith in her to give her one final chance. She'd not let him down, and each of them now harboured enormous respect for the other.

"Mountford is something of a mystery man," said Bob. "A self-made multi-millionaire, we've no clear idea of how his fortune has been accrued. There're apparent links to arms dealers, rumours of drug operations, people trafficking. Money laundering? You name it. All of this predates his time as an MP by a long way, years in fact, and he seems to have made an excellent job of covering his tracks. He got all the required security clearances, probably because he has the PM's ear and faith. Thinking about it, whilst we've nothing to evidence nefarious dealings, there're enough other past MPs who've climbed the slippery pole, despite falling down later."

"There're crooks in every walk of life. Parliament is no exception," added Tammy, thinking about the infinite variety she'd met in her own short solo career.

"That's right," Bob remarked, then added, "but there are some oddities, aren't there. John Stonehouse, Labour, faked his own death to avoid dealing with mounting business problems, went to jail in 1975, but wasn't expelled from the Commons until a year later. Heavens, Horatio Bottomley, first chairman of the Financial Times, had no less than sixty-six bankruptcy writs issued against him. Finally given seven years for fraud and expelled from the Party in 1922."

"And there are more, recent ones," Bob expounded. "Jonathan Aitken, Jeffrey Archer, to mention but two. Remember, whatever the whispers, Oscar Mountford has never been accused, let alone convicted of any crime."

"So how has Oscar climbed so high in government?" she asked.

"He's a charismatic individual. Imposing, educated, articulate with the charm to go with it. A law degree from Cambridge, though he was not in practice for very long, choosing to concentrate on a political career instead. He's a dab hand at dispelling whispers about his current business interests, all of which he will claim are contained within his publishing company."

"Mountford Taylor produces mainly textbooks for schools and universities. That alone would have made him wealthy, but not to the extent of the lifestyle he supports. I mean we're talking about, among other things, a fifty-million-pound yacht in harbour at Monaco. Maybe not on the scale of some of the Russian oligarchs' billion-pound boats, but mega just the same."

"Impressive. That it?"

"No, Tammy. One more thing. We believe the man is dangerous. Gets others to do his dirty work. All gossip again. But be careful. He acts ugly if he doesn't get the results he wants and expects."

Of course she'd be careful. No problems in an investigation of this type of her jeopardising her condition, she reminded herself. All just desk work and talk.

Although she'd already accepted, she'd have to factor in being slowed down, at least physically. Hopefully not mentally. Still there was time.

But then, just how ugly?

CHAPTER 4

TEN DAYS AGO

A T FORTY YEARS OF AGE, while still attractive, if somewhat past her best, Georgia Keith was under no illusion she'd ever find marriage or even yet a long-term partner. Putting on her make-up in the mornings she'd taken to always having the bathroom light dimmed. She didn't need to see the fine lines developing at the corners of her eyes or witness the thread veins beginning to appear in her cheeks. She'd been with her boss, Oscar Mountford, for the past fifteen years, enjoying lamentably little time off, in the early days having harboured vague hopes he might actually leave his wife for her.

She'd finally accepted that was no more likely than her winning the Mann Booker Prize. For one thing, she smiled ruefully, to win the prize you need to write, at least metaphorically, something she'd never done. Struck out. Taken a chance. Similarly, in her life, to have won the man she hoped for she'd have needed to be bolder. To give him an ultimatum. Marriage, or else I go. Her mother, a strident feminist, now in her late seventies and as astute as ever, down to earth and pragmatic, had warned her, men like that don't risk all for a bit of fluff. "Which, my darling," she'd added, "is what you are, or have become, irrespective of your class, your education or your qualifications."

Of course, the truth always hurt. What made it worse was her mother's oft repeated assertion when Georgia was in her teens and starting to date: "Keep 'em guessing, darling. Keep 'em on a string. That way you can haul them in whenever you're ready. Act on your terms not theirs. You're beautiful, you're brilliant, a catch for any man. Just don't give it all away on a plate. You're not a bloody registered charity." But then, Georgia, the incurable romantic, had to her mother's utter exasperation, insisted on the value of declarations of undying love. She was now reaping the rewards of her generosity as, sitting on her boss's lap, she watched him fumble clumsily at her blouse.

* * * * *

Oscar Mountford, junior minister and one of the PM's current favourites, rumoured to be in line for the post of Chancellor of the Exchequer, had risen swiftly through the political ranks. Relying on the power of his wealth he'd been able to achieve what he wanted for both the country and himself a goal his PM was blissfully unaware of, if he gained the promotion he sought. The problem was that Oscar Mountford's ambitions amounted to a form of socio-political terrorism. The PM simply recognised Mountford's business talent and wanted to put it to work in the best interests of the economy, naively ignoring some of the discreet warnings from the security services passed on to him by his colleague, Detective Chief Superintendent Bob Walker.

Originally planning a career in law, Mountford realised his exceptional and unique talents lay elsewhere, and accordingly applied to go for officers' training at Sandhurst Military Academy in Camberley, Surrey. Undergoing the initial twenty-four-hour selection process at the Army Officer Selection Board, comprising interviews coupled with mental and physical tests, Mountford, having come through with flying colours, went on, in common with all other successful applicants, to the three-and-a-half-day AOSB series of tests to assess his suitability for officer training.

It was at this point the Selection Board, in starting to review the young candidate's responses to questions put, decided to invite him to attend a psychological profiling session. Or two. He was reassured all was in order, and that the profiling was merely part of the process, applied where considered useful, but not necessarily to all candidates.

The man brought in for the assessment was not resident at the Academy. Leonard Masters was respected as one of the UK's pre-eminent men in his field. A short and somewhat overweight, balding individual with a nice line in humour, he invited Mountford to join him for a coffee in one of the Academy's several casual areas. A small office with leather easy chairs facing a desk that Masters chose to ignore. The two men, suited but casually tieless, sat back as a young recruit brought in a tray laid with cups, saucers and a cafetière of the steaming brew.

Sipping their drinks, Masters faced Mountford. "So, young man. Tell me something about yourself. I gather you got a First in law at Cambridge."

"That's right," said Mountford. "Not a difficult subject to do well in."

"You surprise me. With subjects like maths and science, where marks are gained for the right answer, there is generally a higher number of top degrees. Law is subjective, unless you can present cast-iron theses to support your arguments. No matter how brilliant you may eventually be in practice, in the exams it is notoriously difficult to score high marks."

"I found it all very easy."

"I'm impressed. But you've decided to aim instead for an army career. Looking forward to shooting a few people, are you?" asked Masters, a twinkle in his eye.

"Something like that," said Mountford.

Masters raised his eyebrows, only very slightly. "What about skills in leadership, teamwork, logistics, and strategies in warfare?"

"Yes, I suppose," said Mountford. "But in the main I prefer to work alone."

"Killing people?"

"Well, if you put it like that… But the soldier has a job to do, whatever is required at the time."

"Do you consider the army has a duty to explore all paths towards peaceful settlements before resorting to war?"

"Unfortunately, we're all too often faced with intractable situations that require an iron fist."

"I see. But how about the velvet glove, Mr. Mountford? Not worth a try?"

"Only as a last resort."

"I should have thought, first resort. However," he smiled, "tell me, have you come across General Sir Michael Rose, by any chance?"

"Never heard of him."

"Admired to the point of being loved by his men, having served in many theatres of war, including Northern Ireland and Afghanistan, and noted for his courage, leadership skills and strategic planning; his view was that war should only ever be used as a last resort. When all other avenues to peace had been explored and failed. What do you say to that, Mr Mountford?"

Mountford appeared vaguely bored. "He's entitled to his opinion."

"Entitled to his opinion?" Masters leaned forward as though to hear the young man better. "You prefer the iron fist, Mr Mountford?"

"Very much so. Nothing wrong in taking a strong hand."

"Would it trouble you at all to kill a fellow human bing?" Masters asked, looking Mountford in the eye.

"Not at all. I'd welcome the opportunity." Mountford stared back unblinkingly.

Placing his cup and saucer on the desk, Masters got to his feet, smiling broadly. "Thank you, Mr. Mountford. I've more than sufficient here to complete my report."

"That's it?"

"Absolutely, young man."

"How did I do?"

"Depending on your aims and goals in life, I'd say wonderfully well."

Sandhurst waved goodbye to Oscar Mountford the following day. The four words that stood out in the report on his suitability as officer material in the British army, were "Functioning psychopath. At present."

CHAPTER 5

TEN DAYS AGO ^{CONTINUED...}

"SOMEONE MIGHT COME IN, darling," she whispered.

"Not at 7.00 am, my lovely. Come on, we've time for a quickie." And so saying he hauled Georgia across his desk, impatiently brushing the copious paperwork away where it fluttered to the floor, then pushing her skirt up to her waist he spread her thighs, dragging aside the crotch of her knickers, and unceremoniously entered her, pushing hard. Georgia, with a constant eye on the office door, responded in a desultory manner to her boss's careless thrusts which ended in mere moments, the man gasping, grunting, then withdrawing and drying himself off with a tissue he discarded in the waste bin.

"Good, darling?" he enquired, settling himself back in his swivel chair and adjusting his trousers and tie. "Good for you, was it?" he asked again, bending and picking papers up from the floor, before shuffling them into order.

"Wonderful," she murmured, recalling her mother's words, somewhat late in the day.

Opened in 2001, Portcullis House, designed by Michael Hopkins and Partners and located in Westminster, houses offices for some two hundred and thirteen MPs. The site has a history dating back to 1400, when it was occupied by houses built for the dean and twelve canons of St Stephen's College in the Palace of Westminster. A magnificent building, the atrium is nothing short of breathtaking. Incorporating Westminster tube station, the building is apparently separated from the station by a slab of concrete, ostensibly to guard against underground terrorist attacks.

The office occupied by Oscar Mountford was oak-lined with Persian rugs on the floor. Books decorated two of the walls, the third and fourth being festooned with a variety of impressive pictures. The man sat behind a vast mahogany, leather-topped desk opposite the door to a small ante room occupied by his PA, which also served as a reception area for visitors waiting to see him. A desk lamp with a cylindrical green glass shade on Oscar's desk, had survived the morning's exertions, although only just. It teetered on the edge of the desk where its owner rescued and repositioned it.

Georgia, having straightened her skirt, rebuttoned her white blouse and primped her long hair back behind her ears, now sat at her own desk and started reading through the early morning emails on her laptop, composing herself as though nothing had happened. Then, as though the thought had just occurred to her, she got up and walked around to Oscar's desk and asked, "Have you heard anything about Letitia, Oscar? I mean, it's been longer than her usual jaunts. How many weeks has it been?"

"Nothing. Not a damn thing," he responded, irritably.

"You don't seem unduly concerned, darling?" It was a question rather than an observation.

"Letitia looks after herself. Always has. She needs no-one."

"It won't look good if the press start nosing around asking questions. We need to know where she is and what she's up to, Oscar."

"I know, dammit." He slammed his fist on the desk making the papers jump.

"Alright, darling," she soothed. "I shan't ask again."

Oscar stared at Georgia. "Look, I've mentioned it to my friend Bob Walker, the Chief Super. He's got someone good looking into it. Okay?"

"Fine, fine."

Oscar had just put his mobile on the desk in front of him when it buzzed. "Mac?" he enquired, anxious for a moment as he ran his fingers through his thick, greying hair. Then relaxing back into his chair, he lodged the mobile in the crook of his neck for a moment and cracked his knuckles. "Good. Glad it's you. How're we doing?"

Georgia sat mute. She'd heard a number of these mysterious conversations about which her boss had not deemed it necessary to enlighten her. He always opened the chat sounding apprehensive before calming down when he'd apparently been reassured all was as it should be. She listened now, trying to fathom just what was going on.

"I'm donating a hundred K, Mac. We need to do something here to stop the rot. England Foremost are organising a demonstration in Trafalgar Square. They need funds. I'm providing funds." He paused to let the other man, Mac, respond. Georgia tried to listen as unobtrusively as possible, but it was all too soft to make out what Mac, whoever he was, was saying to her boss.

And, England Foremost? she thought. Wasn't that an illicit far right organisation? Illicit and largely undercover. There'd been sparse mention in the media about a group seeking to stop all immigration, to repatriate whole swathes of communities. It was rumoured there'd been violence, subject to D Notices. Issued, she wondered, on whose authority? The violence, it appeared had not, as might have been anticipated, been directed at immigrant communities, but instead at a number of homes of prominent politicians. Mostly left wing, but some right leaning too.

A ripple of nerves ran up Georgia's arms and back. She knew her boss could be unpredictable. Accepted he was an ambitious man, used to getting his own way. Knew he had issues with the question of immigrants. But this was something new, something he'd not confided in her. Why, she wondered, would he let her hear about it now?

He went on, "The country's going to the dogs, Mac. We want to see the back of all the Hebrews here, Africans back to the bloody jungle, where they came from, a return of the birch and reintroduction of public hanging, if it's possible."

"Hebrews? Hebrews? Oscar?" She stepped back into his office and spoke over his phone call, interrupting him, and he put the mobile aside for a moment, clearly irritated. "Don't you mean Jewish people, Oscar," she went on. "Some of whom are your supposed friends. At least I thought they were. I don't see the Party turning down their contributions."

Resuming his call as though she'd not spoken, he continued, "Time we got a legitimate government in place, my man. A government the people can show some respect to. I've been in touch with some like-minded people in France, Italy, Germany. I think we could get something moving here. I mean on a grand scale. Anyone gets in our way, deal with like we did with Anderton. Keep in touch," and he cut the call.

Georgia stared at her employer, white-faced. Kevin Anderton, rumoured to be working undercover for the security services, had been found murdered a month ago. A planned hit and run. A professional job, the police so far had no leads. "Oscar," she gasped, barely able to speak. "What are you doing? What are you saying? You've been mentioned as our next Chancellor. What you're suggesting is treason. A crime against the State. It carries a life sentence. Darling, are you crazy. What if this all gets out?" Then, for the first time she noticed the phone he was using. It wasn't his usual one in the distinctive blue cover.

Getting to his feet, all six feet four of him, Oscar hitched his trousers and straightened his jacket, before addressing Georgia. "I'm on my way out now, Georgia. Don't forget, I'm a lawyer, you don't need to read me the Riot Act, I know the consequences of what we're planning. But someone has to act."

"Oscar, we've heard all this before from other far right groups. This isn't you. It can't be you. And what makes you think it will work this time, when it never has in the past? They're always found out, discovered before things get out of hand. You know that as well as I do. And why are you using a burner?" she ventured.

Striding towards the door, Oscar stared pointedly at his PA. "But it won't get out this time, Georgia. And if it does, there's too many on the right of the Party to stop it now. If it's leaked," he added softly, pointing at his PA, "we'll find out where the leak comes from, Georgia, and we'll deal with it accordingly. Should be clear enough. Shouldn't it?"

CHAPTER 6

SOME WEEKS AGO

THERE WAS NO *elevator in the old tenement block located on the wrong side of town. Vinegar Hill, Brooklyn.*

From her fifth-floor apartment she peered down the stairwell at the elderly man who'd just arrived, somewhat out of breath, on the fourth-floor landing below. "I seem to have lost my key," she called out, clearly close to tears. "Stupid of me. Even left my phone in the apartment, can you believe? Whatever can I do?"

She wore her hair in a ponytail, and sported, incongruously, white bobby socks, a red drum majorette skirt and white short-sleeved blouse under a red bolero jacket. She distractedly pulled up one wrinkled sock until it matched its immaculate partner, straightened her blouse and smoothed back a stray lock of hair.

It was hard to tell her age. She might have been twenty-five, thirty-five, even forty-five at a pinch. Impossible to be sure these days, with cosmetic surgery being what it was.

The white-haired old man inclined his lined and sallow face in her direction, smiled up at her kindly, waving his own front door key about. "Come, my dear," his accent was distinctly Eastern bloc, "I make you coffee and we call a locksmith from my flet. I got jem doughnuts too. You like jem doughnuts?"

"I love jam doughnuts," she enthused, happily skipping down the two flights to the old man's landing, where she playfully grasped his shoulders, before heaving him over the balus-

trade. His hollow scream echoing throughout the block, ended abruptly when his feeble frame hit the ground floor with a sickening crump.

"Oh, my!" she murmured, her palms to her cheeks. "I did think the old gentleman looked a bit shaky on his feet."

CHAPTER 7 DAY 2

THE RATCLIFF HIGHWAY murders in the London district of Wapping in 1811 involved more fatalities than those committed by Jack the Ripper in 1888. With seven deaths across two families only twelve days apart, the motive and indeed the identity of the perpetrator have been the subject of speculation ever since. Indicted on a charge of murder, at the time, John Williams was declared guilty on 28 December 1811 but not before he had committed suicide in his prison cell.

It was a warm bright day when Tammy exited Fenchurch Street tube and started the walk to Wapping station. A bit of useful exercise in her present condition. Less than two miles distant, it would take her about twenty-five minutes. She was troubled for no apparent reason. One of those days when something nags at you, but you can't put your finger on it. She hurried on.

A landmark in the area, on the site of the oldest riverside tavern dating back to 1510, stands the Prospect of Whitby. Outside the pub in recognition of the smugglers, cut throats and footpads that frequented the place, on a wood post actually planted in the Thames, is a hangman's noose. In the seventeenth century the pub was 'Hanging' Judge Jeffreys' favourite haunt.

Execution Dock, by the Town of Ramsgate pub, on Wapping High Street, is where pirates and others similar were hanged from a gibbet situated close to the low water mark, their bodies left to swing until they'd been submerged three times by the tide.

Today Wapping is largely redeveloped with hotels and chic eating places. Tourists flock the area to view in neighbouring Southwark, Borough Market, Southwark Cathedral, the Shard or the London Eye.

For all of our sophisticated humanity we still have more than a mere residue of our primordial instincts, she mused. At first it was no more than the slightest feeling someone was watching her. There were few people about at that moment. The buzz of traffic muted what might otherwise have been the sound of footsteps anywhere near. She glanced left and right. There was nothing. Turning round to check the route she'd just come she spotted a leather jacket. Denim jeans. Wire-rimmed spectacles. A small individual. A head quickly turned away from her? Initially dismissed. Imagined problems? Her briefing by Bob Walker had been entirely confidential. No way was she being followed. Yet female instinct still left her feeling troubled.

There were still remnants of the Victorian era, echoes of the harshness of life and poverty of the time, with old factories and warehouses in ancient, cobbled streets, in some cases situated practically at the water's edge.

With no natural light and located in a basement of one of these apparently derelict nineteenth-century factories, a partnership of two unique IT geniuses had established itself. The property was owned in its entirety by a company called Incognita Ltd, registered in the Isle of Man and a one hundred percent subsidiary of another called Prorsus Ignotem Ltd, based in the British Virgin Islands. Incognita meant 'unknown'. Prorsus Ignotem meant 'totally unknown'. All someone's idea of a joke perhaps? After that the trail would grow cold with a further several rafts of ownership to blindside any planned supplementary enquiry. It was how the two had planned it.

There are some twenty-six miles of tunnels under London's throughfares, with some running beneath the Thames. From the street level of Wapping underground run twin curved staircases to the two station platforms below.

Set into the wall close to the bottom of one of these sets of stairs was a door marked 'Staff Only', beyond which ran a passageway leading to a spot where the partnership operated. Tammy was one of a select few to be granted access via that entrance, a privilege she relished.

Entering the enclave itself, through a disguised, armour-plated door secured by a biometric palm-print lock, found one in a well-lit, ultra-modern, fully equipped Aladdin's Cave of computer technology and wizardry. Elegantly decorated in blacks, whites, greys and burgundy, with banks of screens lining the walls and hovering over shiny work surfaces, the place resembled a version of the BBC's Newsroom in Broadcasting House. The added kitchen, bathroom facilities, bedrooms and supplies of food and drink, meant the two owners could work undisturbed, and without the need to emerge into the wider world for days, even weeks at a time. Clearly the partners weren't expecting unannounced visitors to drop by for a quick cup of tea.

Dismissed too soon? she wondered. Several times she'd doubled back on herself. She was used to losing a tracker, but if she was right and she was being followed after all, this one knew what he was doing. Eventually she slipped into Wapping underground, but only when she was absolutely certain she'd lost him.

Tammy arrived unannounced, as she frequently did, to the immense pleasure of the two men. "Hi, guys," she said, flinging herself down thankfully into one of four leather, captain's chairs. That walk? Too far really. The baby was definitely slowing her down, leaving her tired.

The two men, Jamie Steele and George Meekins, both glanced up from the rows of screens they were working at, acknowledging her with broad smiles. The men's names were the polar opposites of their personalities.

Jamie Steele, bespectacled and on the short side, floppy white-blond hair, pale complexion, aged twenty-six, shy and withdrawn to the point of almost total silence;

when he was in the vicinity of Tammy, he'd open up happily. Lads like him were usually the butt of schoolboy bullying, but not so Jamie, who was so insignificant, he was simply seldom noticed by anyone. Always bottom of his class, written off as a non-achiever by his teachers, it was only when introduced to IT that, to the mixed joy and amazement of his blue-collar parents, his genius IQ became apparent. A single man, he'd always been too timid to approach any woman he fancied, and so far none had approached him.

George Meekins, in his fifties, with a dark receding hairline, was anything but meek. A bruiser of a man with ruddy pockmarked skin and scars on his hands and arms from the frequent fights he'd got into as a teenager at his expensive public school. A reckless risk-taker, he'd won and lost fortunes as a professional gambler, mainly poker, and been asked to leave a variety of clubs when his uncertain temper had got the better of him.

On one occasion while playing Texas hold 'em at a Las Vegas Casino, George had caught the dealer manipulating the cards, and challenged him. The dealer had sneered back at George who lost his rag and broke the man's jaw. Not considered by the management to be received etiquette, he was asked by several large gentlemen, working on behalf of the establishment, to leave. He duly obliged, promising, to their astonishment, never to return.

He'd met and got talking to the ultra-reserved Jamie when they'd found themselves inspecting an advanced piece of computer kit at an IT exhibition in Olympia some years before. Also single, for the moment, George's love life was a chequered history of passionate, sometimes violent, affairs. All in the nature of the man.

Apart from computers, gambling was the one other thing they had in common, although for Jamie it was the rather more speculative blackjack that rang his bell.

From a national security point of view, George and Jamie were employed clandestinely by the MoD, the Foreign Office, the Central Office of Information and Scotland Yard. Two individuals whose joint contribution to the security of this country was inestimable. Hence their long hours spent in front of computer screens. Worth noting, none of the various government departments that used their services was aware of the others similarly involved.

Tammy had been introduced to the two men by Dov at a time when he'd uncharacteristically let slip he had himself occasionally been employed by the Israeli intelligence agency, Mossad.

Hoisting his considerable bulk off the high-backed work stool George asked, "Coffee, m'dear?"

The question was interrupted by a faint tapping at the armour-plated door. George, his head on one side in contemplation, remarked, "Someone has come through the Staff Only entrance and is seeking our attention." Despite the levity, George looked concerned.

"I can't have been followed here," protested Tammy. Christ, she'd be mortified if she'd led someone to the place. Her scalp prickled with embarrassment, as though she'd personally let the two men down. "Just a feeling I had. I thought I'd lost him. Now I don't know. Can we be heard in here?"

"No," put in Jamie. "With our acoustics we pick up things like that knocking, but no-one's going to hear us. No need for concern."

A blessed relief, though who else but the little man could have found this place? Practically no-one knew about the location of this place. She'd take extra care when leaving in case her instincts about the possibility of her being followed had been correct. Whoever it was might be prowling about in wait for her, not knowing where she'd disappeared to. If she was right and it was a confrontation he was after, she'd not disappoint him.

"So," resumed George, "where was I just now? Oh yes, coffee?"

"Perfect," she responded, relieved, self-consciously adjusting her specially made belt, its discreet pockets holding four shuriken. Seventeenth-century Japanese throwing stars comprising steel discs which, flung like a frisbee at the neck or head, were lethal. Tammy's were Catherine wheels, with razor-sharp curved points around the edge, made specially for her by a skilled metalworker operating from a tiny West End mews. More than once they'd saved her life where a gun would have proved inappropriate.

"Then you can enlighten us with the purpose of your visit."

Jamie just smiled, said nothing.

Bob's insistence on total secrecy suggested her project was more than just a missing person's search. Politics, politics, she thought. She'd find out soon enough.

"Come on," Tammy said. "I'll help with the coffee."

Walking into the kitchen, newly redone in black and white marble, Tammy observed, "Very smart."

"Jamie's idea. He said it adds a touch of class," George explained as he brought out cups and saucers and filled them from the coffee machine, before hauling himself like a lumbering bear onto one of the bar stools, inviting Tammy to do likewise.

"What about Jamie?" Tammy asked.

"Our frail friend?" said George cheekily, pointing a thumb in Jamie's direction. "Always got health on his mind. He limits himself and doesn't start till later in the day."

"Seems sensible," said Tammy, and pulling at the knees of her black flares to stop them creasing planted herself on a stool on the opposite side of the bar so she could face George.

"I'd love to think this is just a social call, Tammy. But I presume it's business?"

"It's business," she replied, toying with the cup, but not yet drinking from it.

"Fire away, then. I'm all ears," said George, blowing on the surface of the steaming drink.

"You know the name, Oscar Mountford, of course."

"Yes, we've had no reason to deal with the man personally. From all I've seen of him though he strikes me as pompous and arrogant. On the cards as our next Chancellor of the Exchequer. Heaven help. Just about the worst possible candidate."

"Maybe so. He's a shrewd businessman. Maybe not. He's also likely a crook. On a grand scale. We'll have to see. His wife's gone missing, apparently a couple of months ago."

"Where did you get this from, Tammy?"

"I've had my old Guv, Bob Walker of the Met, ask me to look into it. No-one is to know anything. Other than Bob no-one else in the Met knows anything either. Seems it's all very sensitive."

"More to this than meets the eye, if you ask me." George took a contemplative sip from his cup.

"Bob just called for absolute discretion."

"Did he give you anything at all to go on?"

"Bob gave me a date." George nodded and jotted it down as Tammy gave it to him.

"What else?"

"Just that CCTV suggested his wife had gone to Heathrow, Terminal 3, on the date in question. They'd lost her in the crowd when she went into the ladies. Terminal 3 goes to the US, among other places. That would have been just under six weeks ago. So she was somewhere in the UK for a couple of weeks before flying out. I thought I'd talk to you before interviewing Mountford."

Climbing off the bar stool, George nodded towards the doorway and made his way back into the main working area. "Come on," he said. "Let us see what we can see."

"What can you do if we've nothing to go on?" Tammy asked, knowing how George relished a challenge.

"How about starting with her name?"

"It's Letitia. Letitia Mountford."

"Right. Here's what we'll do. We'll poke around through all of Heathrow's CCTV on the day we've got."

"There'll be hundreds of hours…" she mused softly.

"All in a day's work. Let's see now," he said before tapping at the keyboard he'd been working on with the rapidity of a machine gun with the trigger stuck on fire.

"George," Tammy said thoughtfully, "CCTV images are retained for just thirty-one days, right?"

"Yup, police recommendation. Many are kept for longer. If Letitia went missing more than two months ago we might not be so lucky. Up to then, it'll be hit and miss. But we're thinking about, maybe between thirty-five and forty days max? We'll look at whatever we can find on the Earthcam and NYPD networks."

"This is new to me, George. I mean, is it ethical?" Tammy asked, surprised. "Isn't it an infringement of the liberty of the individual?"

"Probably." George sighed. "But the justification would be the protection of society against terrorists."

"And you can hack into it, I presume?"

"Normally we wouldn't need to. Permission could be sought of the Deputy Commissioner for Legal Matters to view video footage."

"And will you be seeking that permission?"

"No. From what you say, if absolute discretion is required, and clearly with a potential future Chancellor in the picture it is, we'll keep the whole thing quiet."

"Do you think you'll pick up much?"

"We'll have to see. But even if it's patchy we may be able to get enough to locate her whereabouts, track some, if not all, of her movements. Fingers crossed. Nil desperandum, m'dear."

"Anything you need right now?"

"So, to repeat. Full name. Rough description of appearance. That is, approximate age, height, colouring. Anything distinctive about her choice of clothing. Distinguishing marks."

"As I said she is Letitia Mountford, née Philips, if that last helps at all. She's above middle height, youngish, mid-forties, shoulder-length, wavy chestnut hair, trim figure, usually in skirts or dresses rather than trousers. Quite fashionable apparently. Oh, and she wears glasses. Got quite a selection of expensive frames. Just Google her. Plenty of clear shots to choose from."

"Jamie, are you getting all this?" George turned to his younger colleague, who nodded with the slightest murmur of assent.

"Ah," George grinned, "Jamie's in talkative mode today."

"Flight manifests?" asked Tammy.

"Of course. We'll race through them all looking for the name. What would normally take a week to scour we can do in an hour. Making progress here all the time. We've also got updated facial recognition software. The tech will select the size and colour needle you are searching for, in any given haystack." He paused, smiling. "Well, up to a point, that is."

"Okay," said Tammy. "I won't get in your way. In fact, I've a number of errands to run," she said, shrugging into the black jacket she'd removed when she entered the place, and left the guys to it.

Outside and about a mile from Wapping station, walking east, she suddenly found herself jostled by a little man in jeans, leather jacket and wire-rim spectacles. Her stalker? Their recent visitor? Hell!

She'd hardly had time to register the incident when he hissed at her, "Keep out of the Mountford affair, Madame Pierre. Way out of your depth. Hmm? You don't know what you're yourself getting into. Neither did the others. The dissidents. They should have listened too. Heh, heh."

CHAPTER 8 DAY 2

JANE CAST HER MIND back several weeks. The recollection hurt.

He'd spat in her face, "I hate you, I hate you, I hate you."

"Now, David, you know you don't mean that," she said, almost pleadingly, the earnestness she was witnessing like a knife to the heart.

"I hate you, I hate you, I hate you."

"David, please?" she said, taking the boy's hands and holding them gently by his sides. But David snapped his arms away from her and ran off to play with some toys in a far corner of the room.

"It's not working is it, Jayne? Admit it." The man spoke with the authority of one unused to being contradicted. Unused to being proven wrong.

Middle-aged and middle class, Jayne thought. His closed mind to her efforts to introduce something innovative to the institution was driving her mad. Do it all by the book, he insisted. Rules, rules and nothing but rules.

Then she berated herself for her own base prejudices. The man was no different to her father after all, and he was making a great success in politics, despite his tunnel vision, or possibly because of it. Maybe it was just this man's idea of focus, the principle. But even so, they were making too slow progress with the children.

"I want you to go back to our tried and tested routines, Jayne. These new-fangled American notions are not how we do it in this country." A tall man, stalking about like a bedraggled heron, his shabby grey suit matching his pasty grey complexion, he sounded furious. "You're unsettling the children, Jayne, and I won't have it. Do you hear me? I won't have it."

"I've barely started, Neville. I need more time. I know this can work. I can make it work." She was pacing the room herself, like a caged animal, her trainers squeaking on the hardwood flooring like rampant mice.

"I don't give a damn about your mumbo jumbo ideas."

"But, Neville!" She had to be given a chance to succeed. Autism need not be a life sentence.

The American youngster Jake Barnett had been born severely autistic. His mother Kristine had devoted all her attention to him over the years, practically destroying her health, the family finances and its equilibrium. Jake had an IQ greater than that of Einstein.

His mother had said, 'When Jake develops a sense of humour, I'll know I've succeeded.'

And succeeded she had, so much so she'd written a book about the development and nurturing of her son Jake, telling of her monumental struggle to get Jake out of his mental prison. Jayne had Googled him and watched as he lectured a theatre of eager listeners, only to throw his papers in the air just after starting to speak, before announcing jauntily, "Only joking."

My God! she thought. Only joking. How long had it taken for Kristine to get that far, to achieve that result?

That's what Jayne wanted for the children in her care at the College for Autistic Children in Chelsea. The book was inspiring, concentrating as it did on encouraging the youngsters to do whatever it was that stimulated and motivated them. It might be cooking, modelling in clay, tinkering about with a musical instrument, drawing, painting. Whatever.

From there the child could be gradually drawn out, as Jake had been, until they started to interact and communicate with those around them. The process was slow requiring infinite patience and understanding. The ability to face setbacks, tantrums, rages. Jayne was inspired. She'd seen how it worked. Nothing would put her off.

And now Jayne had something to prove. She had a guilty secret she couldn't shake whenever the recollection emerged. Because things had changed dramatically, in a way none of them could have foreseen.

The family was shocked when it happened. Her mother found it difficult to accept, at least, at first. Jayne's brother David had been born profoundly autistic, specifically something called Angelman Syndrome, or Happy Puppet Syndrome, because of the child's happy outlook. But he had, in time, begun to emerge from his chrysalis of isolation with the attention, the love and the encouragement of the family in general, but Jayne in particular.

He was her mission. Her goal. Her father seldom had time for the boy, being wrapped up in his own political ambitions. The others got involved superficially, and that undoubtedly helped. But he was Jayne's primary responsibility. She made it that.

In time, as the youngster began to show fragile signs of communicating, he started to develop a personality. Daubing his face, hands and clothes relentlessly with all the colours of the rainbow, he took to painting pictures of his parents and siblings, which despite their crudeness, were all recognisable. Then he'd call for more paper, paints, crayons. It was all done in silence, but with gestures and facial expressions to express his wants.

Now he started to move on, to become playful, surprising people, jumping out from behind doors, or furniture, sofas, armchairs. He needed attention, needed it all the time. But there was discernible progress. As long as there was interaction. And his sister was tireless. The more he advanced, the more committed she became. Little more than a child herself, she was maturing quicker than her fellows at school, because of David. And the process of her development continued in the years that ensued. Until now, in the present day.

It was then that Jayne heard it for the first time. Her mother, distracted by pressures of her own of late, had screamed when David, flinging his arms wide, popped out from behind a tree in their extensive garden. And Jayne, watering some rare orchids her mother had been nurturing in the conservatory, had dropped the heavy can, damaging the flowers. But that was as nothing. Because what Jayne heard. That is, heard for the first time; was something she'd never expected to bear witness to.

And the understanding that came to her, crystal-clear and unmistakeable, was the sound of David laughing. It was like a peal of bells to Jayne. An explosion of joy. He was starting to connect, to act and react to those around him, and it was all due to Jayne. It was all she could do to prevent herself from crying. Instead, she laughed. She went into the garden and laughed and laughed with David.

That evening, Jayne's adored David was found dead in the bath. He'd been left unaccompanied for a few moments by his mother, she'd said, and slipped under the water. He was gone. The family were bereft. All but their father. Their mother was frantic. But Jayne was inconsolable.

That was less than nine weeks ago. Just before her mother had gone missing. Was it perhaps the reason she'd gone missing? For now Jayne was on a mission, working in the College for Autistic Children in Chelsea, from which no-one was going to be allowed to divert her.

But Jayne had that secret to clasp. It had happened a few days ago. Something she could never confide to anyone. Something she would have to live with, for just as long as she could. She could see no solution.

CHAPTER 9 DAY 2

BACK IN THE BUNKER George, happily wreathed in a cloud of blue vapour from one of his perennial roll ups clamped between nicotine-stained fingers gained during his poker playing days, blew a jet of smoke ceilingward. Jamie, unconcerned, flapped away some of the fumes that drifted towards him like an approaching weather front.

Tammy, reclining once more in the captain's chair, experienced a pinpoint of pain in her abdomen. Sweat broke out on her forehead. Jesus, not now. Please not now. Stifling the urge to wince and smiling brightly, she enquired, "Right, guys. Anything for me?"

But George had noticed the spasm, and concerned, asked Tammy, "Is everything well, m'dear? You look a little peaky."

Now was definitely not the time to start dwelling on her immediate issues, though it was sweet of him to enquire. Hoping he wouldn't take it further, she replied, "Just some of the wounds still healing up. The occasional twinge, you know. Nothing to be concerned about."

George didn't look convinced but took the hint and let the subject drop.

Tammy had got back without being followed. The little man had said his piece, but she'd taken extra precautions all the same, doubling back on herself several times just to be sure.

The two men had steaming cups of coffee on their respective worktops, so Tammy had fixed herself a cup before re-joining them.

Jamie nodded at her and concentrated on wiping his spectacles, but left George to do the talking.

"We've been doing some digging, m'dear," he said, drawing absently on his smoke while still staring intently at his screen. "From your description and our software tying up with the Googled images we found, your Mrs. Mountford, something of a woman of mystery."

Unfolding her rangy frame from the captain's chair, Tammy loped across to stand behind George and stared into his vast monitor.

"Look," he suggested, pointing at the screen. "There she is. Unmistakeable, hmm? See? Tallish, in a loose-fitting dark grey back-belted coat, high collar, Gucci shoulder bag, note the motif on the clasp? Smart heels, wavy auburn shoulder-length hair. Note the spectacles, that feature of Letitia you mentioned earlier. Altogether a picture of elegance. Reminds me of Kate Middleton. Lucky man, our Oscar Mountford. I can well understand him being worried if she's always going AWOL. Even if he says he's used to it, you never get used to it. If you see what I mean," he added, twisting round to look up at Tammy.

Cupping an elbow in her palm and leaning her chin in the other, Tammy asked, "So where next?"

"Watch," suggested George. "She goes into one of the ladies' conveniences in Terminal 3." Tammy smiled at George's discreet use of the word. "But we don't see her emerge. Just as Bob Walker outlined."

"Is that it?" Tammy asked.

"No, m'dear. Not by a long way."

"I'm listening."

"The facial recognition software used by the police and ourselves is state of the art, but if Bob had spotted anything, or anyone resembling Letitia Mountford both entering and then emerging from the ladies he'd have told you, of course." He paused.

Then, for effect, "And he didn't."

Tammy offered, "Because he and his team spotted nothing?"

"Correct."

"But you've found her."

"Yes."

"Because your software is better."

"Precisely."

"Because you both wrote it."

George sighed once more. "You've guessed."

Jamie, catching Tammy's eye, looked heavenward, but said nothing. Punching George affectionately on the shoulder, Tammy said, "Come on, George. This isn't Round Britain Quiz. What have you got for me?"

"Just concentrate." George winked at her, twisted back to the screen, and played the recording again.

Tammy watched a lot of women entering the ladies, among them Letitia. At the same time a number of women exited the facilities, but there was still nothing obvious. Then, after another five minutes staring at the screen she said, "Stop."

"You've got her."

"Have I?"

"Well, m'dear, haven't you?"

"Who's she," Tammy asked, pointing to someone resembling Letitia.

"Exactly," added George, stubbing out his cigarette. "Who is she? We spotted her going into the ladies a little earlier. I'll show you," he said, back-tracking.

"See, she limps slightly. Looks a bit like our Letitia, doesn't she. Except that she isn't. Resemblance is a bit too weak. Even without the software, you can see she isn't as tall. Hair's the same length and colour. Clothing is similar to Letitia's. Albeit the coat is tight-fitting and navy, not grey and loose. Gucci shoulder bag."

"And something else." He paused again, deliberately rolling another smoke before continuing, the cigarette drooping from his lips. "She's not wearing spectacles. A slip up? Or deliberate? Also, this person doesn't have that self-assured walk, demeanour, call it what you will, of a member of Letitia Mountford's class of individual. In fact, if you look really carefully, you'll see she has that very slight limp we just mentioned. Has she recently suffered a minor accident? And then, see how she stares about her as though she's afraid of being spotted? She looks hunted." He paused again.

"Definitely not our Letitia. Which invites two questions. First, where is Letitia now? Second, who is this woman. And I'd add, who put this person up to a very obvious and pretty creaking subterfuge. Our Mrs. Mountford is turning out to be something of a very dark horse."

"So we've lost Letitia?" asked Tammy.

"Not quite."

Tammy gulped back some of her coffee. "Not quite? How, not quite, George?"

"Look at the woman behind our duplicate Letitia, as they emerge from the ladies." He pointed to the screen again.

Tammy leaned forward, stared intently at the crowd of people. "That?" she asked.

"That's right m'dear."

"But she's nothing like Letitia. Even if you ignore the different clothes, the denim jeans and blue blazer, her height, and cropped blond hair? I mean, no way. Plus, she's too short. Sorry. It doesn't work for me. What does your software say?"

Showing an interest for the first time, Jamie interjected, "It's her, Tammy. We're as sure as we can be."

"What about her height? You can't disguise that."

"No, but she was previously in heels. We've linked her with our record of people going into the ladies. It wasn't difficult. Look, she's in flats now. The difference means our perception of her is of a much smaller woman. In fact she's actually a bit taller than you might think. And…"

"And?"

"And, she doesn't have that limp."

"The imposter was found easily among women going into the conveniences, at least by us, and despite not entirely resembling Letitia, she had the limp. Our imposter, who is now coming out, is clearly meant to be Letitia, has even changed her coat to grey. The women have swapped, haven't they? But to complete the picture, this one is now wearing spectacles. And she limps. It identifies her for us."

"That means Letitia must have guessed she'd be tracked," said Tammy.

Speaking softly, Jamie said, "She couldn't have known she'd be watched. But it's instructive that she planned on taking precautions. She wanted to be sure to make a clean disappearance."

George smiled up at Tammy. "The clincher, m'dear, is that the Letitia lookalike isn't carrying Letitia's mobile."

"No?"

"No," said George.

"So where is Letitia's mobile? Oh, I see."

"Of course you do. It's with the blond-haired woman emerging from the conveniences just behind this other counterfeit Letitia. That is the real Letitia."

"Did you follow these two women?"

"Of course we did."

"You know where they were both planning to fly? And without the manifest? How could you? It can take a week to get all the information together."

"Tell our friend, Jamie." George beamed. "After all," he added, "it was your work m'lad."

"Using the software we tracked them to their various departure lounges. From there it was easy," Jamie intoned softly, gazing at the screens in front of him.

"Tell her about gait recognition, Jamie."

Settling his glasses on the bridge of his nose, Jamie leaned back on his stool. "Gait recognition software is in the process of development. But we're way ahead of the game when it comes to tracking and identifying people this way; that is, arms, legs, head movement. The limp we spotted. You name it."

Tammy, who'd been walking up and down the room restlessly, faced Jamie. "And?" she asked.

"To summarise. The imposter is the woman now in the grey back-belted coat. The bespectacled one with a limp. She's a complete stranger to us. Letitia is the woman who's changed her hair colour and length, height and clothing."

CHAPTER 10 DAY 2

"**I** DON'T THINK Pa gives a flying fuck where Ma's got to." Built like an international rugby union player, Oscar's twenty-five-year-old son, Pierce, a maker of TV ads, towered over his live-in girlfriend, red-headed estate agent, Petra Cullen, seven years his senior. They were watching a box series on Netflix in his Chelsea apartment, with neither of them concentrating that hard.

"More wine, Pierce?" Hoisting herself off the sofa, Petra, clad only in a white lacy negligee, wandered over to the Hepplewhite sideboard where the wine bottle was sitting, and at Pierce's desultory nod, poured him another glass of merlot, topping up her own glass at the same time.

Sitting back in his boxer shorts and T-shirt, his legs spread inelegantly before him, Pierce fidgeted with his signet ring, a sure sign he was irritable. Not too difficult to sense, Petra asked him, "What's wrong, lover? You're like a bear with a sore head."

"He's up to something."

"Who is? Your dad?"

"Mm."

Petra stood over her boyfriend, an arm stretched forward with his drink, her negligee falling open to reveal stark white breasts, lissom thighs and a newly pink Brazilian, which Pierce in his state of agitation conspicuously failed to acknowledge. "How can you be sure?" she asked. "And anyway, what's he supposed to be up to?"

"He left his laptop open in his study, accidentally I presume. I dropped in at home for coffee, you know the other day, when you were showing a client a property."

"I remember." Failing to arrest his attention with her display of nudity, Petra sat down on the sofa next to Pierce and picked up the remote. "Do you want to go on watching this right now?"

"Later."

"So tell me, lover, what did you find on Daddy's laptop? Which, I might add, you shouldn't have been peeping into. What was it that's so upset you? Tell the mama."

Sitting up, Pierce took a draught of the wine, before setting the glass down on the occasional table. Then he twisted around to face Petra. "I think Pa's involved with some sort of far right political group or groups."

"What!!" Petra sat up, twisted around and stared intently at Pierce, as though her attention might speed up an answer from her boyfriend.

"I chanced to glance at one email, and what I read shocked me. Then as I read more and more of the exchanges he was having I began to understand what I was witnessing."

Toying with her glass, Petra leaned back and stretched her legs forward, crossing them at the ankle, now covering herself modestly at the front with the negligee. "Well, well. So Daddy has hidden depths."

"More like hidden shallows. I don't think my father has experienced a moment of empathy with anything or anyone in his whole life."

"Pierce, how can you say that?"

"Easily. When David drowned in the bath, everyone when nuts. Everyone except Pa. And all he could say was, 'Well, the boy could never have made anything of his life. Probably better this way.' He didn't give a damn. I almost began to wonder if he'd killed David himself. I mean, he was having to pay out all sorts of money. Apart from the autism, David had heart and lung problems. I'm certain Ma's pregnancy should have been terminated when she got mumps early on. But it wasn't deemed necessary."

Pierce shrugged. "Our Davie. Poor little bugger. The medics said his health issues had nothing to do with Ma's illness, but I wasn't convinced. They were just covering their own bloody backs."

"So, poppa wasn't upset," she mused. "Stiff upper lip, do you think?"

"Rubbish. He's just a heartless bastard."

Finishing her glass of wine, Petra ventured, "But attractive, darling Pierce."

Increasingly irritated Pierce asked, "And just what is that supposed to mean?"

"It means, lover, that your pop isn't the old stick in the mud I always took him to be. Bit of a maverick, if you ask me. Takes a pragmatic approach to loss. Extreme political ambitions. Wow!"

"Extreme? Chrissake, Petra; Hitler had extreme political ambitions. For all the good they did him. You sound as though you actually admire my old man."

"He's an intriguing guy." She closed her eyes, as though visualising Pierce's father, making an assessment of him, before sitting up, staring at Pierce right in the eyes, and adding, speculatively, "You have to admit, Piercy poo, your daddy is eminently fuckable."

An explosive crack had Petra spinning round, spitting blood from the punch Pierce delivered to the side of her face.

CHAPTER 11 DAY 2

"SO WHAT HAPPENED next, guys?"

"Need to work out, m'dear," said George, climbing off his stool and wandering around the room, alternately bending and straightening his legs. "My limbs, that is. Go on, Jamie, you tell her. Got to exercise these old bones."

Taking off his glasses and absent-mindedly cleaning them again, Jamie squinted across at Tammy.

"We followed them to the departure lounge for a Virgin Atlantic flight to New York," he said. "They made no show of knowing each other. Acted like perfect strangers. Not a nod or a smile. They sat at opposite ends of the premier economy class on the plane."

"You've got that detail?" asked Tammy. "From inside the aircraft? However did you—"

"Classified info, m'dear," George interjected.

"The manifest, Tammy," said Jamie, taking over animatedly. "Then we took an educated guess at their seating, placing them by triangulating their mobiles before take-off. It's rough and ready, but close enough."

"I feel this calls for a small vodka, gentlemen." She would indulge the occasional treat, ignoring the guilt, despite the pregnancy.

"Why this particularly, Tammy?" asked Jamie. "I mean, what're you celebrating? Bit early isn't it?"

"Oh, it doesn't have to be this, you know," she responded.

"That's right, young lady." George smiled, nodding at Jamie. "Any excuse will do with our Tammy. You know where the drinks cabinet is in the kitchen. Bottle of Bison Grass, kept just for you. Garibaldi in the biscuit tin."

"Doesn't really go with vodka, mes amis." She smiled. Then extracting a heavy lead cut-glass tumbler and bottle from the wall-mounted drinks cabinet, Tammy poured herself a sensibly modest tot, calling out, "Anything for you, boys?"

"We're fine," they both echoed.

Back in her swivel chair, sipping the drink in between chomping on biscuits, Tammy asked, "Were you able to pick them up after they'd landed?"

"I'll say," said George. "Go on, Jamie, tell her."

Trying not to smile openly, Tammy thought, Abbot and Costello. Or maybe, Laurel and Hardy.

Shaking his head almost imperceptibly, Jamie went on, "This is where it gets interesting."

"Talk to me," prompted Tammy.

"We've got them disembarking the aircraft. But from our facial and gait recognition software, they've changed back to their original persona. Letitia is Letitia, and the other woman who pretended to be Letitia, the one with the limp, whoever she is, is back to whoever she was."

"They must know they're being followed. Surely?"

"No way," said George. "We can track them. But they can't track or identify us."

"Why all the subterfuge, then?"

"Whatever it is they're up to, they're clearly not taking any chances on being followed," George explained, absently rubbing his thighs with his palms.

"So what happened next?" Tammy asked, wide-eyed. Then she turned away from the men, just for a moment, to massage her hands, which still gave her barbs of pain with their extensive scarring. God, she thought, irritated, I'm acting like a bloody invalid.

George spoke to her knowingly. "The Black Candle affair?"

"'Fraid so." She smiled.

"Thought it must be. We'd picked up the info from our various sources, as you'll be aware. Nasty business. Still bad, are they? Your hands?"

"Could be better."

"Pity. Great pity," he said, shaking his head.

"It happens." She shrugged.

"So, Jamie," she continued, "tell me more."

"The next piece in our mystery puzzle," Jamie said.

"Come on, then. Don't keep me in suspense," she urged.

"This is the strangest thing," Jamie continued. "Whilst they'd swapped identities back to their original selves, they'd left their mobiles with each other."

"Curiouser and curiouser."

"We tracked number two, our imposter with the limp, to a shabby tenement block in the Vinegar Hill area of New York."

"And Letitia?"

"She's been found or followed, more correctly, by us, staying at the five-star Ritz-Carlton on Park Avenue. At least that's where she was a few weeks ago when she first got to New York."

"New York?"

"Precisely."

"Living it up?"

"Could be." Then Jamie stopped talking, stared fixedly at one of the overhead screens. "Hang on," he said. "I'm getting something coming through. "Do you want to take this up on yours, George?"

Resuming his seat, George started moving his mouse around with ever-increasing rapidity, images of newsreels, interviews and what looked like recent black-and-white film flashing into sight.

"Who's this?" he wondered, staring at the clip as it slowed and finally emerged in colour.

"Well, well. Seems some old boy was found dead in a tenement block in New York's Vinegar Hill area. About a month ago. Isn't that about where our dummy went?"

"I wonder what's so special about an old man's death?" mused Tammy.

"It seems, this old man, in his nineties no less, was found having apparently fallen through the stairwell from one of the upper floors."

"Horrible," said Tammy.

"What's interesting," added George, pausing to roll up another cigarette while continuing to look intently at the screen, "is that he'd been living there incognito for years. Apparently, his name was Isaac Abrahams. He was known to the KGB for being a dissident in the time of Stalin. They've almost certainly been searching for him ever since. You don't escape the KGB, or their successors the Federal Counterintelligence Service of Russia, or FSK, until you're dead. Mr Abrahams has now escaped them," he concluded, turning to them both.

"Will you be telling Mountford we've located his wife, Tammy?" Jamie enquired.

"Not yet. I'll let Bob Walker know, of course. But I think he'll want to wait and see what Mrs. Mountford is planning to get up to from her comfortable base at the Ritz-Carlton."

CHAPTER 12

SOME WEEKS AGO

THE MUSIC *in the club was deafening, a warehouse basement in Greenwich Village. The place was heaving, juddering as though it had an organic life of its own. Hundreds of youngsters were all bouncing up and down to the sounds of Billie Eilish, Dua Lipa, Justin Bieber and others of that genre. The sugary smell of sweat was cloying. Packets of white powder were changing hands conspicuously, and there was too the underlying, but distinctive, aroma of hash in the air.*

The woman danced beautifully. Sensuously. Sexily. She might have been in her twenties, or thirties. A bit old for this crowd of largely teens. Her chestnut hair was drawn back in a ponytail and she wore white bobby socks and a short, red drum majorette's skirt with white T-shirt and a loose-hanging red silk scarf which she occasionally adjusted and readjusted until it sat just the way she wanted it to. She was looking for a particular someone, but knew he'd find her.

A Ukrainian, and the sexiest man she'd ever encountered. In his mid-twenties, and well over six feet tall, with a mass of floppy black hair, he was the type that always sought out the different, the exotic, the seemingly unattainable. He'd found her, and was dancing with her now, touching his chest to her breasts, his hips to hers, his lips to hers. She shuddered as his hands drifted around her back, cupping her buttocks.

"Come with me," she practically pleaded. "I know where."

Grinning happily, he followed her outside of the club to a deserted area occupied only by wheelie bins and strewn rubbish, empty cardboard takeaway boxes and beer cans. He was squeezing her breasts, shoving himself up against her. She pulled at his belt as they sank to the ground. "Is hard on floor, no? Is Cold? But you have lot of bum. Nice to cushion."

He couldn't wait. Her panties in his fist, he ripped them apart and took her in one swift movement. She gasped and rose to meet him feeling herself slipping into uncertain oblivion. Foolish self-indulgence. "I know how to make it last longer," she whispered, slipping the scarf from around her neck and looping it round his.

He smiled. He'd done this sort of thing before. "Is good. Is good, no?"

She tightened the noose, feeling herself practically blacking out with mounting fear. She'd miscalculated. He was too strong for her. Had to keep conscious to enjoy, enjoy; it's only pretence. She could hear someone screaming. Her own voice, drowned out by the sound of the music drifting from the club.

She was gripping him now, feeling him become more insistent. When he peaked it'd be prolonged, and he was getting there now, faster, and faster, the scarf tighter as she frantically dragged the two ends apart, his eyes bulging, her strength fast ebbing. He was finishing now, at last, only moments left.

She screamed one last time and fell back spent, as he rolled over her, dead.

Pity, she thought as she walked away, uncommonly badly shaken. Still, Nikki can't complain. He picked him out. And I never even asked the boy his name. Young lad, inexperienced. Just one of those things.

CHAPTER 13 DAY 3

THERE WAS AN AUTUMN feel in the air, with trees wrapped in shawls of yellow and gold, fallen leaves crunching underfoot.

Pierce Mountford was sunk within himself, as though he were carrying the world's troubles on his shoulders.

They were walking in the park, close to the lake on one side, and on the other, beyond the railings, Horse Guards Road, where a troop of soldiers in brilliant red uniforms with black bearskins rode past. There was a clear view of Buckingham Palace beyond the lake. On its surface and within its environs massed all sorts of birdlife, the squawks of a group of courting mallards floating across to the young couple.

"How are you, Pierce?" she asked.

He shrugged but didn't reply, then turning to his sister, enquired, "So how are you, Davina? Still with tubby hubby?"

"Don't ask," she responded. "He seemed so nice when I first met him. It didn't matter that he wasn't God's gift. But really, he's a complete waste of space. I only stay because it's too much trouble to leave. He earns bloody nothing from his business, I bring in everything from mine. At times I could kill him. I just have to be in the same room and I start sounding off about things. I sound like a raving banshee."

"What things, Davvy?"

"Anything. The world. The news. The weather. The family."

"Our family?"

She turned to her brother. "Who else's? Oh, forget it." Then changing the subject, she said, "Where's the lovely Petra, Pierce? I thought she'd be along with us today. I mean, look at this gorgeous autumn sunshine. St James's Park never looked better. She's always so smart. I put on this new dress just to impress her. The assistant in Harrods said the peach matched my complexion. Very sweet, really. Thought I might find Juliet there, but no. Probably off screwing someone. God help her, she has a problem. But still, Petra? Not with us today?"

"Gone," he responded moodily.

"Gone? What's gone?"

"She's gone." Pierce glared at his sister as though it were her fault Petra was no longer with him.

"Gone where? Come on, Pierce, stop being so damned obtuse."

"I threw her out."

Davina stopped in her tracks. "You did what?"

"You heard." Pierce, hands in his jeans pockets, kicked at a pebble and walked on disconsolately.

"But why? She was nice. Maybe a bit on the mature side?" she ventured, stealing a look at her brother.

"Look, Davina, I think we need to talk." Pierce pointed at a park bench. "Do you mind if we sit for a moment?"

"Of course not," she replied, leading the way to the park seat. "I must say, you sound somewhat portentous, Pierce. Is there something I need to be worried about? Apart, that is, from Mummy still missing. Which I must say doesn't seem to leave Pa the least bit concerned. He just keeps saying she can take care of herself. Which, I suppose she can. But this has been a long absence."

"Davina," said Pierce, sitting down next to her. "For heaven's sake draw breath. First thing. I told Petra to leave after she drew some pretty unacceptable comparisons between Hitler and Pa. Particularly after I told her I'm concerned Pa may be involved with some far right group. She thought it made Pa look terribly sexy. I hadn't realised how foolish she was. So I ended it."

"Oh, Pierce; I'm so sorry. I thought you were really fond of her."

"So did I. For a time."

"What's all this about far right groups?"

"I happened to see some emails on Pa's laptop," said Pierce.

"Eavesdroppers never did learn anything to their advantage, you know."

"I do know. Petra said much the same thing."

"So?"

"I saw what I saw. And it knocked me sideways. Pa's always been very distant, a world of his own, but I realise now, he's a complete stranger. You know, apart from his political career, and now this right wing thing, which I'm presuming is somehow linked in with his political contacts, he's never really shown any interest in anything I can think of."

"I s'pose, now you talk about it," she pondered, staring off into the distance, then out of context, added, "David."

"What do you mean, David?"

"We all loved him. For all he was autistic, there were those times when somehow one of us, usually Jayne, could get through to him. Then that smile of his. Well."

"I know, Davs. It lit up the whole world," said Pierce sadly. "Pa either looked disinterested, or else really annoyed. I think he resented having to fork out so much money. I reckon he positively glowed after David died when he realised he'd have no more bills to meet."

"Come on, let's walk again. I'm restless," she said, getting up and starting to stroll ahead.

Pierce soon caught up with his sister, and let her take his arm as they walked on together. "Davvy?"

"Yes, brother."

"You'll think I'm mad."

"I do already, brother dear."

"Seriously, though."

Putting a forefinger stagily to her lips, she whispered, "Seriously, then. I'm all ears."

"Even if Pa's not worried by Ma's disappearance, I am. But I'm even more worried by those emails."

She matched her steps to Pierce's, as though emulating the troops who'd passed. "Darling, there's nothing you can do about it, you know."

"I think I can. And I think I have to."

"Have to?" she asked, facing her brother.

"Yes, have to." Pierce stopped walking to face Davina. "You know, I didn't want to make an issue out of it, but if you'd seen what I read..."

"Go on, then."

"I think Pa's conspiring with a number of MPs and far right groups, both here and abroad, to engage in some kind of coup."

Stroking her brother's cheek tenderly, Davina said, "Come now, Pierce. You know that's nonsense. Daddy's in line to be Chancellor of the Exchequer. Why would he risk his career for some ludicrous pie in the sky ambitions?" A sudden breeze blew up and she pulled her blouse closer about her neck.

Sighing, Pierce said, "I don't know. It seems absurd, but if you'd read those exchanges..."

Davina thought for a moment, concentrated. "But what you're suggesting Daddy's up to amounts to treason, no less. I mean, if convicted it carries a life sentence. God, Pierce, until the Labour peer Lord Archer banned it, hanging remained the penalty for treason until as recently as 1998."

"You're well informed, Davs. How do you know all that?"

"You know me, Pierce. A mine of useless information."

"I'm not going to let it happen, Davs."

"Darling, you don't know for sure what Daddy's up to. And even if you did, what could you do to stop it?"

"There's something more."

Hunching her shoulders and wrapping her arms about her as though she were thoroughly dismayed, Davina said, "You're beginning to alarm me now, Pierce. What more could there be?"

"You read about the recent murder of that security guy, Kevin Anderton?"

"He was working an undercover project, wasn't he?" Davina asked anxiously.

"That's right. I think, between the lines, he was on to one of those extremist right wing groups."

It had begun to cloud over quite quickly, spots of rain beginning to tap their shoulders. "Better get back before we get caught in a downpour," she suggested.

"Davvy, I think Pa knew about the Anderton thing, too. Maybe he was involved?"

"No!" she whispered. "Not Daddy."

"He's got to be stopped."

"How?"

"By me."

"You? What can you possibly do to stop these sorts of groups, Pierce?"

"I can't stop the group. But I can somehow influence or interrupt Pa's activities."

Davina shook her head. "I'm not convinced."

Pierce gazed off into the distance. Then said, as though talking to himself, "I'm going to infiltrate one of the groups."

"You can't," she gasped. "Even if you wanted to, they're highly secret. And we all know about far right extremists and the almost random killings. Look at that Scandinavian, Anders Breivik, seventy-seven slaughtered by a right wing maniac. What happens if and when you get into a group like that? How will you know who they are? Where they operate from? How to join, or infiltrate, as you put it?"

"I'll go onto the dark web if I have to. I'll do whatever it takes. If Pa is involved, someone will have to stop him."

"You'll get yourself killed one day, Pierce. Don't be stupid."

CHAPTER 14

EIGHT DAYS AGO

"I CAN'T STAY LONG. I need to be back at the House for a vote on a number of amendments to the Finance Act. Damned Opposition never know when to leave well alone. I'd shoot the bloody lot of 'em, given the chance."

The place was cramped, crowded with the hubbub of lunchtime customers.

"Are we okay to talk here?"

The man sitting opposite Oscar Mountford in Costa Coffee, close to the Houses of Parliament, was a sallow-complexioned, jowly, heavy-set man in his late fifties. An ageing British bulldog, without any of the usual characteristics of colonial stoicism on display. His thick, greying eyebrows were knit in an attitude of concern and he fidgeted constantly with the gold chain of a fob watch, hung loose across his immaculate black waistcoat.

"I'd have preferred to be walking outside. You know, no listening devices, and that sort of thing." A plummy middle-class accent. The man might have been an MP himself. But in fact, he was MacDonald Smollett, senior partner at leading firm of London based solicitors Smollett Davis Carleton.

The practice had been established sixty years ago by Smollett's father Angus, a dour Scot who'd come to England to read law at Cambridge and stayed on for good,

forming the practice, Smollett & Co, as a one-man band immediately on gaining his First. It had grown, largely due
to the young graduate's reputation for brilliance as a
lawyer and his integrity as a man, to the present hundred
partners, turning over in excess of fifty million pounds
a year.

Angus had married Edith, an English Literature
graduate he'd met at Cambridge, and their only child
MacDonald had been born a year later. Angus had died,
aged eighty-three, two years ago, never intending to fully retire. His widow Edith lived alone, still fiercely independent and self-sufficient, in the long-time marital home
in Cambridge.

MacDonald Smollett resided in the isolated splendour
of a large detached Edwardian house in Islington, having never married. He was, his father sadly suspected,
discreetly gay. The subject was never broached between
them, nor even alluded to.

Sipping from his espresso, Oscar said, "We're fine,
Mac. No hidden mikes here, and even if there were they'd
pick out nothing from this racket."

"If you say so, Oscar. Still…" He let the sentence hang
in the air, his jowls wobbling, before continuing, "You
know what I'm worried about."

"Of course I do. The killing of the Anderton man."
Smollett looked around as though convinced they could be
overheard. "He was getting too close, Mac. Something had
to be done."

Smollett pulled at his shirt collar. "But he was almost
certainly MI5, Oscar. We're getting out of our depth here.
I have to tell you, I'm not happy with the way things are
turning out."

Oscar, placing his cup deliberately on the table, leaned
forward on his elbows and stared fixedly at Smollett.
"You're involved, Mac. Whether you like it or not. We've a
big demonstration coming up. You know damn well I've
helped finance the thing, remember? I've laid out a hun-

dred K. So don't tell me now that you don't like the way things are turning out."

"Well."

"Well, nothing, my friend. It's not just money we're talking about here. It's this country, Mac. Our bloody country, and we are the ones to stop it going to the dogs. Blacks, Jews, Frogs. Only us. Remember, England Foremost."

"Wherever did that name come from?" Smollett sounded sceptical.

"Me, Mac. It came from me. I coined the name, and it's been taken up by a growing group that I partially finance. Don't pretend you don't know," he added, wagging a finger. "I've kept you in the loop all along."

"I know, but..." Smollett's top lip showed a sheen of sweat.

"But nothing," Oscar hissed. "We're linking up with other groups in Germany, Italy, Spain. This is big, and it's going to get bigger. Much bigger. On the home front I've got at least fifteen MPs from our Party and, believe it or not, a contingent of Labour lackeys."

"Labour?" asked Smollett, aghast. "You've got Labour support? You can't possibly be serious. They're utterly self-seeking and totally untrustworthy."

"There's some might say the same of us, Mac."

Smollett sat unspeaking for several moments, then changing the subject, asked, "Has there been any news of Letitia?"

"None. Thankfully."

"They still haven't identified the body on the Heath."

Oscar started getting up to leave. "You mean the one with the limbs missing and the harem trousers?"

"That's the one. Could it be her, do you think?"

"Doubtful, Mac. Still, one lives in hope."

CHAPTER 15

SOME WEEKS AGO

SHE'D COMBED HER HAIR *several times and still hadn't got it right. There was always a stray hair lurking. Finally she surveyed it, satisfied, the chosen style pulled back into a ponytail. But she still hadn't got the bobby socks to sit at exactly the same height as she wanted. Sighing, she adjusted them yet again, pulled up tight to the ankle. They looked right. Yes. They were right, at last.*

The white silk blouse with its Peter Pan collar took longer to adjust under the red bolero, but eventually she nodded at her reflection in the mirror of the shabby rented apartment in the South Bronx tenement block and left to meet her date. They'd hooked up through one of the online dating sites. She'd used the search function to seek an 'Exceptionally tall gentleman, ideally fifties, looks unimportant, art lover, Renaissance period? Appreciation of Rachmaninov'.

They met, at his suggestion, at an expensive fish restaurant overlooking the East River. He told her his name was Michael, but she was well aware it was really Mikhail. He was almost seven feet tall, shaven bald, with a bull neck and broken nose. In a black tailored two-piece suit, he might have been mistaken for a prosperous retired wrestler. There were one or two odd looks as the two of them entered the place, but people soon got on with their own meals. From what she learned of him he liked young girls. Despite her striking good looks, she clearly wasn't a young girl. But any doubts she may have had on that score were dispelled when he regarded her appraisingly as soon as he met her. He told her, over their meal, that he'd been born in Philadelphia to a pair of English teachers, educated at the local public school and then at Princeton, where he'd gained a degree in fine art. It had remained an interest, but he dealt mainly in property. Buying, selling, renovating and letting. He had a considerable portfolio spread around a number of major US cities.

He'd been in the US for twenty years. Had outlived his usefulness, might even have been turned, though he was far too canny to have been rumbled. His spoken US accented English was impeccable with not the trace of a Russian inflection. His quiet demeanour and confident delivery had her wondering. She was beginning to find him sexually attractive, and although it was dangerously, foolishly unprofessional, moved her leg tentatively against his, only to find him subtly respond. God, she thought. If only. Then feeling one of his giant paws grasp her thigh, she shuddered, found herself wildly wondering, if, and if so, where?

"Do they have rooms here," she whispered.

"No. This place isn't a hotel. But there's somewhere nearby. We can... If you're sure." He caught her glance, stared back at her as though seeking to gauge her intentions correctly.

Putting her hand on his, she asked, "Do you... Do you have? I mean, can you, now...?"

"Wait," he said, pushing his chair back. "Give me a moment."

"You've left your drink. It was so expensive," she offered, indicating his glass of wine.

"I'll be two minutes. Why not finish yours."

He hurried unsteadily from the table, having had considerably more to drink than his date, and she watched him paying the bill at the desk before disappearing through a door marked 'Restrooms'.

Not quite how she'd planned it, but one could always improvise. Slipping a hand into the pocket of her ridiculous little skirt, she unobtrusively withdrew a plastic screw-top cylinder of clear liquid. Five milligrams of gamma-hydroxybutyric acid, or GHB, liquid E, cherry meth, scoop, soap, salty water, the date rape drug. More than three times the usual dose, and enough to knock out a horse. But then Mikhail was a very large gentleman.

Glancing left and right she noted that people nearest to her were concentrating on the big man, not her. Taking a deep breath, she slipped the liquid into his drink and swirled the glass once, hoping she'd guessed the dose correctly. It could take anything from fifteen minutes to an hour to work, and then would be undetectable in the man's urine beyond twelve hours of ingestion.

He was back in moments and, glancing down at the front of his trousers, smiled at her. "Love glove's in place," he offered, then seeing her puzzlement, added, "the rubber, honey."

"Ah." She understood, and raised her glass to him, while he responded with a polite nod, raised his and they both finished their drinks together.

"This way," he said, taking her by the hand and leading her outside.

"A moment," she pleaded. "It's so cool and fresh out here after the warmth of the restaurant. Let's walk along this promenade for a moment. There's no-one around at this time. It's so nice to have the place to ourselves. Do you mind?"

"Fine by me." He smiled. "Got all the time in the world."

"Yes, Mr. Bond." She grinned back.

For a moment Mikhail was puzzled, then said, "Ah yes. Old Satchmo, On Her Majesty's Secret Service."

Palm to palm, they strolled the promenade by the water's edge, its surface glittering with the reflected lights of the surrounding buildings. An occasional river vessel chugged past, but otherwise all was still.

The East River is in fact not a river at all, but a salt water tidal estuary in New York City, connecting Long Island Sound on its north end with Upper New York Bay at its southern extremity. Its tidal flows and currents are subject to unpredictable changes. Coupled with that, it is still comparatively polluted and not generally a recommended spot for amateur holiday swimmers.

Mikhail was in no condition for a midnight dip. In fact, his gait had become noticeably less steady as the drug began to take effect and he lurched from side to side. Turning to the woman next to him, he growled, "Summings wrong here. Whatchoo bin up to, lady?"

"Hold me, Michael," she asked plaintively, seeking to divert his attention. A man his size could be dangerous if he felt threatened or at any sort of disadvantage. She didn't know how long she'd have, but flinging her arms around him, he responded immediately, holding her tight. She could hear his breathing becoming laboured as she turned ever so slightly, manoeuvring him towards a gap in the railings by the water's edge.

Uncertain of what was happening he sought to halt her progress, whereupon she fumbled with the front of his trousers, feeling him quickly respond. Crushing her hips up against his, yet again she thought ruefully, if only. Then he was pulling up the tiny skirt, pressing hard against her. She moaned softly, then abruptly pulled away. Madness, she thought. This sort of self-indulgence could get her killed.

"What is it?" he asked, his speech becoming clearer, his vision less blurred. But he was still on his feet, now unsteady, his bent legs spread, body bent forward, beginning to topple, a hand on the ground supporting his weight as he stared up at her.

She was close to him. Too close. His eyes narrowed to slits.

"Don't fuck with me, lady," he snarled, and swung the flat of his hand up against her cheek, sending her spinning. She landed on all fours, ripping the skin from her palms and kneecaps, and having lost the initiative, she cursed. She was now in real danger.

For a moment she was lost, mentally drawing a blank. Dragging herself to her feet and acting purely on instinct, she backed off several paces. He was standing now. Ready to advance towards her. Without thinking she ran at him, full tilt, crashing into his midriff.

Though making him stagger, he'd otherwise hardly moved. But his arms now hung limp at his sides. The drug was starting to take greater effect.

She backed off and ran at him again and again, gradually moving him closer to the water's edge. But she was tiring as fast as he was.

"I'm gonna have you," he muttered.

Then she made a mistake. "No you're not, Mikhail."

Now he stood up straight, as though he'd been lanced by a bolt of lightning. "Mikhail?" he asked. "Mikhail? Who's Mikhail? Chertovski suka."

"Who's a fucking bitch?" she goaded.

"Stop! Who are you? Where the fuck...?"

But she was frightened. She'd turned around now and was running back. Running at him. Running for her life. He stood with arms folded, a sardonic look, and watched her as she approached, long loping strides.

Then she jumped high, wrapping her legs about his neck, her crotch in his face. He staggered back, and she grabbed his chin, pulling his head back. Disorientated, he lurched several paces towards the gap in the railings, fighting her off.

But she clung on hard. He had his hands on her legs and was disentangling them. Even with the drug taking effect he was too powerful for her.

Then they were toppling over. Over and over into the blackness of the East River.

She still had her legs about his neck as he attempted to struggle to the surface, gasping for air, grasping for a purchase against her. He was still strong. He was going to win. Fighting her off. Manic strength.

She was out of fuel. Could feel herself being dragged down. All over. She was under the surface, barely able to hold her breath. Blackness closing in.

Then quite suddenly it stopped, as though a light switch had been flicked off in the man, and she watched from under the surface of the filthy river, as he floated away from her, floated on with arms and legs flailing uselessly, and finally sank gracefully, the undercurrent carrying him swiftly away from her.

Pushing up, hands clawing, feet working, her head finally above the water, gasping, spluttering, wondering at her own folly. Close. Too close. No joy in the kill.

Floating on her back. Regaining her calm. She'd won. Against the odds.

A smile spread across her face. Joy at last.

They'd moved a fair way from the shore, the gentle wash of an approaching boat, its lights enveloping her; a man's voice called out, concerned, "You okay, lady?"

"I'm fine," she called back. "Couldn't resist a quick dip. Water's lovely."

"Not so clean, ma'am," came the response. "Changing currents. Lotta undertow. People been known to drown out here."

CHAPTER 16 DAY 3

"D^{OV?}"

"Tammy."

"Missing you." Be better if she didn't sound so needy. Trouble was she did need him, not that she'd ever admit as much. Too damn obstinate.

"Don't, Tammy. You know I can't do anything about it."

She'd just returned from an early morning jog in Queen's Park close to her flat, itself situated in a small modern luxury block in an area of mostly Victorian and Edwardian conversions. Comprising a solid grey sugar cube of a building, it gave Tammy a sense of permanence and security within the hazards of her profession. This was the same apartment she'd shared with lover Ginny.

Later in the day, she planned a visit to a small private gym she used, in a cul-de-sac off the main thoroughfare in the area, for a bout of boxing with her occasional personal trainer from Glasgow, Ralph McAllen. Short, squat and powerful though he was, Tammy always gave him a run for his money. He had the skills and experience, she had the height and reach. And she was strong, very strong. That's why she'd survived on her last jaunt in Syria. But the session today with Ralph would be a gentle one.

The morning was fresh, and after the devastating pounding she'd suffered during her capture in the affair of the Black Candles, she was glad to be gradually return-ing to fitness. Her local GP Doctor Aziz had said exercise was alright, but strictly kept within limits. She must not risk her pregnancy again. With her high levels of testos-terone she couldn't be certain she'd conceive once more if she failed to go to term. He'd given her a complete top-to-toe examination, including checking on weight and height. "One hundred and seventy-five pounds and six feet one," he'd announced.

"I've put on weight," she replied.

"You're pregnant. Of course you're heavier."

"Hey, I'm not that far gone."

"Well you're not that much heavier than the last time we checked your height and weight."

"And that's another thing," she added. "I'm six feet tall, not six feet one. Unless I'm growing too."

The doctor, glancing over his notes, ran a finger down the page. "Here it is," he confirmed. "You were six feet one at the date of your last complete check-up, and the one before. Surely I've mentioned it to you every time?"

"It couldn't have registered," she said, doing up her blouse and straightening the collar. Then she smiled. "I think I can live with it. I've managed so far."

Back in the flat, after stripping off her tracksuit she'd stepped into the shower and stood there for fully fifteen minutes, letting the scalding hot water loosen all the muscles and tendons. The feeling was positively sensual.

As she lay back on her bed, naked, mobile in hand, she pressed the call button on her phone as let her mind drift to Dov. Not Ginny, she realised. Perhaps she was finally putting that relationship to rest.

But Dov, more than any man she'd ever known, secure in the knowledge of his own masculinity, constantly reminded her, when she was with him, of her own undoubted femininity. For most other men her physicality, intelligence and that height of hers, was a threat to them.

In a moment she'd be asking Dov to accompany her to the US. Running over what was known. The Letitia Mountford project was becoming an increasing mystery.

Detective Chief Superintendent Bob Walker had not yet felt it necessary to advise Oscar who was apparently untroubled by his wife's disappearance. Tammy had met up with Bob Walker and his CIA contact who insisted on going by the name Felix, in tribute to his name-sake's character in some of the Bond movies.

Still naked, Tammy climbed off her bed and wandered thoughtfully around the bedroom, the mobile to her ear. "Bob Walker's been in touch, Dov."

"I'm listening."

"I've had a meeting with him and Felix."

"The CIA guy?"

"Right," she said, sitting down at her whitewood dressing table and shuffling through her lipsticks and perfumes.

"And?"

There was a pause, then, "They want me to try and locate a woman who's gone missing."

"A woman, Tammy? What woman? And why's Bob Walker involved?"

"You know the name Oscar Mountford, Dov?"

"Up-and-coming politician. I do read the papers."

"He's the one tipped to be our next Chancellor."

"I know."

"It's his wife, Letitia."

"And when did she go missing?"

"About eight weeks ago."

"Eight weeks? And he's waited this long to report it? Any leads yet?"

"She's been traced to the Ritz-Carlton in New York. And here's the thing, she flew out on the same plane as a rather poor double."

"To throw off any trace?"

"Right. Only it seems as though her so-called double is running wild in some of New York's seedier areas. She's killed three people; at least we're pretty sure it's her."

"How do you know that?"

"You wouldn't ask if you could see the outfits she sports."

"Conspicuous?"

"You might say. Ponytail, white bobby socks, a red micro-mini drum majorette skirt and short-sleeved blouse under a red bolero jacket?"

"Isn't she a bit old for that sort of thing?"

"Letitia is. She's in her forties, but wearing pretty well. This woman, the stand-in believed to be carrying out the killings, might be slightly younger."

Tammy heard Dov breathe in and wondered what was coming next.

"Very well," he announced. "I'll stop hedging around and be frank with you, Tammy. You've called me burner to burner, so I can speak freely. We, that's Mossad, know Mountford. And we know his wife too. She's got history. I've not spoken of it till now, as it hadn't come up on your radar. But as it's clearly there, and you're obviously included, let me brief you."

"History?" Tammy stopped fiddling with the items on the dressing table and with her elbow on the surface leaned her chin in the palm of her hand. "What history? Something here I need to know?"

"Her parents are dead. At least, from what we've found, we think they are. Possibly killed in a car crash when she was about ten years old. She was brought up by an aunt. Her birth certificate shows her father to be Ukrainian. A man called Pyotr Filipek. She was called Larissa Filipek. During her LSE days, and possibly before, she became involved with politics, in particular, the Communist Party," Dov explained.

"Good heavens. Why do you think she was involved with politics before university?" Tammy asked.

"Because she changed her name to the far less conspicuous Letitia Philips before starting at university. She's now Letitia Mountford."

"So why do you think the Communist Party, Dov?"

"At first it was the fashionable thing to do. Then it seems she either got committed to it, or else maybe, persuaded. Could be she was bought? Coerced? Who knows?"

"Wow!" murmured Tammy. "Is Oscar aware?"

"He's no idea. At first she was an informant of minor university student or lecturer transgressions that might be of interest to the Russians. Later she was trained to be an assassin, a role, it seems, she was rather adept at, despite protesting to her current handler it wasn't in her terms of employment."

"You know an awful lot about her, Dov."

"We've been keeping a close eye on her for some time. One of our operatives overheard a conversation with one we presume is her UK intermediary. As I said, I didn't realise you might become involved. I can tell you, she doesn't like her present go-between either. Not one little bit. She's been giving him a hard time. Leaving him angry and confused. She's a rebel, and extremely dangerous."

"Dov, does Bob Walker or anyone at MI5 know any of this?"

"Not yet. MI5 suspect something. As do 6. Of course they both know of her university past. But she's been well-managed and it's all been ultra-discreet."

"Shouldn't they be informed?"

"Shortly. We'll see what happens next. We're keeping a close eye on everything."

Picking up a short bristle brush Tammy raked it through her tight curly hair, feeling the welcome surge of circulation in her scalp. The wound at the side of her head where the giant of a man, Bear, had cut her, was all but healed. The scar, about which she'd been so self-conscious, no longer visible.

"It's a mess," Dov added. "On top of everything else, we've found Mountford is involved with alt.right groups. You know all about these extremist collections of misfits."

"Of course. Trouble is, they're not all mentally backward, are they. A lot of them are in positions of power and responsibility, and sufficiently influential to draw in the gullible, the lonely and the misfits. Like our friend Mountford. Though he's hardly a misfit. Quite the opposite, worryingly. I wonder, what are his pet hates? His particular bêtes noires?"

"You'd be a problem for him, Tammy. He doesn't like people of colour. Nor Jews. He's a deadly individual. Mossad believes he may have been instrumental in the murder of one Kevin Anderton, a security man investigating far right groups. Mountford's type are functioning lunatics, and what's more, he could be your next Chancellor. Odd, isn't it."

She'd pulled on a pair of tiny white knickers and sat back down, still half naked, gazing at her own reflection in the dressing table mirror, wondering what colour lipstick to go for, and wishing Dov were with her now. "What's odd?" she wondered aloud.

"His socio-political obsessions don't prevent him from actually doing what might be a good job as Chancellor."

"I hadn't thought of that. But as you mention it. He's a rich man, isn't he, knows how to deal with mega sums."

"True. And there've been plenty of able psychopaths in history. Look at Robespierre. Lawyer and politician. Called 'the incorruptible'. He presided over the executions of thousands during the French Revolution, which his party, the Jacobins, largely initiated in the Reign of Terror that witnessed Paris streets literally running with blood. Then in a supreme irony, he succumbed to the guillotine himself."

"Yes, I know, Dov. And there're lots more you could name. Genghis Khan, Atilla the Hun, Hitler, Mussolini. Then there're the super-rich, criminals with vast organisations to support their enterprises. People like Scarface, Al Capone, whose activities in the twenties brought him in a staggering two hundred million dollars a year."

Neither spoke for several seconds, an anticipatory silence hovering between them.

Then Dov asked, "You called me, Tammy. I'm assuming we're talking about Letitia Mountford? Let me guess. You're going to the US and want me to accompany you."

"In one, Dov."

"You've not forgotten, Esther's expecting."

"Yes, Dov, you told me. Not something I'd likely forget, is it. Really, I wouldn't ask if I didn't think it absolutely necessary."

She went back to that time in the hospital. Her return from Syria. The look of utter despair he gave her when he came to visit. Had he known about Esther's pregnancy at the time? Was that why he'd looked so bereft? The acceptance that he'd be tied to Esther for the foreseeable future? That for Tammy and himself there was no future?

"What am I supposed to tell her?" he asked.

"Come on, Dov, you'll think of something. You always do."

"I'm not so sure, Tammy. She was pretty angry about the Trinidad trip. When were you planning on going anyway?"

"Couple of days."

"And in the meantime?"

"I'm going to talk to her husband. Oscar Mountford."

"Tammy." Dov sounded worried. "I know you can take care of yourself…"

"That's right, Dov, I can. As long as the odds aren't too stacked against me. Letitia has been found. Bob wants to know what's going on. Three dead. How many more? I've got to talk to Mountford."

"But, Tammy, I'm telling you, this man is treacherous. Take it from me. He pays people to do what he wants. Investigate the wife if you must. But leave him out of the picture. Please. I'm asking you. There's more here than meets the eye. Keep out of his sight. Don't have anything to do with him."

Tammy had finally settled on a lipstick, a bold cerise by Dior. "Bit of a paradox, all this, isn't it?"

"How so?"

"Just look at it. Ultra-right wing husband married to ultra-left wing wife. Shakespeare had it nailed, didn't he? In The Comedy of Errors. An apt title. Except, this is no comedy. And there's certainly no themes of love and loyalty. Just hate and betrayal."

"Do you hear me, Tammy? It's possible, even likely, Mountford's been involved in more than just the murder of Kevin Anderton. Once he has you in his sights..." He sounded tired now, spoke softly, a note of something like desperation in his voice. "Please, for God's sake, for my sake, don't put yourself in danger's way."

"Dov, my love," she announced, "I'm seeing Oscar Mountford in his office tomorrow."

It was as she rang off her mobile that the home landline sounded. Few people knew the number, and she frowned, perplexed as she put the receiver to her ear. All she could hear was the hum of traffic and distant noise of children playing.

The hairs on her arms prickled in premonition as she waited, wondering whether to hang up, when she heard a muffled voice say, "Y'ell not find her. Leave well alone, missy, before someone gets really hurt."

She couldn't place the accent.

CHAPTER 17 DAY 3

"WE ARE A TOTALLY, fucking, dysfunctional family." Davina Nathan, Oscar Mountford's eldest daughter, paced the living-room floor of the elegant Chelsea riverside home she shared with her generally ineffectual husband, Jerry.

With her honey-coloured shoulder-length hair and healthy complexion, she looked every bit the English rose she clearly once was. But business pressures, family jealousies and a husband she held in polite contempt, had all contributed to her ageing prematurely. She was twenty-six but could have been years older. She'd started designing jewellery at sixteen as part of a school art project and found she had a natural flair. Now she designed and manufactured for a number of wealthy Middle Eastern gentlemen, mainly introduced to her by her father.

Her husband, a balding, heavy-set but retiring man, whose size didn't compensate for his timidity, ran a small private recruitment agency. It was singularly unsuccessful as Jerry lacked the necessary drive to push candidates hard enough. Their magnificent home was, of course, care of his wife, assisted, unsurprisingly, by her father.

"Why are you all dysfunctional, my dear?" Jerry nursed a glass of sherry in both hands as though it were a pet mouse, and gazed out at the river from their antique-laden living room.

"Why? I'll tell you why," she responded, throwing her hands in the air in exasperation. "Pa's pissing around with his PA, Georgia. He thinks nobody knows."

"Does your mother know about this?"

"How would I know? She's been missing for weeks. Pa doesn't seem to give a toss. Though he does say he's got one of his government security people to look into it. MI5, or something." She stopped pacing the room and stood with her hands on her hips, glaring at her husband as though the family ills were all his fault.

Turning back from the window, Jerry said, "MI5? Why MI5, for heaven's sake. Your mother's not in league with terrorists. Is she?"

"Think about it, Jerry. It shouldn't be too difficult, even for you. Pa is in line to be our next Chancellor. If there's any whiff of scandal, he won't get the job. Ma is bloody missing. Capito? Words of one syllable?"

"Yes, my dear. I do understand."

Jerry took a sip of sherry and smiled benignly at his wife as he sat himself in one of a pair of Queen Anne wing chairs either side of the fireplace. "Tell me, does Pierce know about what's going on? Or Juliet? Come to think of it, how about Jayne?"

"How would I know? Pierce is nosing around, convinced that Pa's up to something. What? I've no idea. But Pierce hinted at some illicit ultra-right wing political activity. You never know with Pa. If he buggers up his political capital it'll be no-one's fault but his own."

Davina had helped herself to a generous dry sherry from the Regency drinks cabinet, and joined George in the opposite wing chair.

"I see." Jerry studied the Persian rug, like a child that has spilt its drink. "And Juliet?"

"Juliet's been showing me some expensive items she's got from the jewellery departments in Harrods. I thought maybe her boss, being a director, might have gifted them to her. But he's not that gullible. No. Our Juliet is enjoying the attentions of as many young men in the store as she can accommodate. So gifts galore. I think she's waiting for the annual Harrods sale when there'll be a quarter of a million customers in the shop, half of them men. And she'll only have a fortnight to work her way through the lot. Shouldn't be too difficult for her."

"My goodness, Davina."

Leaning back in the armchair, Davina crossed her trousered legs and breathed in slowly as though to keep her temper. "Oh, for God's sake, Jerry."

"And Jayne? What's she up to? I remember she was terribly upset when your brother David..." He left the rest unsaid.

"We were all upset. We are upset. He was the one thing that held the family together. Her, and Ma, I suppose, when she's around. Where the hell is she anyway? What's she playing at? Never been gone this long before."

Throwing back the last of her sherry, Davina added, "As for Davie, even now I can't believe he's gone. Jayne's been working for some time with kids who have learning difficulties. You know, Autism or Asperger's. She adored Davie the most. Idolised him. She won't have got over this. All too recent. Blames herself."

"Never knew what happened there, you know." She toyed with the empty sherry glass.

"David could hold himself up in the bath. He didn't need propping, but he'd slipped under the surface of the water somehow. Ma was exhausted taking care of him. Distraught when he died. Blamed herself too."

CHAPTER 18 DAY 4

TAMMY ARRIVED in Westminster at precisely 10.00 am for her 10.30 am appointment with Oscar Mountford. It wouldn't do to keep the man waiting, so she'd taken no chances on being late, mooring the Lexus in Coaches Park on Tothill Street, about five minutes' walk from Mountford's building, the impressive Portcullis House.

Knowing the man's reputation with women, she'd dressed carefully, opting for a sober two-piece flared-trouser suit in clerical grey, with a white open-neck blouse. The twin triangle gold amulet with its Hebrew inscription nestled between her breasts, with just enough décolletage on view to inspire interest, without seeming blatant. Her individually designed three-inch Manolo Blahnik bootees, in finest black calfskin, might give her a slight height advantage over Mountford.

Waiting in the oak-panelled ante room outside his office, she was offered coffee by Mountford's PA, Georgia Keith, a smartly turned out, still attractive woman, Tammy guessed to be in her forties. But with a worried demeanour, badly masked by her attempt at cheerfulness.

Whether it was Georgia's apparent tension, or her own slight apprehension at the prospect of meeting this man that Dov had begged her not to see, she wasn't sure. Bob Walker had counselled against advising Mountford that his wife had been traced at this stage. He didn't seem worried by her unexplained absence, so her job was to try to find out what made the man tick. At least, in her opinion. Bob had known Mountford for some time as an acquaintance but was interested in getting Tammy's views. Plus there'd been a number of apparently motiveless murders in the US by the double of Oscar Mountford's wife, needing to be to be unravelled.

Mountford kept Tammy sitting outside his office until almost 11.00 am before he had Georgia show her in. With that volatile temperament of hers, the wait had had her beginning to steam. He then didn't apologise for keeping her waiting.

Like the ante room, the office was oak-panelled, the walls lined with bookshelves and costly Persian rugs were scattered around. Mountford's vast antique leather-topped desk was devoid of all paperwork, supporting a green glass Art Deco Banker's desk lamp. There were also two landlines and three mobile phones neatly laid out. She observed a couple of Sheraton chairs and a Hepplewhite occasional table in the room. On the walls, in addition to pictures of race meetings and yachts, were arrayed etchings and lithographs by Degas, Lautrec and Renoir, with no less than three Art Deco nudes by Tamara de Lempicka. Clearly Mr Mountford was an individual with a great deal of money. Nothing new there. Also, here was someone with taste. Not unlike plenty of the world's worst dictators, she pondered, with their love of art and classical music.

The soft hum of traffic going past could just be heard, but nothing else.

He'd stood up when Tammy entered his office, and she'd been immediately taken aback by his presence. Seen on TV he came across as attractive enough, but in the flesh he was little short of dazzling, all six feet four of him. In a navy pinstripe two-piece, with plain white shirt and slim silk tie, he resembled what once might have been referred to as a matinee idol. Certainly the square jaw, piercing blue eyes and thick grey hair made for a dashingly handsome individual. No trouble finding candidates seeking extra-marital affairs for this man. He'd be as at home on the parade ground barking orders as he would be instructing a firing squad.

Despite her bootees he was a shade taller than her, and as she sat in the proffered leather button-back chair opposite his desk, he made no secret of his appraisal, brazenly sizing her up as though she were a meat carcass for sale.

Composing herself, her legs crossed and hands in her lap, Tammy began. "Thank you for agreeing to see me, Mr Mountford."

"Oh please," he responded, arms extended expansively. "Call me Oscar."

His nails were manicured, and he was wearing an expensive cologne. Watching his body language, she found his movements almost mesmeric. "You know why I'm here," she paused, then went on, "Oscar."

His eyes locked on to hers, and there was the odd sensation of being trapped. Hemmed in. Unsure of what was coming next. Then quite unexpectedly he asked, "What's that thing between your bosoms?"

Bosoms? She flushed slightly at the neck. What an extraordinary reference in this, the twenty-first century. Feeling almost shy she responded, "It's an amulet given me by my father."

"I can see what it is," he said brusquely. "I was wondering what the hieroglyphs meant."

"They're not hieroglyphics, Mr…Oscar," she corrected herself. "They're Hebrew lettering. An inscription, designed to protect."

He clasped his hands together, interlacing the fingers, his brows knit, concentrating. "You mean, mumbo jumbo?"

"If you like. But really, only if you take that sort of thing seriously."

"And do you?" He grinned.

"Hardly. The sentiments expressed on it are merely an expression of my father's wish to see me protected from harm."

"And have you? Been protected from harm, I mean?" he said, taking in her scarred hands, which she self-consciously grasped closer together.

Gazing over Mountford's shoulder at the sun shining on the building opposite, she let him wait for her answer, then said quietly, "I've had a few scrapes."

"But survived," he added, irrelevantly.

Tammy smiled, but made no comment.

"How can I help you, Ms…?"

"Tammy will do, Oscar."

Reaching into a drawer in the desk, Mountford withdrew an A4 pad and, taking a gold Mont Blanc from inside his jacket pocket, addressed Tammy, "Really, it's about how you can help me. Bob's briefed you of course."

"Of course."

"I don't know where she is. Letitia, I mean. I'm not worried. Not sure I even care." He gazed about distractedly as though he might find her lurking somewhere in his office. "She's always disappearing for days at a time. Never says where she's been. I used to ask, but not any more. She has her life and I have mine."

"But you wanted her disappearance to be investigated?"

"Naturally. Bob must have told you I'm in line for Chancellor of the Exchequer. If Letitia is up to no good it could crucify my chances. Got to be squeaky clean these days."

"Unlike the days of rotten boroughs and purchased seats in the House of Commons," she offered.

A tap at the office door and Mountford's PA came in wielding a silver tray supporting a choice of coffee and tea pots with a dish of biscuits, which she carefully deposited on the desk. Her brows knit when Mountford, without a word, batted her away as though she were a troublesome fly.

"And what do you know of rotten boroughs, my dear?"

Briefly clenching her fists, and keeping her temper under control, Tammy smiled sweetly and responded, "I know enough not to be patronised by you, Oscar."

"Incidentally, that accent?" he enquired, ignoring her last remark. "French, is it? Bob didn't say where you were from. Or that…that…" For the first time Mountford floundered, very out of his comfort zone.

"That I'm black?"

"Well," he shifted in his seat, "mixed race, I'd say."

"Does that make it better, then?"

"Not at all," he replied, recovering quickly and, reaching for the coffee pot, gave a nod in her direction, to which she acquiesced. "Help yourself to a biscuit." Pushing the coffee towards Tammy he poured himself a cup of tea. "And?" he enquired, leaving the question hanging like a loose end.

"My mother was French. Parisian banking family."

"Was?"

"She died of breast cancer some ten years ago. French was my first language."

"Your father?"

"Trinidadian. Elderly. Retired architect."

"Ah, Caribbean. I suppose that's where…"

"Yes, Oscar. That accounts for my colour."

"I didn't mean…"

"Of course you didn't." It was all very polite for now. "You want to know what Letitia is up to and whether it could hinder your chances of the Chancellorship. It's early days, but we believe she may have been spotted in the US, and I'm proposing to go out there in a day or two to investigate."

"That's all?"

"So far." Tammy blew on the surface of her steaming cup of coffee, noting the expensive bone china she was holding. "What I need to know from you is what you know about your wife. Her interests. Her activities. Her political views. Has she been faithful to you? What does she watch? What does she read? Does she seem happy to you? Does she get on with the children? Is she a good mother?"

"Anything else? You seem to have mapped out enough there for a biography. Where do I start?"

"I'll take them one at a time. Her interests?"

"None. Bar maybe gossiping with friends about nothing I can see of any use."

"Her activities?"

"Horse riding in Hyde Park."

"Her politics."

"You have got to be joking. She doesn't know her left hand from her right, let alone the politics of each extreme."

"Has she been faithful to you?"

"God knows."

"What does she watch or read?"

"No idea."

"Does she seem happy to you? Is she, or was she a good mother?"

Oscar sighed, he was starting to look impatient. Deliberately plunked his cup and saucer down. "A good mother? How would I bloody know. Pierce, my prodigal son, is a mystery to me. Davina gets on with Letitia, I suppose. Juliet? She sleeps with men in teams. Usually together, from what I can see. Otherwise, no idea. Jayne likes her mother. They've always got on. Both devastated when David died."

"Does Letitia have any distinguishing features? Birth marks? Visible scars? Tattoos?"

"Not really. She was pretty conventional all round, apart from the behaviour, characterised by the absences." He gazed about him. "There was one thing, though."

"Tell me."

"Hardly what you'd call visible, but she had a tiny navel piercing made years ago. Of all things, a skull and crossbones. No idea why she bothered, it was barely noticeable. Still, not the sort of thing she could be identified by if you bumped into her."

"Tell me about David, Oscar?"

Leaning back in his swivel chair he responded, "What's to tell?"

"You tell me."

Oscar shrugged. "The boy was born backward. Autistic. Angelman Syndrome, they called it. Happy Puppet Syndrome. Rubbish. A cretin, if you ask me. I told Letitia not to bother, get him into care. But she insisted we keep him at home. Madness really. She knocked herself out over the kid. As did Jayne. Both of them made it a sort of personal crusade."

"Is that bad, then? Surely it's admirable. I'm told all your children loved him."

Shrugging with disinterest, Oscar said, "It's tough out there, isn't it? Law of the wild. Law of the jungle. Let the infirm go to the wall, I say. Not the resources in society to support every lame duck."

"Lame duck, Oscar? He was your son. Is that how you viewed him? Did you have anything to do with him at all?"

"Not if I could help it. Couldn't understand a word he said. All gibberish. I had my way, those in that situation would be discreetly euthanised at birth."

"Isn't that a somewhat Hitlerian approach?"

"What if it is?" He was starting to look and sound hostile, hands flat on the desk.

"Where do you stop, Oscar? Hitler killed the disabled, homosexuals, blacks, Jews."

"Not everything Hitler did was wrong. Be fair."

"Be fair? Are you really being serious, Oscar?"

"Got the trains running on time, didn't he?"

"Wasn't that Mussolini?"

"Well alright. It was roads Hitler built. The autobahn."

"Worth killing tens of millions for?"

"Only those superfluous to society. Those not making a contribution."

"Homosexuals?"

"Condemned according to the Bible. Chapters 18 to 20 of Leviticus. 'You shall not lie with a male as a woman. It is an abomination'."

"Blacks?"

"Backward. Should have stayed in Africa."

"What about equality? Abraham Lincoln—"

"Abraham Lincoln said, and I can quote you from his speech, 'I will say that I am not, nor ever have been, in favour of bringing about in any way the social and political equality of the white and the black'."

"I know that speech. You've quoted him out of context. Lincoln was an abolitionist. The Jews?"

"Owned too much. Started controlling everything. Getting too powerful."

"Hitler said the Jews were lower than beasts. How could they also be controlling everything?"

"He had a point."

"I'm a Jew, Oscar. A Jewess."

Appraising her once more, as though throwing out a challenge, he said, "Oh so you do acknowledge you're female?"

"Of course I do. Do I alarm you, Oscar?" She smiled. "Some men appear intimidated by me. My height. My intellect. Mainly those males who like to see their woman as, 'the little lady'."

The atmosphere was clearly becoming strained. They were speaking more rapidly. Tammy began to rein herself in, aiming to gain some sort of insight into the man.

Banging the palm of his hand on the table, Oscar said loudly, "Well, it's time we men wound the clock back and had women learn their place once more."

"You mean waiting on men?"

"Well, what's wrong with that? The Christian Bible insists a woman's place—"

"And whether you like it or not, I'm black too," she interrupted. "What's more, Jesus was a Jew. Whilst being Semitic, some would also say, a person of colour, if not black."

"Jesus was a Jew?" His voice was starting to rise, and there was a sheen of sweat on his brow. "For God's sake woman, Jesus was the first Christian."

At this, Tammy went out on a limb. "You're beginning to sound like an extremist yourself, Oscar."

"What? What do you mean, extremist? What's an extremist anyway?"

"Hitler, Mussolini, both of whom you seem to admire. How many others like them, I wonder. What happened to reason and debate?"

"Where did that ever get anyone? Bismarck talked about the great questions of the day not being decided through speeches, but by blood and iron."

"Some say Bismarck's policies helped introduce the First World War."

"He brought about the unification of Germany."

Tammy crept further out on that limb. "What do you know about alt.right groups, Oscar?"

"I beg your pardon?" He'd been stopped dead in his tracks.

"I was wondering, listening to your views. They seem ripe for that sort of pseudo-political affiliation."

"Hardly pseudo, Ms Pierre. They are gaining in legitimacy and power. Look at Hungary, Italy, Spain. We — They," he swiftly corrected himself, "they will eventually accede to power in most European countries."

"They have a reputation for violence, Oscar. If anyone gets in their way? You may have read about the murder of Kevin Anderton, a security man, possibly with MI5, who infiltrated a number of the extreme right wing groups in the UK and was murdered for his trouble." She then determined to test the waters further. "It's said his killing was planned, organised even, by a prominent up-and-coming Member of Parliament."

Oscar had gone white and his face had turned to stone, apart from a barely discernible tic under one eye. "Unfounded rumour. And what does it have to do with my missing wife? Why are you asking me this?"

"With your various political affiliations, I just wondered…"

Clumsily getting to his feet, Mountford, turning his back on Tammy, muttered through clenched teeth, "You're getting out of your depth here, Ms. Pierre. You're into very deep waters. Over your head. I don't know what you're really up to, but this interview is over."

"HE WANTS TO have you killed. And he can do it. I've suspected it of him in the past, but discounted it as impossible. But I was wrong. I've been a wantonly blind fool. A complete idiot."

The voice was frightened. Terrified. "I need to speak with you, Ms. Pierre. It's very urgent. Please, please, how soon can I see you?"

The tone was familiar, though the last time she'd heard it, it had been polite and efficient. Rather more in control. Certainly not in the sort of state it was right now.

But, just who? Then, it came to her, of course.

"Ms. Keith? Georgia Keith?"

"That's right, Georgia. Oscar's PA. Can I...?"

"It's a bit late, isn't it? But, well, yes. Come over now. I'm in Queen's Park. Will you be driving?"

"No. I'll come by Uber."

Tammy gave Georgia the address, and twenty minutes later she arrived, as breathless as if she'd run all the way, rather than taxied. She hadn't changed out of her work clothes and Tammy guessed she'd been kept late by Oscar and come straight from the Ministry. Walking into Tammy's apartment Georgia was wide-eyed. "Oh, Ms. Pierre, what a wonderful flat. It's quite beautiful. Did you engage interior designers?"

"No, I planned it all myself."

Distractedly removing her mid-length dark blue coat, Georgia said, "Really? Hey, you're a genius."

"I doubt that."

"If I'm not being terribly rude?"

"Go ahead."

"The cost of an apartment like this. Your earnings as a private investigator…"

"Wouldn't cover the cost of this, I can assure you. Papa was an architect. Now retired. Comfortable, but not rich. Maman…"

"Papa? Maman? French? I noticed your slight accent."

"Maman was French. It was my first language for a while. I was educated initially in France. She died of breast cancer —"

"Oh, I'm sorry," Georgia interrupted.

"It was ten years ago, so the hurt softens. She was from a Jewish banking family. She left enough for me to get apartments for myself and Papa in this area."

Sounding slightly embarrassed, Georgia said, "I didn't mean to pry."

"Not a problem. We all have our challenges."

Then, tilting her head on one side, Georgia asked, "What's that music I can hear?"

"I asked Alexa for Oscar Peterson's 'C Jam Blues'. Magic, isn't it? I'll leave it on for a while."

"Yes, do. Odd coincidence of names."

"I hadn't thought of that."

"Would you mind very much if I looked around?"

Taking her coat, Tammy smiled. "Help yourself. And while you're looking can I get you anything? Tea? Coffee? Something stronger?"

"Ooh," she responded. "What have you got?"

"What do you want? I've most things. Vodka? Gin? Schnapps? Cognac? Whisky?"

"Whisky?" she asked, almost timidly. "I quite like a single malt, if you've got one?"

"Vodka's my poison. But, if I'm going for a whisky it'll always be single malt. So, I've got a very nice Glenlivet, twenty-five year old single. Or a more conventional, Laphroaig. I've also got a Port Askaig. Very nice. Or…"

"Oh, that would be fine."

"Which one?"

"The Port Askaig. It's delicious."

"I'll join you with one. Help yourself to a view of the place, then I'll see you in the living room." She pointed to the door. "Loo's at the end of the corridor, if you need it."

A few minutes later and Georgia had joined Tammy, both women occupying easy chairs opposite each other.

Leaning back, her legs crossed, a lead crystal glass of single malt in hand, Georgia observed, "It's all so elegant, with these creams and browns everywhere. These sofas?"

Tammy waited a moment as a police car roared past the block, its siren see-sawing.

Turning to Georgia, she explained, "They're Jasper Conran."

"And, Tammy. May I call you Tammy?"

"Sure you can, Georgia," she replied, sipping from her own drink, feeling it warm its way into her stomach.

"You look stunning. I thought so when you first came into office."

"You're very kind."

"I mean, your clothes. What is that you're wearing? Those flares, slit almost to the hip."

As though acknowledging the observation, Tammy absently ran her palm long the length of her bare thigh, feeling the toned muscle. "Yes," she murmured.

"And the colour?" Georgia added. "I've not seen it that often."

Tammy smiled again. "It's a Louis Vuitton cat-suit, of sorts, I suppose. It's really a two-piece, linked under the cummerbund. And the colour? Well this sort of deep turquoise is what's called kingfisher blue."

"It looks fantastic against your...your..."

"My skin colour."

"I hope I haven't offended you."

"Not at all. I chose this colour just because it suits my complexion."

A tiny mew made itself heard as Tammy's cat wandered in and over to her mistress, where she rubbed her flank sensuously against Tammy's bare leg.

"Oh she's beautiful," said Georgia. "What's her name?"

"Risky, she was a stray who found her way onto my windowsill one night. She was never claimed, so I kept her."

"Frisky?"

"She is. But no, she's called Risky."

"Why Risky?"

"Because it took guts to climb up onto the sill. She could so easily have fallen. So, she's a risk-taker." Tammy stroked the cat's head fondly. "Like me," she added.

"You're very beautiful, Tammy."

Tammy rolled the lead crystal tumbler between her palms. "I'm flattered, Georgia. But you didn't come here to talk about me. You said it was urgent, my dear. You sounded frightened. Said he could have me killed? Now you've had a chance to unwind a bit, how about telling me what's on your mind?"

Placing her drink on a glass-topped side table, Georgia sighed. "Where to begin?"

"How about the usual place, Georgia."

"What?"

"The beginning?"

"Oh, yes. Yes." She paused, collecting her thoughts. "I've been working for Oscar for fifteen years. At first the relationship was strictly professional. Oscar is a very talented man and I think I may have been a bit overawed. Well, I know I was. He is, or was, a commercial barrister. Dealt with a number of high profile cases in his time. In the early years his earnings were good. Then he cut back on the legal work as he became more involved in politics. But his earnings didn't go down, they went up, and on. Until about ten years ago when he started to really earn big money."

"What do you call big?"

Georgia looked around as though afraid of being overheard. "You know about the boat?"

"Fifty million?"

"That's before a host of extras. He spends as though it's going out of fashion."

Tammy drew on her whisky, but Georgia's was left untouched for the moment. "Where do you think all this extra cash is coming from, then?"

"Oscar has email addresses on a laptop he carries in his briefcase. He thinks I'm not aware. And, he runs three mobiles. I don't know where the cash comes from, but when you're that close to someone for fifteen years, you hear snippets, see emails that have gone to the wrong address, put through calls from people who sound, how shall I put it? Unsavoury would sum it up."

"And the money, Georgia? Drugs? Involves stock movements. People trafficking? Involves accommodation, food, possible death or injury, depending on who's being trafficked and from where. So, what is your boss into, do you think?"

"I think he's into money laundering. In a very big way."

"Ah. And what makes you think that? Certainly money laundering can be hugely profitable."

Leaning forward to pick up her drink, Georgia sipped from the tumbler, then replaced the glass on the side table, but not before she'd held the drink for several moments, letting it slide pleasurably over her tongue. An act not lost on Tammy.

"He can't hide everything from me," said Georgia. "I've seen evidence of bank accounts in the Isle of Man, the Cayman Islands, the Turks and Caicos, Belize. And more. I don't think he's too worried by my knowing. He's aware there's nothing I could do about it, even if I wanted to. And he's conscious I've been besotted with him for so long, he has me where he wants me."

"Those accounts don't necessarily mean money laundering, though."

"No. But I've heard about deals involving vast sums. Complaints about over-invoicing. Inferior supplies. The term money laundering has come up several times. Oscar wouldn't be able to keep everything permanently under wraps from me."

"So," offered Tammy, "a history of success. No failures along the way?"

"Oh plenty of those. Umpteen liquidations, recommendations he be disqualified from holding directorships. You name it."

"But?"

"But he knows all the right people. It always gets lost in the mix and Oscar manages to remain, to all intents and purposes, squeaky clean. Not a shred of adverse publicity. Ever."

Re-crossing her legs to accommodate the cat as the little scrap jumped into Tammy's lap, she went on, "Understood. Now, if I'm not being too personal..."

Without waiting for Tammy to finish, Georgia offered, "Of course I am."

"Having an affair with him?"

"In the early days he promised he'd leave his wife. Marry me. Held out the carrot of a big salary too."

"And?"

"He's still with Letitia. And as for my earnings ... I live in a bedsit in Battersea."

"What?"

"It's all I can afford on what he pays me."

"Georgia, he's treating you with utter contempt."

She shrugged in response. "I need the job."

Tammy studied Georgia for a few moments, then offered, "Your call, I suppose."

Then she added, "Tell me about the wife. What do you know of Letitia? She must have some sort of hold over Oscar if he's not prepared to leave her?"

"Not that I'm aware. It's politically expedient, he thinks, not to be divorced. Bit old-fashioned really. He certainly doesn't worry when she goes off for days at a time."

"You know why I saw him today?"

"Yes. Because this time she's been gone for weeks. He may not care, but he needs to know what's happening. And his children are probably concerned. I know Jayne worries. She and Letitia were always thick as thieves. Both of them adored David."

"What do you know of their other children?"

"Very little. I hardly ever see them. Pierce was nosing about the office recently. I've a feeling he's probing his father's other political activities."

"The extreme right wing affiliations?"

"That's right. He's intimated that what he's discovered leaves him horrified. Not surprising really. Then, I was appalled when Oscar started referring to Jewish people as, Hebrews. Much of his electioneering has been financed by the wealthier sections of your community. Oh, I overhead some of your conversation with Oscar," she offered when Tammy looked intrigued. "And, Hebrews? What's wrong with Jews, or Jewish people?"

"Hmm!" Tammy mused.

"And, it surprised me he agreed to see you at all, with his views on Afro-Caribbeans."

"I was recommended to him by Detective Chief Superintendent Bob Walker. Oscar could hardly refuse to see me. Tell me more about his family?"

Smoothing her skirt as she considered it, Georgia said, "Other than Pierce, there's Juliet who works in Harrods. She's always got some new affair on the go. I've watched her grow up into a discontented, disillusioned young lady. She was the apple of her father's eye as a little girl, but he gradually lost interest when she matured."

As she spoke, with Georgia gazing at her exposed limb, Tammy immodestly moved slightly, allowing the slit trouser leg to reveal more flesh. She watched the other woman, fascinated, wondering what was going through her mind.

"That leaves Davina," Georgia went on, adjusting her position on the sofa. "She's married to Jerry. Another malcontent. Jerry has failed to live up to her hopes and expectations. She's become more exasperated with him over the passing years. Jayne and David, you know about."

"Happy families," said Tammy. "Your Oscar Mountford sounds every bit as disreputable as you suggest."

"He's a lot worse than disreputable. I'll tell you a story that came to me through some misdirected emails."

"I'm all ears."

"Oscar has contacts everywhere. Many in the States. He's got a share in a fringe bank there, New York. I believe a lot of the laundering has been facilitated by the bank, which to all outward appearances is perfectly respectable, and indeed it carries on a lot of legitimate business, lending to high-risk clients and charging exorbitant rates accordingly."

"And the story?"

"An English businessman working in New York, Michael Dennison, American wife, was building a small company. I forget the nature, but work was coming in. He needed cash to buy up-to-date machinery but couldn't get any of the main banks to lend him unsecured. With orders flooding in he reckoned he'd be where he wanted to be in three months, and Oscar, who got to hear about it, got word to him that his affiliated bank in New York would look at it."

"So far so good." Tammy who'd been stroking Risky, now put the little thing, protesting volubly, on the floor and went over to the sideboard where she retrieved a packet of Henri Wintermans panatellas, one she'd forgotten to discard, and withdrawing a slim smoke, lit the tip with her Dunhill lighter before returning to her seat. Then remembering she'd elected to eschew tobacco during her pregnancy, was instantly guilty. Oh, well, she thought, just the one won't hurt.

Georgia watching her, totally perplexed, looked as though she was about to say something, then changed her mind.

"And so?" Tammy enquired, sending a plume of smoke curling towards the ceiling.

"Oh, yes. Well Michael went to the bank which occupied a single floor in the Citigroup Centre at 601 Lexington Avenue."

"Very smart," offered Tammy.

"You know it?"

"Yup. Been there on more than one occasion."

"The story he told his wife when he got home was that they'd lend him all he wanted, but because of the risk factor and the newness of the company the rate they'd charge would be colossal."

"Don't tell me," said Tammy. "He took the loan."

"What else could he do? If he didn't fulfil the orders coming in his business would fold before it had even got properly off the ground."

"Let me guess what happened next? He couldn't pay back on time."

"He went back on the appointed day, and told the truth. Everything was on track and about to take off, but he needed the repayment period to be extended by just one month."

"The bankers disagreed?"

"The manager, a man called Jack Naseby, explained quietly to Michael that the deal was written in stone and had to be repaid by noon that day."

Tammy took another drag on the panatella, it tasted sweet and smoky.

"I can see something unpleasant coming."

"Mr Naseby, so Michael told his wife, made a telephone call, and the name Oscar was heard."

"Oh dear."

"Then, when he came off the telephone Mr Naseby explained that there was no leeway, and the loan had to be repaid, in full, as agreed. When the Englishman explained that that was totally impossible, the cash simply wasn't there, 'You know,' he'd added, 'Blood out of a stone, and all that,' Mr Naseby buzzed in a man called Frank Tullogh, and turning to Michael, had commented, 'Blood out of a stone, hmm?'"

"Then quite politely to Tullogh, said, 'Frank, will you take this young man into your office and explain how the bank works. He doesn't believe it's possible to get blood out of a stone.'"

"Presumably he wasn't giving your Michael a lesson in bank liquidity ratios."

Georgia hung her head. "Michael got home about an hour later. He was able to walk, just, but he was in a bad way. I mean, a very bad way. Internal bleeding, nothing visible. He refused to call the police or go to hospital. Said he'd report things later in the day, after he'd dealt with matters. His wife was hysterical, insisted he must do something. He couldn't simply ignore what had happened to him."

"And? The money?"

Georgia faced Tammy squarely. "Michael went back to the bank at one minute to noon, with the money."

"All of it?"

"All of it. Every cent. In cash."

"How did he find it in time?"

"I've no idea. But when you've a threat to your life hanging over your head…"

"And that was it?"

"No."

At this point Georgia began to weep.

Going across to her, Tammy sat down next to Georgia and put an arm about her shoulders. "Hey, hey, hey. There's no need for that, my dear. He'd paid it all back. What else could happen?"

In between sobs, Georgia replied, "Before he could report the issue to the authorities, Michael was found in a back street of New York in the early afternoon."

"Another terrible beating, was it?"

"No, Tammy. This time his throat was cut."

"My God, Georgia. How much do his children know?"

"I've been dropping hints to Pierce. Not sure whether or not he takes me seriously."

"Well, I think it's about time he did."

"What should I do, Tammy?"

"Call him, my dear. Call him right now."

CHAPTER 20 DAY 4

"PA'S GOT THIS black woman out searching for Ma. She's been brought in by one of Pa's colleagues, Chief Superintendent Bob Walker. I know nothing about her, except she's supposed to be formidable."

Pierce was sprawled back on a sofa in the living room of his fourth-floor Chelsea flat in an Art Deco block close to the Thames, a property, like those of his siblings, purchased with some considerable financial assistance from his father. It was his favoured period and he'd furnished the place with as much as he could find of the style. A large mirrored sideboard took pride of place in the room, to which had been added an Art Deco cocktail bar in cherry wood, with a centrepiece comprising a couch table with ivory-coloured applications made of macassar wood. And of course, the loungers, like the one he was on. Pierce was casually dressed in dark blue chinos, white trainers and a white T-shirt, exposing muscled biceps.

There were few traces of his recently departed girlfriend, Petra, save a pair of expensive black leather gloves Pierce had bought her, and a faux gold bracelet, both left on top of the sideboard.

It was late evening and getting dark outside.

Pierce's three sisters occupied other sofas in the room, the three girls in blouses and jeans. They were all drinking glasses of red wine.

"Has there been any feedback from this woman?" Davina put her glass down on a side table and studied the backs of her hands, clearly strained, as usual. Problems with Jerry, presumably.

"Nothing," said Pierce. "Although Georgia picked up that she might have gone to the States. Maybe the private investigator will be able to shed more light there, when we get to hear from her."

"What a load of rubbish," interposed Juliet. Middle height with short, straight, dark hair and arresting blue eyes, like her father's, she was liable to explosions of temper. None of her innumerable boyfriends had the slightest idea how to cope with her.

"What's rubbish, Julie?" enquired curly fair-haired Jayne, the youngest of the siblings, the smallest in stature and the most reserved.

"Everything," Juliet responded. "We've for ever made out Ma was our angel, our rock. But she was always off doing her own thing. Gone for days at a time. We were left to fend for ourselves while Pa made his millions and sucked arse in the Tory Party."

"He's going to be Chancellor," said Davina, sounding morose.

"He's not there yet," said Juliet. "We know all about him, don't we. He's always been pretty close about how he made his loot. Just think, if he's the shyster I've always suspected, he may, as Chancellor, turn the UK into a prosperous ally of the Sicilian mafia."

"And we can hardly complain about him, can we," added Davina. "Face it, he contributed to the purchase of all our homes. This flat."

She swung her arm indicating the room. Then addressing Juliet, she added. "And both of ours."

Juliet merely shrugged sullenly. "Blood money. He knows it'll keep us in line."

Jayne said quietly, "I suppose. But I still like living with Dada. I think he prefers me staying at home, especially when Mama's away."

Changing the subject, Pierce added, "I think, in fact I'm sure, Pa's involved with some far right groups."

With one leg hanging over the arm of the sofa, he swung his foot listlessly back and forth. "I nosed about his office when I got a chance. Georgia, the long-suffering, has been dropping hints to me about what Pa's been getting up to for some time, but she's been clearly nervous of divulging too much. To be honest I'd not paid too much attention to her comments. That's until now."

"And what's the bastard been getting up to that we should know about?" Juliet asked.

Sitting up straight, Pierce said, "I'm pretty sure he's been involved in financing some sort of far right demo, like that pathetic one in Trafalgar Square a couple of weeks ago. Georgia said Pa was in cahoots with a number of similar far right organisations on the Continent. She'd whispered to me, he doesn't like blacks. That's a joke, isn't it, he's got one working on Ma's case. He doesn't like Jews, forgetting how many are financing him. And there's more."

The girls all gave Pierce their close attention.

"So get this," he whispered confidentially, pointing to them each in turn to emphasise his point, "Georgia thinks he's working on some lunatic international scheme to take over the country."

"A coup, Pierce?" asked Jayne.

"On the head, Jaynie."

Davina blinked incredulously. "You're talking treason."

"I'm talking treason. What Georgia says she told him."

"Know what?" said Davina.

"Go on," encouraged Pierce.

"To digress a moment, and with all this, I miss David."

"We all do," said Jayne. "He was the thing that held us all together. Remember how Mummy freaked when we lost him?"

"Remember how Daddy didn't?" added Juliet.

"You fainted, Jayne," said Davina. "Always the fragile one," she mused.

"Georgia thinks Pa was involved in the killing of that security guy, Kevin Anderton, who'd infiltrated a far right group." Pierce had got up and was pacing the room restlessly. "What's the betting he was closing in on Pa? Got too close."

"Dada, a murderer?" offered Jayne, leaning forward animatedly. "No. He's a businessman, a politician, a fraud, a liar, a cheat. But he's not a killer. Not that he wouldn't if he could. But he hasn't got the guts. And he's not enough of a psychopath."

"So, you don't think David's death might have been suspicious, then?" Juliet was sitting back moving her wine glass idly from hand to hand, drinking from it in tiny sips. "The pathologist didn't seem to think so. 'Nothing suspicious,' he said. Tragic accident."

"Juliet, if you mean Dada? Kill David? Then again, no way," returned Jayne. "He complained all the time about what David was costing him. Insisted he shouldn't have been kept alive at birth. Horrible. But he knew Mummy adored him. There was nothing suspicious there. Dada even made the effort to get through to David. Sometimes. When he had nothing better to do. As the pathologist said, a tragic accident."

Pierce's mobile bleeped, interrupting Jayne, and they heard him say, "Georgia? Bit late, isn't it?"

The conversation lasted about five minutes, then Pierce addressing his sisters announced, "Georgia just told me that that private investigator, supposedly working for Pa, has confirmed Ma was spotted flying from Heathrow weeks ago. On the same plane was a woman who might have been Ma's double. I want to know what the hell's going on, and I'm going to start nosing around a bit more."

"It might be better if you leave well alone, Pierce," advised Davina. "Dad's surrounded himself with some pretty unsavoury characters, by all accounts. I'm beginning to realise, heaven help us all, he's pretty unsavoury himself. You never know what could happen to you. Some bad people out there. Really, better if you don't do anything rash."

"Try to stop me." Pierce paced the room ever more agitatedly. "Any of you, just try to stop me."

CHAPTER 21 DAY 4

"I WISH YOU DIDN'T have to go, Dov. I'm feeling the baby beginning to move."

In appearance, quite unlike Tammy, Dov's wife Esther was blond, with an hour-glass figure. Despite her effervescent sense of humour, which served as a foil to Dov's frequent brooding interludes, Esther could be bad tempered, her moods often lasting for days.

Tammy, on the other hand, would have explosions of temper which would quickly fizzle out. In her case, very much the storm before the lull.

A year older than Dov, Esther, a clever interior designer, already had two grown sons, but had wanted to bear another child, ideally for Dov, who had no children of his own. Basically, Esther regarded herself as the best thing that had ever happened to Dov.

Ironically, she also regarded him, as indeed she regarded most men, as little better than a helpless child. Something that rankled with Dov, though he was too diplomatic to ever make an issue out of it.

Clipping his suitcase shut, Dov said, "I'll only be gone a few days. I have to go. As you're well aware."

Standing over Dov as he bent to the case, Esther asked, "But what about the baby?"

"Yes, Esther," he sighed, standing up and stretching, "what about the baby?"

"Don't you care?"

"Of course I care," he responded patiently. "But you know I have to do this. And the baby will still be here when I get back, won't he? Or she."

"Won't he? He? You said that first, didn't you. You really want a boy, don't you. You know I was hoping for a girl." She was starting to sound, edgy. As though this might be the onset of another of her capricious tantrums.

Folding his arms, Dov looked down at his wife.

"Esther, what I want is a healthy baby. I don't care whether it's a boy or a girl. As long as it's got ten fingers and ten toes."

In a gesture Dov recognised as one of frustration, Esther ran her palms erratically down the sides of her flowered dress. "Are you seeing that woman again, Dov. Are you? The private detective? The one you went to Trinidad with?"

"That again? We had all this last time. A serial killer was stopped. Tammy nearly died…"

"Oh it's Tammy is it?"

"She has a name, Esther," answered Dov wearily. "What do you expect me to call her, Ms. Pierre? That woman?"

"You haven't answered me yet. Are you seeing her?"

"Esther, I have a job to do. You know that."

Stamping her feet one at a time, Esther shouted, "Are. You. Seeing. Her?"

"No, Esther. I am not seeing her."

"Swear it," she snapped.

"Don't be ridiculous," he growled. "I will do no such thing."

"Swear it," she urged, her voice shrill.

Shrugging into his suede leather bomber jacket, Dov sounded annoyed. "Stop it now, Esther. You're getting hysterical."

"Hysterical? Hysterical, am I? I'll show you what it is to be hysterical."

"I'm leaving," he said, picking up his case and making for the door. But Esther ran up behind him, started punching him on the back with both fists. Dov, placing the case on the floor, turned around slowly, catching her wrists so she couldn't hit him again.

"Leave me alone," she screamed. "Leave me alone. You're hurting me."

The door now open, Dov let go and glanced at her one more time before retrieving his luggage. "Calm yourself, Esther. This can't be good for the foetus."

"What would you know about that? You idiot."

Sighing, Dov said, "What is this all about, Esther? You wanted a baby. My baby. What's happening to you? To us?"

"You said you had to go. So go. Go! Go! Go!"

"I'll be incommunicado while I'm away. Then, when I get back we need to talk."

Closing the door behind him before she could say anything more, Dov made his way out of the block of flats. He wondered then whether he'd see the inside of their home again, other than to collect his things.

* * * * * *

At first she ran to the window to watch him walk towards his parked car. Then before he could look back she shrank from sight.

She waited until she heard the car drive off, then speed dialled a number on her mobile. A deep voice replied, "Shalom, Esther."

"Shalom, Reuben."

"He's gone?"

"He's gone."

"For how long?"

"He wouldn't say. A few days, at least. Knowing Dov, it could be a week or two. Who knows?"

"Shall I come round?"

"I'll come to you."

"How's our baby?"

"Starting to kick, darling. Starting to kick."

CHAPTER 22 DAY 4

GEORGIA LEANED against Tammy tentatively. "I shouldn't have to remind myself how threatening Oscar is. But if he ever suspected I'd betrayed him in any way..."

Sounding calm and reassuring, Tammy counselled, "Just keep doing your job, as you have been for the last fifteen years."

Catching her eye, Georgia said, "You know, I do feel safe with you, Tammy."

Giving her shoulder a gentle squeeze, Tammy said softly, "I have a job to do, Georgia. A job whose dimensions I'm just beginning to grasp. Look, I've been asked to locate Oscar's wife, Letitia. We have her in New York less than two months ago. Her present whereabouts are unknown."

Her back against the sofa, an arm still about Georgia's shoulder, Tammy added, "But now, obviously, I need to start investigating Oscar Mountford's activities. These far right affiliations, talk of some sort of political shenanigans, suggestions he's been involved in a murder or murders... Do I need to elaborate further? And then, possibly to see him appointed Chancellor of the Exchequer? God help us all."

Lacing her fingers together nervously, Georgia said, "It's all been staring me in the face for, I don't know how long. But I've chosen to ignore, or else been too frightened to do anything about it."

"And so now you've made the call to Pierce."

"That's right. Finally."

"Did he sound convinced?"

"Very much so. Judging by the sounds in the background I think he was with his sisters. So, if they didn't know before, they will now."

Tammy got up and started pacing the room, undecided, then she said, "I am going to need some help, Georgia. Do you think you could? It'll be risky. Could be really dangerous, from what we both know of the man. I shouldn't ask, I know. I will understand if you'd rather not."

"Oh, no I will. I will. You know I will."

"Do I?"

Lowering her eyes for a moment, then taking Tammy's hands in her own, Georgia asked, "May I ask, what happened to your hands, Tammy? I don't mean to pry or offend. But you have such lovely long fingers. And. And, the scarring…"

Gently stroking Georgia's cheek, Tammy wondered aloud, "How does an intelligent and independent woman like you allow herself to fall so completely under the spell of a man like Oscar Mountford?"

She was aware Georgia's breathing was becoming uneven, her chest rising and falling in expectation of something. Leaning towards the other woman, Tammy placed her palms on Georgia's cheeks and kissed her on the lips.

It was meant as a gesture of friendship, nothing more. So she was astonished at Georgia's reaction, the older woman immediately grasping Tammy's head and kissing her back, hard and deep. To Tammy it was as though Georgia had been starved of love and needed the affection as much as the physical satisfaction.

Sensing her own attraction for Georgia aroused, Tammy began exploring Georgia's body, at first cautiously, then more deliberately, feeling the woman's response heighten under her skilled touch. The kiss went on, long and sweet.

Georgia's hands ran along Tammy's naked thighs the flesh the woman had so blatantly been staring at, the slashed trousers providing no barrier to exploration.

"You're not wearing...?" she breathed.

"Not when I'm home," whispered Tammy in between kisses, easing Georgia's tight skirt gradually up revealing miniscule white panties. "Mmm," she added. "I see you came prepared."

"No. No, I..."

"I'm teasing, Georgia. Don't be silly. They're lovely," she said. "You're lovely," she added, slipping out of the blouse-top to reveal breasts swollen with her pregnancy. Breasts she was not embarrassed to display.

"Tammy," gasped Georgia, gazing up and down the younger woman's body. "Those scars. Whatever happened to you?"

"I know. They're ugly. I try to forget, but they're still too recent. I'm sorry if they put you off. Not very feminine, are they?"

"They're just scars, Tammy. They don't mean you're any less feminine. I think you're the most feminine woman I've ever come across in my life."

"Well," said Tammy, somewhat bemused. "I'm glad someone else does."

"Someone else?"

"My special friend, Dov Jor—"

She was interrupted by a loud banging at the front door of the block, and a hoarse voice shouting, "I know you're in there. Let me in. Let me in now, I say."

"Mon Dieu," muttered Tammy. "Who the...?"

But Georgia had gone pale, quickly pulling her skirt down. "Don't you recognise the voice, Tammy. That's Oscar. My God! What do we do?"

"We ignore him. It's very late. He won't keep banging for ever. The neighbours will probably call the police if he goes on. He won't want a scandal. You don't step outside. You spend the night here, then we'll take things a day at a time."

CHAPTER 23 DAY 5

EARLY HOURS

"HE'S STILL THERE OUTSIDE, Tammy." Gazing through the window, Georgia whispered as though she might be heard down in the street.

A light breeze swept a cluster of dead leaves skittering across the road, briefly illuminated by the twin beams of an SUV's headlamps as the vehicle drove silently by.

Pulling the borrowed negligee tighter, she peeped through the glass, standing to one side where she'd not be noticed. "I can see him clearly under the lamp post."

"Come back to bed, darling." Tammy yawned. Leaning up on an elbow, she ran her fingers wearily through her hair. "Viens, chérie, he can't spend all night there."

"He's looking up," Georgia panted. "He's looking up here."

"Let him stare. But don't let him see you. If he doesn't see you there's not much he can accuse you of in the office tomorrow. Not that you're doing anything that's any of his business," she added.

"But what will I say if he asks me where I was?"

"You were at home. If he says he went to your home and you weren't there, you'll tell him you took a sleeping tablet. You heard nothing."

"Very well. I only wish I had your cool." Georgia was about to turn round when she stopped dead, her face white in the darkened room. "My God, Tammy."

"What, darling? Whatever is it? You look as though you've seen a ghost."

"Not possible. It can't be. He's spitting up at the flat. He's spitting! At us! At us, Tammy!" she said, her voice breaking with fear.

With the situation now threatening to escalate out of control, the woman was becoming hysterical. Not unusual where reason counter-intuitively produced the opposite of calm. No telling what Georgia might do right now, even so far as insanely running down into the street to seek some sort of closure.

"Is he now?" Addressing Georgia in an undertone, Tammy patted the bed, placing an arm protectively around the other's shoulder as the terrified woman sat down next to her. "Don't you see, Georgia? He's presenting us with his professional credentials. Spitting is clearly the best he can do. Relax. There's absolutely nothing to fear from that fool."

* * * * * *

THAT EVENING

It was dark, with a slight chill in the air. Tammy was meeting Bob at their previous rendezvous on the Thames Embankment, close to the snack stall. Traffic was light, and there was the same sprinkling of leather-jacketed youngsters with parked motorbikes chattering away.

She'd made Georgia spend the night with her. Studiously ignoring Oscar's yelling, he had eventually sloped off. He must have had her followed at some time to find where she lived. Not too difficult to do. Georgia, she'd advised to simply go into work as though there were nothing untoward. Oscar would hardly attack her physically in his own office, and depending upon his attitude she'd be able to judge whom it was he'd hoped to confront last evening. In the event, there were no frantic calls from Georgia, so presumably there was nothing at this stage to get alarmed about.

Earlier in the day she'd been to see her father at his two-bedroom Victorian garden flat situated close to her own in Queen's Park. Her mother's legacy had been sufficient to cover the cost of this flat and her own, with something left over for the offices off Bruton Street in Mayfair, together with decorations and furnishing.

Tammy had made a flying visit to the office, but there was nothing so urgent it couldn't be dealt with by Mrs. Gilchrist, her brilliant PA, found for her by Ginny Jones at the time they'd split up.

The tall, retired architect had never fully recovered from the shock of his wife's early death, his close-cropped hair now white, contrasting starkly with his ebony complexion. The old man was ageing visibly as his body and nervous system were attacked by the deadly disease with which he was afflicted.

They were seated on canvas-backed easy chairs in her father's sunny garden, long glasses of chilled fruit juice sitting on the umbrella-shaded table. Matthew's walking stick lay on the ground by his feet. Tammy was in flared taupe trousers with an open-neck blouse in café au lait. Her father in black trousers, pressed to a knife-edge, and white shirt, as usual, his black brogues were polished to a mirror shine. She'd learned from him never to let yourself go. Even when slopping around indoors, clothes should still be spotless, pressed and fresh.

"So tell me, chile, why y'all have come to see me today? Somting on your mine?"

"Some advice from you, Papa?"

"Oh, ho," said her father. "It's Papa today, is it? Not Daddy. Got to be somting serious."

Taking a long draught of the juice before replacing the glass on the table, Tammy said, "I wasn't sure when, or indeed whether, to tell you."

"Let me guess. Y'all expectin' again."

"Papa!" she said, shocked. "How could you possibly know? I've told no-one. Not even hinted at it."

"Tamsin, dahlin', y'all my darter. You tink I ain't see you smile to yourself when you tink no-one lookin'. Course y'all pregnant. Jus' one ting, sweetheart. Tell me, y'all happy? Or you have a problem you want to tell you Daddy."

"I have a problem, Papa."

Matthew took a drink from his glass, then absent-mindedly rolled his shirt sleeves up from the wrist to the forearm, making sure the cuffs sat evenly. All the time he was listening intently to his daughter.

"Where to start?" she pondered, thinking Georgia had only recently posed much the same question. She smiled as she got the anticipated response from her father.

"The beginnin' am a good spot, Tamsin."

"Okay. Well, just before I went off to Syria, I got an unexpected visitor."

"You boyfriend from Israel." It was a statement, not a question.

"Yes, Papa." She cast her eyes cast down guiltily. Somehow her father always managed to remind her that to him she would always be a little girl. His little girl.

"The one who you say marry Esther?"

Tammy nodded.

"An' now you expectin' his chile? Hmm?" Matthew stared straight at his daughter as if the revelation had just struck him. "Aaaah! Now Papa unnerstan. You ain't know if it his babby?"

Again, Tammy said nothing. The silence stretched on without Matthew attempting to prompt her. "It's not that simple, Papa."

"When is it ever?" he said, shaking his head. "So, darter, you gonna tell me?"

"Yes, of course. I have to. When I was in Syria lying injured in that makeshift Free Syrian Army hospital, the man leading that group of men, when I was drugged…"

"He have you?"

"I don't know for sure. But yes, I think so."

"His babby, then?"

"It could be, but I simply can't be certain."

"Dey call dis ting rape, Tamsin," Matthew said quietly. "He have rape you. How you feel about dat?"

"His name was Nabil."

"Was, Tamsin? He gone somewhere?"

"He saved my life, Papa. Then he got killed."

Matthew considered that for a while. Then he asked, "Dis man, Nabil. A Muslim?"

"Yes, Papa."

"Y'all know dey read de Old Testament."

"I know."

"Like Maman."

"Like Maman."

"And you."

"And me."

"So, don't really matter if de chile am Dov or Nabil."

"Not really."

"Either way, he gonna be Jewish?"

"That's right." She held her breath, waiting for her father's next remark.

"And you happy?" he asked again, uncertainly.

"Awestruck."

The seconds ticked away once more with Matthew lost in contemplation. She simply could not anticipate his mood.

Then, apparently frowning at his daughter, Matthew said simply, "Me too." Then, smiling broadly, he repeated, "Me too, Tamsin."

"Oh," she said, her eyes brimming as she flung her arms around him. "I love you so much."

CHAPTER 24 DAY 5

SHE'D BEEN ON A HIGH all day after her father's ebullient reaction to news of her pregnancy, but now the reality of what was expected of her was starting to become apparent as she spoke with Detective Chief Superintendent Bob Walker.

"Thanks for coming out at such short notice, Tammy." Soberly dressed in suit and dark overcoat against the evening chill, Bob blew on the surface of his tea, cupping the Styrofoam mug in the palms of his hands to warm them. He glanced discreetly at her outfit, a navy two-piece, jacket and slimline trousers, with a lavender silk scarf tied at the side of her neck.

"Tammy," he said, with the hint of a smile. "I hope you won't think me impertinent, but is there ever a time when you don't look as though you should be gracing the catwalk of some haute couture fashion show?"

"Let me see now," Tammy said thoughtfully. "Well, yes. Come to think of it there is."

"I'm all ears, Tammy. Tell me, when don't you look stylish?"

"When I'm in the shower." She grinned, at which Bob burst out laughing.

"And so to business," he said, becoming serious all at once.

"And to business," agreed Tammy. "Is this going to be about Letitia?"

"No, Tammy," he said. "We're talking Oscar Mountford now."

"Okay. I'm listening."

"Thanks for keeping me in the loop, by the way. Emails, WhatsApps. I gather you weren't too impressed with the client."

"At first I thought Mountford was just a nasty piece of work. A pseudo-macho bully. Now I realise different. From my interview with him, and from what his PA knows and suspects, I think we're dealing with a pretty dangerous individual. He certainly doesn't give a damn about his missing wife."

"You gave no indication to him of her being spotted in New York? The double, and so on?"

"No. Not at all. What worries me is what his PA, Georgia, had to say about his apparent far right affiliations."

"Mm, yes. We'd been looking into that. Rumours at the moment, with up to now nothing concrete on the man."

"Georgia thinks he was involved in helping finance that big right wing demo which took place in Trafalgar Square a couple of weeks ago. She's agreed to discreetly nose around Oscar's office for me. I know, Bob," she said, holding up her hands before he could express any reservations about Georgia's safety. "She will be careful."

"I sincerely hope so," countered a worried-looking Bob.

"She also thinks he may be conferring with a number of European groups of the same type, to attempt some sort of coup."

"Well there's ambition for you. Worrying, nonetheless. We need to try to prevent him becoming Chancellor. He's far too dangerous to be allowed to gain that sort of position of influence. God alone knows what he might get up to. Failing that, we'll have to find some way of discrediting him. You know, force him to resign. But we can't just go to the PM with our suspicions."

"Plus, Georgia thinks he's got support from a number of other MPs."

"Tammy, I've asked DCI Rosemary Sharpe at the Yard to start making some discreet enquiries. This has got to be nipped in the bud. Would you mind very much giving her some assistance? I know you two didn't hit things off immediately when you first met her. I wouldn't ask, only..."

"Bob, it's okay, really. I like Rose, and I learned to respect her over the Black Candle affair. She had her own issues. A dying husband. A crooked sergeant. We'll be absolutely fine."

"Tell me, what do you know of these far right groups? The so-called alt.right."

Wandering back and forth as she worked it through, Tammy said, "There are innumerable such groups throughout Europe. They aim to seek political power through disruption of the normal democratic processes. They post fake news on social media and foster fear and suspicion wherever they can, hoping at some stage to show themselves as the so-called saviours of society. When in fact they're the exact opposite."

"So far, I'm with you. And, we're both up to speed on this. Of course you know their credo."

"It's all a mixture of the bizarre and the contradictory. They're anti-Semitic, racist, want all ethnic minorities returned to their countries of origin. Not sure where that leaves mixed heritage like me." She looked across at Bob, who nodded in understanding. "But everything is suffused with the idea of, whites only. They also believe in what they call, trad wives. It's something gaining increased internet interest."

"A new one on me, Tammy. Trad wives? Is it what I think it is?"

"Probably. They want women back in the kitchen, a return to their view of perceived roles. Theirs is an openly misogynistic attitude. The irony is that the view is promoted to an extent by some female anti-feminists. The Russian-American alt.right activist Lana Lokteff, claimed on the white supremacist Radio 3Fourteen, that white males were effectively being attacked by feminism. Can you credit that?" She shrugged.

"The feeling is," she went on, "that a woman's principal value to men is in her sexual value, her SMV, or sexual market value. She needs to be regarded as sexually pristine, however they choose to interpret that. Believe it or not there are even apps available to women to advise them how they rate in terms of sexual value."

"God, what next?"

"You name it. There's a community of so-called Pick Up Artists, or PUA, aiming to coach men into getting women into bed. Then there's the Men's Rights Activists lot, or MRA. How about the anti-marriage movement called Men Going Their Own Way or MGTOW? There's even a group seeking revenge against women who they regard as responsible for men's frustration if they are unsuccessful with women. That's the Involuntary Celibacy or Incel movement."

"My heavens! You've done a bit of homework, Tammy."

"Not really. Some I've picked up on an almost daily basis on my travels. Some, my PA Mrs. Gilchrist has researched for me. You must have had MI5 fill you in on some of this?"

"Certainly. It's well up on 5's radar. Less so on mine, personally. I'm mainly involved with routine policing. Still, I'm in touch with 5, and they won't object to any intel you come up with."

"Don't look yet, Bob, but there's a dark blue Ford Fiesta parked on the other side of the road. Did anyone know we were meeting here tonight?"

"Only Control. And she's totally discreet. It is, after all, her job."

"I could be wrong, but it looks to me as though the driver of that Ford has a long-range listening device. He's wearing headphones, and I suspect he's recording whatever he picks up. Even from here, I think I recognise the make of device."

"Which way is his car facing, Tammy?"

"He's facing east. My car is close to his, on the same side of the road, but facing west."

"Very well, let's walk west for a moment, away from our listener, and wrap this up."

"I'll get in touch with Rose. Meet her away from the Yard so no-one there is aware of my involvement. We'll feed each other info as we get it and see where it leads us."

"You'll need to work quickly, Tammy. Announcement of the Chancellorship is due any time now." He sighed. "Mind you, things frequently have a habit of spinning out over a longer period than anticipated."

"What about Letitia? She seems to have drifted off the radar, about a month or so ago, when the New York drum majorette murders appear to have ceased, and whilst Oscar isn't interested in her whereabouts, I think we need to pin her down. She's a real mystery. A totally unknown quantity. About as predictable as the UK weather. Why has she been killing people? And is it her in fact, or is it her double? Indeed, is she still in New York, or has she crept back into the UK unnoticed? Don't want her coming in from stage left when we least expect it and upsetting the applecart."

"Agreed. What do you recommend, Tammy? I'll be guided by you on this."

They'd stopped walking for a moment and stood facing each other.

"While there may still be time, I'm going to take a quick trip to New York. See what's happening at the Ritz-Carlton with our high spending Communist. The Party would not be impressed."

"Tammy." Bob sounded seriously concerned. "Are you up for all this? I mean you took a terrible hammering…"

"I wouldn't take it on if I was in any doubt I couldn't manage. After all, you don't need to have another liability on your hands right now. You've more than enough on your plate."

"If you say so. I'll talk to our contact, Felix. He's back in the US. He'll organise CIA backup if you need it."

"Thanks, Bob. I've anticipated much of this, and have already asked my colleague, Dov, if he'll come along."

"Ah." Bob smiled. "The Krav Maga expert."

"The very same."

"I presume he's given you all his credentials?"

"You mean, Mossad?" she offered candidly.

"He's worked with MI6 on occasions. Good man to have around."

"He is." She smiled.

Bob turned away for a moment, gazed distractedly across the Thames to the illuminated buildings on the other side. "You know, I'm concerned, for all her Socialist credentials, is Letitia Mountford blindsiding us?"

"How do you mean?"

"I was wondering, could she be a secret weapon of the alt.right?"

"Who knows, Bob. Oh for the days of the clear-cut two-party political system, when the only terrorists were striking students seeking grant increases." She turned to leave. "Look, I better go now. Our friend is probably out of range, but we don't want to encourage him any more than we need."

"Tammy." Bob suddenly sounded urgent. Leaning forward, his hands brushing her shoulders, he kissed her lightly on the cheek. "Be careful. We don't want to lose you." Then he stepped back, embarrassed. "Apologies, apologies. Most unprofessional of me. Am I blushing?"

"A bit," she laughed, "am I? Of course, you probably can't tell."

CHAPTER 25

TWELVE DAYS AGO
THE DAY OF THE TRAFALGAR SQUARE RALLY

IF HE'D HOPED FOR a turnout of tens of thousands Oscar Mountford was destined to be disappointed. Despite extensive social media messaging, word of mouth and announcements that found their way, or were otherwise directed via the dark web, on the day there were fewer than a thousand people in Trafalgar Square.

Unbeknown to Oscar there'd been a move to sabotage the event. It seemed that Pierce, who made ads for TV and was a lot more clued in to social media than his father, had been active on Twitter, Facebook, WhatsApp Messenger, Instagram, LinkedIn, Snapchat, Pinterest and Reddit, Gab and many more.

Apparently, he'd had no small measure of success in trashing the whole event, persuading people of the futility of their attendance. He'd also been at some pains to organise a counter-demo, which saw a few hundred noisy anti-fascists making their presence felt with waving banners and catcalls.

It was overcast and cool on the day, both calculated to dampen spirits on what Oscar had hoped he could organise into a fun day out for followers and possibly new recruits to his brand of extremism.

Taking as his cue the Charlottesville rally of 2017, Oscar had sought to present to the world's media a taste of what he saw as the British leaning towards the extreme right, with its desire to see a return to traditional values, without actually revealing his personal involvement. As the planned rally slowly built up steam around Trafalgar Square, police riot vehicles were readied, but maintained a discreet presence in side streets.

Oscar watched the whole thing via drones he'd organised with some friends in the police, ostensibly, as a senior MP, concerned for the safety of demonstrators.

The mood in the square was sombre rather than festive.

There were banners out, proclaiming, 'We must secure the existence of our people and a future for white children.' Tammy had come across this for the first time when investigating the Black Candle killings; an alt.right expression used by crooked cop Sue Thompson in threatening emails sent to her and signed simply '14', the number of words in the phrase.

Other streamers announcing, Blood and soil, from the Nazi blut und boden, a slogan of nineteenth-century German nationalists, later an element of Hitler's Lebensraum, the policy adopted by Germany as a justification for expansion into the land of surrounding territories, and a contributory element to the beginning of the Second World War.

Then there was, Russia is our friend, comprising admiration for Putin and Russia's authoritarian regime, which it was reckoned had played a powerful part in advancing far right movements in Europe in recent years.

Some wore the white hoods and gowns of the Ku Klux Klan, but were left alone by police, who maintained their distant presence.

There were burger and hot dog stalls, drink stalls and ice cream counters. The whole event was supposed to harvest an atmosphere of sunny afternoon fun. Oscar had paid for the banners, the installation of stalls, marshals to ensure that order was maintained. A dais where speeches could be made. Amplification equipment, speakers, mikes. Floodlights if the event went on into the night.

Georgia had heard Oscar muttering that he'd hoped for a hundred thousand people. In the event, and according to a whispered telecon Georgia overheard the following day, the numbers showing up amounted to a major disappointment. There'd been a number of speakers reported on the news, none of whom Tammy had ever heard of.

None of Oscar's MP supporters were to be seen. Perhaps understandably. And the event which started off at around 3.00 pm gradually petered out as people started leaving within a couple of hours.

Perhaps the biggest single element in the failure of the rally, overlooked by Oscar, was the disinterest of the British public in extremist politics. Oscar, aware of the build-up of the far right in Europe and the US, wouldn't be so easily discouraged. But in the office next day he was apoplectic with rage, realising there was little if anything he could do about the reverses in his ambitions at this stage.

CHAPTER 26

THE DAY OF THE RALLY

THE HOTEL IN ST. JAMES *was a five-star Victorian boutique with period furnishings and traditional iron bedsteads. A five-minute walk from Trafalgar Square, which was why she'd chosen it. Cosy, well appointed, elegant, discreet. It also had a useful back entrance for deliveries, she'd noted.*

Once the last of the speakers had finished his ranting about reclaiming the old world order, the proper place of women within this traditional confederacy and the superiority of the white race with its coming victory over those who'd seek to sully it with ethnic intermarriage, the motley crowd had gradually dispersed. All ages, all white and with a bizarre choice of clothing, a proclamation of their individuality and independence, she didn't stand out from the rest with her purple harem trousers and balloon-sleeved white blouse.

He was average height, with a pot belly and comb-over of greasy strands of black hair. Wearing a rumpled blue suit with crooked tie and a shirt that was shredded at the collar, he wasn't the picture of sartorial elegance. Close up, his lips were purple and his complexion florid. A likely sign of high blood pressure. He smelled of perspiration and sour breath. He was certainly very out of breath. Scheduled as the penultimate speaker, he'd tried desperately to keep the dwindling crowd from dissipating through his hoarsely delivered oratory, before the final key celebrity came on. Someone she'd never heard of before, and wouldn't remember in the future.

He was leaving the rally himself. It had been a failure, he had to admit it. "Hello," she said, standing directly in his path, arms folded, legs slightly apart, leather shoulder bag resting on her hip. "I'm Larissa. Larissa Filipek. I liked your speech. You've got real passion. I like that in a man."

"What!" He hauled up in front of her. "Really?" He didn't seem to know what to do with his hands, so he stuffed them in his jacket pockets.

"Oh yes," she said. "We need to reclaim this country for white Anglo-Saxons. Clear it of the rubbish. Blacks, Jews, disabled, mental cases."

"That's right, that's right. Men back where They. Sorry," he corrected himself, "where We, belong. What do you think about that?"

"Absolutely. I'm looking for the sort of a man who fits the bill. But they're all such wimps these days," she said, taking his arm, gradually imposing herself on him as they walked along together.

"Your name?" he tried cautiously, glancing over to her. "Russian, is it?"

"Mummy and Daddy were born here. Grandparents came over from St. Petersburg years before."

"Ah." He nodded. "We, on the right, have a lot of time for Putin's Russia."

"I know." She smiled, happily. "That's one of the things I like about the movement. And," she breathed, "we're gradually gaining in power, aren't we."

"Oh yes, we are indeed. Clear out the wogs, that's what I say. All of 'em."

"Absolutely."

"I'm Toby, by the way," he said, enthusiastically. "Toby Trimble."

"That's a nice name," she said.

They walked on for a while, then he asked, "Where are we going?"

"I hope you won't think me forward, Toby, but I'd like to spend a little time with you? I find you very attractive."

"Oh really? Would you? Where would you like to go, then?"

"Well, I'm here from Switzerland, where I live, just for a couple of days. I came for the rally. I'm staying at the Victoria, five minutes from here."

"I know it. I know it." He gasped, clearly running short of breath, his jacket flapping open, shirt stretched, stomach bulging over his trousers. Then he stopped as though struck by a sudden idea. "Tell me," he asked hesitantly, "are you always this forward? This quick? I mean, I mean…"

"Not always," she said reassuringly. "Only if I really fancy a man."

"And you fancy me?" He could barely keep the surprise out of his voice.

"Oh yes."

He stared at her, openly perplexed. "Why? What have I done? What have I said?"

"Who can say what it is that attracts? The magic? The electricity? But when I heard you giving that speech, I just knew."

"Really?"

"Oh, yes. Really. And then too, the way you spoke to those counter-demonstrators before the police stepped in. You know, there must have been hundreds of them."

Trimble's neck flushed. "Oh it was nothing."

"It showed you to be courageous and resolute, Toby."

"Shall we go on, then?" he asked, hesitantly. "Would it be alright?"

Nodding at him reassuringly, she said simply, "There's a back entrance to the Victoria. No deliveries at this time of day." She giggled and gave him her room number and key. "I'll see you there in ten minutes."

She delayed for about ten or twelve minutes to give him time to get to her room, then marched into the hotel through the lobby herself.

He was waiting for her when she arrived. "Did anyone see you come in," she asked.

"Not a soul," he leered, starting to hurriedly undress, and glancing pointedly at the red ribbons she'd left on the bed-side table.

She reckoned she knew the type but couldn't risk getting it wrong. He'd seen the iron bedstead and kept looking expectantly from it to her. That much she had right. But was he the one who wanted to be in control? Or like so many of the alt.right, an inadequate man who paradoxically preferred to be dominated. The public-school accent suggested the latter.

Quickly getting undressed, she smiled encouragingly at him. Naked himself now, he approached her, and cupping her breasts in his hands, muttered, "Nice tits." Underneath the hairy stomach flab, he showed the suggestion of arousal, and she tried not to think of what was in store. Responding to him tantalisingly, she murmured, "Lovely." Then, "Oh my, Daddy, what a big boy you are."

She could smell his breath and sweat more closely now. Burgers and beer, presumably bought at the rally. And although she found it revolting, his hands working away at her were producing the suggestion of a reaction. "Like that, do you, bitch?"

This was exactly what she'd been afraid might happen. Her own damn fool fault. Dragging herself away from him before she could lose any more ground, he faced her, then, pointing at the bed he shouted, "On the bed, fucking whore." Then he punched her in the face, bursting her lip. "I said, on the fucking bed. NOW! Who the fuck do you think's in control here?"

Now she was frightened. The man sounded as though he was losing it. Totally. His voice rising to a pitch of mania. He'd entered the hotel, unnoticed. Anything might happen, and he'd never be tracked. She hoped he couldn't see her shaking.

She paused for just a moment. Looked him up and down, insolently, her heart beating a tattoo in her chest. There'd only be one chance to get it right. If she misjudged it…

She punched him back. Hard. In the face, drawing blood from his mouth. The two stood facing each other, unspeaking. The si-

lence expanded, filled the room. Then she punched him again. As hard as she could. Her fist was throbbing, and she waited for his reaction, which to her amazement was followed by him covering his face with his hands, before bursting into tears. "Now," she barked. "On the bed, little man. Before I get really annoyed. Now! Now! Now!"

Heaving his bulk onto the bed, he said, "Yes, yes. I will. I will."

"What you need, young sir, is a taste of discipline. And I'm about to give it to you."

He whimpered softly, cowering before her. She didn't let him see her breathing with relief, before ordering him, "On your back, mister. Arms and legs out."

He immediately complied. As she'd hoped, he was happier being dominated once she'd shown who was in absolute control. Now she took the ribbons from the bedside table and swiftly tied his wrists and ankles, so they were securely held by the bedposts. He was struggling slightly, uncertain now. Not sure whether he'd done the right thing with this complete stranger. She'd need to subdue him before he decided he'd had enough. Leaning over the sagging gut, she straddled him as he started to move with her, matching her as best he could. His face getting redder. "I can prolong it, darling," she whispered. "Make it more exciting. Yes?"

"Fuck, yes," he gasped. "Anything. Anything."

She'd left the plastic bag on the side table, and grabbing it, she quickly placed it over his head, tightening it around his neck before he could realise what was happening and could call out. She hadn't thought about getting him to use a condom. Very short-sighted of her, as it was clear he was choking, at the same time moving more and more quickly. She shifted with him, encouraging his rhythm, pushing him to finish. But then, biting her lip to quiet herself, she thought, dammit to hell, too late, as she flopped forward against him, finally exhausted. Overcome by a fresh shudder of fear, aware she'd used up all her credit. What now?

The plastic bag removed, his face showed rage. Helplessly twisted.

But he lay still.

Done, just as her lover had asked, even down to the name she'd checked in the hotel with. The name she'd given to Mr. Trimble, Larissa Filipek.

Find someone at the Trafalgar Square rally. Your judgement who. Then, you know what to do. That'll throw them off the track, Letitia had argued. The final killing. Letitia would follow her accomplice in due course, having completed her work in New York.

Close. Too close. But job well done.

Moments later she left unseen by the back entrance of the hotel.

CHAPTER 27

THE DAY AFTER THE RALLY

"ARE YOU FUCKING INSANE?"

"What's the problem, Nicolai?"

"Is Nick. Is Nick, you stupid bitch. How many times I got to tell…"

"Alright, Nicolai. Look, let's do a deal, okay? I'll call you Nick if you'll stop calling me Filipek. I'm Larissa, as you damn well know," she said, her voice rising with irritation.

"Alright, Larissa. Larissa," he muttered, resigned. "Fuckin' women."

"So why are you calling me? What's on your mind. Nick?" she added with deliberate emphasis.

"You playing games with me, missy?"

"What are you talking about? And can you speak more slowly? This is a bad line, you keep breaking up."

"You killing people in the UK? Who tell you to start killing here? You tell me you don't like to kill. Bullshit. Of course you liking it. You loving it."

"I don't know what you're talking about, Nick."

"Trafalgar Square. You forget? You kill so many you don't remember?"

"No idea what you're going on about. And anyway, I'm nowhere near Trafalgar Square. I'm in the States."

"Is in the papers and in the news." He was shouting now. "Is a dead body find in hotel in St James's. Lady sign in as Larissa Filipek. You think this is coincidence? You got two Larissa Filipeks? You make a fool of me, lady. Make me in trouble. My people show me the CCTV. Is you Fili…Larissa. Don't tell me you in America."

She could practically see the sheen of sweat on the man's brow, the spittle forming at the corners of his mouth. A rank amateur, way out of his depth.

"Oh but I am, Nick. That's exactly where I am right now. I don't know what you think you've seen. Or who you think you've seen. But I can assure you it wasn't me."

"I not argue with you," he growled. "But we got work for you. Meet me in the usual place in Soho. Usual time."

"Next week," she said, smiling to herself. "When I'm back. I'll call you."

"Try not to kill nobody till then." He rang off before he could hear the peals of laughter at the other end.

CHAPTER 28 DAY 6

SHE WAS DUE to meet DCI Rosemary Sharpe, the detective with whom she'd worked after their initial run-in on the Black Candles case. Tammy had suggested the bar of the Sofitel Hotel in Waterloo Place opposite the Institute of Directors on Pall Mall. It would not likely be frequented by any of Rose's team from New Scotland Yard and gave a pleasant atmosphere, with soft background music, for an informal discussion.

She'd left Bob Walker the previous night and made for her vehicle, the Lexus SUV, parked close by the Ford occupied by the driver they'd thought might be attempting to listen in to their conversation.

She recalled a slight breeze last evening, letting her recollections meander over an unplanned and unwanted occurrence. Despite the hour, close on midnight, there had still been some pleasure cruisers plying the Thames, light traffic humming along the Embankment. A few cyclists had wound past her, crossing each other on both sides of the road.

I love Paris. She'd gazed across the Thames, pairing it with the Seine. My birthplace. But London. My adopted home. Special. She'd walked on briskly. She still got tired easily after her recent ordeal, but soon would be back in Queen's Park to a hot soak, and a late Bison Grass straight from the freezer. A bit of cheating in view of her pregnancy, but an occasional one wouldn't hurt.

He was about her height, broad-shouldered, in a black tracksuit, Nike trainers and pulled-up hoodie, which failed to hide the livid scar under his right eye. A knife crime? The accent was what she'd have described as UK Caribbean. Pointing at her, he said, "Heard what you have to say, lady."

"Well then, I hope you found it interesting," she offered quietly.

"All recorded."

"Sensible," she added. "Means you won't need to try to remember everything later."

"Y'ain't get fonny wid me, innit."

"I'm not laughing, sir. Are you?"

"Fockin' coconut."

"Presumably you weren't recording my conversation for your own amusement. And coconut? Why, delicious if grated in salad. Or, come to think of it, on its own," she added, smiling sweetly.

She started to move on but he barred her way, staring her down. "Now we're not going to be a silly boy, are we?" she insisted.

"Talking to dat fockin' toff."

"Aren't you rather exceeding your brief, sir? If you were retained to make a recording? It seems to me you have what you want. Now why don't you let me get to my car, hmm? Without any unnecessary fuss."

"I can take you, lady. Anytime." He was standing closer to her now, breathing heavily, his eyes bloodshot. If it was drugs, she couldn't think what or which it might be. Ecstasy? Very possibly. If he'd been snorting it, there'd be a quick reaction, not unlike that she was witnessing right now.

"You might try, young man. But I really wouldn't advise it. I'm used to dealing with thugs, you know. Before breakfast. With my muesli."

"Who you callin' a fockin' thog?"

"Well, nobody specific, you may have noticed. But then, if the cap fits." She pondered the shuriken at her belt, but dismissed the idea as quite unnecessary. Then she had another idea. Holding out her ruined hands, palms uppermost, she said, "See these?" and observed his eyes as they widened in disbelief. "Had a fight not long ago," she informed him. "A gentleman with your somewhat negative approach to life. Got quite rough at times." Noting his continued horror, she added softly, "I won."

The man rocked back on his heels as though he'd been struck across the face, then stared at her fixedly as she swept past him to her car.

Setting aside her musings over the previous evening, she noted Rose was already there seated in a corner, a coffee in front of her, waiting for Tammy. Stocky as ever, she was in her usual two-piece working suit, but older now and more tired. The effect of husband Frank's recent death? Getting up immediately, Rose beamed at her. "Tammy," she said, the smoker's rasp unchanged. "Love. How're you doing? Must say, you're looking fine. The hands?"

Taking Rose's hands in her own, she leaned forward and kissed her on both cheeks. "Getting there slowly, my dear. Slow but sure. Doc tells me be patient. They say it's a virtue. But then, when was I ever virtuous?"

Rose laughed, and said, "What can I get you, darling?"

"Coffee's fine, Rose."

A few moments later, with both of them sipping from hot mugs, Rose cast an ear, cocking her head to one side. "Nice music they play in here. I wonder what that is?"

"It's boogie-woogie, Rose. Sounds like 'Dancin' the Boogie' by Silvan Zingg, who composed it. Google him. It'll knock you for six."

"God, Tammy. You know your stuff."

"Not really. I come here sometimes because it's conveniently placed. Plus, I like the jazz and boogie they play. But, give me Mozart or Bach any day. And maybe, a smidgeon of Laura Pergolizzi."

"Who's that?"

"Oh, she was one of Ginny's favourites."

"Do you still miss her, Tammy?"

Tammy considered the question. Considered Ginny, of how she'd lost her. Then she smiled, raised her eyes to meet Rose's, but said nothing.

Taking the cue, Rose changed the subject. "Bob wanted us to liaise in the Oscar Mountford business. He's really concerned Mountford might get appointed Chancellor. I know he'd like to see him out of government altogether."

"I'm sure he would," said Tammy.

"Is there anything we can do? Look at? Investigate?"

As Tammy gave it some time a group of business people came in, laughing at some shared joke, and seated themselves on the other side of the bar. Others came and went, the occasional sound of traffic filtering into the place as doors opened and closed. The muffled sound of a police vehicle could be heard rushing by. The music had switched to jazz, and the sound of Miles Davis on trumpet. "Nice," murmured Tammy. Then turning to Rose she said, "There's really not a lot anyone has to go on. But I was wondering if there might be some mileage in taking another look at the Kevin Anderton case."

"The security man who infiltrated a far right group?"

"That's right. Georgia Keith, Mountford's PA, is doing her best to keep me informed about what Mountford's up to. She heard him on the phone telling someone called Mac, to deal with anyone that got in their way in the same manner they'd dealt with Anderton."

"Wasn't Anderton MI5?"

"Possibly. My friend Dov Jordan thinks he was. But Bob hasn't said anything to me about Anderton. No doubt 5 will be making, or have made their own enquiries. They don't play about. But Mountford's a slippery customer, with all sorts of contacts. Who knows. Anyway, worth a snoop. Bob might be a bit more forthcoming with you as it's ostensibly a police matter rather than a political one."

"Fine," said Rosemary. "I'll talk to him, see what he's got so far. I know when we first got the murder on our plate we drew a blank. File's still open though, as you'd expect."

Drinking from the mug, Tammy stared vaguely across the bar at nothing in particular. Her usual attitude when considering issues, alternatives.

"How did Anderton die, Rose?"

"A hit and run. The vehicle, a Ford Transit Custom, picked out on CCTV. Not false numbers, as you might expect. That would have suggested murder, of course. No, this was a stolen hire vehicle, turned up dumped in a side street about three miles from the accident."

"I see. Genuine numbers on a stolen vehicle would suggest a joy rider. False numbers on an untraceable motor would point to a planned killing."

"Exactly. But one little slip told me it was planned."

"Let me guess. No DNA traces in the van."

"Exactly. Everyone leaves a trace, unless they specifically don't want to be found. But. Absolutely nothing."

"I see the problem. So it's all on hold?"

"For now. But Bob wants me to take another look. Have another think."

"You still have the van?"

"Oh yes."

"Mind if I take a look sometime?"

"No problem, Tammy. Just say when."

"Thanks, Rose." She nodded, making a mental diary note. "Now back to my original brief, which was to look for the wife, Letitia Mountford. Although, with things changing all the time there're now a lot of overlapping enquiries. I'll concentrate on the alt.right terrorist aspect of this. Georgia is doing what she can. But I'm worried she'll be taking too many risks. She's very frightened of her employer. With damn good reason. I'm beginning to think that perhaps I've asked too much of her." Tammy sighed.

"I'm sure you know what you're doing, Tammy. And as long as this Georgia is sensible."

Resting her chin in her palm, Tammy said, "Something here doesn't add up. Come to think of it, a lot here doesn't add up. You won't know at this stage, but I'm ninety-nine percent sure we've located Letitia to New York. Letitia and what appears to be her double. A woman who flew out to the States on the same plane on the same date as Letitia."

Rose looked astonished, asked, "Does Mountford know this?"

"Beyond a mere suggestion, we've said little, if anything else to him about Letitia being spotted in America, or any possible double. Bob is aware. But Rose, here's the thing. What we've got is a series of murders, all apparently carried out by Letitia, or possibly her double. All, bar the one in a tenement block, on CCTV."

"Crikey. How'd you manage that?"

"Fact. There are over four hundred and fifty homicides a year in New York. No way can they all make the news. But what I can say is that whilst the New York police precincts tend to compete with one another, unwilling to exchange much information, a case like this attracts attention anyway. The odd outfits were mentioned on CBS and NY news channels, one of them called her, the Bobby Socks Killer. It's got to be the same woman, Rose.

"And here's the thing, the murders were all of Russian dissidents. Three of them. However, paradoxically, the far right in this country idolises Putin. That means Mountford should by rights be a Putin fan, like Letitia his wife, but for different reasons. In fact, I'm getting a nagging hunch that if there are efforts somewhere out there to bring the two political extremes together, seeking to gain more than just a foothold in the West, when Mountford finds what his wife has been up to, instead of castigating her, we might expect them to join forces."

"Hell. It's a long shot, Tammy."

"Stranger things on heaven and earth, Rose. With nothing at all to go on, I'm open to any suggestions."

"No, Tammy," she said. "We're talking Oscar Mountford now."

"Okay. I'm listening."

CHAPTER 29 DAY 6

THE HEAD TEACHER was visibly shaking with rage. "I've told you NO. NO, a thousand times NO," he practically shouted.

"It doesn't work. It will not work, and even if it did, we want nothing to do with it in this institution. Do I make myself bloody clear? All this American rubbish. Short-sighted. Infantile. Regressive. Counter-productive. Not what educated middle-class people in this country want to find themselves paying for. We could end up losing students this way. It's not on. No way." He looked grey and drawn, ill. Like someone trying to shake off a wasp that had landed on their arm.

At last she'd recognised some tangible progress with the boy who showed a natural aptitude for drawing. He focused very much on people, cleverly drawing out some of the aspects of their character with his insightful obser-vations. In fact he had a genius for it. He could depict humour, deceit, anger, love, all with speedy flourish-es of the pencil, or the black ink drawing pen Jayne had bought him.

She'd already climbed mountains with her brother, he was hard to reach, but she'd get there. Was getting there. Sooner or later. Just as long as she was given some sort of chance by Neville Quaid, the Head.

In time there would be gentle encouragement to start experimenting with colour. Jayne would show him how to mix paints and explain by demonstration the basics of per-spective. If it could work for Jake Barnett, the maths genius, it could have worked for David, as it had begun to. Too late for that now.

But still time for others. She just needed time to work with more of the children.

Young Edwin Matthews was a boarder at the school and, very much like David, a gifted artist. Edwin's parents, who lived abroad, visited the boy as often as they could, and were thrilled with his progress. With Jayne explaining what she was attempting she gained their absolute agreement to continue in the manner she'd adopted, despite its unconventional approach.

All of this was conducted under the nose of the Head, but with such subtlety, he'd hardly realised what was going on. Absent-minded as ever, it wasn't too difficult for Jayne to discreetly pursue and implement her own techniques, producing the result she'd hoped she would.

She was standing over Edwin now, having left him to his own devices for the last half-hour. He'd not heard her quiet approach, and she watched, holding her breath, entranced and unmoving, as he sketched a likeness of the school's Head. He'd captured the man to perfection. The tall stooped posture, thinning grey, side-parted hair, rumpled suit, even the worn, scuffed shoes.

Edwin had also done a headshot, a portrait of Quaid, next to the full-length drawing, as though to add something further to the character study of the man. He'd spotted the small, barely noticeable mole at the side of his nose, the beetling, angry eyebrows, even the pallid complexion and fine lines at the corners of his eyes and mouth. It was masterful and if Edwin could be persuaded to let it go, Jayne would show it to his parents on their next visit in a couple of days' time.

Then Jayne sensed someone breathing down her neck. The heaving rasp of one in a whirling eddy of rage.

"You've heard what I have to say. I've made it abundantly clear. I want you to go back to our tried and tested routines, Jayne," muttered Quaid, his voice gaining in volume.

"I've told you, these new-fangled American notions are not how we do it in this country. You're unsettling the children, Jayne, and I won't have it. Do you hear me? I won't fucking have it."

"Neville, for heaven's sake," whispered Jayne, twisting round to look up at Quaid.

"Not in front of Edwin."

"Not in front of Edwin. Not in front of Edwin," mimicked Quaid.

Then examining the sketch, and realising what he was witnessing, he spluttered, "And what the hell is that? Hmm? Supposed to be me is it? Boy taking a rise out of his head teacher. And you encouraging it? Against my specific instructions. Well we'll see about that."

Reaching down to the desk Edwin was working on, Jayne watched in horror as Quaid grabbed the drawing and before she could stop him, tore it to shreds.

Seeing what was happening, the child let out a slow moan and started crying. "Drawing? Drawing?" Then, "Nasty. Nasty." Finally, a whispered, "Why?"

Close to tears, Jayne said, "Never mind, Edwin. We'll think of something else to do." But the child had become quite indifferent to her and his surroundings.

Aware he might have gone too far, Quaid sought to calm the situation, attempting to sound reasonable.

"Look, Jayne, how many times do I have to tell you, we don't get the children to respond to what they want to do. We get them to respond to what we instruct them to do."

Just for a moment Jayne let her annoyance get the better of her. Something she hardly ever let happen. "No we don't," she said angrily. "You know perfectly well the US approach works. You've seen it for yourself."

"But look."

"Look nothing. All you're interested in are the fees from wealthy middle-class clients. And let the children go hang."

She was breathing heavily. Shocked at her own brazen outburst. But with no intentions of taking anything back. She knew she was right, and so did Quaid.

CHAPTER 30 DAY 7

"**Y**OU'RE SUPPOSED to be trying to find my wife," he hissed. "Aren't you?"

"And so I am, Mr. Mountford."

Tammy was seated at the rosewood desk in her office on Bruton Street, in London's Mayfair, the mobile to her ear, and made a point of no longer addressing him as Oscar. She ran the tips of her fingers longingly over the packet of Henri Wintermans panatellas, quickly crushing the urge to smoke, stuffing them in a drawer. No point in risking the baby's health, size or intelligence. All things that could be influenced by smoking, drink or drugs. She'd more or less cut out the vodka and ditched the smoking altogether. Well, almost altogether. That just left the cocaine habit. The stash at home had been flushed. She ached for a line, but wouldn't. Not under any circumstances. She'd been sick a couple of times recently, in the mornings, and needed no further reminders of what she may or may not do.

She was in the office for the morning, catching up with a pile of pending left on her desktop by Mrs Gilchrist. Her PA had also placed a small vase of fragrant freesias in pink, yellow and white on Tammy's desk, their delicate scent brightening the day.

She'd be leaving for America as soon as... Possibly within the next forty-eight hours. Right now it was Oscar Mountford demanding her attention. His manner was less threatening than it had been when she'd last seen him in his own office. But the underlying mistrust and dislike of her were manifest just the same.

"Not having much success in finding her, are you."

She drummed her nails irritated on the desktop. "It's only been a matter of days."

"Bob Walker insists you're the best."

"I'm flattered." Tammy smiled at Mrs. Gilchrist who'd just planted a hot mug of coffee in front of her.

"But I hear you're poking your nose into a lot of troughs, not part of your brief, Ms. Pierre."

"Everything is part of my brief, Mr. Mountford. I take a holistic approach to my investigations, sir."

"And just what the hell does that mean, when it's at home?"

"It means that in seeking answers to question A, I may examine events surrounding events B, C and D. Together with anything else I feel may assist."

"Look, I've got the feeling someone's looking up my backside, Ms. Pierre."

"What a truly appalling prospect, Mr. Mountford. I hope you don't imagine it's me."

"Don't you get clever with me, madam."

"Understand, Mr. Mountford," she attempted to soothe, patiently, "that if you want me to find your wife, in particular to avoid the possibility of any potentially embarrassing press reports, bearing in mind your political ambitions, I'll poke, as you put it, in as many troughs as I think necessary to get to an answer."

"I do know you're bloody rude."

"I wouldn't call you the soul of courtesy, sir."

"I'm paying your fucking fee," he yelled.

She was gripping the phone so tight the whites of her knuckles showed. "Actually, you're not. Bob Walker will cover my fees and exes. And if you raise your voice to me again, I'll hang up."

She could hear him breathing at the other end of the line, as though wondering what his next move should be. Could imagine him walking around the room like a caged baboon.

"You talking to my children?" he snapped.

"I've got calls scheduled with them this morning."

"Leave them out of this. They've got nothing to do with what's been happening."

"Oh, really? And what precisely has been happening, Mr. Mountford? You got very annoyed when I mentioned at our first meeting the murder of Kevin Anderton, the security man. What do you know of it? And what do you know about the disappearance of your wife you're not telling me about?"

"Why do I get the feeling you've been doing more snooping around than you should, Ms. Pierre? Who have you been talking to?"

Then, as though a notion had just struck him, said, "Has my PA Georgia been feeding you with any sort of rubbish? She sees and hears plenty of what goes on here, enough of my activities and connections to be able to form all sorts of the wrong impressions. Bloody stupid woman. Another hysteric."

"Ah, but then all that'll change in the future, won't it, Mr. Mountford?"

"What? What are you talking about?"

"Well, when women are re-established in the household performing their traditional duties. At least according to your view of the Old Testament, as I recall you telling me."

"I need you right now, Ms. Pierre," he muttered through what sounded like gritted teeth. "But when your investigations are over, we won't be needing you further. Will we."

"That sounds like a veiled threat."

"Take it any way you want. Everything has its period of use. Its lifespan. Then we discard it."

"And that includes me, does it?"

"As I said. Any way you want to interpret it."

Tammy let the silence that ensued sit for at least half a minute, then she said, "Where's your wife, Oscar?"

"What?" He sounded flustered, taken off guard, but quickly recovering said, "I won't have you play games with me, young lady."

"I think you know where she is, and want this investigation to simply legitimise your position prior to your being considered for the Chancellorship."

"Rubbish!"

"Have you killed her, Oscar? Hmm? Or have you had her killed? You seem to know little enough of your wife and the life she leads. Did you find out something about her that might have threatened your political ambitions? You were in no hurry to report her missing, I note. Two weeks was it? Or is she still alive. In America? Getting up to no good?"

"You tell me. And I'm warning you, leave my children out of this." He paused for a final comment. "And, if Georgia's been spreading any nonsense, I'll make damn sure she doesn't add anything further."

"Oh, really. What and how are you proposing to go about that, Oscar?"

But he'd rung off without another word.

CHAPTER 31 DAY 7

SHE'D SPENT THE last hour or so talking with both Davina, who'd thrown no new light on anything, beyond her obvious dislike and mistrust of her father, and Pierce, who'd confirmed his own suspicions and Tammy's regarding Oscar's far right activities.

Pierce had done a lot of snooping, even going to far as to meet up with some alt.right extremists. He flippantly dismissed them as a bunch of losers, misfits and thugs, not likely to be a real threat to anyone. Full of hot air, he'd decided.

Tammy had expressed her genuine fears that where Oscar was concerned, no-one, not even his own children, could be safe from his ruthless ambition. The alt.right clearly amounted to far more than Pierce's views of the few he'd come into contact with. Their known activities and political advances throughout Europe were clear testament to that.

In his turn, Pierce had reassured Tammy that he'd be safe, and with his strength and physique, unlikely to come to any harm. She ended the conversation plagued with doubts. Concerned at what she perceived as Pierce's well-meaning naivety.

Juliet had proved to be a total mystery. Ostensibly loathing her father and his questionable politics and life-style, she then astonished Tammy by appearing in some measure to support some of her father's more extreme views.

She then surprised Tammy even further by asserting, "Ma was a bloody bitch. She certainly didn't give a damn for Pa or David. David she found heavy going, whatever she pretended. Left him as far as possible to Jayne, who adored him, got through to him better than anyone. Pa was simply a boring stick in the mud, an arse-licker sur-rounded by more arse-lickers. Ma craved excitement. Dis-

appeared for days at a time. Probably had some fellah secreted away."

Something Juliet wasn't letting on here? Did Juliet,
in fact, know where her mother was at this moment? She
did not, she insisted. That left Tammy with the ongoing
mystery of Letitia's and her double's whereabouts. Which
she'd be chasing up herself shortly in New York.

An image flashed up in Tammy's mind. Apropos
nothing in particular. Just something she'd been speculating
on, but couldn't make sense of. The headless, semi-limb-
less corpse on the Heath? There'd been enough speculation in the press since the discovery, with nothing clear
so far. Letitia? Possible? she wondered. The bizarre clothing on the corpse on the Heath. Letitia's eccentric choice of
dress? A link?

Unlikely, she sighed, shelved the idea. Letitia was
a survivor. A killer, who could take care of herself. And
anyway, she'd been located travelling to New York. If not,
could the corpse be her double? It didn't figure. Still, she'd
talk to Rosemary. Get an opinion. Perhaps seek to view the
body. With the age of the corpse and the timing of Letitia's
or her double's disappearance in New York, might one of
them have returned to the UK?

Tammy had been warned off by the man in old-fashioned NHS type wire-rimmed spectacles, the one she
thought she'd spotted following her when she visited Jamie and George in Wapping. Had Letitia gone too far? A
lot of flamboyantly carried-out killings in New York. Someone intent on being noticed. Had a Russian handler decided to bring the spree to a halt?

Juliet had agreed to come to Tammy's office, and
duly turned up an hour late, with neither explanation
nor apology. She was dressed in an absurdly short
black miniskirt and burgundy bolero jacket, contrasting
shocking pink blouse and black lace-up Doc Martins, with
her bobbed black hair immaculate. The impression was startling. No wonder the guys all fell for her. Come to think of it,
Tammy mused, noting the acres of thigh on display as Juliet
sat and crossed her legs, if circumstances were other.

Then, being practical, she accepted that women like Juliet weren't interested in relationships. They wanted conquests, vanquished enemies, cringing wimps. Not exactly where Tammy was coming from. And, Tammy had no idea which way Juliet leaned. Plus, there was Georgia now. Just thinking of her made for a warm feeling in the pit of her stomach. Attractive, if vulnerable. But gutsy too, it had to be said.

One thing was clear however right now, and that was that Juliet could not sit still for a minute. She crossed and re-crossed her legs. Consciously or unconsciously flashing red underwear. She leaned back, sat forward. Animated one moment, apparently bored the next. Drugs? Tammy wondered. Or just a self-centred neurotic who couldn't relax for a moment.

"I don't understand you, Juliet. Do you favour Oscar's extreme views? Or are you just an old-fashioned rebel?"

"We need strong government in this country, the Tories are too weak. An effete organisation. But Pa's racist and sexist. That's his trouble. Come to think of it, he must find it problematic working with you?" Then, "Do you mind if I smoke," she asked, unexpectedly switching her attention and extracting a pack of king-size cigarettes from her clutch bag.

"I'd rather you didn't."

"Oh very well," she responded, flicking her hair over one ear, irritated.

Tammy patiently clasped her hands together, laying them on the desktop, Juliet's face registering her horror at the damage on view. Clearly not wanting to be presumptuous she simply looked questioningly at Tammy, who smiled back but made no comment, other than, "What do you know of your father's close associates?"

"Absolutely nothing," she responded, sounding nervous. But the exchange had calmed her. As though someone or something had demonstrated that she wasn't the only person on the planet with personal issues.

She carried on slowly, "Nothing, that is, apart from his daily screw."

"Georgia?"

"Poor woman is entirely in awe of him."

"That's it? No-one else? How about an accountant? Doctor. Dentist. Lawyer."

"Lawyer. Yes. A man called MacDonald Smollett. His father, Angus, originally from Scotland, established the prestigious law practice of Smollett Davis Carleton, which MacDonald now heads up."

"Anything you can tell me about this man Smollett?"

"Not much. I've seen him on the odd occasion if he's been in Pa's office when I turn up. Could be sixtyish, bit overweight, jaundiced complexion, bushy eyebrows, bushy hair. Old-fashioned dress sense. Waistcoat, fob watch. About it," she said.

"Another of Pa's lackeys. He jumps if Pa raises a finger. Don't know what Pa has on him, but whatever it might be, he'll do anything to preserve the reputation of the firm his father set up. And his own, come to think of it. God knows, but I think Pa has him involved in some shady stuff. Anyway, Pierce is doing his own researches. Asking questions."

"Isn't that dangerous?"

"Pa?"

"No. I was thinking, some of the far right associates your father may not have under his thumb. They're gaining strength. No doubt about it. Pierce won't be as invincible as he thinks he is."

"Oh yes he is." Juliet smiled. "Pierce is a man-mountain. No-one's going to take him on," she said confidently. "Or take him out."

"Not good being overconfident, Juliet. One gets slapdash. You can take a risk too many."

Gazing over Tammy's shoulder at the sunshine outside, Juliet said almost dreamily, "You don't know Pierce. He only takes calculated risks."

"I'm all ears," said Tammy with a sigh.

"He joined an extreme sports group. They do mad things, with caving, coasteering."

"Sorry, coasteering?"

"Oh, it's where you explore a rocky coastline by climbing or swimming. Or jumping."

"Jumping? Wow! Okay."

"He also does skydiving. You know, free-falling."

"Thrilling, I'm sure. But hardly dangerous these days."

"Pierce has taken it to a whole new level."

"You mean ten thousand feet instead of five?"

Ignoring the joke, Juliet went on animatedly, still fidgeting, changing position in her seat, flicking her hair behind her ear. "He jumps without a parachute," she breathed.

"What? He must be totally mad. Where did that idea come from?"

"That amazing James Bond free fall in GoldenEye. The one where the light aircraft takes off without a pilot on board and Bond zooms over the mountain edge leaving his motorbike to crash on the rocks below, while he, using a base-jumping technique without the necessary base jumper's outfit, manoeuvres himself through space and into the plane.

Pierce was obsessed by it. Said he could do it. Had someone work out necessary heights and thousands of feet per second of the light aircraft, gravitational pull and air density. All that. He's no fool."

"And he did it?"

"Twice. Said it was the greatest rush he'd ever had. See, he has to jump out, then the plane circles, drops beneath him, and he guides himself towards it. He wears a sort of webbed suit. Looks like a bat, but it slows his fall so there's time for the plane to lose sufficient altitude. He lands flat on his stomach, squarely on top of the high, fixed wing where there are harnesses to prevent him falling off while the plane comes in to land."

"Okay, Juliet. I'm convinced. Anything else I need to know?"

"About it," she replied, and got up to go, extending a hand to shake Tammy's, as tentatively as though testing the heat of a nearby flame.

"That's alright," said Tammy, "not necessary," noting the relief on Juliet's face as Mrs Gilchrist showed her out.

That just left a call to Jayne, before a visit to either or both the morgue to view the corpse and a look at the Ford van that had mown down Kevin Anderton. The Ford, maybe. The corpse she'd look at on her return from the States. After viewing the New York haunts of Letitia and her shadow.

Before she could ask Mrs Gilchrist to get Jayne on the line, Tammy's direct line on the desk rang. She picked it up, perplexed. As with her home landline, only a handful of people had the number. "Tammy Pierre," she announced.

The voice had a familiar central European turn to it, one she recognised. Short black, greying hair, those glasses again, and a warning not to get involved, which she was already.

"I have tell you not to get involve. You waste your time go to America. Filipek not there anymore. You try find her, we stop you. You learn. You go, you maybe don't come back. Maybe you do come back." The voice paused as though for effect, before adding, "In pieces."

Cold palms ran over her skin. Some threats you don't take seriously. They had her private number, knew her movements. Ergo, this threat was real. "Who are you? And who, or what is Filipek?"

"Filipek. Larissa Filipek. At university, she call Letitia Philips, like English version of Russian name. Now Letitia Mountford. Working with us. Stay away, Ms Pierre. Else you dead. Heh, heh, heh."

CHAPTER 32 DAY 7

"IS THAT HIM?"

"Where?"

"Look, over there," the man said, pointing unobtrusively. "Across the road."

"The boy?"

"Hardly a boy."

"You know what I mean. He can't be more than twenty-three or four."

"Well whatever. Pretty big though, isn't he?"

"Yes, well, there's a pair of us, and we aren't exactly undersized."

The two men, in their forties, wore immaculate three-piece suits, with trousers ironed to a fine crease. Everything about them was smart. They stood together on a corner of the busy street surveying Pierce Mountford as he loaded shopping into his car, a blue BMW X1 SAV. Their muscled physiques showed visibly under their attire.

"Who is he?" asked the taller of the two.

"Apparently, he's the son of one government wallah," the other responded.

"Which one's that?"

"I've not been told."

"Well who's paying us, then?"

"Some Caribbean gentleman. Also large, about our height and build."

"So, big then."

"Very."

"Come on then, Charles. You can do better than that. You must have some idea who he is?"

"Not really, Tristram. I met him not long ago in a pub near Kew Bridge, overlooking the Thames. He was drinking copious amounts of Jamaican rum. Never seen a man put so much of it away. Must've got through a whole bottle on his own. Well, you know what these people are like. Water it down, drink it slowly. Get through pints of the stuff, with no apparent ill effect."

The two went on idly watching Pierce finish loading the car. Then the taller of the two, Tristram, asked, "So, who engaged whom first in conversation?"

"We were on adjoining bar stools and drifted into a sort of unplanned conversation. I let slip I was ex SAS. Now retired, but filling time as a club doorman and bouncer. He latched on to that, as if it were something he could use. Which, of course, was what transpired. Had far too much to drink myself. Trying to show I could match his input, I suppose," said Charles.

"Not very discreet of you," observed Tristram, shoving a pebble with the toe of his well-shined Chelsea boot. "Did he proffer a name?"

"Ainsley."

"Just that?"

"That was all."

"Hmm. Scottish name. A lot of Caribbeans, particularly Jamaicans, descended from Scots. People like General Colin Powell, born in New York of Jamaican parents, themselves of mixed Scottish, African ancestry, known for his handling of the Gulf War. And then the Crimean nurse, Mary Seacole. Various others."

"You seem to know a lot about names."

"Scottish names, perhaps. Got family in Edinburgh myself," Tristram explained.

"Hadn't realised. So, here we are, Tris."

"What are we supposed to do with this young man?"

"Ainsley's brief is to simply rough up the boy."

"And why can't your friend Ainsley earn the full fee himself, if he's so big?"

"Complications, apparently."

"Like?"

"From what he said, I got the impression our Mr. Ainsley had a number of other commissions pending, and he was concerned there might be some degree of conflict of interest in fulfilling his tasks."

"Tell me more about Ainsley."

"What's to tell? Put it this way, I can't think of anyone who'd want to meet him on a dark night," said Charles.

"Menacing?"

"Showed me a retractable blade he carries in his inside jacket pocket. Told me he only uses it if he has no choice. He struck me as a smouldering tinder box of rage. An original psychopath. So when you ask if he's menacing, I'd say, yes, very."

"But then, so are we."

"Hardly in the same vein, Tris. I'm a bouncer. You collect debts from a few unsavouries who refuse to pay monies they owe. This man had killer written all over him. A bit different to our situation."

"So, why are we roughing up this individual?"

"I could use the cash," said Charles. "Like you, mine's a lousy pension. Neither of us from the right background to get the promotions that would see us well provided for right now. Always looked down upon by our military and social superiors, hmm? And from what you tell me, you're more than just a bit short right now. That new young lady of yours? Somewhat demanding?"

"Okay," responded Tristram. "In truth, one's life, post all arenas of conflict, has become a bit dull anyway. Also, it's a bit too dangerous these days being a mercenary, though it was fun for a while. And, I could use a bit of excitement. It's what we're good at, after all. Money for old rope, I suppose. A bit of a rough and tumble, with care not to let things go too far."

"Agreed. We're just supposed to teach him a bit of a lesson."

"Will he know why?"

"Ainsley says he'll know. We shan't need to give chapter and verse."

"Know what, Charles?"

"What, Tris?"

"I think this might just prove to be a bit of fun. Teach one of our middle-class betters to know his place."

"Couldn't agree more, Tris. Give the bugger a session he'll remember."

"HE'S FALLING, HE'S FALLING. We've lost him, Pete, we've lost him. Shit, Christ, he's dead. He's fucked. We're fucked," the man screamed.

"We should never have supported this lunacy. Madness. Insanity. How could we have been so bloody idiotic. No parachute? Man's a total fucking maniac. And we've gone along with it."

The co-pilot was shaking uncontrollably, the sweat pouring down his face mingling with his tears.

"Pull yourself together, man. For God's sake," growled the other, older man, pushing the centre stick forward and to the right to take the nicknamed push-pull, twin-prop Cessna 337 Super Skymaster through a clockwise, curving downward spiral, in an attempt to position it below the fast accelerating free-faller. His own pulse was racing, but he was still in control of himself and his emotions.

"He needs to spread his arms and legs wider to slow the fall. He's dropping too fast for us to get underneath him. I'm going to be shoving down into a virtual dive."

"No! No! Please God, no!" yelled the younger man.

The twin engines were screaming as Pete forced them to their limit, his armpits starting to perspire as he attempted to maintain a firm grip of the stick. "Shut up, Nat. For crying out loud, man, I need to concentrate."

The Cessna angled in a wide looping arc, falling heavily out of the sun-bright sky like a spinning autumn leaf, the airmen's view of the horizon a crazily tilting geometric line.

The pilot, Pete Matthews, his jaw clamped shut, shoulders squared, was trying desperately to get far enough under the falling man to give him the chance to guide himself towards the plane. But as they all sank lower, Pete recognised, with growing horror, he was going to have to resign himself to the first death ever recorded on his watch.

And though he tried to put the suspicion out of his mind, he was going to have to admit he'd been guilty of an unforgiveable error of judgement. It would probably signal the end of his career and a lifetime's regret at the needless death of one with the whole of his life ahead of him.

The individual plummeting to earth, a powerfully built, fresh-faced, good-natured young man, maintained he'd done the fall before. Twice, he insisted. But he neglected to say where, so there was no way Pete could follow up and find whether the previous pilot or pilots had experienced any difficulties or problems.

Pete Matthews had been a pilot for most of his working life, initially securing a degree in maths and physics at Bristol University. Then he'd gone through the process of interview selection and medical checks, followed by a six-month full-time course in theory. And then basic training, building up his in-flight hours before gaining a CPL, or Commercial Pilot Licence, and finally completing his MCC, or Multi-Crew Cooperation course, to allow him transition to an airliner.

He loved flying, lived for it, even after decades in the air, still got a buzz the moment one of those big birds he was piloting lifted off the runway. Touchdown, and the satisfaction of a safely completed flight, gave him the same thrill.

Having married his Gillian, Jilly, who was five years younger when he was nearly forty, they'd had two children, thirteen and ten years of age. Not wanting to miss out on his youngsters' early years, Pete had retired from the airlines at fifty and now at fifty-five had been in charge of a small flying school, run jointly with the owner, Tom

Selby, at Fairfield Aerodrome in Oxfordshire for some five years.

Nat, his co-pilot, at thirty-five and single, was only licensed to fly light aircraft, and was now agonising over the folly of his decision to go along with this catastrophic jaunt. They'd been offered a substantial fee, but money was no longer the issue. If indeed, it ever had been.

Pete had managed to direct the plane until it was under the young man, but they'd both misjudged when Pete had moved towards the falling body, only to have his erstwhile passenger float away, out of reach of the flat surface of the single wing positioned over the fuselage that was being aimed for.

Close to, he'd seen the lad's eager expression under the peculiar black and yellow flying suit he'd insisted would give him the necessary aerial buoyancy to let him descend at a pace slow enough for the plane to get under him. A base jumper's suit, the boy had called it. Except he wasn't jumping from a static base, he was leaping from a moving plane, and at several thousand feet. Seeing him splayed out star-like gliding away from the aircraft, he was no more than a blur fading as fast as Pete's hopes for his survival.

The Cessna had initially been taken up to twelve thousand feet, around the comfortable maximum before oxygen would be required. Technically the plane could climb to nineteen thousand feet, but that would present the pilot and free-faller with other issues.

At twelve thousand feet, the young man had exited the plane. He was slightly nervous.

Or perhaps, just excited.

Experienced free-fallers exiting at thirteen thousand five hundred feet generally allow thirty-five to forty seconds of free-fall time before using the chute, at approximately six thousand feet, with maybe three to four thousand feet in reserve, to be comfortable. Pete reckoned that a fall rate, computed by the lad, of thirty feet per second, would see him at the planned six thousand mark after just three minutes and twenty seconds, way after a parachutist would deploy their chute, thereafter hitting the deck after six minutes forty if plane and man completely failed to rendezvous.

Everything depended on relative wind speeds, the weight of the young man, who was big, his forward speed and his ability to control his rate of descent in that extraordinary outfit. All of it involving Pete mentally adjusting his timings.

But they'd need to have the Cessna under the flyer no later than two thousand feet from the ground, minimum, as at that height they'd be just one minute and six seconds from disaster. And that must not be allowed to happen.

Pete had reckoned they'd have to get it right first time. There'd be no useful second chances. Now at six thousand feet, with man and plane nowhere near each other, Pete was praying there'd be that second chance, a prayer he knew was in vain.

They were three minutes and twenty seconds into the fall, way beyond the point when a parachutist free-falling would have been expected to open their chute. But this young man had no chute. He'd clearly misjudged his rate of descent, failed to link up with the Cessna and was falling to an unavoidable and totally unnecessary death.

What in God's name would Pete tell his wife, and his kids, both of whom idolised him, their daddy was their hero. But this was all too selfish. What would he tell the next of kin of the young man? That would be the hardest thing of all. It may have been his client's choice, but he might have refused.

An indefinable aspect of him, something in Pete's make-up — a flaw perhaps? — persuaded him to consider the chance of something exciting. Something truly electrifying. After all, hadn't his client assured him he'd done a leap like this before?

Yet, this whole jaunt and Pete's place in it, was nothing more than a self-indulgent quest for the sort of buzz he was accustomed to experiencing when piloting the big airliners.

At six thousand feet, they'd had just three minutes and twenty seconds left. But they didn't have that time anymore. Time was whipping by. With that in mind, Pete had swept the plane down to below the absolute minimum he'd calculated, that was below two thousand to just one thousand feet. If they missed the boy this time, the lad'd be just thirty-three seconds from death.

Forgetting his long years of experience in keeping calm, he was now becoming frantic, his palms wet, shirt soaked with sweat, as they entered swirling, low-flying cloud. Pete couldn't see the boy anywhere, so unless he was below them, and effectively dead, he had to be above the Cessna. But if so, where? He was invisible.

Nat was screaming now, and trying to grab hold of Pete's arm in a flat panic, with Pete almost savagely shoving him away. "Off," he barked.

Then Pete spotted him, away to his left, apparently attempting to wave and catch the pilot's attention? Or perhaps to steer himself towards the aircraft. Even from that distance Pete could see the terror on the lad's face. He was manoeuvring himself as best he could towards the plane, and Pete was dropping ever lower to allow time for the young man to connect.

Down to nine hundred feet.

Eight hundred, seven.

Pete was close to uncontrolled panic himself. The boy was nowhere to be seen, but they were providentially over the runway. They'd planned the flight in this way, without ever considering the consequences of failure.

A few seconds from touchdown they experienced a moment's low-level turbulence, or wind shear. Possibly similar to that pedestrians can experience from time to time, when say, crossing an open space on the way to a tall building when a strong wind stream circles the base of the block.

The wheels of the light aircraft touched the runway, the squeal of rubber on tarmac as Pete taxied towards the main building, finally bringing the Cessna to a halt. For several seconds he sat unmoving, his head in his hands. There was the gentle ticking of the engines cooling down, but otherwise an oppressive silence.

Nat was sobbing uncontrollably. "Dead! Dead! Fucking dead. Where the fuck is he?"

Sighing, before taking a deep, resigned breath, Pete unbuckled his seat belt, when to his horror the limp body of the young man fell from the side of the plane and hit the ground with a muffled thud.

The brief moment's turbulence experienced on their approach must have been the impact of the lad hitting the plane. He would barely have had time to grasp the safety harness, so it was impossible to know…

Pete stopped trying to make calculations as, staggered beyond belief, he witnessed a slow movement of the corpse. Arms and legs shifted about erratically. The head appeared, trying to raise itself from the runway.

Any second there would be blood. Lots of it. Pete fought the desire to vomit, while bile rose in his throat. He swallowed back hard.

There was further movement, the young man apparently coming to life? Not possible. A ghost? The thing was getting shakily to its feet. What's more, it was beaming. Literally beaming.

Dragging open the plane door, Pete practically tumbled out of the plane. "My God, son. Not possible. How did? How did…?"

"Jesus, Joseph and Mary." The lad held his arms aloft like a lottery winner. "By God, Pete. By God. That's the greatest high I have ever experienced. Peter Matthews, you are a bloody genius."

Nat had followed Pete out of the plane, and gazed stupefied at their client.

Pete stood back with his arms folded, merely faced the young man silently.

Then to Pete's astonishment, the boy said, "My man, that was awesome. Never experienced a rush like it. Better than sex. Way, way better. Not in the same street. Not on the same planet." He sounded out of breath.

"I presume you left your name at reception when you booked this flight?" Pete muttered.

"Correct."

"But you neglected to tell me."

"Since you ask, I'm Pierce Mountford." Then he added, "When can we do it again?"

"I presume you're joking, sir."

"No way. Best buzz ever, and I mean it. When can we go again?"

"Not on my watch, sonny," said Pete, glancing down at the back of his hands.

"Never again on my watch, sonny."

CHAPTER 34 DAY 8

"PIERCE, IT'S ME." The voice was hesitant, small, almost frightened. A murmur of traffic in the background.

"Yes, I know who it is. What do you want, Petra? I'm busy right now." Pierce sounded irritated.

"I'm sorry. I'm so sorry. I was stupid."

"On that we're clearly agreed."

"It was a dumb thing to say. I wish I could take it back. God, Pierce, I'd cut my tongue out if I could."

"That wouldn't do either of us much good, would it, Petra?"

"It was so great."

"What was?"

"We were."

"Yes, we were, come to think of it. While it lasted. Trouble with you, Petra, is you never know when to leave well alone."

"I know. I know." She was breathing heavily.

Pierce sat back on the sofa in his apartment. The afternoon was still sunny, the Thames, which he could see from where he sat, was sparkling. The Johnnie Walker he was sipping was excellent.

And Pierce was beginning to make ground on his father's activities. Maybe the private investigator, Ms. Pierre, could give some advice. If she was that good. Nothing to lose by asking. And, furthermore, the cuts and bruises didn't look too bad.

"And now it's over," he said coldly to his ex.

"Oh, don't say that, Pierce."

"I just said it."

"What do you want me to do? Prostrate myself in front of you? Beg you?"

"Don't be ridiculous, Petra."

"Anything. I'll run down Piccadilly stark naked if you want me to." She paused, awaiting a response. "I love you, Pierce. You're the most exciting man I've ever known."

"I wish I could say the equivalent about you, Petra."

"You're being terribly cruel. I never knew you had that streak in you. Okay, I asked for it last time. It was uncalled for."

"I'll say." He drank some more of the whisky, feeling it plough a path to his gut.

"I'll do anything."

"Anything?" he asked, giving her offer some space.

"Anything."

"Hmm! I wonder," he pondered, giving it some brief attention. "Okay. I'll tell you what. There could be a couple of things you might be able to do for me."

"Go on. Go on."

"First, if you really want to assist. I mean, if you're being serious. I'd want you to help me nose around into Pa's activities. These far right groups are a damned menace. They're threatening all sorts of social and political disruption. It's genuinely worrying. I've got some names and addresses I don't have the time to follow up. Will you though, for me? Good-looking woman like you should be able to make some headway, get some inside info."

"You know I will. Of course I will. I'm good at squeezing information out of people. Anything else?"

"Yes," said Pierce. "There is one thing. Only I'm not sure…"

"Go on."

"Well," he said slowly. "I recently did a free fall. From twelve thousand feet."

"Wow! That is amazing. Was it sexy?"

"I'll say," said Pierce, getting into the mood for what he was going to suggest.

"More. More." She giggled, gaining in confidence.

"I did it without a parachute."

"What? Are you being serious? Really, Pierce? Without a... No! You couldn't have. That's absolutely crazy. You might have been killed." Her voice was trembling.

"Too true," he replied. "The biggest buzz I've ever experienced."

"Better than...?"

"Sex?"

"Better than me?" She sounded shy.

Pierce let her wait for several moments before responding graciously, "Well, maybe not better than you, Petra. But, you might say, on a par."

"What was it you wanted me to do, then?"

"I'll tell you what I want you to do, Petra." He counted to ten.

"Yes? Yes?" she said breathlessly.

"What I want you to do, Petra, is...I want you to jump with me. That is, without a chute. Do you think you could it, Petra? I know you're a gutsy lady. But this would require a slice of madness. Are you mad, Petra? Are you just a bit insane?"

A full half-minute passed, with Pierce allowing Petra to digest what he'd suggested. Then she whispered, "I'll do it." There was a moment's silence, then the sound of traffic once again.

"You will?" He could hardly believe it. "My God, Petra, you really are the sexiest gal I've ever come across."

"I'll come with you," she added. "We can cling together on the way down. Soooo seeexxxyy. We'll come together, darling. You know what I mean."

"You know, I think I may have underestimated you, my love. Tell me, where are you right now?"

"I'm in my car, across the road from you. Shall I come up?"

"The door's already open." He chuckled. "Your spare keys are on the sideboard."

"Yeeeooow!" she squealed happily.

She was in at the door of Pierce's apartment within minutes, to witness what turned out to be the biggest shock of her life. "Good Christ, Pierce, what in God's name...?"

His face was yellow, mauve and purple, with livid cuts on both cheeks. He was barely recognisable. But he was grinning, a grin that was unmistakeable even beneath the ghastly distortion in his appearance. "I was attacked," he said, as though it were an everyday matter.

"Attacked," she asked, dumfounded. "By whom?"

"Two men. Quite large. Something they said let the cat out of the bag."

"You mean, it wasn't a random mugging?"

"No way."

"So what was it they let slip?"

"They were strong. Very strong, and there were two of them. Told me to stop snooping where I wasn't wanted. But, what they didn't know, what they couldn't know, is my years of training in..."

"Martial arts, my lovely man."

"In martial arts, my lovely girl," he replied, taking her in his arms.

"And what was it they let slip?" She laughed. "I can't wait to hear."

"See these cuts and bruises?" Pierce asked, and Petra winced as she surveyed them, putting a palm tenderly against one of his cheeks. "I gave them both back five-fold."

Petra gasped with pleasure. "Fuck, Pierce. You are the sexiest man on earth. I'm practically coming just listening to you. Darling, before I pass out with want, what was it you heard?"

"As I beat the hell out of them both, I mean, really pasted the backsides off them, one of them said, 'I don't care which bloody member of the government put the black up to this. It's not worth it. He can have his money back.'"

"You think it was your father who paid them?"

"Absolutely. Or paid someone to find them. The black? Neither of them were. Presumably someone black was retained by Pa, and he in turn found them."

"Oscar? Paying to have his son beaten up?"

"Paying to have me reconsider my investigations into dearest Pa's nefarious dealings."

"My God. My God."

"Still want to help?"

"Just try to stop me."

"Could be dangerous."

"I said, try to stop me," she repeated, sinking deeper into Pierce's arms.

"Okay," he murmured. "But I won't try to stop you just now."

CHAPTER 35 DAY 8

"MISS PIERRE, I HAVE. an urgent call for you. In fact, I have a raft of calls for you to return. I know you're hard pressed for time, but really I think you might want to take this one."

"Alright, Mrs Gilchrist. If you say it's urgent." Tammy sighed. "What's the nature of the enquiry?"

"It's a business problem, Miss Pierre. Seems as though it'll need some of your own type of accounting experience."

"And you're not able to deal with it?"

"It looks like an insolvency, and the caller sounds frantic."

Mrs Gilchrist, as she insisted on being addressed, Mrs Florence Gilchrist, Tammy's PA, a qualified chartered accountant and member of a dying breed who believe in old-fashioned courtesies, sounded uncharacteristically urgent.

She didn't have the time for this, but recalling how many insolvencies her researches revealed Oscar Mountford to have been involved with, and the smug manner she imagined he would have dealt with them, Tammy decided to take the call. "Put them through, please, Mrs Gilchrist."

Picking up the handset, she announced, "Tammy Pierre. How can I help?"

The voice at the other end of the line sounded desperate, close to breaking point. "My name's Sheila Simmonds. It's my husband, Ms Pierre. He's threatening to kill himself."

People who threaten suicide always need to be taken seriously, the issue dealt with immediately. "Where is your husband right now, Mrs Simmonds?" Tammy asked quietly.

"He's here at the moment. Sitting next to me." The woman was weeping now. "He won't listen to anything I have to say."

Leaning forward, the handset squeezed between her shoulder and her chin, Tammy extracted a panatella from the pack on her desk, and wistfully remembering her condition, put it between her lips, without actually lighting it. Nonetheless, she could smell it and taste it. In a few months she'd be able to smoke one. But then, maybe not with a baby around. "Mrs Simmonds, I need you to try to calm yourself and tell me what the problem is."

"Martin's business is the problem."

"Not doing too well at the moment?"

"You could say that. Ms Pierre, his business is bust. His in-house accountant has gone missing, possibly with some company funds. We don't know how much."

"And what is his business, Mrs Simmonds?"

"He's in IT."

"Do you think he'd be willing to talk to me?"

The sound of muffled conversation could be heard through the handset while Tammy waited for the answer. Then, back on the line Mrs Simmonds said, "I'll put him on, Ms Pierre."

"Hello." The voice was strained, hoarse. The sound of someone at the end of their tether.

"Mr Simmonds?"

"Yeah!"

"Talk to me. Tell me what the problem is. And take your time. As long as you want."

"My business is falling apart. Bloody bookkeeper's gone missing. If he's taken money, I'll skin him alive when I get my hands on him."

Another missing person. "I might be able to help on that front," Tammy suggested.

"Yeah? How?"

She'd attracted some interest from the man. "I'm a private investigator, with an accounting, business background," said Tammy. "Among other things, I do missing persons."

"Well you better find the bastard before I do…"

Ignoring the threat, and glancing at the time, Tammy asked, "Does your company have business debts?"

"Yeah!"

"To whom do you owe money, sir?"

"The Revenue."

"And?"

"What do you mean, and?"

"Who else do you owe money to?"

"Who else should I owe money to? Isn't it enough I owe the government a pile of money."

"Well, for example, do you have any trade creditors?"

"None."

"Bank loans or overdraft?"

"Nope."

"Leasing or HP debts?"

"None."

"Rent due for business premises?"

"I work from home."

"Staff back pay? Holiday pay? Redundancy?"

"I employ no-one, other than my so-called self-employed bastard part-time bookkeeper."

"Okay, well we'll take it a step at a time. How much do you owe, or think you owe, in tax?"

Tammy waited as the seconds ticked away, wondering if she should prompt the man. Absent-mindedly, she shoved the panatella back in its box and pushed the pack away from her. Then she heard the man sigh, and say, "I owe the Revenue over two hundred and fifty thousand pounds. So what do you say now? Hmm? How am I supposed to deal with that, eh?" His voice was rising as he was demonstrably panicking.

"Mr Simmonds, please listen to me. No, listen to me," she urged as the voice at the other end of the line interrupted her and began rising to a peak, bordering on a scream. "Please, Mr Simmonds. Please listen to what I have to say." But he was gone.

"I did say you can't talk to him, Ms Pierre," begged Mrs Simmonds.

Tammy noted the time again. Mrs Gilchrist nodded, tapped her watch and mouthed, "Running late."

"I know, I know," muttered Tammy. "Got to try to deal with this now, if I possibly can." Then back with Mrs Simmonds. "Please try to bring him back to the phone. This can be dealt with. But I have to speak with your husband first."

"I'll try to get him back, but..." Again, there was the sound of muffled conversation, the tone pleading.

A few moments later, he said, "Sheila says you want another word. It's a waste of bloody time. They've got me and they won't let go. They're threatening all sorts of proceedings. I can't take it. I say, I can't take it any more."

"Listen to me, Mr Simmonds. No, again, stop for one moment and listen to me," she insisted as he began to speak again. "If you won't let me talk I can't deal with this."

"Alright," he said, sounding resigned, tired, beaten.

"Now. How do you trade?"

"I told you, I trade from home."

"No, that's not what I mean. Are you self-employed?"

"Of course I am. No-one employs me."

"I see I'm not being clear. What I'm asking is, do you trade as an individual, that is as a sole trader, or do you trade as a limited company?"

"I'm a limited company. M. Simmonds IT Consultancy Ltd."

"Okay. Excellent."

"Excellent? What's bloody excellent?"

Not responding to the comment, Tammy continued, "Now this two hundred and fifty thousand pounds you owe the Revenue. Is it VAT?"

"No."

"PAYE, on your own earnings?"

"No, it's Corporation Tax. And I think I'm going to hang up. This is getting nowhere."

How do you stop a charging bull in its tracks? Tammy wondered. "Before you do, Mr Simmonds, there's something you ought to —"

"No, Ms Pierre, you've been very kind, but I'm ringing off now. Then I know what I must do."

You don't stop the bull, you divert it. "You don't owe anybody anything, sir."

In the background Tammy could hear Mrs Simmonds. "What's she saying, Martin? Oh do let her finish." Then Martin came back on the line. "I'm listening. Though it won't make a blind bit of difference."

Heaving a sigh of relief, Tammy said, "Mr Simmonds, are you not aware that Corporation Tax is a company debt, not a personal one? You don't owe anyone a penny."

"I don't?"

"Not a brass farthing. And you might be interested to learn they stopped hanging bankrupts in the eighteenth century."

"They did?"

"Yes, John Perrott, he was the last, hanged in 1761 for debts of around twenty-five thousand pounds. That's about five million in today's money, give or take."

"Bloody hell!" he breathed. "But I've got this official letter talking about High Court hearings, and that sort of thing."

"Mr Simmonds, do you have the document to hand?"

"Hang on a bit. Yes. Alright, go on. What am I supposed to do with it?"

"Read it to me."

"Okay, it says here, Petition for the Compulsory Winding Up..."

"Stop there, Mr Simmonds. Stop right there."

"Really? What have I said?"

"That document is not directed, nor even addressed to you."

"It isn't?" The relief in the man's voice was practically palpable.

"It's addressed to the company. Your company, Mr Simmonds. Not you."

"So then...?"

"So then, your company owes HMRC, Her Majesty's Revenue and Customs, a sum of money it is unable to pay. The company is insolvent and needs to be wound up and its affairs dealt with. That's what is happening."

"My God. So... My God."

"You know, if your company owes that sort of money in Corporation Tax it must have been making substantial profits."

"It was. It was going swimmingly, till..."

"Until?"

"We signed a big, I mean, very big contract. International company. Promised us years of work."

"What happened? They wouldn't pay? Or maybe, they couldn't pay?"

"Couldn't pay. They went bust owing us over half a million. We'd have been well in, but for them."

"Does your company have any other monies due from customers right now?"

"About a hundred thousand."

"All good?"

"Should be."

"Tell me, when is the hearing date in that document?"

The sound of paper rustling drifted over the phone. "Three weeks' time," said Mr Simmonds.

"In that case, two things need to happen now. First it's necessary to have set aside the Compulsory Winding Up Petition, for that's what it is. Then you need to organise the liquidation of the company yourself."

"How do I do that?"

"Through a licensed insolvency practitioner, whose name and number I shall text you in a moment."

"How do I pay for that, then?"

"You don't. Your company will pay, from the monies you say are due from clients. Costs will be a fraction of what's due in."

"And that's it?"

"That's it. I'm surprised your own accountant didn't give you this information."

"We fell out a while ago over his fees, they were becoming ridiculous. But I need to earn an income, and IT is what I do. How do I get on now?"

"You start a new limited company."

"Won't I be barred or something, from directorships?"

"Of course not. You've committed no offence. Your company has failed through a massive bad debt. That could happen to any business."

"That's amazing."

"No. It's the law."

"I feel as though I'm floating."

"You'll need a new accountant."

"Can you…?"

"I'll text you details of one. Incidentally, he doesn't overcharge either."

"How can I thank you?"

"No need. Tell me, Mr. Simmonds, how did you find me?"

"I Googled 'insolvency and forensic accounting'. Your name came up as a forensic accountant. All five-star reviews. Someone described you as a sort of boutique outfit. And also, I reckoned if you were in Mayfair you must be pretty good at what you do."

"Then you didn't want to talk to me."

"I was going downhill pretty fast."

"Seems Mrs Simmonds got to me just in time."

"Bloody hell! I was done, you know. Ready to end it. Hey! I'm forgetting. What do I owe you. Christ, you've saved my life."

"Nothing."

"What's that?"

"I said you owe me nothing, and I absolutely have to go now. Really."

"But surely I must owe you something?"

"No you don't. All I've done is give you some advice and passed you on to the right people. I hope all goes well from now. Incidentally, when you're ready, get in touch and we'll see what we can do about finding your bookkeeper and maybe locating the embezzled funds."

"I don't know how to thank you, Ms Pierre. You're amazing. Christ, I shall sleep tonight, for the first time in months."

"Sleep well, Mr Simmonds," said Tammy, smiling as she replaced the receiver.

Mrs Gilchrist, facing her way, added, "How nice, Miss Pierre. We've heard that comment a few times before, haven't we."

"We have, Mrs Gilchrist," said Tammy, hurrying to leave. "Makes the whole job worthwhile. May have a new client there as well, if my current clients don't lynch me first for being so damn late."

* * * * *

"Someone's been busy here," Mountford snarled, spittle forming at the corners of his mouth. "Going through my desk, my papers. And if I ever find out who."

Georgia had risked discovery in securing as much information as she could to relay to Tammy, thence to Walker. Terrified of discovery, she'd crept into Oscar's office when he was out, either at meetings or simply in the loo, on more than one occasion having to excuse her presence there saying she was bringing in or taking out papers. Perfectly natural for a PA, but feeling perfectly unnatural in circumstances such as these.

She had a feeling he suspected something, witnessed some odd looks he gave, but covered up well, forcing herself to look confident and untroubled, despite the huge effort it took. It extracted its toll, however, keeping her awake at night, leaving her unusually drawn and pale, something else Oscar noticed, and was moved to remark upon.

"What's wrong with you, woman," he asked her irritably one morning. "You up to something I should know about?"

"No I'm fine," she said brightly, her pulse racing. "That time of the month."

"No it isn't," he barked. "You're not due for another week. I should damn know, shouldn't I."

"I'm starting to become a bit irregular these days." Not wanting to harp on about her age, she left it at that.

"Bloody women," Oscar murmured, dismissing the subject. But the brief exchange had left her trembling. Something she found hard to disguise.

As often as she could she phoned Tammy, mainly for moral support, both using burner phones. Other relevant information she relayed via WhatsApp, or in person whenever she got the chance to see Tammy, whom she was quickly coming to regard as her anchor. They'd spent more than one night together and she was aware of the growing attraction between them, her own insecurities countered by Tammy's absolute self-assurance. This liaison was the first she'd ever experienced with another woman, and she marvelled at how natural it was.

Then turning to Georgia, he demanded, "What do you know about this? My things have been disturbed. I'm certain of it. Do you know anything? Anything at all? Because if I thought for one moment..." His silence hung in the air like a petrified spectre.

Her hands shaking, legs like jelly, unable to talk for fear, Georgia turned away from him so he wouldn't see her swallow, clearing her throat in order to reply. It was as though she were choking, and while the powder on her face absorbed the perspiration there, she thanked God he couldn't see the line of sweat that ran down her back between her shoulder blades. The moments she took collecting herself allowed Georgia to give the impression she was perfectly calm about everything.

"Oscar," she announced coolly, "I don't know what you're implying. But if it's what I think it is, then unless you clarify your statement I will not remain in your employ." Having started, she became more emboldened, faced him now with hands on her hips. "It's been fifteen years, Oscar. Fifteen years when you've never once had to question my loyalty or commitment..."

"Very well. Very well," he muttered, one placatory hand held up. "Let's leave it there shall we?"

On the brink of taking the matter further, Georgia stopped herself, realising she'd gained the upper hand.

Oscar retreated to his office, and Georgia made herself a cup of strong, sweet, steaming coffee. Off the hook, thank God. It took her nearly an hour to stop shivering.

CHAPTER 36 DAY 9

"**I** LOVE YOU, DOV."

"I love *you*, Tammy," he'd responded softly.

They were seated side by side in first class, holding hands like a teenage couple as the Virgin Atlantic A350 came in to land at New York's Kennedy, the hum of the big jets barely disturbing the plush peace of the aircraft cabin.

"What are we going to do?" she asked, feeling a confusion of melancholy and joy.

He shook his head but didn't reply.

"Dov?"

"Tammy, I don't know," he answered, more roughly than he'd intended. "I've told you Esther's pregnant. We're here to do a job of work. Let's talk when we're done and on our way out."

Linking her arm through his, his bicep bulging in response. "Okay, boss," she whispered, nuzzling his cheek. "Whatever you say."

"You know I'd marry you tomorrow…"

"Hmm. Not such a good idea."

"No? Why not?"

"With my morals?"

"I know all about your morals."

"Not sure you know all about them." She sighed, leaning closer to him, smelling that unique freshness he always carried, no matter the hour of day or night.

The daytime flight had been smooth and they'd slept part of the way in each other's arms. She hadn't wanted the journey to end, but Dov was right. They were here to do a job of work, and to get in as fast as possible. It would be late when she finally made it to where she planned on going. This might all be a wild goose chase, but she had to know if there was anything linking Letitia Mountford with the flamboyant murderer who'd apparently been occupying an apartment in that rough district of New York they'd identified. Was it Letitia? Was it her double?

Finding out what was going on was what Bob Walker wanted to know. Might Letitia be linked to extremist groups on the left? How did that figure with her husband's support for the alt.right? They'd planned a trip incognito, she and Dov. A quick hop in and out. But that wasn't going to happen. Now, this was going to be a step into the unknown, and she was straining to get things underway.

She'd hired a vehicle similar to her own in the UK, a Lexus 450h, hybrid SUV, as she didn't want to risk using a motor with which she was unfamiliar. The Ritz-Carlton had organised it for her, the hotel either Letitia or her double were reckoned to be staying at, and where she would now be residing with Dov, for as long as it took. The SUV was ready for her as soon as they arrived.

They had hurried showers, and Tammy barely had time to check her appearance, rushing off before Dov was ready to go with her, despite his insisting she wait for him. She was lagged after the long flight, but time was of the essence, though she was tired and wouldn't be at her best.

Having driven around the area several times, looking to see if there were any spots she might find herself trapped, she concluded there were none that could be regarded as safe. Once she alighted the vehicle she'd be on her own. Nothing unusual in that, it was a position she'd been in many times before. But this one in particular called for extra vigilance, with as much mental preparation and forethought as possible.

A car key offered a useful weapon, particularly if the stem was left extended. Other than that she'd come unarmed. Depending upon whom and how many might be facing her, any visual armament would be both provocative and allow an assailant an excuse to attack with weapons of their own. It was a risky strategy, being open-handed, but one she judged the best policy, however tempting it might have been to slip on the belt with the pockets of secreted shuriken. Not that she'd have been likely to get them past customs checks.

Pulling over to the curb into a spot clear of other vehicles, she climbed out of the Lexus, palmed the car key, with the stem protruding between her fingers, and glanced down at her clothing. Always dress for the occasion, she'd decided. Look the part. Smart, chic, in control. It had to be assumed they, if it was a they, wouldn't be expected to be aware she was a private investigator more than capable of handling herself. A two-piece suit in clerical grey, knee-length flared skirt, together with a pale blue blouse completed the ensemble. The bootees with their four-inch heels comprising a further potential weapon, they also had the effect of raising her height to six feet five.

It was dusk and the square appeared deserted. Derelict and deserted. A breeze sprang up, wafting leaves and torn newspapers over the blacktop. A crushed basketball lay at the base of a rusting hoop, presumably abandoned. The area smelled of rotting garbage, drains and general decay.

The ancient block was on the far side of the square, an eight-storey hostile brownstone, the apartment she'd come to search situated on the fourth floor, number 452. Her stomach twinged. Too early for the baby to be moving. Doctor Aziz had been adamant, no undue physical stress if she wanted to keep this child. She recalled the medic's advice, no guarantees with her levels of testosterone she'd be fortunate enough to conceive again. Dov had told her to wait, said he'd be no more than ten minutes behind her, max, but she was impatient. As ever.

It was a mistake, she was to find. A big one.

The unidentified text she'd received, presumably from the little man in the wire-rimmed specs, had said to stay away, there'd be nothing to find there, a sure sign there would be something they didn't want to her to see. If anyone else was proposing to search the apartment, she'd be there first. At least that was the intention. She was already running days late. Her fault. Too many diversions, too much prep she decided was needed.

Squaring her shoulders she breathed in deeply and strode forward purposefully, the bootee heels clacking emphatically. There still appeared to be no-one in sight. Another flutter of moth's wings circled the pit of her stomach. This time it was nerves. But if there were to be any attempt to obstruct her, she'd be clear and cool to deal with it when it happened. And it could be any time now.

Halfway across the square, she heard soft padded footsteps hurrying up behind her, the hooting of laughter from over to her left and right. Sounds in the square echoed, but it was impossible to locate their precise source.

Then things started happening, unpredictably and out of sequence.

Three men appeared from nowhere, all shiny shaven-headed and decked out in navy tracksuits and white trainers. Smart, she smiled. Thugs should always look as smart as their victims. It made for a sort of elegant symmetry with her own attitude to dress.

The fourth man she could sense, breathing behind her. She could smell him. What was that cocktail? Hash? Sweat? Sure. And something else. Something she could easily identify as her own preferred poison. Cocaine, particularly noted by those who embrace it as coke, snow, big rush and others. The man might be high on it right now. It wouldn't give him much of an edge, she imagined, possibly quite the reverse. But judging by the source of the scent, from above the back of her head, the man was clearly a deal taller than she was. Something to bear in mind if things got difficult.

She smiled. Let them see her smiling, she decided. It can be so thoroughly disarming in socially awkward situations such as these.

So this was to be her welcoming committee. A board pledged to impede her progress. Not the most sophisticated of panels in her experience. Might they be open to debate? To persuasion of her good intentions? She was about to find out.

"Hey, guys," said the biggest of the three facing her. "Whadda we got here? A babe or a guy?" The accent was pure northern Manhattan. Pointing at Tammy he rasped, "Ho, sister? Y'all got up in drag, mama? Or be it papa?" Joking as he squealed with laughter.

Facing the three, her back erect, legs slightly spread, a hand on one hip, she replied, "You talking to me, cowboy?"

"I'm talkin' to you, honey. So where'd you dink ya goin', hmm? What's poppin', babe?"

"Now what has that got to do with you, sir?"

"Sir? Sir? Fuck me, the chick's callin' me sir. Can ya dig it? I mean, you sound like a chick. Sure don't look like one, fam. Whatchoo say, Des?" he asked, turning to his left. "She look like a chick to you?"

"Not me, man," responded the one called Des.

Turning to his right, the big man said, "Beau?"

The other man merely shrugged his acknowledgement.

Then the mood changed. The men had stopped smiling. Tammy sensed the accompanying shift in the pattern of movement, body language, behaviour and braced herself, ice cool now.

The first thing she was aware of was the hands of the man behind her closing around her neck. Hands that were slick with sweat. Great bear paws. Fingernails like talons bit into her neck, constricting her breathing. In mere seconds, curtains of grey clouded her vision as though she might black out at any moment. Her legs were like rubber.

She'd not factored in to this jaunt just how exhausted she still was from the events surrounding the Black Candle investigation. A regrettable miscalculation.

The three men ahead of her were laughing again, and falling about.

"Go, man," said the apparent ringleader. "May as well finish de job while we gots time to get to t'de bar, see de rest uh de guys. Dump her in the water soon as ya're done, man. S'cool, bro. Catch up wid us." And they made to leave.

Reaching up to lay hands on her assailant's, now barely able to breathe, Tammy caught further raucous mirth ricocheting from every side of the square. It was all hugely funny, and she'd soon be dead.

They thought.

For all of her accumulated exhaustion, she knew better.

But the curtains of grey were turning black. She was out of time. Legs beginning to give way.

Using her thumbs and curled forefingers, she grasped the little fingers of the man behind her, those pressing hard into her neck, and heard his agonised shriek as she pulled down smartly, snapping them both.

Feeling him fall away from her, she heard, "She fucking broke mah fingers, man. Broke mah fucking fingers."

The other three now approached intently, the middle man muttering oaths under his breath, "Jokin's ova, lady. Time for bed."

Dragging her skirt deliberately up to her hips at the same time as she sucked blessed air into her protesting lungs, Tammy, both fists bunched, adopted the stance with thighs spread wide and legs bent at the knee as the men closed on her.

The main man, practically on top of her, stopped in his tracks, pointed straight at her crotch, staring in disbelief.

"What da damn fuck, Jesus, man," he shouted to the other two, turning away from Tammy in shock for that one moment. A moment just long enough for Tammy to high kick the man under the chin as he turned back, the pointed heel of her bootee piercing the soft tissue beneath his jaw.

Dropping to his knees, hands scrabbling under his mouth in an attempt to staunch the flow of blood which gurgled out from between his lips, he muttered, "Kill the fucker. Don't let the fucker…"

But he'd fallen unconscious.

That left the other two.

The one to her right said, "Don't know what Jack saw waaay down dere, lady, but…" He stopped when Tammy turned to face him, her legs still spread. "Fuck me," the man muttered.

But before he could do anything more, the man to her left had drawn a long-bladed knife. She swayed to her right in an attempt to avoid the shank as he sprang at her, her quick reflexes probably saving her life, but the weapon pierced her jacket and blouse anyway, cutting into the left side of her abdomen, a red hot poker, carving a trail of fire.

She gasped, winced, but recovered quickly. With the blade sticking out of her like a barbecue skewer, the man snapped his hand away as though he'd been stung by a wasp. Smothering the pain, Tammy said softly, "No way to treat a lady, young man," and, reaching down, dragged it out by the handle, feeling its serrated edge savage her own flesh.

"My turn now," she muttered, lunging forward and thrusting the blade into the man's solar plexus, pushing up hard so it would pierce his heart. He gasped once, then went down hard.

But she was tiring fast, realising the folly of having come unaccompanied, and accepted she couldn't cope with the last of them when he drew a gun and pointed it straight at her. Facing down the barrel was like staring into a black unseeing eye and her heart stopped, as a microsecond of hollow silence ensued.

"Merde!" she groaned as the explosion of a high-powered semi-automatic ballooned in her head and the man collapsed like a sack of lead.

Spinning around, she exclaimed, "Dov," as he holstered the gun. "Dieu merci. Where were you, for God's sake?"

Furious, he replied, "I told you to wait, Tammy. Couldn't you do as I ask, just for once? Another minute… And what were they so staggered when you readied yourself they were thrown? Haven't they ever seen a pair of knickers before?"

"Ah," said Tammy, breathing with vast relief.

"Ah?"

"Yes, ah. You see I came prepared."

"How prepared was that?"

"Very prepared. My secret weapon."

"I daren't ask," he said, shaking his head. "But let me ask?"

"I'm not wearing knickers." She grinned. The poor man looked totally nonplussed.

"I knew I shouldn't have asked. But God, Tammy, you're bleeding. Look at you. We need to get you to a hospital. Now."

The adrenalin rush was quickly subsiding as she floated back to earth and reality. The stark presentiment, my baby. Will I lose my baby?

Barely pausing, "No," she announced, firmly banishing the vision. "I'm going to finish what I came for."

"Hell, Tammy. You're crazy. I said, you're bleeding."

"I'm going in to see what's so important in that apartment they're prepared to kill to stop me finding out." Then, with one unconscious, the other whimpering over his broken fingers, she noted, "Dov, two dead, two injured. Who's going to deal with all this?"

"Who do you think?" He sighed.

"Your people? Mossad?"

"Do you have any other ideas?"

She shook her head. "Felix might have helped, but Bob called him off just before we left. Not a CIA matter, he said. This is a UK problem."

"Tammy? Please…? Come! Now!"

He might not have spoken for all the notice she took. "Will you wait for me? I'll try to be quick."

"What a question. Who else do you think is going to insist you get to the hospital?"

"Back soon, darling," she whispered, and turned to walk away, a hand grasping the injured side, her body shaking with an overkill of delayed shock. It had all been a bit too close for comfort.

"Tammy, slow down," he called in a seeming afterthought. "I'll come along anyway. Two sets of eyes."

"If you must." She hurried on.

Then, "Hey," called Dov, brandishing something in one hand.

"Yes?" She spun round, impatient now for him to catch her up.

"You dropped your car keys."

CHAPTER 37 DAY 9

"**M**A'AM, YOU'VE LOST a lot of blood." The doctor, a young Asian man in the customary white coat, had left his tie loose; he looked concerned.

Gazing up from where she lay in a plain white hospital nightdress in the small private ward Dov had organised for her, Tammy remarked, "I imagine I might have." Her recent wounds were burning with the efforts of the evening's exertions, the current injury throbbing, despite the analgesics administered. She was bunkered in flame.

"A lot of sutures holding you together, Ms Pierre. We need to keep you in overnight. Or at least, for the rest of the night," he added, checking his watch.

She was surrounded by medical apparatus, a number of tubes attached to her arms and one hand. Screens and meters registered all her vital signs. Dov was at the back of the room, his arms folded, saying nothing, although from his angry expression it was as though he might at any moment step forward and tie her to the bed.

"I appreciate the advice, doctor," Tammy replied. "And would you kindly remove all this?" She indicated the spaghetti tangle surrounding her with an imperious wave.

"Don't you want to know about your condition?"

"I'm sure if there were anything untoward, you'd have told me before anything else."

"You've only just come round from the anaesthetic, Tammy. You've been out for two hours while they put you back together. When was he supposed to have told you?"

"Thank you, Dov. I'll let you know when I need your advice." She didn't have to be mother-henned. Then, addressing the doctor again, "Is there anything I should want to know about my condition?" There was one thing she had to know, but preferably not when Dov was in the room.

But before she could ask him to leave, the doctor put in, "You know you're pregnant, Ms Pierre?"

"Of course I know."

"From what you've been through I'd say you're lucky not to have experienced a spontaneous termination."

"That's right. I am aware," she said, feeling foolish, cowed. But she added nothing further. There was no point.

"I'd say, about three months," the doctor went on. "We can be reasonably accurate in the first trimester."

She watched Dov fixate, mentally counting off the weeks, as she'd seen him do before, then observed him visibly relax. It was his. Of that he could be certain.

But then, depending on a whole set of indeterminate factors, might he one day in the distant future have cause to query the baby's paternity? That was one question she'd have to leave on the back burner for now. If Dov were to be disabused eventually, how could Tammy ever explain the circumstances of her having conceived and then kept a Muslim child? Nabil's baby. The freedom fighter from the Free Syrian Army who'd saved her life, effectively at the cost of his own.

"What time is it, Dov?"

"It's 3.00 am, Tammy," he said without checking his watch.

"Alright, Doctor. Give me three hours to relax, then one of us will be undoing all this paraphernalia."

"But," the doctor said, appearing thoroughly alarmed. "You can't…"

"Actually," said Tammy resolutely, "I can, and I will. Unless you do, of course."

The doctor started to say something, then clearly thinking better of it left the two of them together.

As soon as he was gone Tammy said to Dov, "Darling, don't give me advice or instructions when they're not needed. Hmm?"

He went over to the window and stared into the darkness. "What are you proposing to do when we leave here at 6.00 am, Tammy?"

"Have you got the carriers I brought out of the tenement block, Dov?"

"There." He turned and pointed to a corner of the room where two large white plastic carriers were placed, one apparently filled with clothing, the other with a profusion of papers.

"Have you had a chance to go through them at all?"

"Only given them a cursory glance while you were in theatre."

"And? Uhhh!" she said, wincing as she attempted to make herself more comfortable.

"Drum majorette's costume in one bag, somewhat torn and looking as though it's been in muddy water."

"That fits, doesn't it. The fight outside the restaurant where she might have drowned in the East River. And, what else?"

"Sundry other filthy clothing. Looks like she left in a hurry."

"What about the papers?"

"I've riffled through them. Here's the puzzle. We've guessed that Letitia stayed at the Ritz, leaving her double to do a lot of the dirty work in the shabbier end of town. This whole exercise suggests Letitia, knew? Guessed? Found out? She was being watched from very early on and was out to confuse as far as possible. We still don't know whom the murders were committed by, and we've not found for sure who it is that's staying at the hotel. Letitia? Presumably. Her double? Unlikely."

"Tell me about the papers, then?" Tammy asked, knowing his Mossad ties would render anything he deduced to be of value.

"As you well know, irrespective of how secure apps like WhatsApp claimed to be, some terrorist groups take no chances and issue messages, instructions, guidances on paper. What I've found in the paperwork was as you suspected. We've got a stack of instructions, with dates, times and places where targets can be found and dealt with. We've seen three murders here in New York. The mass of correspondence here suggests there've been more, not necessarily carried out by one of our two ladies, but certainly within the last year or so."

"No idea why the whole lot hasn't been burned. Someone slipped up, didn't they," offered Tammy. "But there were lots of angry printed notes about the need to use ricin, and the fact that it wasn't being utilised as instructed. So I ask myself, just who was it staying in the tenement? The double? As we've assumed all along. Or was it actually Letitia? I'm beginning to wonder whether our rebel madam was aiming to escape her controllers, while at the same time running from us, before we could get to question her. In which case, who is it staying at the Ritz?"

"Whatever. Whoever. She, whichever one she is, certainly seems to have been misbehaving badly. We'll find out soon enough once we get back there. I know. I know," he protested, holding up his hands in surrender. "You're leaving here at 6.00 am. With me."

"That it? Nothing more?"

"What were you hoping for, then?"

"I'm not sure. Something. Something at the back of my mind. Some little thing."

Stroking his jaw, he returned his gaze to the darkness outside, then noted, "There was one other item."

"Go on."

"In a small white envelope, three tiny bits of tin? Base metal? Silver? Don't know. Not sure what they're supposed to be for, but I found them on a shelf when I was searching the bathroom. Looked interesting, so I thought I'd pick them up and drop them in the bag with everything else."

"Can I see?"

"Sure you can." Reaching down into the carrier with the paperwork he withdrew the envelope he'd referred to and handed it to Tammy. "There you go."

Pulling back the flap and peeping inside, she said, "I think I know what this is. I won't tempt providence by guessing just yet. I'll let you know as soon as I'm more certain."

"Fair enough. Suits me."

"Okay, Dov. We'll start to make our enquiries as soon as I get out of this place and back to the Ritz."

He nodded, but said nothing.

"Oh, and Dov, while I'm resting, could you possibly get back to the hotel and fetch me a change of clothes. I can't walk out in the bloodstained things I have here."

"You can't? Whyever not?" A half smile played about the corners of his mouth.

"Well what would I say if I were stopped by one of the hospital staff?" she asked him quizzically.

"Tell them you've just had an op and didn't have time to wait about."

She burst out laughing. "Dov?" She suddenly felt unaccountably foolish, even bashful. "Thank you."

"What for?" He shrugged.

"Everything," she replied. "Just everything. That's all."

CHAPTER 38 DAY 10

SHE WOKE RAGGEDLY, the space behind her eyelids protesting at the blaze of morning sun. Her body ached, racked with pain, the knife wound biting like a steel man-trap. She moved fractionally, and grunted involuntarily as the wounds, old and fresh, mocked her.

"Quelle heure?" she wondered, half to herself.

"It's 8.00 am," said Dov.

"Quoi?" she snapped, sparking awake.

"8.00 am," he repeated.

"Connard!" she spat. "Imbecile! I said we were to leave here at 6.00 am. Where's that damn doctor? Why isn't he here?"

"He was here at 6.00 am, but you were sleeping sound-ly. So we thought…"

"You thought? You thought? Aaaarrgghh!" She tried to sit up, but the combined effort and pain were too much, and she flopped back against the pillows.

"Rest, Tammy. For heaven's sake, can't you see you'll be in better shape to chase up your investigation if you're clear-headed. Which you can't be if you're in so much pain."

She finally managed to unstick her gummed up eyes and focused on Dov standing over her. He'd changed from the denim jacket, jeans and trainers of last night into the smarter set of navy chinos and blazer with loafers and white T-shirt. It was always like the first time with Dov, no matter how she tried to ignore it her heart hammered in her chest. He was just so beautiful.

"Go away," she snarled, instantly regretting her out-burst, before muttering, placatingly, "I don't need you to tell me what to do."

"I think you do, Tammy. And if you try to get out of that bed I'm going to stop you. If I have to damn well sit on you."

Too tired to argue, she could feel herself drifting off into blessed unconsciousness. She faintly heard, "Just give yourself twenty-four hours. Till this time tomorrow. I'll make some enquiries in the mean…" But she was oblivious to his suggestions.

She was still asleep when Dov returned the next day at 7.00 am, and she continued sleeping until around 11.30 am, when she awoke abruptly, stared up at Dov angrily, and said, "What's the damn time?"

Drawn and with shadows under her eyes, she was as obstinate as ever when he bent to kiss her. "Go away," she said, half-heartedly.

"Very well," he said, and made for the door.

"No wait," she called after him.

"Make up your mind, Tammy. Do I stay or do I go?"

"Bladi nar!" she muttered under her breath.

"It was French yesterday, Yiddish today? And anyway, who's a bloody fool?"

"You are. Damn pest," she said, grimacing and gasping as she struggled to sit up.

"Let me," he offered. But she pushed him away.

"Okay, Tammy. Can we be serious for just a moment? Tell me, how're you doing? You don't look too brilliant to me."

"I've had better days." No point in going on about it. His sympathy was all very welcome, but a luxury she couldn't afford if she was going to move on. Dealing with volatile extremist groups, the murders committed, the threats made, there was no telling who might be next in any given firing line.

"Will you stay in another day?" Dov asked. "They seem to think you should."

CHAPTER 38 DAY 10 • 213

"No, Dov. We need to move on."

"Fair enough. You're the boss. So what's next?"

"Well now, big boy," she smiled at last, "what have you found in the twenty-four hours since I let you loose?"

Pulling up an armchair to the side of the bed, Dov sat down and made himself comfortable. "Starting with the hotel, they were very helpful when I explained who and what we are and what we're trying to find out."

"We're not police though, Dov."

"No, but I do know how to contact your Felix and Bob Walker."

"You do?"

"Of course I do, Tammy. You know very well I can easily establish my credentials."

"Yes, Dov." Thoroughly admonished, she couldn't argue the point. She must be wearier than she'd been prepared to admit to herself.

"It seems, if our duo were seeking to confuse us they've been to some trouble."

"I'm listening." She linked her fingers together in her lap and tried to relax.

"As soon as they both arrived in New York they split up. Letitia then checks into flat 452 in Vinegar Hill, ostensibly as her double using her double's passport for ID, while her double checks into the Ritz as Letitia using Letitia's passport. That's how they played it out."

"How did you find out about the double renting apartment 452, then?" she enquired.

"It's not too difficult to locate the owners of freehold properties in New York. It needed no persuasion to have them confirm who they'd let the apartment to, giving them the date of the pair's arrival in New York."

"And?"

"The apartment was rented to one Polonia Filipek."

"Filipek?" Tammy exclaimed. "Wasn't that Letitia Mountford's surname before she started changing things around?"

"Precisely. So I called Bob and he started nosing around for us."

"Always reliable, isn't he. I'm very fond of Bob. You know, he gave me a peck on the cheek the other day, then he jumped back with embarrassment. Totally harmless. But you know Bob. It's all about protocol."

"I do know Bob, of course. Anyway, it seems there's not too many people with the surname Filipek in the UK. His people found, among a few others, a single mother in North Wales called Filipek. Here's the thing though, she was originally called Morgan, Sarah Morgan. She changed her name a long time ago by deed poll. And, wait for it, she has or had a daughter called Polonia. Smaller communities sometimes gave single mothers a hard time in the past. And all this was, of course, about forty years ago."

"My, my, Dov. Everyone has been busy. Polonia Filipek," she mused. "Apart from the fact she looks enough like Letitia to play her part, I wonder what else connects them?"

"One thought."

"Go on."

"Clearly, the name, Filipek. I'd bet Letitia's and Polonia's father are one and the same. It'd be too much of a coincidence for the two to share a surname and appearance but have different fathers."

"Half-sisters. Pyotr might have strayed."

"Could be."

"Sarah Morgan takes Pyotr's surname, gives her credibility in a small local community that she was once married."

"Hence the physical resemblance. The management at the hotel have been helpful and shown me CCTV of the day Letitia booked in. And, Tammy, I'm pretty sure it's not Letitia, but this so-called Polonia."

"So, to make sure I have it clear," said Tammy, "Letitia booked into the apartment at Vinegar Hill, calling herself Polonia Filipek? And Polonia checked into the Ritz-Carlton hotel calling herself Letitia. They simply swapped passports, and presumably credit cards, and got away with it?"

"Looks like it. In which case some? Or likely all of our three murders will have been conducted by the wife of the UK's next Chancellor of the Exchequer."

"No wonder the Security Services in the UK are intent on finding where she's disappeared to. Plus, who knows where she'll pop up next and who might be in her sights? And will it be here, or will it be back in the UK? We need to question whoever it is that's staying at the Ritz now. I mean right now, Dov. No more delays being bullied out of me."

"Wait, Tammy. No wait." Dov held his hands up in protest.

"Wait? Wait? What for, man? We've no time to lose."

"No point in hurrying, Tammy."

"For goodness' sake, why not?"

"Because Letitia or Polonia, whichever, has already checked out of the hotel."

"How? What?" She held her hands out, questioningly. "When?" She sounded nonplussed.

"Days ago, Tammy."

"I'll bet you forgot to ask who paid. Whose credit card they accepted at the hotel."

"No, Tammy. I'm really slightly more competent than you give me credit for. It was Letitia's credit card that was used at the hotel, not that that helps, given what we know of their swapping arrangements.

"Finally, Letitia, I'm presuming it's her, having committed the East River murder makes a quick escape from apartment 452, leaving all sorts of incriminating evidence behind for us to find. She must have been very frightened to have been so slapdash.

"Then, one of the two, almost certainly Polonia, pays the hotel bill and leaves. The CCTV images aren't that clear. What's happened to the other, must be Letitia, we don't yet know."

"Wow, Dov. Well done. I'm impressed."

"I'm delighted you're impressed, Tammy." He sighed patiently. "So what's next? Can your people at Incognita see if they can track either or both of the women back to the UK?"

"Won't be easy. We got them exiting the UK because we had a date. Without a date to go on, pinpointing their return will be like searching for a needle in a haystack. In short, well-nigh impossible."

"Actually, we've got a couple of things to go on," offered Dov.

"I'm listening."

"We've got the date, that whoever it was left the hotel. That'll give your boys something to work on regarding date and time of a return to the UK. They've got the two names to work with as well."

"And we have the clothing worn by our murderer. In that carrier." She pointed.

"Additionally, we know whoever checked out of the hotel did so before the East River murder was committed. Thus, one of the two, probably Letitia, was still in residence at the time in flat 452."

"We need to get back to the UK. See if we can track down anyone."

"I know. As long as you're really up to it."

Tammy's mobile on the bedside cabinet bleeped an incoming text, and she glanced at Dov before picking it up. Staring at the screen, she read out loud, "Tammy, we're getting news that there's been another murder we need to look at, this time in a hotel in St James's, close to a demo that took place in Trafalgar Square. It happened about seventeen days ago. Details are still sketchy. CCTV shows a bizarrely dressed woman with cropped blond hair booking into the hotel. She'd been picked out earlier at the demo talking to the same man later found dead there. It's been brought to our attention at this time because of the woman's clothing. The SIO has made the link with the investigations around the New York killings.

"The woman isn't seen again, although facial recognition software picked out a woman of the same height, build and facial characteristics as the one that booked in leaving the hotel, but this one has long auburn hair and is dressed conservatively in a grey skirt and jacket.

"We're pretty sure it's Letitia. Contact me urgently on your return. BW."

CHAPTER 39 DAY 10

IT WAS BRIGHT SUNSHINE with the merest smattering of cumulus clouds and the finest of fine breezes. An ideal day for a jump.

Fairfield aerodrome set in the Oxfordshire countryside, not far from the M4, catered to a class of individual who could afford to rent, or better yet buy, any one of a variety of exclusive executive jet aircraft. Presently gracing the airstrip, among others, a Cirrus Vision SF50, an Eclipse 500 and a Stratos 716. All modest jets in terms of size, but each one able to produce an impressive performance. For a small private aerodrome, Fairfield boasted a notable collection of flying hardware.

"Now that we're here, I have to admit I'm a bit apprehensive, Pierce." Petra was turned out in a bright red jumpsuit, with matching helmet and trainers that had that look of an outfit bought specially for the event. She and Pierce were strolling about on a grass verge close to the strip upon which several aircraft were parked.

Standing back with arms folded to survey his girlfriend Pierce, decked out in jeans and T-shirt under an impressive black and gold flying suit of sorts, observed, "I can't decide whether you look more like a tomato or a peeled prawn, darling."

"Be serious, you idiot," she said with a giggle, punching him playfully on the shoulder.

"You'll be fine," he reassured her. "I've done this pretty frequently. At any rate, hundreds of free fall parachute drops."

"How come I never knew anything about this hobby of yours?"

"Ah," he said, touching the side of his nose. "Lots you don't know about me."

"So I see. Well then, master, tell me, how does this work?"

"You'll piggy-back on me," he explained. "You'll need to hold on tight when we jump."

"Ooh!" she said. "Sounds promising."

"It will be." He grinned.

"Pierce, did you really mean it when you said, hold on tight? Is that all?"

"Of course not. We'll be harnessed together."

Giving Pierce the once over, Petra remarked, "I have to say you look very swish in that black and yellow outfit. What did you say it was called?"

"It's a wingsuit," he said, extending his limbs to reveal the webbed joins under the arms and between the legs.

"So, who are you, then? Billy the Bee? Or Batman?"

"Very droll, Petra."

"What about that thing on top of your very macho black spaceman's helmet?"

"That, my persistent interrogator, is a GoPro video camera. So we can all watch a film of the event later over a dry martini."

"Hmm. No comment."

"No comment?"

Changing the subject, Petra asked, "Will you have a parachute for this jump, darling? You will, won't you?"

"No, Petra, I shan't," he said, sounding stubborn.

"But after what nearly happened last time?" she protested. "Oh, Pierce. Is that really such a good idea?"

"I'll be fine. We'll both be in very capable hands. This is after all a reputable establishment. And," he added, "you will very definitely be wearing a parachute. When I let loose the harness that joins us, you'll pull the handle that releases your chute."

"Which plane is it?" she asked, pointing to an eight-seater Learjet 75 parked nearby.

"No. 'fraid not, Petra. To buy one of those you'd need to be rich as Pa. To hire it for an hour or two we'd be forking out around eight thousand pounds."

"Oh," she said, suitably crestfallen. "I see. So you don't think I'm worth eight thousand pounds?"

"You're worth it, darling, any day. Trouble is, I'm not."

"My comic boyfriend. In which case," she asked once more, "which one is it, then?"

"That one over there." He indicated the push-pull he'd flown in last time, on that near disastrous drop.

"Not quite so glamorous, is it."

"It's not meant to be. As long as it can get us to about twelve thousand feet…"

"How high?" She sounded astonished.

"Twelve thousand feet."

"It does seem a helluva long way up, Pierce."

"You'd be surprised how awfully quick you come down. Just you wait, it'll be the biggest buzz you've ever experienced."

"Who's the pilot, then? Is it someone you always use?"

"There's two I've used at this airport. Peter Matthews, very experienced. But he won't take me again. Got annoyed with me last time for risking things the way I did. Really, I behaved very foolishly. My own fault. On too much of a high, if you'll pardon the pun."

"Darling, you won't be taking too much of a chance with me, will you?" She'd paled slightly. Stood staring out at the variety of aircraft.

"No, I won't. It's one thing to put oneself at risk, quite another to chance another's life. Particularly yours, my beloved."

"Am I your beloved?" She put a hand on his shoulder, and he drew her to him and kissed her affectionately.

"Now, now, now? What's all this. What do we have here?" In khaki overalls, Tom Selby, the owner and joint manager of the flying school, a balding, ruddy-faced man in his sixties, approached the couple, all beaming smiles. "Do I detect wedding bells, boys and girls?"

"Hi, Tom. Good to see you," said Pierce, extending a hand to shake Tom's. "This is Petra, my girlfriend. Petra, Tom."

"Hello, Tom," said Petra. "Have to tell you, I'm a bit uncertain about this little excursion of Pierce's. You know how persuasive he can be."

"No need to be concerned, love. All experienced pilots here. And apart from that bout with your young man last time, he is reasonably responsible, you know. Usually. Maybe not always," he added pensively, staring quizzically at Pierce, as though hoping for an answer to an unspoken question.

"Okay, that's very reassuring. I suppose. Pierce says the thing is magical," Petra observed.

Shoving his hands in his pockets, Tom responded, "That about sums it up, my dear. Magical."

"But really, without a parachute, Tom?"

"I told him he was crackers when he booked earlier on, Petra. I know he's done it before. But do you think he'll listen to me? Still, you'll be in a chute. I presume you've done this before?"

"What, free-falling?"

"Well, no. I meant parachuting."

"No, Tom. I've never parachuted in my life. Pierce seems to think it's all so easy. And safe. But isn't one supposed to go on some sort of course for this sort of thing?"

"One is very definitely supposed to go on some sort of course before ever attempting a jump. It'd be totally irresponsible – Pierce – ?"

"I don't suppose Pete's changed his mind?" Pierce interrupted, sounding hopeful.

"No, lad. He's still annoyed about that last jaunt you had with him. But look here – "

"Who've we got, then? said Pierce, interrupting Tom again. "I'd like Geoff if he's around today."

"He was supposed to be, but he texted to say he was on his way with a colleague he was going to be taking up with you. Another pilot. But he's had a bit of a prang. Car's a mess. No-one hurt, thank heavens, but he's had to stay behind and give particulars to the police. His pal's coming on though. Mini cab, I s'pose."

"Do we know this colleague?"

"I don't, but I've checked his credentials, just so's we know he's got the necessary experience. He's fine. Man called Noel Kember."

That's probably him now," said Tom, as a tall figure with an old-fashioned RAF moustache approached the trio. Sporting a brown tweed blazer, highly polished brown shoes and grey slacks, he was a distinguished-looking individual, probably in his mid-fifties.

"Sorry I'm late," he called before he'd reached them all. "Bit of a shunt, don't ye know."

The accent was distinctly British middle class. Pierce recognised the type and was instantly at ease with the man.

"Noel Kember," he extended a hand to each of the three, "we all set, then? Parachutes at the ready?"

"Didn't Geoff tell you?" asked Pierce. "We're doing a tandem jump."

"Nothing unusual in that, old boy. See 'em done all the time."

"Have you been involved in a tandem before, then?" Pierce enquired.

"Can't say I have, old boy. But then I'm just taking the kite up for you. I'm not doing the jumping. I say, m'dear," he said, turning to Petra. "Looking a bit peaky, dontcha know."

"I'm fine. Really, I'm fine," she replied. But she was becoming more than somewhat hesitant.

Addressing Tom, Kember asked, "Paperwork now? I presume?"

"This way, then," said Tom, sounding resigned as he led the way to the airport building.

Facing on to the airfield, the building was a long low brick structure, with an office at one end and a club restaurant and bar at the other. The office itself was small and cramped, with a counter, like that in a lockup shop, maps decorated the walls with flags dotted about them. A couple of easy chairs and a battered occasional table with flying magazines comprised the rest. A number of flying trophies consisting of mainly antique planes adorned the place.

From what one could see of it, the restaurant presented a sharp contrast being exceptionally well appointed, with some tables laid for meals, others closer to the bar left bare for drinks to be had.

Tom, busying himself behind the counter, eventually brought out a number of forms to be completed and signed, and it was at this stage that Petra's nerve finally failed her. That, or else her common sense had eventually kicked in.

"Pierce, you know, thinking about it, I've decided I'm not doing this jump. And please don't ask me to," she said, holding up one hand as though to forestall further argument. "If we were both using parachutes I'll admit I'd be pretty keyed up about it. But if you're flying without a chute? No. Definitely not. This whole thing is much too dangerous. I mean really, not to put too fine a point on it, darling, utterly barmy."

Pierce smiled patiently. "Okay, Petra. I won't press the subject if you're really not happy about going up."

"Quite right, if you must know," put in Tom. "You ask me, you'll do this thing without a chute once too often, me lad. Then what'll your father say? Come to think of it, what about your beautiful young lady here?"

"Yes, alright, thank you, Tom," said Pierce, sounding slightly put out. Then, after a moment he said to Petra, "Look, darling, why don't you just come up for the ride with Noel and me. You can hold my hand right up to the time I jump."

Commenting for the first time since they'd entered the office, Noel wrinkled his nose doubtfully and said, "If the little lady's scared, won't be much fun for her, whether she's jumping with you or sitting in the plane with me. No-one told me you were going without a chute, young man. Geoff never mentioned it. And taking the young lady along with you? Not very wise. Better off, if you ask me, if she stays behind and watches the whole thing from the ground. Be quite a sight watching the lad float down." He smiled at Petra encouragingly.

"Well, Petra, why not come up with me anyway — ?" Pierce started, but she interrupted him.

"No thank you, Pierce. I think I'll do as Noel's suggested and watch it all from down here."

"Okay." He sighed. "Well, if it's only me we don't need any paperwork, do we, Tom?"

Then, addressing Kember, Pierce said, "The agenda is, we go up to, I'll say twelve thousand feet, no higher else we'll both be needing oxygen. I'll make my jump, and you'll throttle back, point the nose to take the Cessna down directly I exit the plane, and with an aircraft descent time of one minute per two thousand feet you should be at six thousand feet, our primary target, in three minutes, carrying on down two thousand feet if, heaven forfend, we don't link up immediately. Unlikely, I know. But best to be prepared as far as one can."

"See you've done yer homework, laddie. Well done. Should be a breeze, what?" he guffawed.

Petra breathed in deliberately, shaking her head, but made no comment.

"My own rate of descent," Pierce continued, "at say, twenty miles per hour, achievable, will be about thirty feet per second, a shade under, giving you time to get well below me, so we'll rendezvous at the six thousand mark, in three minutes and twenty seconds after I jump. That's twenty seconds after you reach the planned rendezvous. I can slow my drop a bit further with this wingsuit, it's the latest state of the art, circling, if need be, until you've reached the right height."

"State of the art, Pierce?" Petra interrupted. "Tell me, what's the normal rate of descent in a wingsuit, then?"

"Darling, it depends on conditions, but anything from thirty to forty miles an hour. Could be much faster, if you choose. But my suit is specially adapted to drop at twenty miles an hour. Cost me a bloody fortune. That'll be six thousand feet in three minutes and twenty seconds for me."

"Crazy," muttered Petra. "Just twenty seconds leeway."

"I've got an altimeter on my wrist," Pierce continued as though he'd not been interrupted, "so, I can judge where I am to match your altitude, Noel, when you flatten out. In the event we miss at six thousand feet we'll have another two minutes and thirteen seconds reserve to meet up at two thousand feet. That's you thirteen seconds ahead of me. Give or take."

"Give or take? Only thirteen seconds reserve? And you've allowed just twenty seconds leeway on the initial plan to meet at six thousand feet. Bloody hell!" exclaimed Petra, wringing her hands in exasperation. "What about turbulence?"

"Possible, but likely more of a problem above twelve thousand feet, m'dear," chimed in Kember.

"Wind speeds? Air pressure?" Petra asked, increasingly frustrated. "Isn't this all totally insane?"

"Lap of the gods, dontcha know." Kember beamed. "Lad's a risk-taker. Life's a risk, ain't it?"

"Twenty to meet up on the initial plan? Just twenty seconds?" said Petra, holding out her hands in exasperation. "You're like a couple of bloody schoolboys playing tag in the air. I give up. Your game, darling, not mine. I've got too much life to live yet."

"Darling, it is a risk, I'll admit," said Pierce. "But remember, I've done it before, and really it sounds a lot riskier than it is. As for the imponderables, we'll deal with those as we need. Noel can squeeze a bit more out of his descent time and I can slow mine to allow a slightly greater margin of safety."

"Really?" said Petra, hardly convinced. "Safety, did you say? Don't make me laugh. I'll repeat, your funeral, Pierce."

Smiling at Petra, Pierce then turned to Kember, and said, "All in order?"

"Gotcha, lad," agreed Kember. "Have to say, never seen a jump done without a para. Still, I s'pose you know what you're about. Done it before, you say?"

"Exactly," said Pierce encouragingly.

"Then what, son?" Kember went on, grinning. "You're going to float into the aircraft and take over the controls, what?" He laughed.

"No," said Pierce patiently. "There's straps and a harness attached to the surface of the wing over the fuselage for me to grip, or else climb into if there's time."

"Do what I can, lad," observed Kember doubtfully. "Must know what yer doing." Then added as an afterthought, "Darned if I do."

"Are we fit?" asked Pierce.

"As we'll ever be," replied Kember.

As the two men strode off towards the plane, Pierce turned for a moment and winked at Petra, who in turn looked enquiringly at Tom. "Can't you stop him, Tom? This is totally crazy. If I hadn't realised it before, being here now I can see it doesn't make any kind of sense. He's not a bloody professional stunt man, for God's sake."

"You know how he is, Petra. If he won't listen to you, he certainly won't listen to me." He scratched his bald head thoughtfully. "To be honest, my love, it's probably more of a spectacle than a danger. As long as the lad doesn't go in for any daft heroics, he should be fine."

A few moments later Kember had the door of the light aircraft open and hauled himself in, ushering Pierce who, encumbered by the wingsuit, clambered in clumsily behind him, tossing in the black crash helmet first.

"Pierce said they'll be going up to twelve thousand feet, Tom," said Petra. "It does seem an awfully long way up. Will it climb to that height easily?"

"Oh yes. She'll get to fifteen thousand feet, max. So, twelve thousand is no problem."

"What'll it do? Anything like those jets?" She pointed at some of the other aircraft not far off.

"No, my dear. Those beauts will do four or five hundred miles an hour. Our little Cessna 182 here will manage one hundred and eighty-eight miles an hour, max. But that man Noel seems to know his stuff. He'll keep her well within capacity."

"What about the push-pull," asked Petra. "Pierce said he'd done the jump in a Cessna push-pull last time."

"Bad planning, that. A slight miscalculation and he could have been chopped to pieces by the rear prop."

"And this is good planning, is it?"

Shrugging, Tom said, "Talk to Pierce. This is his jaunt. He's confident, so I suppose he knows what he's doing."

"I doubt anyone else does," murmured Petra.

With both men strapped securely, the plane coughed into life, the two props spinning elegantly at either end of the pod-shaped fuselage, before the plane moved off slowly and taxied onto the runway. Humming like an angry wasp the Cessna trundled along to the end of the strip, then gently turned on its axis until it was facing in the correct direction for take-off.

Tom said, "ATC will've cleared them to go. You can see there's been no delay. It'll be straight out now, departure approved."

"Tell me, what's ATC, Tom?"

"Oh, that's our air traffic controller, back in the shop." He inclined his head towards a small building Petra hadn't taken much notice of, tagged on to the end of the main building.

"Shouldn't they be in a tower, or something?" Petra asked.

"We don't have one here. Not really necessary in an aerodrome this size."

Then, taking Tom's arm and pulling at it as if she might dislocate it, Petra pleaded, "Tom, it's not too late to stop them. Can't you talk to Noel through that hand-held device of yours?"

"Not now, love. They're accelerating, can't you see? It's not the time, not now, it'll only distract the pilot. They'll be fine, really, they will. Don't fret, my dear."

Walking away from Tom, Petra pulled off her foolish crash helmet, throwing it away in frustration and watched as the plane quickly picked up speed, its nose lifting as the aircraft became airborne, the nose wheel and twin rear wheels neatly retracting. From where she stood watching the Cessna make height, she could hear Tom talking to the pilot on his portable radio receiver.

It should have been reassuring, but it had the reverse effect, leaving Petra more worried than ever.

"How long does it take to get to twelve thousand feet, Tom?" He'd come to stand next to her.

"The Cessna 182 climbs at a max of seven hundred feet per minute," Tom explained. "So if there's no unusual turbulence, it should reach twelve thousand feet in about seventeen minutes."

"Give or take, I suppose?" said Petra glumly.

"Give or take," said Tom softly, before continuing, "looks to be smooth and calm today. Just what your young man was hoping for."

There'd been some thickening of the sparse, low-hanging cloud, the plane ploughing into the pillowy white, at first vanishing, then swiftly reappearing, still climbing steadily. Petra sighed audibly, permitting herself a small measure of relief, while glancing over at Tom, who was smiling broadly. She listened as Tom and Kember spoke to each other.

"Ground control to Major Tom. Over," said Tom to Noel, aware he'd deliberately got things the wrong way round.

"What's that, old man?" said Kember, blissfully unaware of the joke. Then, almost as an afterthought, "Over."

"What's your height, Noel? Over."

"We're about ready to go, old boy. Twelve thousand one hundred feet. Over."

The plane was now making a wide circle about the aerodrome, preparing for Pierce's jump. Noel hadn't noticed his transmitter PTT had stuck in the on position, so those on the ground were able to hear the two men in the Cessna conversing.

Tom said to Petra, "Hey. Listen to this. The transmitter's PTT's stuck so we can hear what they're saying."

"Whatever is a PTT, Tom?"

"Sorry, love. It's the press to talk on the radio transmitter in the plane. Here," he said, handing her his unit. "Listen in. He's about to jump. Sounds cool as a cucumber. I said he'd be alright."

"You hold it, Tom," she said, as a momentary gust of wind ruffled her red hair. "I'll listen from here where I can watch."

They both heard the slightly muffled sound of Noel saying, "Ready, old chap?"

"Yup. Level out a bit, Noel. Thanks, got it. Door's jammed? No, we're okay. See you on the deck, chum. Fly safely."

From the ground, Petra held her breath as she watched Pierce floating smoothly away from the plane, arms and legs spread-eagled in the usual manner of the free-faller, his wingsuit slowing his descent and allowing him to glide in a wide controlled parabola.

In that moment, she couldn't decide whether she was in love with one of the bravest, or one of the most stupid men she'd ever known. But as Pierce's descent gradually, almost imperceptibly, gathered pace, using the wingsuit to best advantage, her mind switched to the Cessna which had turned in a tight circle and was aiming to be directly underneath Pierce in time for him to land on its single high, fixed wing.

"He's doing okay, love," said Tom to Petra. "Pierce said to pick him up at two thousand feet, failsafe, if they don't rendezvous at six, but Noel's at around six thousand now, going for that early catch, so… Look, look. Here he goes. Here he goes." Tom pointed up excitedly.

The plane was directly under Pierce and he floated gently towards it, undulating gracefully. A bird in flight. Petra had her fist up against her jaw with tension.

"If he survives this bloody nonsense, I shall kick his backside to hell and back," she murmured.

Pierce gradually sailed closer and ever closer to the plane, losing height all the time, cleverly manoeuvring himself until he was directly over the Cessna. They'd been airborne for barely twenty-five minutes.

A moment more and he'd drop safely onto the aircraft. Then, just for an instant there was an apparent loss of control, Pierce swerving slightly to one side. But, flapping his arms and legs expertly he restored attitude and worked his way closer until once more he was where he needed to be. Petra sighed with hoped-for relief.

Pierce was now about to land securely on the surface of the fixed wing, his hands thankfully outstretched to within touching distance. A moment more and he would grasp the harness, pull himself within the straps and safety.

But quite unexpectedly, the light aircraft veered away, and Noel was heard to mutter over the transmitter, "Damned wind factor. No matter, lad, we'll have you next time around."

"What happened?" Petra protested to Tom. "Do you have any idea what is supposed to be going on up there?"

"No problem, love. Noel knows what he's doing. Like I said, that's why he had the first attempt at six thousand feet. Room for a second go. Still a hundred and thirty-three seconds available, we reckoned, if they didn't link up first time round. Which they haven't it seems."

"But, Tom, what happens if they don't link up second time around." She sounded angry. "What happens then?"

"They will. I promise you they will." But Tom was starting to look concerned, his brow furrowed with worry.

"You think so?" shouted Petra.

"He'll pick up the lad at two thousand feet, like I said. That was the original plan Pierce had."

In fact, Noel had swiftly brought the plane about and was readying it to receive Pierce, who once more was able to glide elegantly in the right direction to land on the wing. But again, as Pierce approached the plane, the aircraft sheered away from him as they both disappeared into cloud.

Tom wasn't making any further comment, merely walking about, muttering something inaudible to himself and clenching and unclenching his fists in obvious distress.

But Petra was raging now. "What the hell is going on up there? This is just a fucking circus. At this rate he's going to die, isn't he? Why don't you bloody admit it? They must be below two thousand feet by now. What does that leave them, according to your reckoning, no more than sixty-six seconds."

But in the same instant, Tom, about to say something, pointed to the Cessna as it appeared through the clouds.

"There she is," he called, pointing up at the plane. "She's in time. We're all fine. The old girl. In safe hands with Noel. Didn't I say she'd be fine?" shouted Tom, jubilant with relief as the plane vanished into the mist once more, only to emerge at the same time as the sight of a tiny body appeared through the clouds, seemingly waving triumphantly to the watchers, as it hurtled down at increasing speed to smash into the ground at one hundred and twenty miles an hour.

There was a moment of shocked silence. Tom stared off into the distance, aghast, then turned to Petra, unspeaking, a look of utter horror on his face.

"Is that it, then?" she screamed, pointing to where Pierce had plunged.

"All under control, is it? How it's meant to happen? Tell me, Tom, explain it to me. I'm listening. What does it all mean? And where's the fucking plane gone?"

"It means, love, your boyfriend's dead," Tom said quietly, his head bowed.

"And that man Kember's fucked up and by the looks of it, he's fucked off too," he added as the Cessna disappeared into the clouds.

CHAPTER 40 DAY 11

IT HAD BEEN A LONG FLIGHT and they'd slept late. Sun streamed into the bedroom, warm and welcoming as Tammy turned over in bed and stretched out for Dov, ruffling his thick copper hair. "You smell delicious, darling."

Leaning up on one elbow, hovering over Tammy, he asked, "And precisely what do I smell of?"

"Mmm." She closed her eyes, the better to think about it. "You smell of musk, soap and clean shirts."

Dov burst out laughing. "Clean shirts? I've had a lot of compliments in the past, but clean shirts?"

"That's right. A nice cottony smell," she said, punching him on the chest. "I know what I mean, even if you don't."

"So, who am I to argue?"

"And me? Or shouldn't I ask?"

"You, my darling, smell of honey."

"Hold me, Dov," she said, enclosing him in an embrace. "I'd love to...love to, but..." she said, wincing slightly.

"I know," he responded quietly. "You very sore?"

"Bit. Stitches pulling. Give me a few days. Hmm?"

"You really should have stayed in the hospital a while..."

"No, Dov." She sounded cross. "Not now."

"Okay, okay." He sighed. "We'll do it your way. Don't we always?"

"Yes, darling. We do. Avoids arguments that way, doesn't it," she said coyly as she climbed out of bed. Then, as though aware of the scars starkly clear in the bright light, she self-consciously shrugged into the white negligee that lay across the bottom of the bed.

"You showering?"

"Yup," she replied, as a small furry black creature jumped up onto the bed and nuzzled up to Dov.

"Plans for the day?" he asked, tickling Risky behind the ears and kissing her on the forehead while she purred happily.

"I need to speak to Bob. Let him know what we know. Which isn't a great deal," she said wistfully. "I want a catch-up with George and Jamie at Incognita. See what they can find out about Letitia's and or Polonia's return to the UK. Then there's the St James's murder. I wonder?" she pondered.

"A busy day ahead. Are you sure...?"

"Yes, Dov, I'm sure," she snapped. "Let's not go there now." Then, before she could reach the bathroom her mobile rang.

"Miss Pierre?"

"Hello, Mrs Gilchrist. Is everything in order?"

"You won't have seen the news?"

"We got in late," she replied, feeling strangely uneasy.

"It seems that Oscar Mountford's son Pierce is dead."

"Good heavens. How? When?"

"It was just yesterday. The young man was attempting a foolish manoeuvre..."

"Let me guess, Mrs Gilchrist. He was skydiving without a parachute?"

"I'm afraid so. The family are distraught. That is the sisters. The father is threatening to sue the aerodrome for wanton irresponsibility in ever allowing the event to happen."

"Do we know who owns or runs the airfield?"

"A gentleman called Tom Selby owns the Fairfield Aerodrome near to Oxford. Your colleague, the Detective Chief Inspector Rosemary Sharpe, called to say she would be interviewing Mr Selby this morning. If you're not too jet lagged...?"

"Don't worry, Mrs Gilchrist, I'll have Dov Jordan drive me to the aerodrome." As if in acknowledgement, Dov nodded back at her.

Tammy, not wanting to look too official, or indeed officious, wore a simple roll-neck jumper with plain black trousers. While they'd got ready Mrs Gilchrist had called Rose to say Tammy was on her way.

Taking Tammy's Lexus, with Dov at the wheel, they arrived at Fairfield around midday. The weather was much the same as it had been the day before, being mostly bright with a smattering of fluffy, white cumulus clouds.

Police tapes cordoned off a wide area around where Pierce had fallen. The site was well clear of the runway and judging by the cars parked within view there might still be some flights available to take off. A couple of uniforms patrolled the area, ensuring no sightseers got close enough to risk contaminating the scene. Otherwise it was almost like business as usual.

They found Rosemary with an ashen-faced Tom Selby sitting in armchairs in the cramped aerodrome office with untouched mugs of coffee on the occasional table between them.

As they both walked in Rose immediately got to her feet, a look of concern on her face as her eyes roamed over Tammy's, taking in the deep shadows under her eyes, the drawn demeanour. "Tammy? Are you? Are you...?"

Raising a reassuring hand, Tammy said, "I'm fine, Rose. Just a bit lagged, that's all."

Glancing at Dov, Rose asked, "Can we get you anything? Coffee? Tea?"

"I'm fine. You, Tammy?" he asked.

"I'm okay too," said Tammy, turning to Rosemary. "Rose, some quick introductions. You've not met Dov. I hope you won't mind him sitting in? He has some experience in matters of this nature."

Her eyes searched Rose's.

"No problem, Tammy," said Rose, extending a hand to shake Dov's. Then, as Tom Selby got to his feet, Rose made the further introductions, before the four of them sat down again, opposite each other.

"How far have you got?" asked Tammy, noticing Tom constantly wiping perspiring palms against the greasy legs of his khaki overalls. Poor man. Unfortunate casualty of one young buck's arrogant overconfidence in his own indestructability. No amount of professional indemnity or public liability insurance would cover the folly of what he'd allowed to take place. His ill, grey complexion was testament to his probable lack of sleep. He wouldn't be sleeping for some time, Tammy mused. Would the aerodrome still exist a year from now?

Leaning forward for a moment, his head in his hands, perspiration beading on the man's smooth scalp, Tom then looked up at Tammy pleadingly, before asking Rose, "Shall I, Detective Chief Inspector?"

Rose might have been about to suggest a more informal approach, but apparently thinking better of it, merely responded, "That's fine, Tom. Go right ahead. Take your time. As long as you need."

He sat back now, locked his fingers together and gazed up pensively. When he spoke it was hesitant and nervous, as though he'd already been pronounced guilty and was awaiting sentencing. "Lad said he'd done it before. Done it twice. Once only I know of, from this aerodrome."

Breaking off to take a handkerchief from a pocket in the overalls, Tom ran it over his perspiring pate, then wiped his palms with it before shoving it back in his overalls again. "I told him it was madness, but he wouldn't listen. Wanted to take his girlfriend up. She was too frightened to go. That, or else she simply had more sense."

"Tom," said Tammy quietly, assessing the overall damage. "Did you get Pierce to sign any form of disclaimer? Too late to save the boy, but might have helped in any claims for compensation, damages and so on."

Tom's voice was breaking when he responded, "Don't even ask."

Tammy let the man sit unspeaking for several moments, that is until he'd recovered himself sufficiently to go on, then she asked, "Tom, you said he'd done the jump before?"

"Like I just said, told me he'd done it twice."

"Do you know who the pilots were on the previous flights?"

"As I said, I know of one. Our own Pete Matthews, runs this place with me. Very experienced. Took the boy up last time. Not so long ago. Said he'd never do it again. He'd got caught up with Pierce's enthusiasm, allowed himself to be convinced it wasn't all that dangerous. Of course, it was. As we now know. Pete said he thought they'd lost the lad that time he went up. Was kicking himself for his amateurishness and stupidity. Matches mine, doesn't it? He told me it was the closest run thing he'd ever been involved with." Shaking his head, Tom added, "He should talk."

The door to the office opened and a freckle-faced youngster in overalls like Tom's poked his head in. "Mr Collins is here, Tom. The Lear. He wants to know, is it good to go?"

"All good, son. Tell ATC he's here."

The boy nodded, and in a moment was gone.

"You said Pierce claimed to have done the jump twice?" Tammy asked.

"He was lying. No-one here admitted to having taken him up other than Pete. Pierce just wanted to sound convincing."

"So," Dov put in, "who took him up yesterday, Tom. If it wasn't one of your crew?"

"A man called Noel Kember."

"Do you know him?"

"Never met him before. He was on his way here with Geoff Howard, who, Pierce claimed, was going to pilot him."

"But he didn't arrive?" Dov pressed on.

"There was an accident. Geoff was driving. He hit a parked car. Seems Kember called out a dog running across the road and he grabbed the wheel from Geoff. At least, that's what Geoff told me later yesterday. Claims he never saw any dog. It was broad bloody daylight. He's a pilot for God's sake. He'd hardly have missed it."

Dov raised his eyebrows, glanced at Tammy, who nodded back.

"Tom," asked Tammy. "What do you know about this man Kember?"

Before Tom could reply, the freckled-faced boy came in again, carrying a tray of Styrofoam cups. "Coffee, anyone?" he asked, noting the mugs of stale coffee on the table. "They're all black," he added. "But I've got sachets of milk and sugar if anyone wants."

Tammy and Dov, in a change of mind, took black without sugar, Rose was white with one and Tom merely shook his head, but said, "Thanks, Sean. Good boy."

They all glanced up for a moment as the jets of the Lear resounded in the room, a gale-force whistle as the aircraft taxied to the end of the runway then turned around, pausing for a moment before a rising hurricane scream accompanied the plane's powerful acceleration to take-off speed, the roar quickly subsiding as the Lear lifted up and disappeared into the sky.

"So, Tom," prompted Tammy, blowing on the surface of her coffee, the cup nestled between her palms as she took up the narrative once more. "Kember. Tell us. What do you know about the man?"

"Not much."

"Come on, Tom. I know this is difficult but help us out here. You must be in shock. But tell us what little you do know. Did you check him out at all?"

Sounding utterly worn, Tom offered, "I called the airport he said he was from."

CHAPTER 40 DAY 11 • 241

"Which one was that, Tom?" Dov enquired quietly.

"Blackthorn."

"I know." Tammy nodded. "In Hampshire. Dov?"

"Yeah. Same one we picked up those two Israeli media-tors. How could I forget?"

"Go on, then, Tom. You checked him out. How?"

"I called Blackthorn to see if they knew him, and they did. Said he was an experienced pilot and he'd been with the airport for fifteen years or more."

"Okay. And when he arrived, did he show you any ID? Driving licence or other?" Tammy pressed.

"Well, no."

"No, Tom? Why no? Surely you'd have needed to see something?"

"Well…I mean. He was a pilot." Tom shrugged. "What was I supposed to think? He was one of those tall, distin-guished types. You know, air force moustache. Sounded public school."

"Tell me," asked Tammy. "Have you spoken to your colleague Geoff about this man he invited along with him? This Noel Kember?"

"No. No I haven't."

"Why not give him a call? Right now. See what light he can throw on Noel, and what made him want to invite Noel along yesterday."

Picking up his mobile from where it lay on the table, Tom dialled Geoff's number. "I'll put it on speaker," he suggested.

It rang three times before Geoff answered. "Geoff How-ard." A pause, then, "That you, Tom?"

"Yeah it's me."

"How're you doing, mate? Bet you didn't get much sleep last night."

"You could say that again. Listen, you alright after the crash?"

"I'm fine. Bit of a jolt. But otherwise fine."

"Look. The man you were coming with yesterday. The one you invited."

"Sorry, old man. I didn't invite anyone."

"But wasn't he your friend?"

"Not really. Only someone I knew slightly. Met at the clubhouse at Blackthorn once or twice. I say, met. More like, saw."

"Noel Kember?" Tom sounded increasingly hesitant. "Your friend Noel?"

"No, Tom. Not my friend Noel. But a man called Davenport. Bill Davenport. And I didn't invite him. He called me. Said he'd heard I was doing a drop yesterday, and could he come along? Never said how he knew, so I didn't bother to ask."

The four people said nothing for several moments, Tom squirming in his seat, staring this way and that, increasingly bewildered.

Then Tammy suggested, "Ask him what Noel looks like, Tom?"

"Geoff? You heard that?"

"I did. Noel. Lovely guy. Has problems keeping his weight in check. Whenever there's a medical due he has the devil of a job dieting. But yes. He's what you'd call short and dumpy, I suppose. Great pilot. But no way could he be described as tall. And as for a moustache? Nope. Noel is clean-shaven."

"Thanks, mate. Thanks," said Tom and rang off. Then he said, "If this man Davenport wanted to come along, why didn't he just ask Geoff, and tell us his real name?"

"Could be that if he'd offered to fly with or instead of Geoff, that Geoff might have turned him down," Dov suggested. "He wanted to be sure he was the one piloting the aircraft to do whatever it was he had in mind, unobserved. Say, Tom, come to think of it, did you notice anything unusual about Davenport's handling of the plane?"

Tom took the handkerchief from his overalls and wiped his scalp again. "Yes," he said softly. "Now you come to mention it. I ignored it at the time. But I could see the whole thing from down here. Except when they were in cloud. For all Davenport's convincing talk about the risks involved, I think he deliberately steered away from Pierce."

"You're saying you think Pierce was murdered by Davenport?" asked Rosemary, speaking for the first time since Tammy and Dov had arrived.

"That's exactly what I'm saying," said Tom. "Mad though the jump was, from where I could see what was happening, Davenport could have caught him. I'm saying, I think at the very moment Pierce might have connected with the Cessna, it left him to fall."

"And then he flew off?" Rosemary asked.

"And then he flew off." Tom nodded.

"So, why didn't he land here? Where'd he go to when he flew off?" Dov put in.

"Blackthorn?" Rosemary suggested.

"I think you should call them immediately?" said Tammy.

"I will," answered Tom.

A few moments later he was speaking to Lennie Cole, the manager of the airport. "Hi, Lennie."

"Tom," came the friendly reply. "Got something of yours here, chum."

"The Cessna?"

"That's the one. Bill brought it in yesterday. But then you'd know all about that, wouldn't you." Lennie sounded cheerful. "Said there'd been an accident at your end. I got it on the news this morning. I must say, Bill looked pretty beat up about the whole thing. Not like him to get uptight about much. The little we know of him. He's not actually tied to this airport, just turns up occasionally for a drink. Chats up Tilly behind the bar when she's on duty. Still, if the kid died."

"Did he say why he flew off, Lennie?"

"Said after what happened he couldn't face any of you. Said he felt sort of responsible."

"I'll bet he did," murmured Tammy, drinking some more of her coffee.

Then Dov suggested, "Ask Lennie if they have any contact details for Davenport?"

Lennie, having overheard the question, responded, "He only stayed long enough to check in the Cessna before shooting off. Left a pair of expensive Ray-Bans behind. It was then I realised, no-one here has any contact details for the guy. No mobile, no address. A mystery man."

"Thanks, Lennie," said Tom. "Appreciate it." Then addressing the others Tom announced, "He murdered Pierce, but will we ever prove it?"

"Oh I think we might," said Tammy. "Davenport's been in a bit too much of a hurry. He hasn't thought it out properly. Look at it. Why would he apparently contrive a car accident? Obviously that was to be sure Geoff wouldn't turn up. But why would he use a false name when he got here, when he might just as easily have used his own? I'll tell you why. He was known to Geoff as Bill Davenport. Okay, good. But he introduced himself to us as Noel Kember. He reckoned if anyone checked his credentials with Blackthorn they'd know enough about Noel to credit him as a competent pilot. They couldn't have done the same for Davenport. He was hardly known to them.

"Someone paid him, if you ask me. Who? That'll take some working out, but I have my suspicions. Naturally he flew off. He could hardly have landed and stayed here while there was the near certainty he'd be identified. You're right, Tom. Pierce was murdered."

CHAPTER 41 DAY 12

TAMMY WAS PREPARING to leave for work when her mobile buzzed. "I've got more information." The whispered voice was tremulous, frantic. The fear of being overheard? "How soon can I see you. Best not over the phone. Could be being tapped."

"Is it about Pierce, Georgia?"

"He was on to something."

"Oscar?"

"Can't talk now."

"My place, darling. Any time this evening after 7.00 pm."

"Not sooner?"

"What time do you finish work?"

"Around 6.00 pm."

"Don't want to raise suspicions at this stage."

"Okay, then. See you. Have to go…"

Mrs Gilchrist had suggested the bar on the eighth floor of the OXO Tower on the Thames South Bank as the ideal venue for an informal chat with the sisters. Tammy had let it be known to Rosemary Sharpe she'd be talking to the three aside from any official questioning the DCI herself might want to schedule. The death of Pierce was not yet an official murder investigation, but enquiries were ongoing. In particular attempts to locate one William Davenport.

It was a bright sunny day, with scattered pearls glinting on the surface of the busy river as a variety of pleasure cruisers, police craft and commercial carriers chugged past in both directions.

Sitting around the low occasional table offering a selection of snacks, Tammy couldn't help observing the different reactions to the tragedy of their brother's death. She had spent several minutes gazing at her open wardrobe that morning pondering what to wear for this meeting and had finally chosen a cardigan and flared skirt in mid-blue. Her hair, now in a longer curled crop, a sort of soft Afro, had finally bulked out so that the scar at the side of her head could not be seen.

Davina, in jeans and grey sweater, her usually immaculate auburn hair hung lank, and her cheeks were blotchy from crying.

Jayne wore jeans too, and a denim jacket. She appeared pale and subdued, as though she were somewhere else entirely.

Only Juliet was true to form. She'd had her short black hair fashioned in a Vidal Sassoon pixie. Her two-piece navy blue suit, in a nod to modesty, still bore Juliet's signature micro-miniskirt. There was something wild about the woman and the ever-wanton display. Again, Tammy mused, a kindred spirit, if the circumstances were different.

A selection of teas and coffees were ranged on the table, together with the as yet untouched snacks.

It was early afternoon, and the low conversational hum of lunchtime diners finishing off meals drifted across to where the four women sat.

Twisting in her seat, trying to get comfortable, the wound in Tammy's side pulling and pinching as the sutures dragged, she glanced away from the sisters so they wouldn't see her grimace with pain.

"You okay?" asked Juliet. "You look a bit, I don't know, tense?"

"No, I'm good. I'm fine," said Tammy, forcing a smile.

"If you say so." Juliet shrugged.

"So where do we start?" Jayne asked.

Glancing at the three of them, Tammy said, "Your call. Anyone?"

Reaching into the pocket of her jeans, Davina pulled out a handkerchief and wiped her streaming eyes, blew her nose then pocketed it again. "He thought he was invincible," she lamented.

"No-one's bloody invincible," broke in Juliet. "That jump was asking for trouble. It was a damn fool thing to attempt."

"He was invincible," Davina said. "In any normal circumstances, which these weren't."

"Oh for Christ's sake, Dav. Grow up. He wasn't God, you know."

"It was sabotage. That pilot who's disappeared? Pierce could have done it. He could have made it. He'd already done it before."

"Listen, Davvy darling, ever heard of The Flying Wallendas?"

"Who are they?"

"Were, not are. The old man, Karl Wallenda, was a tightrope walking genius. Had been since the age of six. He could do anything. He was invincible. Just like our Pierce."

"What's the point of all this, Jules?"

"At the age of seventy-three, while walking between the twin towers of the Condado Plaza Hotel in San Juan, Puerto Rico, the invincible Karl Wallenda appeared to be losing his balance and, making every effort to regain it, taking a full thirty seconds, eventually fell ten stories to his death. He, my dear, was a tightrope walking legend with more than sixty years' experience."

"How do you know all that, Jules?"

"Stick around, Davs. You know me. A fund of useless facts."

"I still think he was murdered," insisted Davina.

"Rubbish. Pierce was a chancer with absolutely no experience. If you ask me the man who piloted the plane just made off. He was scared witless, as well he might be. By all accounts he tried to dissuade Pierce, he certainly agreed that Petra shouldn't go up."

Glowering unintentionally as the jagged rip in her side spasmed, Tammy got a sudden confused flashback of the attack she'd suffered in New York, mixed with the Syrian episode. Before anyone could question her further she reached into her leather clutch and extracted a couple of analgesics, swallowing them dry. Then, glancing to her left and right, Tammy continued, "We'll know more about what really happened when the police eventually catch up with this man Davenport. Meanwhile, can anyone think who might want to harm Pierce?"

"There will have been any number who might have found out what he was up to with his poking around these far right groups. Daddy was linked with them, and Pierce was trying to get information on Daddy's involvement," offered Davina, as she reached for the handkerchief to wipe her eyes again.

"You don't think...?" Juliet began.

"If you're going to suggest that Daddy had something to do with Pierce's death, forget it. He was upset when he found out what Pierce was doing. I think he may have hoped he'd have Pierce's backing on the right wing stuff. But no way. Pierce was absolutely against that sort of extremism. My feeling, anyway. But otherwise Daddy doted on his only son. Though I doubt he understood him one iota."

"I told you last time we had this conversation, when we were at Pierce's." Jayne gazed out at the river, unseeing as she spoke for the first time. "Dada may be up to all sorts when it comes to money. You know, laundering. That sort of thing. Everyone who doesn't know him properly calls him ruthless. Maybe in business. But not where his family are concerned. Think about it for a moment. He part financed all your homes. Helped furnish them. Mummy was always away, but he hardly ever complained. I think I know Dada better than most people. After all, I still live at home, don't I, and see him more than anyone. He is lovely. That's all." With that Jayne lapsed back into silence.

"Tell me," said Tammy. "Changing the subject for a moment. You've all suffered a terrible tragedy. Do you have the support you need at this time?" If the question appeared intrusive, even disingenuous, Tammy wanted to gauge their reactions to any sort of emotional probing while they were all at their most vulnerable. "You don't need to answer if you'd rather not."

"That's okay." Davina sighed, leaning forward to pour some tea from the pot into a bone china cup. "For once in his life my Jerry's come up trumps. That great overweight lump. Couldn't run a business to save his life. But he's there for me. Night and day. I'd forgotten how much I love him."

"How about you, Juliet? Job okay? Support from work colleagues? Any chance of bereavement leave?"

"I s'pose." She shrugged. Now seeing Davina help herself to tea, she reached for the coffee pot and poured herself some of the still-steaming brew. Then acknowledging Tammy's nod, she poured a second cup for her.

"So Juliet, that's all? You s'pose?"

"Davs was closer to Pierce than anyone. And it hasn't really hit home yet. Maybe in the next day or two." She drank steadily from the coffee cup, angling her knees insolently in Tammy's direction, watching her, as though there was something she wanted to ask, or say, but didn't know how to. Tammy recognised the gesture but ignored it. She'd seen before at some of the clubs she'd frequented. Some other time, perhaps. For now, file it away.

"How about you, Jayne? How're you coping," Tammy enquired. "Won't you have something to eat or drink?"

"No thank you, I won't," said Jayne, sounding terribly correct.

It was as Jayne spoke that Tammy caught sight of someone in the corner of her eye. He couldn't have been there earlier, or Tammy would have spotted him. She'd scoped out the place before settling down to wait for the others. Of course, now she could see him, she recognised him. The brown leather jacket and blue jeans, the open-neck white shirt and distinguishing wire-frame glasses. He was the little man with the mid-European accent who'd collared her in the street and warned her off when she was meeting up with the guys at Incognita in Wapping.

What was puzzling, was how did he know Tammy would be here and at this hour? Then it struck her; could he have had anything to do with Pierce's death? She just couldn't make the link. He'd approached her when she was first looking into Letitia's disappearance, before the Pierce event. Now the man was grinning and pointing his fingers at her like a gun.

Dragging her attention back to Jayne, Tammy asked, "And how are things at work for you?"

Staring straight back at Tammy, she responded timidly, "My boss is a first-class bastard."

The comment was so out of character that it left Tammy momentarily nonplussed. "Really? You surprise me. Actually, you shock me. Is he really all that bad?"

"Every bit. He won't let me use the techniques that he knows damn well work with autistic children, the same techniques I used to bring David out of his withdrawn state. He needles me endlessly, and when I asked for time off as I was bereaved, he said not possible as I was required to be available at all times."

"He sounds like a piece of work," Tammy observed.

"That about sums him up. I wouldn't shed a tear if he walked under a bus. Someone needs to shoot the man."

"Hey! Hey! Jayne. This isn't you talking."

Putting her head in her hands, Jayne said, "I'm sorry. What with losing Pierce and work being what it is. I'll be okay in a moment. I just get the odd flare up when I'm really peeved."

"Can we change the subject, please?" Juliet suggested, replacing her empty cup on the table. "You were hired at Pa's request to find our mother. Have you made much progress? Come to think of it, have you made any progress?"

"I don't know what you've heard up to now, so at the risk of repeating things of which you may be aware, I'll paraphrase. Your mother disappeared some several weeks ago. It's almost certain she remained in the UK for a fortnight, we know not where, until my IT people found her flying out to the States, apparently with a lookalike in tow."

"God, that is weird," offered Juliet. "Why would she do that? What the hell is she up to?"

"It gets very much stranger because we have reason to believe a number of murders were committed in the US, either by your mother, or else her lookalike."

Davina had stopped crying, and now sat open-mouthed, staring at Tammy. "Murders?" she whispered. "Ma? Not possible. I mean, how do you know?"

"The killer made no attempt to disguise themselves, instead wearing the sort of flamboyant costume that would pick them out," Tammy explained.

"You've seen all this?" Juliet asked.

"There's enough CCTV evidence to show either your mother, or her double, committing at least two of the acts. I'm sorry to have to say this, but it is almost certainly not the double."

Several moments passed before any of the girls said anything. Juliet was the first to break the silence. "Why? Why the hell would she be killing people? It makes no kind of sense. She's a bloody housewife, for Christ's sake. Even when we were kids, and now, she's always been away from home half the time. What is she, then? A contract killer? No way. I'm sorry, but no way. There's something else going on here. Do we have any idea who the victims were?"

"According to US reports, it rather looks as though the victims were all Russian dissidents."

Shaking her head in disbelief, Davina added, "Who is she, then? Who is this woman we don't know? This isn't our mother. It is just not possible."

Opting for the youngest of the three, Tammy asked, "Jayne? Can you offer anything? Help us out here? Anything? However inconsequential it may seem?"

"I'm as bewildered as the others," she said, hoping for some sort of moral support from the other two. "Do we know where she is now? Is she still killing people?"

"We think she may have left the States. Could be some weeks ago? Possibly be back in the UK. My IT guys are trying to track her movements right now."

"A bloody nightmare if you ask me," said Juliet.

"Does Pa know about all this?" Davina asked.

"Your father's been kept up to date, as far as possible by Scotland Yard. Albeit the DCI working with me, Rosemary Sharpe, hasn't given a complete briefing to her team. The whole thing was meant to be handled with utmost discretion in view of your father's position in government. He's due to be promoted to Chancellor any day."

"We pretty well know," said Juliet.

"I believe he's been working behind the scenes on an Autumn Budget speech in anticipation of that promotion," said Tammy. "It wouldn't do if anything like this came out now."

"Is she back yet?" Davina wanted to know.

"Rose is liaising with the US authorities. That's all I know."

"And no more killings?" Davina pressed.

"I have to tell you, there was a killing a couple of weeks ago in a hotel in St James's. You'll have seen it in the press."

The sisters nodded in unison.

"It occurred the same day as the pro-right demo in Trafalgar Square. On CCTV images it could be either your mother or her double. We just don't know right now. Let me ask you all, from your knowledge of your mother and her lifestyle, is there anything else at all you can tell me?"

The sisters exchanged uncertain glances. Then Juliet said, "We always promised Ma we'd say nothing, but it's time to talk." The other two nodded their assent. "We know Ma had been having an on off affair with a wealthy hedge fund manager, called Caspar da Silva."

"Did your father know about this?"

"Probably," said Davina. "He didn't care. They led largely separate lives anyway. He found it amusing when she turned up with bruising, cuts and scratches on her face. He didn't bother to ask her, and she never offered to tell." Davina shrugged.

"And what do you know about this man da Silva?" Tammy probed.

"Only that he's a financial risk-taker, and a lunatic par excellence," said Juliet. "A real alpha male, he looks like Brad Pitt, drives a Ferrari everywhere. Like a bloody maniac. Gambles on anything and everything according to Ma. He'll pick a fight at the drop of a hat. He's been banned from several of London's finest restaurants after some of his rows. I'm not surprised Ma came home showing signs of his attentions. But I think she found him exciting, and Pa boring by comparison."

"Can you tell me where he works?" Tammy enquired.

"In the City," said Juliet. "He's a joint owner of Maerland da Silva Capital Management."

"I think I need to have a chat with this man," said Tammy, suddenly overcome with tiredness. It would wait until tomorrow for her to follow up.

Right now, she needed to be at home resting. She'd already pushed herself too much for the day. Doctor Aziz would not be amused if this pregnancy failed to go to term because of her obsessive work ethic. In fact, never had the prospect of being curled up in freshly pressed white sheets with Risky snuggled next to her been more appealing.

At that moment her phone beeped. A text had arrived which made the blood in her veins run cold and her adrenalin spike overcome the exhaustion. It showed the sender to be Georgia.

It read simply, HELP.

CHAPTER 42 DAY 12

"YOU DID WELL, WILLIAM. It was to all intents and purposes a genuine accident."

"Thank you, Oscar. Praise from you…"

"When I think of that counter-demo, care of my beloved Pierce. God knows what else he was planning."

"All dealt with now."

"A huge relief, William. Another obstacle to my planned promotion eliminated."

"God, Oscar, you are one cold fish. Your own son?"

"Yes, William. My own son. A backstabbing traitor to our cause."

"If you say so."

"But then you ran off. Why didn't you stay? Watch the fun? See all their foolish faces as they tried to evaluate precisely what had happened?"

"You know why. What was I supposed to tell the police when they arrived? That I wasn't Noel Kember? That I am in fact Bill Davenport?"

"Might have been amusing."

"For you, perhaps. Hardly for me."

"You disappoint me, William."

"I wasn't aware you wanted entertaining."

"So where are you now, dear boy?"

"Geneva."

"Geneva?"

"My place here."

"Overlooking the lake?"

"That's right."

"What's the weather like there?"

"For God's sake, man."

"You could have stayed on at Fairfield."

"And said what, Oscar? Tell them I was a paid killer?"

"Don't you think you rather panicked?"

"Hardly. What else did you think I was going to do? What would you have done in my place?"

"Well let's see now. For one thing I would not have behaved like a scared rabbit."

"Nothing scares you though, does it."

"Correct. No. I take that back. There is one thing that scares me."

"Well. Why don't you let me in on the big secret?"

"Failure."

"Really? When did you ever fail at anything?"

"So far, dear boy. Never. Perhaps it's not failure that scares me. Merely the idea of failure. The fear of it."

"So, tell me, how would you have handled the situation? You've carelessly let a young man fall twelve thousand feet to his death. You're dashed terribly sorry and all that. Also, you're not really Noel Kember. But there was no ulterior motive in adopting a false name and being seen to deliberately direct the Cessna away from the falling figure."

"All too, too hasty, dear boy. Running off makes you look guilty, which of course you are."

"And so?"

"If you'd stayed, pretended to be suitably devastated, protested at the stupidity of the boy, they'd have listened, at least that far. You'd have had a head start."

"Then what? How would you have handled the alias?"

"Not as difficult as it might seem at first blush. Initially, you'd have garnered some sympathy. After all, you made

it clear you thought the venture was high risk. Even counselled the girl against going. And, of course, taking your
advice saved her life."

"You still haven't answered the question about my
identity."

"Well, think about it, William. If you'd landed at Fairfield, as you should have done, it wouldn't have occurred
to anyone at that time to call Blackthorn to verify your bone
fides."

"They'd have found out eventually."

"No they wouldn't. If you had any sense you'd have
volunteered the information there and then, right after the
accident, so nothing would have looked suspicious."

"Hello, everyone. Sorry about the death, and I'm not
really Noel Kember I'm actually William Davenport, paid
assassin."

"Don't be damned stupid, William. You would have
pre-empted any enquiry by saying you'd asked Geoff
Howard if you could accompany him on this jaunt he'd
mentioned to you, and that following the car accident you
used the name Noel Kember when you arrived at Fairfield,
as one that would be known at Blackthorn more readily
than your own if they chose to check you out before the
flight. Which is precisely what they did. They may have
been put out, puzzled, perplexed even, but with the death
to contend with they'd have left the question of your identity for another time."

"I'm not as thorough as you are."

"Evidently."

There was a long break in the conversation, interrupted
only by what sounded like nervous breathing from the Geneva end of the line.

Eventually Davenport broke the impasse. "You've got
what you wanted."

"A bit messy though, don't you think?"

"I'm not being paid to do spring cleaning."

"Neither to leave a host of questions in your wake, dear boy."

"Not my problem. There's just the question of my fee for a job carried out to a successful conclusion."

"Ah yes. Two hundred and fifty thousand pounds, my man tells me you negotiated. Pretty steep, I'd say. But a deal's a deal, I suppose."

"I'm on the run now."

"Bad planning, old boy. Should have thought things out sooner. Now's not the time."

There was a hesitation, then, "I want a million."

"Do you now," came the softly intoned rejoinder. "Isn't that being just a tad presumptuous, William?"

"I don't think so. I did the job, just as you asked, didn't I. I'm going to need funds. Lots. I could be on the run for years."

"Not my fault." The voice sounded circumspect.

"I mean, if any of this got out."

"Are we getting on to fresh ground here, William?"

"What do you mean?"

"Beginning to sound suspiciously like blackmail."

"Call it whatever title you like. I believe you're due to present a Budget imminently."

"Word gets around."

"It's common knowledge."

"Gossip."

"A million, Oscar. Or I go public. Prospective Chancellor pays to have meddling son killed."

"You wouldn't dare."

"I've little to lose. Face it, Oscar, you're nothing but a bloody psychopath."

"Hah!" he guffawed. "That's a bit rich, William, coming from you. Still, they say it takes one to know another. Alright," he said with a sigh, resigned at last. "You've made your point. Same address in Geneva as before."

"Yes."

"Swiss bank account details?"

"Unchanged."

"Name?"

"As before."

"Tomas Breuillon?"

"That's right."

"Of course, you're fluent in French, aren't you?"

"Years living and working here."

"However did you manage to get that French passport?"

"I'll let you know one day, Oscar. In my account by close of business tomorrow."

"None of the usual courtesies, William? No please and thank—" But he'd rung off.

A moment later and Oscar had dialled another number. "Oscar," came the reply.

"Who else were you expecting?"

"Okay, okay."

"You've got the address. He wants a million."

"Good heavens. A million?" came the incredulous reply.

"You heard."

"When does he want it by?"

"Tomorrow, close of banking."

"Can you get it together that fast?"

"If I had to, yes. But I don't have to. Do I?"

"What are you going to do, then?"

"What we always do with people who step seriously out of line."

"Like your son."

"Precisely. According to my associates, he was getting close. Too close. A little longer and I'd have been faced with a number of unanswerable questions. You see, we've plans, my friend. Plans for the UK and plans for Europe. But first things first."

"But, your own son, Oscar? I thought he was the apple of your eye."

"Save the tears. I want the usual drill. You've got till tomorrow."

"It will be done, Oscar. Isn't it always? I'll organise it."

"No, Mac. You won't organise it. You'll do it."

"What?"

"Yourself."

"But...but...I'm a lawyer, a professional man. I've never..." The voice was close to tears.

"That's right, you're a professional man, Mac, so do a professional job. No clues. Understood? Dynamite the place if you have to. Nothing's going to stand between me and the Chancellorship."

CHAPTER 43 DAY 12

SHE'D PARKED THE LEXUS in the surface level Doon Street car park, opposite the National Theatre and bare moments from the OXO Tower. She'd been fortunate to find a spot in the normally overcrowded place but had opted for that rather than the slightly more distant Cornwall Road underground facility.

Despite the proximity, it had taken her longer to get to the car than she'd anticipated. The fresh wound in her side tore at her relentlessly, slowing her progress so that by the time she was in the driving seat, she was practically passing out. Leaning her head against the steering wheel, she closed her eyes, taking slow, deep breaths. What the hell was happening to Georgia? And where was she right now? The only option was to get home, and fast, to see if Georgia had made it there. But she couldn't drive in her present state. Reaching into the glove compartment Tammy extracted a box of Nurofen Plus 500 mg capsules and dry swallowed four, then allowed herself five more minutes before pressing the starter button and firing the engine of the hybrid motor into whispered life.

As was to be expected there was an agonisingly slow queue waiting to trail out at the exit. Aware of a slight fluttering in her stomach as she waited impatiently to leave the place, she wondered if all was as it should be with the baby. She'd sensed a possible minor discharge, common with any pregnancy, but in her case a source of real concern. No chance to examine herself here or now. All she could do was to hope. And hope. Then lock the fear away.

Finally, onto Upper Ground, the road fronting the OXO Tower, she swung left making for Waterloo Bridge where, flouting protocol, she raced along the unoccupied bus lane. Then veering right, ignoring the protesting horns of the traffic she was cutting up, she made for the Strand underpass, through that and up onto Kingsway, weaving in and out of slow-moving traffic, until she reached Euston Road, where she hung a left, before jumping an amber light. More angry drivers sounding their horns, waving fists at her. She didn't blame them.

The minutes were ticking away, and she couldn't push herself and the car any faster. Now aiming for the bus lane, progressing up the Euston Road, she spotted a police car ahead and had no choice but to remain in the clogged-up mainstream heading for the underpass. Again, at the last moment, she swerved left onto the bus lane in front of the University College Hospital and hammered across the intersection at Hampstead Road where she pulled right, before roaring up towards Camden Town, horns blaring in her ears. At this rate, and with traffic cameras everywhere, she'd be facing a long-term ban before she even reached home.

'Help'. What did it mean? She chewed the inside of her cheek till it bled. Oscar! Who else? Already berating herself for having leaned on Georgia to snoop on her boss, she swore she'd never forgive herself if she were responsible for anything ill happening to the woman.

In light traffic the journey home, according to Google, should have taken twenty-seven minutes. It was now fifty minutes since she'd received the impassioned plea, but she was on Kilburn High Road, with Willesden Lane and Queen's Park in sight.

She was a cool driver in any circumstances. Any circumstances that is, but these. Her body was running with perspiration, stomach, back, legs, palms. She gripped the steering wheel all the more firmly to stop it slipping from her grasp. The analgesics had already run their course, her head and body throbbing in harmony.

At the back of her mind was the chance that as long as her street were clear there'd be no immediate cause for concern. Unless of course Georgia had been intercepted before getting that far. It was an illogical thought, a desperate hope, but one she clung to as she turned into the Queen's Park area.

Slowing to a crawl, she opened the car windows to listen for anything untoward. It was quiet. A couple of kids playing with a football on the pavement. A mother loading a toddler into the child seat in the back of a black SUV. Otherwise not a sound. Just a lump of plastic some fool had left lying in the road adjacent to her own vehicle. A black lump. A length of bumper from a small car.

Her heart sank and she blinked at the profusion of flashing police car, ambulance and fire engine blue lights discernible through gaps in the crowd.

She parked her vehicle and climbed out, legs shaking. Georgia drove an ancient Golf. Tammy couldn't see what make of car had been involved from where she was, but it didn't have to be Georgia's. She'd deliberately not called Georgia while driving home, both from the point of view of the need for a degree of concentration in her driving, and also in case Georgia were in a compromising situation.

There was blood and oil in the road. Shattered glass, more bits of bumper. Uniformed people everywhere. Police, paramedics, firefighters. Her throat tightened, a knot forming at the back of her mouth. Surely not. Surely not.

Then she experienced a moment of utter relief as her racing pulse slowed. It was a newish red car. Certainly not an ancient banger. A write-off. Crumpled like used up aluminium foil.

"What happened?" she asked a scruffy youngster close by.

"Hit and run, miss," he replied, pointing at the red car. "Them two was lucky to get out alive." Two women, wrapped in silver foil, possibly a mother and daughter, badly shaken, sat huddled on the floor seen through the open rear doors of an ambulance.

"Anyone badly hurt?"

"I should say. Those old Golf's is a bleedin' death trap, you ask me."

"Oh. A Golf, you say?"

"That's right. They've took it away. Police. Left the other one for now. They got the bird out of the Golf though.

Good lookin', what I could see." The youngster scratched behind one ear thoughtfully, then added, "Badly smashed up she was. Load a blood."

Swallowing to hold back the tears, tears she prayed were premature, she asked, "Did anyone say anything."

"Nah! Only the bird."

"The bird? You mean, the driver of the Golf?"

"Thass right."

"Did you hear what she said?"

"Not really. Sounded a bit like, 'Sorry Tams.'" He shrugged. "Whatever that is."

"Oh God. Where is she now? In the back of the ambulance? I must go and find out. Someone there can tell me."

"Here, lady. She's gone."

"Gone?"

"In the other amb'lance, innit. They sent two amb'lances case there was two for the 'ospital. Just as well. The other two was hurt, but not so bad. The other bloke drove off. White van. Like I said, hit and run."

"Do you think she was alright? Do you know which hospital?"

"Someone said Saint Mary's in Paddington."

"So, she might still be okay?"

"Doubt it, miss. After she said 'sorry', they's all hurryin' round her, banging her chest. Putting them electric things on her, makin' her jolt an' that."

"Did she come round, do you think?"

"Don't think so. Cos then the two amb'lance mans looks at each other, and shakes their 'eads. Covers her over and shoves her in the back of the amb'lance 'fore drivin' off."

Sorry Tams.' Putting her head in her hands as she made her way home, she sobbed.

CHAPTER 44 DAY 13

"I**T'S DONE, OSCAR."**

"Are you on a burner?"

"No, I didn't think it would be — "

"What the hell do you mean, you didn't think? That's your damn trouble, my friend. Never thinking. Hang up, man, and call me back on the burner. If you haven't got one, get one. Or use a public call box. They do still exist in hotel lobbies, among other places, you know."

Ten minutes later the caller came through again. "It's me." The tone was tremulous.

"Well? Tell me. Did you keep it clean?"

"Yes."

"I don't need to know the details."

He paused for a beat.

"No, tell me anyway. PM's going to announce my Chancellorship any day. Possibly tomorrow. Budget's all but ready. Been burning the midnight oil with the Treasury boys. Economy's in a state. They need me to sort it. A businessman, like Trump. A man who knows what he's doing, not a bloody academic. Carstairs knows he's for the chop, making way for me. Not best if there're any messes left to clean up... God help you. Though on reflection I doubt even he'd be able to. When I think; the Anderton thing nearly blew up in our faces. That idiot, Ainsley. A sledgehammer to crack a nut. Well, go on. I'm listening."

"I took the jet, like you said, Oscar. Alright? I went to that small private aerodrome near the main Geneva airport. Told the pilot I'd be a couple of hours. Hire car was waiting for me under an assumed name. Thanks for organising things." The voice was hesitant, almost pleading.

"Least I could do for a paid killer. Even one as bloody incompetent as you. Next time I'll use my man Loughty. Knows what he's doing. Trouble is, he wasn't available this time. So what next?"

"I got to Davenport's place around 5.00 pm. It was getting dark, but I could see he was in, silhouetted against the lights indoors. The place is pretty plush."

"Get on with it. Get on with it."

"When he opened the door, he looked around suspiciously as if he wasn't sure who or what to expect. He acted very jumpy. That is, until I told him I'd been asked by you to personally agree details with him for the transfer of funds on a deal he and you had made. He wanted to know why you hadn't told him I was coming."

"What did you say?"

"Only that the funds were ready, and you'd asked me to come at short notice as I happened to be available."

"Very well. Then what? You had the Rohypnol?"

"Of course I did, Oscar. What do you take me for?"

"I won't answer that."

"We spent a while, with him giving me bank account details. He wanted the cash in several different accounts around the world, and in several different names."

"You kept all the details?"

"Yes, I did. I have them here, right by me. Let's see now, where are my spectacles?"

"You and your bloody spectacles. I've never known a man lose so many pairs."

"It's alright, Oscar, I've found them. Always carry spares anyway. Oh my!"

"What's wrong, man."

"Nothing, Oscar. Nothing at all."

"God help you if you've fouled up."

"I haven't, really, I swear it. I've done exactly as you asked." The voice sounded frightened now.

"Very well. Anyway, you have all the bank details. That's something. He'll have reserves in all of them. We'll raid them if and when we need them. Failing that we'll use them for laundering. Mr William Davenport, alias Monsieur Tomas Breuillon, has been most accommodating. So then?"

"Once all the details were sorted, he said we should have a drink to celebrate. The cognac was within reach on the occasional table. I made as if to leave, saying I had to get back. But he insisted, as I was sure he would."

"You got something right, then."

"Thank you, Oscar. He poured us both a generous Remy, and I slipped in the drug when he went rooting for some snacks to add to the festivities."

"Next?"

"He fell unconscious, out after no more than ten minutes."

"You gave him a big dose?"

"Ten milligrams. More than that I couldn't have got into his brandy bowl without him noticing. I should say, before the celebrations began, while he was giving me chapter and verse on his various accounts, he'd already had a couple of shots. He can put it away, which was useful. He'd quickly downed several to my two. Then, when he was laid out, and on the floor, I tipped some of the Remy over his shirt front."

"That wouldn't have killed him. What did you do after that?"

"I got a towel from his bathroom and held it over his mouth and nose till he stopped breathing. I believe that with the drug undetectable after a number of hours, by the time he's found with alcohol in the system and on his clothes, it would look as though he'd had too much to drink and suffered a heart attack. Obviously, there wasn't enough drink in him to kill a healthy man, but with no suspects, no motive and no-one seen in the area, what other conclusion would a medic come to? Probably an open verdict in due course, if there were any sort of inquest. I don't know how it's done in Switzerland, but you're aware he carried a French passport, so nothing to immediately link him to the UK."

"I assume you cleaned up afterwards? No prints?"

"Of course. I wiped everything down, left only the one brandy glass out. I did one or two other things to make it all look like some sort of accident."

"Do I need to hear this?" Oscar was starting to sound bored.

"I dragged his body into the kitchen."

"Why, in heaven's name?"

"He had something ready to cook on the hob, so I left his body close to the stove, with the gas running and an aerosol can of beer close to the flame."

"I don't need to hear anymore."

"You did say, dynamite the place if you have to."

"Not literally, you idiot. I was speaking metaphorically."

"I thought it was all quite tidy. Drink, the aerosol and a small but apparently lethal explosion. And I was well away from the place. A plausible cause of death, and no clues left behind."

"You sound quite pleased with yourself."

"Hardly. I've done what you wanted. And it ends here. You can keep your threats. From now on, I've had it. No more."

"We'll see about that," Oscar replied, and ended the call.

He'd barely hung up when his phone went again. "Yes?" he snapped.

"Boss?"

"Ainsley?"

"Assright."

"Done as I asked?"

"She dayde, man. Was easy. Pokey little toy Volks. All mash up."

"Very well. I'll have the cash delivered to our usual spot. You're sure she was dead."

"Have a garlfren, work at de Saint Mary. She see da body bring in. She dayde alright, man."

"Very well. I may have something else for you short-ly. A meddling private investigator, getting too big for her boots."

"Yuh means di big black one yuh have me check out, dat night on di Embankment?"

"The very same."

"Any time, man."

"While we're about it, Ainsley, what about the van? Last time they got hold of the bloody thing. It's still in po-lice custody. The Anderton thing is still an open bloody sore."

"Nah, man. No slip ups, dis time. Me tek di mota to de breakers. It all crush."

"Thank heavens."

Oscar smiled as he hung up. "God is clearly on my side."

CHAPTER 45 DAY 13

CIRCLING TAMMY'S HEAD like a swarm of angry bees was the stench of formaldehyde. That and other unidentifiable aromas, which to the uninitiated, together with the sight of a mutilated corpse, could induce pronounced vomiting.

She'd made the appointment and agreed to meet with Rosemary Sharpe who, as it happened, had been first on the scene when the body was initially discovered, along with SOCO. The DCI's presence at the premises of the pathologist ensured the necessary continuity required when dealing with the further examination of a corpse in what looked like a pretty clear case of murder.

She'd cried most of the night. There were reasons, she pondered, but no excuses. She should never have involved Georgia. It had been a mistake from the word go. Maybe it was tempting to have someone that close to Oscar to keep an eye on him, but Dov had warned her early on how dangerous Oscar was, and she'd planted Georgia right in the line of fire. It was exhausting, but she couldn't ease up now. In some ways the investigation seemed to be spiralling out of control. If she didn't come up with something soon, Bob Walker would begin to question her competence and ability. And anyway, she owed it to Georgia to do all she could to reach a conclusion. That is, if there were one to be reached.

In the morning, fortified with copious cups of strong black coffee and an enormous bowl of fruit and nut muesli, she dressed in a working two-piece grey suit and left the flat.

The bruising and knife wound she'd sustained in America still left her tiring easily, and Tammy wouldn't want to spend an undue amount of time on her feet. Nonetheless, she was working on a hunch.

The pathologist, Raymond Hawley, a shortish, middle-aged, harassed-looking gentleman with the relevant Home Office credentials, led them into the mortuary. The room was chill, and Tammy instinctively wound the pashmina she'd remembered to bring closer about her neck. "Over here," he announced wearily, pulling open one of the drawers. "The body found on the Heath. Limbless, that is hands and feet, and headless." It was a statement rather than a question. "Still no ID from you people I understand."

Rosemary was about to add a comment when she started coughing, a dry hacking rasp that left her red-faced and puffing.

"Still smoking, Rose?" Tammy asked, concerned.

"I know, I know," she replied, holding up one hand in surrender. "I will get around to stopping. Eventually."

Turning to the pathologist, Tammy enquired, "Rose tells me the likely cause of death was drowning?"

"We have conducted hydro-static tests and taken the view that drowning was very likely the cause." The man spoke with the ghost of an American accent, which Tammy noted for future reference. He could have been in the UK for enough years to have a US accent mellow. "But we simply cannot be certain because of the length of time the body lay undiscovered. Hydro-static testing is imprecise, and without something more to go on, such as, for example, evidence of submersion in perhaps the sea, or a river? Here, I'm thinking trace evidence of salt on the body or perhaps specific pollutants common to certain rivers, we cannot be unequivocal. Incidentally, there were traces of what might have been some sort of detergent on the skin."

"Detergent?" Tammy asked. "What would detergent be doing on someone's skin?"

"I've no idea, ma'am."

That American inflection once more. Something stirred at the back of Tammy's mind, but she couldn't immediately isolate it. "Could we have the body on the slab, do you think."

"Sure. You'll need to get into gowns, masks and gloves." Turning towards the door they'd just come through the pathologist called out, "Sean, can you organise the necessary, and give me a hand here?"

A tall, willowy young man wearing horn-rimmed spectacles came in with the items for Tammy and Rose to change into, while he and Hawley organised the moving of the body from the drawer onto a trolley, and from there into the main room where it was shifted onto one of the slabs.

"Pretty grisly, isn't it," offered Rose.

Tammy had seen plenty of bodies in her time on the force, particularly when working as a DI on the murder squad. But this was about as bad as it got.

"Body appears to have been savagely assaulted," offered the pathologist. "The extensive bruising and multiple lesions together with a clear lack of bleeding suggest the attack took place post-mortem."

"Someone appears to have been pretty angry," murmured Tammy.

"You might put it that way," responded the pathologist. "Bit of an understatement, I'd say. I can print up the report before you go if you like. But there's not much more in it to help you, I'm afraid."

Rose stood back to give Tammy space, while Tammy thoughtfully regarded the partly decomposed body with her chin cupped in her palm. Then concentrating particularly on the lower abdomen of the corpse, she remarked, "I see she had auburn hair, right?"

"That's correct," said the pathologist, looking at Tammy with interest.

Glancing up, Tammy added, "Age, around mid-forties? Judging by the slight greying in the pubic region."

"Again, you are correct."

"Anything occur to you, Tammy?" asked Rosemary.

"I'm not sure yet, Rose." Then, addressing the pathologist once more, Tammy asked, "Do you have a magnifying
glass I can use?"

"Yes, but…I mean, we've been very thorough. I'm not
sure what you'd hope to find that we haven't already noted."

"Bear with me, if you will, Mr Hawley?"

"Of course, of course," he said hastily. Then called,
"Sean? A magnifying glass please for Ms Pierre."

A few moments later Sean produced what he described
as a DermLite Lumio magnifying exam light. About the
size and shape of a small frying pan, it was the sort of thing,
he explained, that would pick out skin lesions, hair folli-
cles and even minor changes in pigmentation. In short, exactly what Tammy needed for her further examination of
the corpse. Costing over three hundred pounds, it would
prove to be undeniable value for money.

Starting at the top of the body, in the area of what little
was left of the neck, Tammy worked her way down, examining everything minutely under the illumination provided by the implement. "Jagged cuts at the neck and base of
limbs," she muttered. "Hacksaw?" she asked Hawley.

"Almost certainly. It would easily work its way through
limbs, joints, tendons and so on. Leaves the jagged mess
you can see."

Stretching back, her hands on her hips, Tammy took a
breather.

"You okay, Tammy? Look a bit peaky to me," said
Rose, sounding slightly worried.

"I'll be fine," said Tammy, suddenly bending to examine the corpse's navel under the surface of the magnifier,
pulling at it this way and that, as though it might be hiding
something beneath or between its folds of skin.

The pathologist, with his arms folded, defiantly said,
"Not sure what you think you might find there, Ms Pierre."
He couldn't seem to decide whether to sound surprised at

Tammy's interest in this area or annoyed at what he might have perceived as the tacit questioning of his competence.

"Yep. Got it," Tammy announced, squinting at the umbilicus and experiencing a moment's satisfaction that her long-shot hunch had been proven correct. "Something I remember being mentioned a while ago. Take a look, Rose," she suggested, handing the magnifier to the DCI.

But after several seconds Rose, who'd been leaning over the body, staring intently, stood up and, shaking her head, handed the DermLite back to Tammy. "Blowed if I can see anything there. What am I supposed to be looking for?"

"Take another look. Take your time. It's there. I promise you."

"May I, perhaps?" the pathologist ventured.

"Absolutely," said Rosemary, handing him the magnifier.

Leaning over the body as Rose and Tammy had been a few moments before, he stared intently, moving the magnifier this way and that, before straightening up, shrugging and handing the implement back to Tammy. "There's nothing. Believe me, we've checked the body thoroughly and if there was anything to see either Sean or I would have spotted it."

Handing the magnifier back to Rose, Tammy said, "Take another look, Rosemary, and search for the smallest sign of anything. Anything at all. Then tell me what you see."

This time the DCI stared intently for minute after minute, then said, "Nothing. Absolutely nothing here to see."

"Stay with it, Rose. Don't give up just yet."

"Wait a moment."

"Yes?"

"A pinhole."

"Ah! Okay. Good. Just the one?"

"No, there's two. I can see two of them," she added, pulling the umbilicus this way and that. "And, hey, what's this? It looks like a third one, largely healed over. Tammy, they're so tiny. But wait, there's others. If I move this flap of skin," she said, moving the umbilicus to view it the better. "So tiny. More like freckles. Six, now. I can see six altogether. What could…?"

"Yes, Rose?" Tammy leaned back, satisfied. "What could?"

The pathologist's brow was creased. "Are you saying…?"

But Tammy held up one hand. "Let's wait for Rose's assessment."

"They can't be piercings, Tammy. They're too small, surely."

"They're not too small, Rose. And the reason there's six of them is that they accommodated one tiny skull and two crossbones. A pair of piercings for each item."

"How could you possibly know that?"

"Because, I was given information about a woman who'd had a miniscule set of piercings to allow a tiny trio of metal embellishments to be inserted in the umbilicus. Though what the devil's happened here and by whom this individual was killed is another mystery entirely. But, I do know who this is. And if you organise some DNA tests you'll find I'm right. You see, I was given the detail about the piercings by, none other than Oscar Mountford himself about his wife," said Tammy.

"Rose, this is the corpse of Letitia Mountford."

CHAPTER 46 DAY 13

THE BAR IN THE BUNCH OF GRAPES was crowded and noisy. An ideal place for a confidential conversation. The place smelled of beer and sawdust. An oddly comforting atmosphere in a typically English pub.

Outside was dark, but a mild evening with a crowd of the younger drinkers standing or else sitting at tables in the open. Tammy could still sense the aroma of formaldehyde on her clothes. She wrinkled her nose, resisting the temptation to grimace. She was bone tired, but thankfully this wasn't going to take long. The stitches were pulling in her side, but she needed to concentrate, be clear-headed. She'd cope.

"Thanks for agreeing to see me at such short notice, Tammy." Bob Walker was in his customary dark blue suit, with white shirt and impeccably knotted tie. A whisky sour sat on the table between them.

"Strong stuff." She nodded at the drink.

"Long day," he replied. "Helps me unwind."

"You're not driving?"

"Heavens no. With this inside me? Let's see now," he murmured. "Double whisky, lemon juice, egg white, red wine. Don't tell the wife." He grinned.

"I won't if you don't." Tammy smiled conspiratorially, toying with her own double Stolichnaya.

"Anyway, my driver's nearby. Unmarked car." He inclined his head. "Of course."

"Of course."

"Tammy, if I may say so, and I know I've said it before, you've been through the wringer. Are you really still okay to proceed with this investigation?"

"I'm fine."

"You look…"

"Bob, I'm fine. If it gets too much, I'll let you know."

"Very well," he responded, sounding chastened.

"Go ahead."

"Tammy, I wanted to talk to you about Oscar, but you go first."

"Okay. So, I've just come from the mortuary."

"The mortuary?" He sounded surprised. "Which one?"

"Dewhurst Street."

"I know. Near the Yard. Ray Hawley's the pathologist there."

"You know him?"

"Yes. Good man, very thorough. Naturalised British citizen, you know."

Nodding, Tammy enquired, "American, by any chance?"

Bob nodded. "Originally. Been here over twenty-five years. The accent flattens out in time. You'd hardly know he wasn't born here."

She'd been right. But whatever it was that had nagged at her when she was at the mortuary listening to Hawley still remained lodged at the back of her mind. "I think I may have found Letitia Mountford."

Bob's eyes opened wide. "Well done, Tammy." Then after a moment he asked, "In the mortuary?"

"That's right."

"What was it took you there?" Lifting the glass, Bob took a long pull on the drink, murmuring in satisfaction.

Tammy followed suit, holding the vodka for several seconds, feeling it run over her tongue, so that when she finally swallowed she got the slight buzz the drink always gave her. In reply to Bob's question, she said simply, "It was just a hunch, no more."

"I'm listening. Your hunches never fail to impress me, Tammy."

"Well, it wasn't all that brilliant, just an idea that I reckoned worth investing a little time in. You see, comparing dates, the final murder that took place in New York by either Letitia or her lookalike was some three weeks before the St James's Hotel murder, also likely committed by one of the two women. The last of the New York murders seemed close to, but obviously before, the date that the mutilated corpse was reckoned to have been dumped on Hampstead Heath.

"With that in mind, I've got the guys at Incognita trying to track down possible dates for the return of either of the two women. They're concentrating on dates around the time of the last US murder, or a day or two later, as the most likely time for the return of the first woman. It'll be harder to confirm the date of the second return as the St James's Hotel murder occurred three weeks later. Someone clearly went to ground for a while.

"Purely on the basis of the date the corpse was found on the Heath, I wondered if it might perhaps be Letitia."

"A long shot, Tammy. There're over one hundred murders a year in London. That's roughly one every three days. But, as you say, worth a look."

They stopped chatting for a moment as a crowd of customers eased their way past them both. Bob finished his drink at the same time as Tammy, and inclined his head enquiringly indicating another. But she shook her head.

Then Tammy spoke again, "It's her, Bob. I know it. I've got Rose checking the DNA with what she'll find at the family residence. But I know it's her."

"How can you be so sure, Tammy."

"When I asked him for any distinguishing features, Oscar Mountford told me his wife had a tiny skull and crossbones piercing in her navel. He said he couldn't understand why she'd bothered as it was barely visible. Dov found the items, three small bits of metal, while going through everything in Letitia's apartment in New York and I kept them. At first, I didn't know what they were. A tiny skull and crossbones. Then I remembered what Oscar told me about them. So when I went to the mortuary, I specifically searched for and found six minute marks in the folds of the umbilicus where the pinholes had been. So small, they were even missed by the pathologist."

"Well done, Tammy," Bob breathed. "If you're right, and I've no doubt you are, this is a real breakthrough."

"A breakthrough, yes. And it can be kept quiet until after this Budget speech I gather Oscar is due to make, which was the object of the exercise."

"Do you think Oscar killed his wife, then?"

"No. I don't. For one thing, he couldn't have known, any more than we could have, when his wife was returning from the US. Consequently, he'd have had little time to plan it, even if he'd wanted to. And then, why kill her at this stage and jeopardise his career? He was certainly uninterested in her. Made little fuss when she disappeared for periods. He's known to you, Bob. A colleague?"

"Hardly. More an acquaintance. In my line you get to deal with all sorts in government and the Opposition too, of course."

"Fair enough. Well, with her political affiliations the polar opposite of his own, whilst it would hardly have endeared her to him, it would more likely have left him puzzled. I mean, he would have asked himself, why on earth had she, an avowed Communist, married an extreme right-winger in the first place. Unless, of course, her Russian handlers had somehow engineered it."

"That's eminently possible. MI6 are constantly looking at ways the Russians might seek to destabilise the West," said Bob.

"The irony of Oscar Mountford's far right ambitions is that with that political grouping's admiration for Putin's brand of Communism, we have a possible alliance of extremes, ably echoed in the marriage of Oscar and his wife. Instead of ignoring her, Oscar might have done better to cultivate his wife."

"So then, if Oscar Mountford didn't murder Letitia, who did? Any ideas at all on that subject?" Bob enquired.

"Not yet." Tammy shook her head.

"Even if we had grounds to arrest him, we couldn't. Not right now. The economy is in a mess, Carstairs is on the way out. We need the sort of steadying hand, the certain direction that someone like Oscar Mountford can give it. Only a matter of days. We sit tight. The speech must be given, no matter what. If nothing else, whatever the question of his money laundering, or other nefarious activities might be, make no mistake, he is a brilliant businessman, and what we need right now."

"Scarface Al Capone was a brilliant businessman, Bob. It didn't stop him from killing all seven of the Irish American Bugs Moran gang. In the dead of night. And in cold blood."

"We don't know for certain that Oscar Mountford is a murderer."

"I'd lay odds he is."

"I suspect you're right, Tammy." Bob sighed.

"Now, of course, we've other things to cloud the waters. There's the death of Oscar's son Pierce. I wonder how he's taking that. I gather the boy was the apple of his father's eye. But with his nosing into his father's right wing dealings, what would Oscar's feelings towards his son have been? There was no love lost between us when we he and I met, so I got precious little from him. Dov told me to take care, said the man is truly dangerous. And I can believe Oscar might well have had intentions where his son was involved. The man is totally unreachable. A classic psychopath, if you ask me. I wonder if there's ever been anyone in his life that's come close to getting through to him."

"I've mentioned money laundering, but of course we both know that's only the part of it." Bob linked his fingers together, resting his hands on the table.

"Kevin Anderton?" Tammy enquired.

"Kevin Anderton," Bob agreed. "And possibly Pierce? I'm keeping an open mind on that one. Then there's Letitia? Although, as we've agreed, that seems highly unlikely."

"And now there's another."

"Another? Murder?"

Several seconds passed while Tammy toyed with her empty glass. Then catching Bob's eye, she said, "Yesterday, Georgia sent me a text while I was talking with Oscar's daughters."

"She was helping you. Transmitting information regarding her boss, I presume?"

"I should have mentioned it earlier, Bob. I'm still trying to get my head around it. It was a huge mistake getting Georgia involved. My fault entirely." She glanced at her hands resting in her lap and swallowed, holding back the tears that threatened.

"Tammy?" He sounded anxious. "What's wrong. What happened? What's this about a text?"

"It just said, Help."

"My God, Tammy."

"She's dead. Bob. She's dead. And it's my fault." As she said it, she put her head in her hands and sat unmoving for several moments. When she looked up again her face was streaked with tears.

She put her palms on the table and Bob rested his on hers. "You feel guilty? Responsible?"

She nodded, turning away, unable to meet his gaze.

"Let me guess. You'd begun to form an affection for her?"

Bowing her head in tacit acknowledgement, Tammy said nothing.

"Oscar, is it, do you think? Again?"

"Who else?"

"What do you want me to do, Tammy. Have Rose haul him in for questioning? Just say the word."

"Not yet." She sighed, brushing her cheeks dry with the backs of her hands. "We've nothing at all to go on; nothing to charge him with. Let's wait and see what he does next. Incidentally, I assume you're keeping the PM up to date?"

"Of course. He's fully briefed. And, one might add, concerned, and finding it hard to believe his star could turn out to be an international criminal, and possibly a murderer to boot."

"Not too many past Cabinet ministers among the criminal fraternity," she observed. "Though I believe we did have one Prime Minister murdered."

"That's right. In 1812. Spencer Perceval, killed by a merchant who had grievances against the government," said Bob.

"There've been other MPs jailed though, haven't there. We've spoken about this before. The most recent, Fiona Onasanya, lawyer and Labour MP, Chris Huhne for perverting the course of justice over a speeding ticket. Others I could name. None for murder, so far."

"As we're aware, that may be about to change. Incidentally, one piece of information that's come my way." Bob stroked his chin pensively. "An odd death in Geneva."

"Odd?" Tammy asked. "Odd how?"

"We got the heads up at 5 from Interpol. A man called Tomas Breuillon was found dead at his home overlooking the lake yesterday."

"How did he die?"

"That's a bit of a puzzle, because it looks as though he'd been preparing a meal when an aerosol can of beer he was using, apparently too near a gas hob, exploded."

"And that killed him?"

"Well now, here's the question. The explosion made a mess of his kitchen, but on first cursory examination, the police in Geneva feel the explosion shouldn't have been powerful enough to have killed an apparently fit man."

"Anything else?"

"A lot of drink in his system. But again, not enough to kill. Unless there were any sort of heart condition. We'll know after the autopsy."

"Any clues at all?"

"A pair of spectacles was found at the scene."

"Just the one?"

"Apparently."

"I see. The point being that no-one who wears glasses has only one single pair. Everyone carries spares. Is that it? Why you were contacted?"

"No, there's more. It seems the Geneva police found a second passport in the property when they went through it, in the name of one William Davenport. The photograph was the same as that on Breuillon's passport. Interpol texted me the two passport pictures. Look," said Bob, fishing out his mobile to show her.

Glancing at the two pictures, Tammy noted, "They're the same man. Our fugitive pilot. Isn't that a turn-up for the books? Seems someone paid our criminal pilot a visit."

"I should say very much so. Now the question is, was the death a genuine accident or did someone want Mr Davenport out of the way?"

Without warning Tammy grunted involuntarily as a needle-sharp point of agony cut into her side. Unwilling to acknowledge her exhaustion, and now experiencing flashing white lights, she was aching to do a line or get a smoke to ease the pain. She'd promised herself she wouldn't during the pregnancy. But the temptation was there just the same, teasing, mocking.

Bob could see it, of course, her distress, and said quietly, "You need to go home, Tammy. Get some rest. Please."

"Okay, okay."

"How did you get here?"

"Drove," she muttered through clenched teeth.

"Leave the car, Tammy. Get a cab."

"I'll be okay," she said, feeling anything but.

"Come on, then, I'll see you to your car. Is it far?"

"Couple of minutes from here," she replied, wondering if she'd make it that far. Once behind the wheel the adrenalin would kick in and the drive home, about twenty minutes, would be okay.

As the two of them struggled through the packed bar, she was suddenly shocked cold when she spied through the heaving bodies, on the far side of the place, the Caribbean man who'd accosted her on the Embankment after her first meeting on the case with Bob. The one who'd called her a coconut. The one they'd both debated might be listening in to their conversation. As before he was in a black tracksuit with hoodie, that same livid scar under his right eye. There was no mistaking the man. He was grinning at her broadly, swiftly disabusing her of the notion his presence at The Bunch of Grapes was mere coincidence.

CHAPTER 47 DAY 14

IT WAS 4:00 AM and the M4 motorway ahead was empty as the young man eased the $2.5 million all black liveried Bugatti Veyron Super Sport up to two hundred and fifty miles an hour. "She'll do more," he announced over the purring engine, the car making barely a shudder over the surface of the road.

"Christ, Theo, I'm on the verge of an orgasm. I've never known anything like it." Her skirt, already absurdly short, had ridden up until it was effectively around her waist, revealing an all but transparent red thong.

"Can you wait till we get to the hotel, Juliet?"

"No way. I'm screaming for it," she said, reaching over to push a hand against the front of his black chinos, noting his immediate reaction.

"There's a motorway service station up ahead," he said. "Hang on till we get there."

"Aren't there speed cameras on this motorway? Surely you must have points on your licence?"

"About sixty at the last count."

"Shouldn't you be banned by now?"

"Several times over, angel face."

"How do you manage to get away with it?"

"Erm!" He smiled. "Actually, my father has contacts."

"Really? What sort of contacts are those?"

"He knows the Metropolitan Police Commissioner."

"What you might call friends in high places."

"A bit like your pater, Juliet. Don't knock it. We're the people that get things done."

"Can you slow down in time? How many miles a minute are you doing?"

"We're eight miles away, and we'll be there in two minutes, so I'm slowing down now. Hard," he said, taking his foot off the accelerator and applying the footbrake. The car barely murmured as it swiftly lost speed. A little over a minute later they were approaching the exit slip at just seventy, and then slowing to a sane speed of thirty. Theo steered the car into the almost deserted service station car park and pulled into a designated spot. Juliet was on him in a moment like a starving animal, pulling at his trousers, trying to climb onto him.

"Car's too fucking cramped," she complained. "How am I supposed to fuck you?"

"For Chrissake, just blow me," he said, rearing up in his seat as far as he was able. "You do yourself now, Juliet, I can't reach you. We'll finish this properly later." Another moment and she was groaning softly, her body shuddering, feeling him swell as she neared her peak. Then everything stopped abruptly when Theo suddenly murmured, "You do it just like your mother." He sounded mildly irritated.

"What?" she snarled, pulling back from him and flopping down in the bucket seat, pulling her skirt down over her hips again.

"No, don't stop," he complained. "Why have you stopped?"

"My mother? You shit? How long?"

"I thought you knew. She said everyone knew."

"What? You think she announced it to everyone? Like. Hey, guys, thought you'd like to know I'm fucking my daughter's new boyfriend?"

"Yeah, well."

"Yeah, well what? You piece of shit," she stormed, turning her face away from him to stare out of the side window. "Take me home."

"But!"

"Now," she screamed. "Did my Pa know about this?"

"You mean, me and you?"

"No, you dunderhead. About you and Ma."

Starting the engine, which replied with a deep-throated rumble, Theo backed out of the parking space and started to drive slowly towards the service station exit. "Juliet?" he asked.

"What?"

"Why do you call your folks Pa and Ma? Why not Dad and Mum, like most people?"

"Because, you dummy, we're middle class. Christ, which grammar school were you educated at?"

"Actually, I went to a secondary modern."

"God above. What the hell have I landed myself with?"

"You know very well I earn megabucks as a hedge fund manager."

The car trailed onto the entry slip and picked up speed as they approached the motorway.

"Keep it to seventy, buster."

"Okay. Okay."

"Secondary modern. Daddy and Mummy? God help. You're just working-class trash."

"Rich enough for your father to work with. I made him a lot of money. All legit. Something he wasn't used to."

"I'll bet. I want you to tell me, did he know about you and Ma?"

"Of course." Theo pulled at an earlobe. "What he doesn't seem to have known about was the affair your mother was having with my partner Caspar da Silva. He's the senior guy at Maerland da Silva."

"Who's Maerland, then?"

"Retired. I'm joint owner of the practice, but with Caspar's length of service, age and so on, we split profits sixty forty in his favour. I don't complain," he said, indicating the interior of the car. "We both do okay."

"I'll say," she said quietly.

"There was, or is, a peculiar relationship, da Silva and your mother."

"How?"

"Well, she seemed to get off on him beating her up. Did you never see her with scratches and bruises? The trouble is, once you start down that path it leads to ever greater excess. Caspar was starting to get high himself on beating her up. I think she came to me for a bit of respite, believe it or not. And, as I've said, it suited Oscar who knew nothing of the other goings on."

"And so?"

"He encouraged it. My affair with Letitia."

"What?" She stared at Theo, as though trying to read his mind, but could see nothing. She hadn't realised how vacant he looked most of the time; began wondering what she'd ever seen in the man. "Sorry, I don't believe it. Try the other leg, Theo. It rings bells."

"He wanted shot of her. Oscar, that is. But later, once he got the job he was after. Meantime it was enough if she were kept occupied. He thought the affair with me might get things started in the right direction."

"I'll bet."

"Did you know about your mother's left wing games?"

"Which were those? The ones with Manchester United?"

"You can take the piss, Juliet. But your father did a lot of checking when he began suspecting she was up to no good with those long absences from home, and never any explanation or excuse."

"What do you know about my Ma's so-called left wing games? For crying out loud, she lived the life of Riley. Mansion, staff, mega yacht, high society. Left wing, my foot."

"Your father found she'd been involved with the Communist Party when she was at uni. He thought all that was in the past, but he was beginning to find out some things he didn't like about her present."

"Such as?"

"Secret assignations with someone, or someones, with links to the Communists in this country."

"I don't believe a word of it. She was a dyed in the wool Tory. Just like Pa."

"Ask your father. I'm telling you, when he realised what was going on... Your father's an ambitious man, Juliet. He was very concerned your mother was going to get in his way, stymie his ambition. Wouldn't do if the media got wind of the Communist activities of the new Chancellor's wife. He told me he had plans for your mother. He wouldn't say what. But he sounded pretty determined. And you know your dad. Once he gets an idea, nothing, but nothing, and no-one is allowed to get in his way."

"You'll be telling me next he was planning to have her killed."

Theo said nothing, merely shrugged evasively.

"Theo? Say something. Don't tell me Pa was planning on killing Ma?"

"I'm saying nothing. Juliet, your father is a man devoted to his country. You should know that."

"And that involved killing Ma, did it? God, Theo, we don't even know where she is. Are you telling me she's dead?"

"I don't know where your mother is, Juliet. I do know her activities concerned your father. Anything left wing did. In his opinion Russia and the Far East are real threats to the West. The pandemic?"

"What about the pandemic?"

"He never believed it was caused by those pangolin creatures."

"Well what else, then?"

"He believed it may have been started deliberately, with the object of weakening Western industry sufficiently to allow a Far Eastern takeover."

"Isn't that a bit fanciful?"

"He may have had a point."

"But he was a Brexiteer. Wouldn't he have thought we'd be stronger as part of a European political bloc?"

"Oscar said Europe was a corrupt and effete organisation, run by self-serving idiots." He paused and smiled. "A bit rich, coming from him."

"I do know Pierce was really worried about Pa's right wing tendencies," she added. "I still can't believe he's gone. I really saw him as indestructible."

"Your father talked to me, Juliet. Said we were like-minded. He believed only the far right would have the strength to counter Communism in its many guises. He was trying to build an alliance of the right in various European countries. He felt the West was ripe for them to step in and take over."

"And you? Where do you figure in all this? Do you have a view? A political grain in your head?"

"I know you think I'm stupid, Juliet, and yes, I went to secondary modern because I wasn't an all-rounder, and couldn't be bothered when it came to the eleven plus, which I failed. Despite that, I was good at maths, very good, which is why I am where I am. My school in Buckinghamshire, George Sand, after the French poet, novelist and ironically a Socialist, was the best of its type. More than fifty percent of the students got university entrance. And you can call me working class, if you must, but my mother is a nurse, my father a doctor in general practice. Humble beginnings, but they've done well."

"I just can't accept you and Ma were getting it on together."

"Don't imagine I enjoyed it."

"What? You expect me to believe that?"

"I told you, your father simply wanted her fully engaged until the Chancellor's post came through. He couldn't risk her disappearing then reappearing at an inopportune moment, so he persuaded me to keep her busy."

"Then she disappeared anyway."

"Right."

"To America."

"Correct. And how did you find out? The private investigator your father employed, I presume."

"Recommended by Detective Chief Superintendent Bob Walker. Apparently, she's good. We met her, Davs, Jayne and me. After Pierce…" She waited a beat, feeling suddenly terribly sad, then went on, "She's very tall. Very bright. Impressive altogether."

"Oscar didn't like her. Called her an arrogant bitch. I'm guessing she was pretty powerful, something he doesn't much like in women. He sees them as chattels to be occupied in the home, attending to men's needs."

"Hmm. Sounds like Pa."

They drove on in silence for a few miles, then turning to Juliet, Theo said quietly, "He's dangerous, you know."

"Maybe," she responded.

"Not maybe, Juliet. He confides in me. I wouldn't tell anyone else, but as you're his daughter…" Theo frowned, worried. "You know the Kevin Anderton thing?"

"The security man who was murdered?"

"I'm pretty sure it was Oscar."

"In that case why would Bob Walker have anything to do with Pa? He must surely know?"

"If Bob wants to nail Oscar, now is not the time to let him have any idea he may be on to him. Also, I've a feeling they want to get this emergency Budget underway. And anyway, there's no concrete evidence linking your father to the killing. So Bob will have to bide his time."

"She was attacked in the States, you know."

"The private eye?"

"That's right. She was knifed. We don't know who they were or how they discovered she'd be there at that precise moment."

"I can tell you," said Theo.

"Really? Go on, then."

"Oscar had the Pierre woman followed out to the States, fully aware she'd be on the hunt for Letitia. He wanted Letitia left alone in the hope she'd remain in the States for as long as possible. At the same time he wanted the PI out of the way, so he organised a welcoming committee for her. His instruction, he told me, was kill her if you have to. Funny thing is, I've got a feeling someone else got there first. Somehow they must've fouled up because Oscar said that things hadn't gone as he'd planned. He refused to be specific. But they lost sight of Letitia."

"You've taken your time giving me all this information. Why now?"

"As I said, I'm not supposed to whisper a word to anyone, but I'm starting to feel very uneasy. I'm a hedge fund manager. I don't want to be involved with anything that smacks of major criminality. Still less murder. That's not what I signed up to when I agreed to give your father some investment advice."

"However did he persuade you to go along with any of this? You could have refused, couldn't you?"

"He finds out things about people, Juliet. Makes sure he's got something on everyone he works with."

"And what did he find out about you that kept you under his thumb?"

"A minor financial irregularity going back years. Not important, except I couldn't risk my partner finding out. I might have lost everything. My name in the industry? Too risky. I like what I earn. This car? The Mayfair flat? Need I go on?"

"Bloody hell!" Juliet muttered.

"He's a loose cannon, Juliet, your father, and he's beginning to scare the shit out of me."

CHAPTER 48 DAY 14

"LOUGHTY?'

"Yes, Oscar." The voice was soft, high-pitched, almost feminine.

"Have you read the papers today?"

"Not yet. What should I be looking for?"

"They've tumbled EncroChat."

"That's a turn-up. Hardly expected."

"Oh, I don't know. We're talking on Lokchat right now, aren't we."

"Always. Your phone to mine. Totally safe from snooping government security ears."

"The NCA haven't a clue. Don't know we exist. As it should be. Trouble with the boys using EncroChat is they're too high profile. Too many of them as well. Someone was bound to put their foot in it. Give the game away. Sixty thousand idiots. All a crowd of sad nouveaux. No idea how to conduct themselves. Like kiddies opening their Christmas stockings. A pile of relatively poor millionaires, if that isn't an oxymoron. Too many big cars, boats, houses. They're not the people who really run things. What I call the Ancienne Riche. Us, in other words. We number just fifteen hundred, all billionaires; and we know how to conduct ourselves.

"The NCA, run by Lynne Owens, now there's a lady, organised a sting against EncroChat, run by her deputy Matt Horne, Gold Commander of Operation Venetic, which netted fifty-four million in cash, can you believe, two tons of hard drugs, seventy-seven firearms, including AK-47s, machine guns, pistols and eighteen hundred rounds of ammunition. Like a bloody revolutionary's shopping list. On top of all that they uncovered plots to murder, kidnap and torture rivals. Pathetic. Absolutely pathetic. Amateur. Bungling. Reprehensible. Literally brings everything we're aiming for in the far right into disrepute."

"Hmph!"

"What was that, Loughty? Were you laughing at me?"

"No, Oscar. I would never laugh at you. We've the same aims, after all."

"My main contention here is that committing amateur crimes like these dabblers is one thing. But guns? Ammunition? What were they after? Robbing banks? Or political power. If the latter, you don't get that in a society as civilised as ours. You get it at the ballot box. That's where real power is secured. With the will of the people.

"Face it, man, even Hitler used the ballot box. He was elected. He didn't shoot his way into becoming Chancellor of Germany in 1933, then President the following year. I shall shortly be Chancellor of the Exchequer in the United Kingdom, not quite the same as Hitler's chancellorship, but ultimately leading to the same sort of power when I become Prime Minister."

"But, Oscar, you've used me to bring about the occasional termination. Extreme unction, as you seem to like calling it. That's what you employ me to do. I won't mention names, even though we're secure on this line."

"Only when absolutely expedient, dear boy. We use finesse. We're selective, not a band of anarchic thugs."

"But what about your boat, the Jayne? You told me it cost fifty million. Doesn't that stand out? Mark you out?"

"It's owned by a Panamanian company, which is part of a web so tangled I'm not even sure I could trace the owners if I wanted."

"But you are the owner, aren't you?"

"Of course I am, dear boy. But who's ever going to find that out."

"Named after your youngest, wasn't it?"

"Correct. I had her built after Jayne's birth. All my other children were thrusting, self-sufficient, pretty much from the word go. You know I can't stand disability. Wipe 'em out, I say. Hitler's view. The disabled. The queers. Blacks. Gypsies. Jews. Burden on society.

"You see, Jayne's type start off helpless, retiring, shy. But with encouragement they can make a real contribution. Jayne works with autistics, the mentally sub-normal; she's mad, if you ask me. Waste of valuable resources. Still, it's given her the confidence to do something she thinks is worthwhile. She's proud the boat's got her name. Helped build her self-esteem."

"You're doing this Budget shortly?"

"That's right. It's all but up and running."

"Will the PM approve it?"

"Don't joke, dear boy. Of course he will. With the present state of the economy he really has no choice. I've got the PM in my pocket. He's surrounded by toadying cretins. Hasn't a clue himself. Never had a proper job. Turns to me now for advice on every subject. I'm a businessman, turned politician. He's a politician and that's it. When I'm ready I'll gently oust him and when I'm in position we'll start to really shake things up, here and in Europe."

"You were never a Remainer, were you, Oscar?"

"God no, man. That bloody shambles run by commie frogs and Nazi krauts. Corrupt, wasteful, with no chance of change when twenty-eight countries need to agree how many sugars you need in your morning coffee? No, lad. Divide and rule. When we're out, properly out that is, we can show the buggers how to do things. That's when we'll be making the running."

"Any news on Letitia?"

"Yes, I heard from Bob. That's Detective Chief Superintendent Bob Walker."

"I know, you've mentioned him in the past."

"Bob thinks they've found her."

"Where is she? The UK? Abroad? Alive? Dead?"

"Dead."

"Dead? Where?"

"They found her headless, limbless corpse on Hampstead Heath."

"You don't sound too bothered."

"I'm not. Stupid damn woman. Thought she'd kept me in the dark about her Soviet games. I've known for years. Said nothing as long as it kept her occupied and out of my hair."

"Hmm. How were they able to identify her, then?"

"They're not yet certain, but they're working on it."

"Who's the one that's found her?"

"That private investigator recommended by Walker seems to have worked it out. The Pierre woman."

"The big black Jew you mentioned?"

"That's her."

"The one you said looked like a bloke?"

"I've changed my mind."

"Why?"

"I looked again. She's big. All of six feet and more. But, Loughty, she is all woman."

"But black."

"That's right."

"And Jewish."

"Right again."

"How does that square with your views on inferior peoples?"

"I'm still working on it. But, Loughty, I want her discreetly terminated. You understand? Walker likes her. And I have to tell you she's tough. I mean, like SAS tough. Her Israeli boyfriend teaches her martial arts. She knows how to kill. But she's wounded. Took a caning in the States. She's still operating, but right now she's weakened and she's vulnerable. Strike while you can."

"Isn't this one for Ainsley? He makes everything look like an accident."

"That's his trouble. Where I need him, he's little more than a clumsy labourer. Much like the rest of his brethren. Don't know why I ever used the man. The Anderton thing was a bloody mess. At least he got it right where my PA was concerned. Given the chance I'd have choked the bitch myself. Employed her on a fat salary for years, and what does she do? Starts snooping into my affairs. Almost certainly going to provide information to the Pierre woman. I couldn't have that.

"If you need to, lean on her old man. Matthew Pierre. Got Parkinson's. Lives near his daughter and they dote on each other. Should be some mileage there. Work on it, Loughty."

"Leave it with me, Oscar. I'll maybe give her something to think about first. A little gift that any Caribbean would appreciate. Something she'll understand. I might rope in her old man too."

"On second thoughts, leave it till after I've delivered the Budget. Then you can dispatch our black beauty. Worry about the old man later. Take your time. Enjoy yourself."

CHAPTER 49 DAY 14

THE CANE WAS LEAD-TIPPED, dripping blood, as it slashed the girl's lower back and tight round buttocks, already criss-crossed with weeping tramlines of red.

She screamed, "It's enough. Enough. Stop it now. Stop it, Cas."

The man, ginger-haired with ginger chest fuzz, also naked and sporting a huge erection, sweat running down his face and front, continued beating the girl who lay chained, spread-eagled and face down on the bed. "Lucinda's been a naughty girl," he snarled. "And what do we do to naughty girls?"

But she didn't respond. Her long blond hair was stuck to her neck and back like threads of straw. She too was bathed in perspiration which ran from her body, soaking the sheets beneath her. The rise and fall of her abdomen showed she was still breathing, just.

The man looked down at her, his lip curling in disgust. Reaching for a Kleenex on the bedside table he started wiping the semen off her back, but thinking better of it, threw the tissue into the waste basket.

Then he undid the padlocks securing her chains to the four corners of the bed, and turned her over onto her back, noticing that in her unconscious state she didn't wince. He made no attempt to rearrange her limbs into a more modest attitude, merely glancing with the same disdain at her arms lying across her face, her legs indecently wide.

The bedroom in the luxury St John's Wood apartment, close to Lord's Cricket Ground, was vast. The bed, a super king size. The room, decorated lavishly, if somewhat tastelessly in golds and white, to resemble someone's idea of a harem. Magnificent, Oriental rugs in pink and turquoise adorned the floor. The furnishings comprised mainly over-elaborate Louis Quinze. Sitting atop a burr walnut commode, decorated with brass corners and handles, a black packet of Treasurer cigarettes. Extracting one of the gold-tipped black smokes, Caspar lit it from the gold table lighter, inhaled deeply and sauntered over to an armchair, where he sat back with legs sprawled, waiting for the girl to recover consciousness.

It was an hour before she stirred into wakefulness, groaning and twisting as she tried to accommodate the pain in her back and buttocks.

"You'd better get showered, Lucinda. Can't get dressed with all that muck on your backside."

Twisting around, she made to sit up, hanging her legs over the side of the bed, wincing in agony. She remained like that for several minutes, her head bowed, hands on the bed either side of her. "All that muck happens to be my blood, you bastard. You said we'd play around a bit. Teacher and pupil, you said. How long have I been out?"

"'Bout an hour," he responded disinterestedly, pulling on what amounted to his fourth cigarette, its ash falling unnoticed on the fabulous rug from where a faint smell of burning issued.

"These wounds need proper dressing. You'd better take me to A&E."

"Don't be ridiculous. If I do that, they'll ask where you got the injuries from and I'll be done for common assault."

"No you won't," she said. "I'm hardly going to bring charges, am I?"

"Look, Lucy, it's late and I'm tired. I'll pay for you to get a cab, if you must. Otherwise there's plenty of plasters in the bathroom cabinet." He nodded in the direction of the en suite.

"God, Caspar. Wherever did you come from?"

"I'm heaven sent, darling. Plenty of women would give their eye teeth—"

"What? To have the shit beaten out of them."

"You didn't object."

"I begged you to stop."

"Isn't that part of the game? You begging me to stop, really meaning me to carry on. With you women 'No' always means 'Yes', doesn't it? Don't tell me you weren't having multiple…"

"No, I fucking wasn't having multiple anythings."

Groaning again, Lucinda gingerly stood up and padded softly into the bathroom where she found plasters and Savlon antiseptic which she brought out and handed to Caspar where he was sitting.

"What's this for." He stared up at her in amazement.

"What do you think it's for, you idiot. I want you to smear in on my back and then apply the plasters."

"Sorry."

Lucinda stood in front of Caspar, arms folded across her chest, medical things in hand, her long legs spread in what in any other circumstances might have been regarded as an erotic pose. "What the hell do you mean, 'Sorry'?"

"No can do."

"No can do?" she said, her voice rising. "You did this to me, now move yourself and help me put on the cream and plasters."

"I would, but I really can't stand the sight of blood."

"Fucking hypocrite. Where in Christ's name did I find you?" she enquired again.

"At a rather chic party, where I picked you up. I guessed you liked the car."

"The Testarossa you mentioned? I wouldn't have minded a ride in it sometime. Very nice, I suppose. I've seen better. You could afford better. Look at all this." She swept an arm around. "Doesn't your partner run something a bit more exotic? A Bugatti, you said. Now there's style."

"More to depreciate."

"Ever the finance man. Christ, you hurt me," she said, carefully reaching over her shoulder to apply the cream and plasters. "You're a real menace, you know. One day you might just kill someone."

"Or I might have already." He grinned.

"Boasting again. Do your other women put up with all your shit? What about that MP's wife you told me liked a good flogging?"

"She's not around at the moment. Seems her husband's been looking for her." He grimaced, as though some unwanted memory had disturbed the calm of his afternoon.

"How do you know?"

"Theo's going out with her daughter. They've no idea where she is."

"And you do?"

"This is getting boring, Lucy. Time for you to go. Get yourself an Uber."

"Just a minute," said Lucinda. "Don't just leave everything hanging in the air."

She'd been walking around the room, retrieving clothing as they talked, and was now dressed in a smart blue, off-the-shoulder frock, her shoulder bag hitched up. "What do you know about this missing woman?"

"Only that the silly bitch got what was coming to her," he muttered, sounding angry.

"Meaning what?"

"Meaning it's time for you to go, Lucinda. I mean now." He pointed to the door to the apartment. "And by the way, I'll send you a bill for the sheets."

CHAPTER 50 DAY 14

"**S**HE LIKE A FUCKIN' LOOSE CANNON." Nicolai was seated in the same Soho bar he'd last met with Letitia, a burner phone held to one ear. With his free hand he fidgeted nervously with the wire-rimmed spectacles on the table in front of him.

He'd waited more than two hours while the place, initially empty, had gradually filled up. His coffee had long since gone cold.

The voice at the other end of the connection was softly spoken. English. Educated. Amid the hubbub in the bar it could barely be heard. "Then do something about it, Nicolai."

"This the third time she stand me up. She take the piss."

"Didn't you hear me? Do something about it. It's expected of you."

"She get away with it in America."

"All badly planned, my friend."

"Not by me."

"Of course, by you. Who else?"

"Her husband. He fuck up my plans for her in America."

"Really? By all accounts the only person who fucked up your plans was the Pierre woman. It seems she acquitted herself rather convincingly when faced with the Harlem contingent. She and her Mossad boyfriend."

"I know, I know."

"And anyway, what were your plans for Letitia in America? Whatever they were, you didn't make them known to the Party. Furthermore, loose cannon or no, she fulfilled her obligations. No thanks to you."

"Now, she go crazy. St James killing. She say she in America. Not her. I say bollocks. What next? She go too far, too far." Nicolai was becoming ever more agitated.

"On that, at least we're agreed." The voice was beginning to sound bored.

"What I do now?"

"You finish off what you say you'd planned for this Filipek woman in America. I'm not interested in the details of what you had in mind. Just be grateful you didn't interrupt her before she completed her assignments. The Party would not have been pleased."

"Okay," Nicolai reluctantly agreed.

"And this time, don't trust the job to someone else. Do it yourself, Nicolai."

"Me?"

"Yes you, man. Who do you think I mean?"

"I Filipek's handler. I not a killer."

"Well you are now."

"Alright. Alright. If I got to. I'll kill the bitch," he said, determined now. Then added, "And I'll enjoy too. Maybe drag it out a bit. I know how."

Getting to his feet, he picked his glasses off the table and placed them resolutely back on the bridge of his nose.

"Just the ticket," said the voice. "Have fun."

CHAPTER 51 DAY 14

THE TINY BIRD WAS DEAD, its throat cut, feathers torn and shredded, blood seeping onto the shiny grey marble floor outside her flat. She stared at it for several moments, as though transfixed, wondering, *What in God's name…?*

Early evening, presumably none of the other tenants had arrived back from work to witness the plight of the poor little thing. An envelope propped against her front door contained a greetings card with an artwork depicting *Judith beheading Holofernes* by Artemisia Gentileschi. Her messenger was someone apparently educated. But then, inside, the printed note said:

Is time you stop investigation.

What sort of language is that? she wondered. A central European flavour? Russian? The little man with the old-fashioned glasses who'd already called her off? But then, the dead bird? Voodoo? Nasty.

Entering the apartment, she quickly fetched paper towelling to clear up the mess before anyone saw it. Then she wrapped the small creature in newspaper, to afford it some dignity, and deposited it in one of the waste bins outside the block ready for the council's litter people to collect.

"Poor little bugger," she murmured as she re-entered the apartment.

She wasn't fazed by the experience, more made sombre, perhaps. She'd need to look into the block security to find out how anyone might have entered without a key. Her own flat was secured with Banham locks, a central station alarm and there was CCTV both in the flat and in all the corridors and by the front entrance. She'd check it out in the morning. Right now, Risky was prancing around, demanding food and a cuddle.

Then her mobile rang. "Tamsin?" The voice sounded concerned.

"Yes, Papa," she replied, slipping off her jacket with one hand, then climbing onto one of the bar stools.

"How you doin', chile?"

"Still a bit sore. Stitches pulling. Could use a few days off. How about you, Pops?"

"Doin' fine. I have walk as far as de park today, and no wobbles."

"Hey, that's great. As soon as I'm done with this job we'll do a walk together."

"Listen, darlin', I have something to tell y'all."

At that, Tammy's heart sank into her boots. "I hope it's not bad news, Papa. Are you really okay?"

"Not me, chile. But when I get back from de walk, I fine a dead bird on my doorstep. Someone who know about Obeah."

"God, Papa."

"And dey have a card saying call off your darter from de investigation."

"Alors, merde," she murmured, feeling her throat tighten in fear for her father's life. "Tu dois faire très attention, Papa." (You must be very careful, Papa.)

"Bien sur, Tamsin."

"Toujours en français quand tu es inquiet." (Always in French when you're worried.)

"Oui, chérie, je dois et je vais," (Yes, darling, I must and I will), he responded, in perfectly accented French. Then he said, reverting to his familiar patois, "Whoever do dis ting don't frighten me none."

"No, Papa. But where you're concerned they frighten me. Listen, try not to go out for the time being, at least until I think it's safe for you. You can shop online, and I can supplement whatever else you need. I'll bring things around. Okay? And keep the front door locked at all times."

"You startin' to sound like my own mama now." He laughed.

"I wish I could always be as positive as you, Papa."

"Have to give life a smile, my chile."

They rang off. Their brief conversation left her exhausted, and so, quickly putting out a bowl of Risky's favourite chopped lamb with an additional bowl of crunchy cat food, she stripped off and wandered naked towards the shower. Standing under the scalding hot water, head up, eyes closed while it splashed all over her, she suddenly considered how she'd be if anything ever happened to Papa, and found herself weeping, her face cradled in her hands, her body convulsing.

He was the one constant in her life. The one person she could turn to for straight, unbiased advice. From a Catholic background, he was never judgemental about her own erratic lifestyle or promiscuity. He even accepted her baby might have been fathered by either a Muslim or a Jew. She suspected he'd also guessed about the habit. Not that either of them ever talked about it. It was there as a prop, not an obsession. She wouldn't be doing any lines, she told herself for the umpteenth time. At least, not yet. This baby was to have every possible advantage.

Lying naked on the bed after her shower she glanced down at her damaged body. The scars from the Syrian interlude at her neck, shoulder and leg, still throbbed from time to time, were still livid and would take months before they healed completely. The further scar she'd picked up in New York was still fresh, pink. She sighed. With white skin they would have eventually faded and blended in. Not so with black where, despite the best efforts of the two surgeons who'd attended the earlier, and now current injuries, they would remain forever as white lines, albeit as fine as could be achieved.

She sighed again. Hazards of her profession she'd learn to live with, she told herself. At least she was alive, and not facially or otherwise bodily disfigured, apart that is from her hands, badly scarred by the shuriken she'd used to free herself from plastic bonds in the Black Candles affair. Her once beautiful hands. With an involuntary shake of the head, she turned her mind to something else.

Thinking about the pregnancy, she smiled now, stroking the gently increasing bulge with her palms. She was expecting a baby, something that had never occurred to her she would want. Now, she wouldn't under any circumstances want to be without.

With a meow, one fully sated pussy cat leapt onto the bed and lay across Tammy's swelling tum and purred loudly. Stroking the cat behind the ears, Tammy watched as Risky gently kneaded and then licked her stomach, before gazing up at her mistress as though she understood about the pregnancy.

"You know, don't you, my darling," Tammy whispered. "You sense it all. And here we are, two black cats in love with each other."

CHAPTER 52 DAY 15

SHE'D SLEPT FITFULLY and woke with the remnants of a bad dream nudging at her. Risky, who'd slept cuddled up to Tammy under the duvet, now jumped off the bed, scampered into the kitchen and started protesting loudly that it was time for breakfast.

Having fed the little imp, Tammy fixed herself a bowl of muesli and a coffee. She was meeting Rose this morning at nearby Gail's bakery and café in Salusbury Road for an English fry-up. Not her usual, which generally comprised a toasted hunk of wholewheat bread, cut into quarters, with Marmite, peanut butter, cheddar and honey on each portion, eaten strictly in that order. Healthy, fulfilling and, she accepted, a tad eccentric. Selling over thirty different types of bread, real bread that is, Tammy's mouth watered at the prospect. Dov had agreed to attend the bakery this morning as well.

It wasn't necessary to dress to impress, and Tammy chose a pair of black jeans and a pale blue V-neck sweater.

Rose was seated at a corner table when Tammy arrived, in her usual two-piece grey working suit. Glancing up at Tammy, she smiled broadly. "Wow! You could grace any catwalk in the world."

"Thank you, Rose. You know Bob Walker said exactly the same thing. Almost word for word. You're both too kind. You don't compare notes, by any chance?" She grinned. "But really, I'm far too old, too cynical and too weather-beaten."

"You could have earned a fortune as a model," said Rose.

"What?" responded Tammy. "And given up the chance of being attacked, beaten and scarred for life? Never!"

"Well, it was just a thought." Rose smiled sheepishly.

"Sweet of you, but truly, I'd have been bored witless."

"I can well believe it." She was flushed, as though she'd been wheezing.

"Rose?" Tammy enquired. "Have you been coughing again?"

"No, no, love, I'm fine. Really I am."

"Okay, darling. If you say so," said Tammy, bending to kiss her on the cheek. "Have you ordered?"

"I'll just have a coffee and croissant, sweetheart."

"I'll go order," said Tammy, and went off to the counter to organise the food and drink for both of them.

About two minutes after she'd sat down opposite Rose, Dov arrived in jeans and sweatshirt, unshaven, drawn and distressed. He sat next to Rose so he faced Tammy.

"What's wrong, Dov?" asked Tammy, guessing what the answer would be.

"Esther's divorcing me." He slumped, so lost Tammy could have hugged him.

"I'm so sorry, Dov. I know you've had issues, but thought maybe you could reach some sort of accord."

He shrugged. "I think she's going to get difficult. We own the apartment jointly, but she says she wants it all as she's going to need somewhere to bring up the baby."

"Can't you get a divorce lawyer to advise you on both joint custody and a share of the value of the apartment?"

"It doesn't look that way at the moment. And I think she's going to play hardball. I mean, I'm not sure I recognise her at all right now. She's been saying some terrible things."

"For example?" asked Tammy, fearing she could guess what might be coming next.

Leaning forward, his elbows on the table, Dov said, "Esther claims the baby isn't mine. She says she's been having an affair for months with a man she says she's in love with."

She couldn't look him on the eye. It had been rape, after all. But if she were carrying Nabil's child would she ever be able to confess it to Dov? Never! He'd be devastated.

"Dov, it's just dreadful," said Tammy, gently clasping his hand.

"I know I deserve it, Tammy. I'm as much to blame as anything. But still, it comes as a shock."

"Listen, let me get you something to eat, won't you?"

"Just coffee for me, thanks. Really," he said, as Tammy got up to order for him.

The food and drinks arrived a short while later, and Tammy, her mouth watering, contentedly surveyed the contents of her plate. The fry-up looked delicious, comprising two rashers of streaky bacon, chipolatas, fried eggs, mushrooms, tomatoes, baked beans, French fries, fried bread and black pudding. Glancing at the steaming black pudding, Tammy couldn't help thinking, Hmm. Not exactly kosher. Maman wouldn't be pleased.

An unkempt individual on the next table of the now rapidly filling restaurant, surveying Tammy's plate, observed, "You forgotten anything, darlin'?"

"Oh my, you're right," exclaimed Tammy, jumping up to the astonishment of Rose and Dov.

"Woss that, love, the bleedin' kitchen sink?" he said and let out a loud guffaw.

"What can you have possibly forgotten?" asked Rose, wide-eyed.

"A knife and fork." Tammy grinned, scuttling off to retrieve some cutlery. Settling down again, she turned to the other two. "Are you sure you won't join me? It's so good." But they both demurred.

Eventually, finishing her breakfast, wiping her mouth on the paper napkin and allowing herself a sigh of satisfaction, Tammy took a gulp of her coffee, then said to Rosemary, "So, talk to me, Rose. What have we got? DNA back on the corpse?"

"Not yet," Rose responded. "I've told them to move it along. Said it's urgent."

"Well, let's talk about the New York murders," she said. "Three Russian dissidents, according to the press. Each murder might have been undetectable, even though two were recorded on CCTV, but for the fact that our killer insisted the world recognise her by her outrageous costumes. We know it's either Letitia, or this double of hers."

"Then there's the St James's Hotel killing," said Rose. "About three weeks after Letitia apparently returned. So, was that Letitia too, or was it the double?"

Shaking her head, Tammy said, "We're still in the dark. If the DNA is a positive ID for Letitia, which it will be I'm sure, then if my boys at Incognita can get a fix on the return of the two women we might be a little closer to unravelling this mystery."

Dov then added, "You still need a motive. Her husband may have detested Letitia, but would that be enough to want to kill her? And right before getting promoted to Chancellor? I don't think so."

"Juliet let me know that her boyfriend Theo, a hedge fund manager, is the partner of a thoroughly disreputable character. A wealthy young man who delights in beating up women. Caspar da Silva was seeing Letitia, Juliet tells me, and that Letitia was frequently decorated with bruises and scratches. Those that could be seen. God knows what was hidden by her clothing."

"Hmm," said Rose. "So could the death of Letitia, if it is her, be due to a sex game gone wrong?"

"I'll talk to this da Silva, see what I can find," said Tammy. "Unless you want to, Rose?"

"No, I'm good for now."

"Okay, my dear. I'll chase that one up."

"Anything else we need to think about?" Rose asked.

"There is still the question of Pierce's death. Was that murder? Bob Walker tells me he learned from the Geneva police of the peculiar death of one Tomas Breuillon."

"Peculiar?" Dov asked. "Where does that fit in with everything else?"

"Smell of booze, but not enough in his system to kill. No pre-existing conditions like heart, stroke et cetera. An explosion in his kitchen. A beer can too close to the stove. Might have burned him, but again not lethally."

"So? What's the connection you see with the present killings?" Dov asked again.

"I'll tell you," said Tammy. "In Tomas Breuillon's property the police found a second passport, with what was clearly Breuillon's photo."

"And what is the significance of that?" Dov enquired.

"It was the passport of Mr William Davenport, pilot of the Cessna that failed to catch Pierce. The one that flew off when he fell to his death."

"I'll make some enquiries," said Rose. "See what I can find out."

"When is Mountford due to make his Budget speech?" Dov wondered.

"Any day now. It seems we still haven't a date fixed. Also, Bob tells me that whilst it was intended Mountford should never be promoted to Chancellor, it doesn't matter if he is. When we've got what we want on him, we can have him arrested anyway."

"Good to hear," said Dov, nodding.

"The thing is," Tammy went on. "If it transpires he's not in any way involved in these murders, the PM and certainly Bob both still want him out of the way. The man, on the political front alone, is a menace, quite apart from his likely proclivity to murder. But with his extremist views, an individual like that can do untold damage."

"How will you get rid of him, if there's nothing linking him to any of the killings?" Rose asked.

"I'll discuss that later with Bob and the PM if it's needed. People don't realise the danger to society of the so-called intellectual terrorist. I don't just mean the Kim Philbys of this world, who defect. I also mean some MPs. Think of Tony Wedgewood Benn, a so-called committed ultra-left Socialist, who on his death left nothing to any left wing party. A man who in true Socialist fashion, kept his wealth tied up in the Stansgate Trust, so there'd be minimum death duties," Tammy added cynically, before continuing. "A man described by the KGB, plus Oleg Gordievsky, the defecting Soviet spy, as an Unnecessary Simpleton given to lying and fantasising. A man too stupid to recruit. One who, if he'd been elected to the deputy leadership of the Labour Party, would, in their joint opinion, have overseen a catastrophic upset in the East–West balance of power during the years of the Cold War."

"A frightening prospect. Socialism in the UK used to be a passport to equality of opportunity," said Dov dolefully. "Now? There are elements I simply don't recognise within the Party any more."

"So you see, right wing extremism, of the type fostered by Mountford, himself an apologist for Hitler's brand of fascism, is as potentially dangerous as the left wing variety with which we are so familiar. Finally," Tammy went on, "there's the highly suspicious death of Georgia Keith and also the St James's killing to look at. Come to think of it, a further view of the Kevin Anderton death might be worth investigating as well. It seems Mountford and his wife are a pair of ideally suited psychopaths, aren't they, albeit at opposite ends of the political spectrum."

"What about the Geneva death? This man Davenport? What will you do there?" asked Rose.

"I'll confront Mountford with that. See how he reacts. He's prone to bouts of rage. It might be interesting. I'll leave you to snoop around a bit on the matter of Kevin Anderton and the St James's murder. The first is on hold, the second, not specifically linked to Letitia or Mountford. At least not quite yet. Take a look. Keep me in the loop."

"So, Tammy, what's on your agenda for today?" Rose asked.

"I'm in the office this morning," she replied. "Then I'll try to get hold of Mr da Silva. See what he has to say for himself. Let me know the minute you get the DNA results, won't you."

"Of course I will," Rose responded.

As the three of them got up to leave a tall man in a tweed sports jacket and brogues approached them. Smooth-shaven with pallid skin, he had an athlete's build, and when he spoke the voice was curiously effeminate. "Ms Pierre?" he enquired.

Turning to face him, she had a feeling this was someone she didn't particularly want, or need, to meet. "Who's asking?" she said.

"The name's Loughty, Ms Pierre." He smiled, revealing tiny, pointed shrew-like teeth, and breath, or else body odour, like ammonia. His pupils, dilated to black marbles, bored into Tammy's, leaving her feeling unsettled.

"Do I know you, Mr Loughty?"

"No, Ms Pierre, you don't. Not at the moment," he said, walking away. "But we'll get to know each other by and by."

CHAPTER 53 DAY 15

SHE'D DELIBERATELY CHOSEN to wear a short skirt, and made no attempt to stop it riding up further as she sat down, crossing her legs, and letting it reveal an eye-popping expanse of black thigh, together with the very obvious, and still angry, scar caused by the sniper's bullet.

She'd judged correctly the scar would fascinate him, watching his gaze arrow in as soon as he caught sight of it.

With the pregnancy her small bust had filled out somewhat, giving the man something more to cast an appraising eye over. And cast an eye he did, as though weighing up the offerings of a back-street Middle Eastern brothel. Ignoring her face, his attention focused on her bosom, which he lingered over, before returning time and again to her legs and in particular the blemish.

It was easy to see why women found him fascinating, the dark brown eyes were piercing and gave Tammy the impression that he was not only undressing her, but fondling her wherever he stared. A slight flutter in her chest confirmed he'd be a challenge. Men like this always were. Dominating him would be an adventure. A dark place she'd walk into without a moment's hesitation. But as with her interview with Juliet, it was something to leave on file. Right now, she was all too aware, she might be facing a cold-blooded murderer.

He was the senior partner, together with Theo Cranfield, of Maerland da Silva Capital Management, the hedge fund business. Situated in a modern block in central London, it presented an impressive sight on approach, with its dignified café au lait decorative vertical girders straddling towering Gothic windows, all within a framework of pale grey mottled concrete.

Inside was no less impressive with the exterior colour scheme carried throughout the reception area and common parts.

Caspar da Silva had agreed to see her and assist in any way he might, although Tammy hadn't given him chapter and verse for the reasons she wanted to talk to him.

The décor in the reception area was an amalgam of muted browns and beiges, mixed with magnolia and splashes of gold. It all oozed wealth, the thick-pile carpet alone so lush it cushioned the soles of her feet like a sponge mattress.

There was no gainsaying the affluence of the man, who, when he emerged to greet Tammy, was wearing a tight cuff, balloon-sleeve, white open-neck shirt Tammy guessed was charmeuse silk. She appraised the slim-fit style of the Yves Saint Laurent black chinos and the garish gold chain and medallion around the man's neck. Neat shiny black shoes, she reckoned, by Jimmy Choo. A fashion fiend, much like herself, if somewhat overstated in his case.

It was common knowledge hedge fund managers earned colossal sums. Ray Dalio of Bridgewater Associates, head of a $160 billion hedge fund. George Soros of Soros Fund Management, Ken Griffin of Citadel and others, all earned vast sums in managing their clients' money, hedging investments against unpredictable world stock exchange fluctuations.

Dalio alone was reckoned to earn in the region of two billion dollars a year, and to be worth around eighteen billion dollars. He made his first share purchase in Northeast Airlines, age twelve, tripling his investment when the airline made a merger. His bachelor's degree was in finance.

George Soros gained bachelor's and master's degrees at the LSE in philosophy, believed by many to be the ideal vehicle for advanced computer scientists. Today his estimated wealth is put at eight billion dollars.

Ken Griffin, with an estimated thirty-two-billion-dollar fortune, graduated in 1989 with an economics degree.

What all these individuals had in common was an absolute belief in their own skills, ably demonstrated by their success, a maverick desire to take risks, albeit calculated ones, and in all cases a facility in finance and mathematics second to none.

Caspar was going to be an interesting case to investigate.

With a boxer's chest and shoulders, but otherwise no more than average height, he exuded the confidence of a man who might have been well over six feet. Indeed, ushering Tammy into his office, she towered over him.

Tammy would later describe his office as extraordinary. A vast ebony desk sat squarely on a rich black carpet. The walls were white and decorated with an array of pictures depicting an assortment of artistic puzzles. In particular there were several of a never-ending staircase, by a variety of artists, including the most famous, Penrose Stairs, but also a number of far more elaborate paintings in a mixture of Gothic and other styles.

Seeing her staring at the pictures, da Silva asked, "You like them?"

"They're fascinating," she said, aware of how much they reflected the owner's proclivities.

"All originals," he announced proudly.

"Amazing," she acknowledged, turning to face da Silva and surveying the array of executive puzzles on the desktop. What caught her eye in particular was what looked like a six-sided, diamond-shaped Rubik's Cube.

Tammy was gazing at it when he said, "It's far harder than the ordinary Rubik's, which I can complete in about twenty seconds. Watch," he said, pulling the pyramid shape in all directions till it was no longer recognisable. Then, almost faster than she could follow, spinning the toy, this way and that, he rearranged it into its original diamond, pyramid shape. Seeing her astonishment, he laughed. Once more, Tammy could see why women found him irresistible. That combination of charm, faux modesty and success.

"You wanted to see me?" he asked, glancing at the gold amulet between her breasts. Then, before going further, he said, "Are you French? You've got a sort of accent?"

"My mother was French. I spent the first years of my life in France. It's really my first language."

"That slightly throaty R?"

"Not unique to France. A Norfolk dialect is similar."

He nodded, then changing the subject, he said, "What is that thing around your neck?"

"It's an amulet given me by my father. The inscription is in Hebrew, designed to protect."

"And does it?" he said, emulating Oscar Mountford's similar enquiry.

"Of course not," she said. "It merely expresses a sentiment."

"Why Jewish?" he asked. "You're not a Jew."

"Quite right," she replied. "I'm not a Jew. I'm a Jewess."

"Oh!" For the first time he appeared bemused. "But. But."

"But I'm black."

"I didn't mean."

"I'm sure you didn't, Mr da Silva. And I suspect some of your best friends are Jews."

"As a matter of fact—"

"Shall we get on, then?" she interrupted.

"Of course, of course," he said, settling back into his huge executive chair with something resembling relief, and indulging himself the luxury of ogling Tammy who permitted her skirt to ride up even further.

"Before we start, Mr da Silva, I wonder if I might ask you to tell me something about yourself?"

"Sure." He smiled. "And it's Caspar, please. Well, what would you like to know?"

"How you started in this business? Something about your background, your education. It may seem as though I'm prying, but it may help me to get a fix on what it is I'm trying to work out."

"And just what is it you're trying to work out? You weren't very clear when you asked for this interview."

"Bear with me, Mr da Silva. It'll all become clear as we go along."

"Okay." He shrugged. "Whatever you say. The business was started by my father, Emmanuel, together with a partner, Rodrigo Maerland. Both their families originated in Portugal, coming here in the first half of the twentieth century. Rodrigo is retired. My father bought him out at the time he stopped work. He died some years ago, and I inherited the business. Theo is brilliant, and I was happy to make him a junior partner, at the right time."

"Your education?" enquired Tammy.

"Harvard, a mathematics degree, followed by an MBA. All top honours. Extremely easy." He smiled. "They wanted me to do a PhD and then become a lecturer. I wasn't interested. No money in it."

He had the disconcerting habit of turning left and right while talking as though on the lookout for predators, so she was never quite sure whether he was talking to her, or merely thinking aloud.

"And now?"

"And now, you can see for yourself." He swept an arm around indicating the room they were in.

"You're in your element."

"Entirely. I think in numbers all the time. I can tell you the exchange rate on a daily basis of the pound against dozens of other currencies. I know the workings of all the world's major economies, and innumerable minor ones. When it comes to company results, I can reel them off by the cart-load."

"I'm impressed," she said, deciding it was time to test the water, to seek a reaction. In between gazing about, da Silva's eyes still roamed the length of Tammy's thighs, as though mesmerised by them. Concentrating on the reaction she might get, Tammy said, "We believe Letitia Mountford is dead."

"What?" he said, his face hardening as he glanced slightly to the right. In her book, left suggested the truth, right and the speaker was lying? Hardly scientific, but worth noting. "What do you mean, dead?"

"I should have thought I was being clear enough. A headless, limbless body was found on Hampstead Heath a few weeks ago. It had lain undiscovered for a number of weeks."

"How do you know it's her, if it's just a body?"

"We're conducting DNA tests, but we're pretty sure we've found her." It was too soon to gauge anything from his reaction. So she moved to the old ploy of asking him a question which would elicit a truthful reply to see which way he turned his head. "You knew Letitia, didn't you, Mr da Silva?"

With only the tiniest of hesitations, he said, "Yes," and she observed he turned slightly left as he replied.

"I'm led to believe you and she were conducting a clandestine affair."

"Rubbish," he snarled, looking to the right. All pretence of friendly good nature vanished. That glance again.

"She frequently came home with cuts and bruises. Did you assault her, Mr da Silva?"

"Don't be ridiculous," he muttered, bowing his head.

"You've a reputation for violence with women, sir. I mean, extreme violence."

"Really? And where did you hear that?"

"It's not important where I heard it."

"She was a kickster."

"Who was?"

"Your precious Letitia. Alright, so we did have something going for a while."

He wasn't concentrating on Tammy's legs any more. "At last, we seem to be getting somewhere. So tell me, what's a kickster?"

"Someone who needs more and more highs to get the sort of satisfaction they're looking for."

"Like being beaten?"

Da Silva shrugged. "The sex was never enough. She got weirder and weirder. Wanted me to cut her, on the arms. Did it herself when I wouldn't. She wanted threesomes and more. I took her to some singles clubs where she'd pick the first bloke she came across, irrespective of his age or appearance, and go off with him, then she'd be gone days at a time."

"Which clubs, Mr da Silva?"

"Mainly one in Sloane Street called Rags. Pretty upmarket place."

"What was Oscar's view about all this?"

"Total disinterest. He wanted to get rid of her, but couldn't while he was waiting for this promotion. It would've looked bad to the press and public."

"You worked for him in a professional capacity."

"Yes."

"What was he like to work for?"

"Nothing unusual. He trusted my judgement and let me get on with things for him."

"Tell me more about Letitia and what she got up to. For example, what happened when she got back from one of these club jaunts?"

"More than once she came back with traces of blood on her clothes. She refused to tell me what that was about. I saw her go off with one unlucky sod, and recognised his face in the papers a few days later when he was the subject of a report into a terrible beating. I asked about it, but she said it was nothing to do with her. Then she started taking it out on me. Where she'd been happy if I slapped her around a bit, she now started getting rough, and I mean really rough, this time with me. Punched me in the face more than once. Threatened me with a bloody kitchen knife. She wanted to know what it'd be like to kill someone. Hinted that she knew already. How could she know? She needed to be stopped. Permanently. She was becoming a bloody menace."

"Did you decide to stop her, Mr da Silva?"

"What?"

"Did you kill her? Did you kill Letitia Mountford?"

"No I didn't." Nonplussed? It was impossible to interpret the response's veracity.

"But you thought it was necessary to stop her?"

"That's not what I said. I said she needed to be stopped. Not that I felt it was my job to do that."

"Mr da Silva, your Ferrari is on the ANPR records as having been in the vicinity of the Mountford home and later on the Heath at the same time as we believe Letitia returned from the States."

He went white. "You're not suggesting I could get Letitia into the boot of that vehicle?"

"That's exactly what I'm suggesting. Your vehicle has eight hundred cubic feet of cargo space when the rear seats are folded in. More than sufficient to stow a body."

"I didn't kill her," he muttered.

"Then you won't mind if we subject the trunk of your car to DNA testing."

"Help yourself. It's all clean."

"Meaning what, Mr da Silva? That you've eradicated all trace of Letitia?"

"I'm not saying anything more. If you want to question me further, it'll be by the police with my lawyer present. You're not police, you're nothing but a small-time private investigator."

"That's correct," agreed Tammy, getting up to leave. "Thank you for your time, Mr da Silva. I'll be in touch as you've suggested, with the police."

"You'll forgive me if I don't shake hands." Da Silva scowled. "Bitch got all she deserved. You won't find anything more in the car. Look all you want. While I think of it, have you spoken to the angelic Theo yet? You might find some surprises there."

Instructive, she pondered as she left. 'Bitch got all she deserved?' What did that mean? And, we 'won't find anything more', he'd said. Motive? Not too hard to find. A sex game gone wrong. Over to DCI Rosemary Sharpe for an in-depth session with Mr da Silva. She couldn't wait.

And Theo, she wondered. Angelic? What was that supposed to mean? What light might he be able to throw on events?

"NICOLAI?"

"Is Nick. Please? Is Nick. Everyone say Nicolai. Filipek, she call me Nicolai."

"Okay, Nick. For Chrissake."

"Da Silva?"

"Yeah, it's me. Who the hell else were you expecting, then?"

"Is done?"

"Yeah, yeah."

"She dead? Filipek? Larissa?" The voice was earnest, probing.

"Yeah. Like I said. Larissa. Letitia. Filipek. Philips. Mountford. Whatever the fuck you want to call her. She's dead. Okay? You can get off my case now."

"It is you who have kill her? I have to know."

"Who else do you think killed her, then? The man outside Catesby's?"

"What is this, Catesby's?"

"Nothing, man. Nothing. Just an old-fashioned phrase." He sighed, exasperated.

"You have not answer my question. Have you kill her? Has to be you. No-one else, or deal is off."

"Deal? Deal?" he shouted. "Since when did you call blackmail a deal."

"What you like to call it. Is our terms. Please. She is dead? You have kill her? We have arrange welcome for the black lady in America. Oscar try the same, but we get there first. Filipek see signs something happening, but don't know what, so she panic, run away. Leave evidence behind. Stupid woman. Think she so clever. Kill and wear clown's clothes. She is dead, yes?"

"I told you, she's dead. And yes. For the record, I killed her. I don't need to keep thinking about it or being reminded of it."

"You go to America to kill her, yes?"

"Enough of this bloody interrogation."

"Where you dump her body?"

"I said it's enough. I'm not answering any more of your damned questions."

"You have debt to pay."

"Well it's fucking paid. Now will you get off my back?"

"Money laundering and insider dealing for Mr Mountford." The voice sounded more confident now. "Make lot of, lot of money. You go to jail long time."

"Do you think it needs repeating?"

"American jail not nice place. You get extradited. You get well buggered in American prison." He started laughing, hiccupping and coughing with what sounded like the mirth of the victorious.

"No more, Nicolai. You got what you wanted."

"Filipek is silly woman. Pretend she not want to kill. She told be discreet. She disobey instruction. Kill dissidents, is good. But she make a game. Stupid. She mad. I think she want excitement. Rebellion. Perhaps bored?"

"Sure, she was bored. I'm getting bored too, Nicolai."

"You don't cross the Party, my friend. She have her fun. Now she pay the price. Oscar Mountford be relieved. Off the hook. Shot of wife. Kill birds with a stone."

"Oscar knows nothing about our arrangement. And he doesn't need to know."

"Of course. Oscar the Chancellor." The voice chuckled, then changed abruptly, sounded concerned. "Is nothing in press? Why not?"

"There will be. Any day now."

"Good. Perhaps the Party make contact with Oscar soon. Make a useful ally."

"Oscar? An ally? To whom? You Russkis? Do me a favour. He'd rather have his balls cut off."

"Still."

"No 'still' about it. And if you lean on me any more, I'll take my chances here or in the States. With the right lawyers, and I can afford the very best, I reckon I could justify enough of my trades to keep me out of prison. Or at worst, to get a suspended sentence."

"Up to you, da Silva. I say, bye, bye." The voice paused. "For now."

"**B**OB?"

"Oscar."

"What news? Is your black friend any closer to verifying what's happened to my wife?"

"We think so."

"I'm listening."

"Oscar, as I've already mentioned, Tammy Pierre is pretty certain she's identified the body found on the Heath, those weeks ago, as being that of Letitia."

"I know, you've told me this. We've been all over it. Nothing new. The limbless one in the newspapers?"

"That's right."

"But are you saying the Pierre woman's still not absolutely sure? Taking her time, isn't she? How much longer till we can nail it?"

"We're conducting DNA tests right now, as you will of course be aware."

"I knew you had some of your people nosing around here with their cotton buds, jars of liquid and evidence bags, but I never questioned what it was they were hoping to find."

"Oscar, please accept my condolences. I'm only sorry to be the harbinger of such sad news. You must be devastated."

"On the contrary, dear boy. You know perfectly well the woman was a thorn in my side. Never knew where she was going or what she might be up to next. Truth be told, I'm delighted she's gone."

"I see. Well, there's not much I can add to that. Of course, the body, when it is formally identified, won't be released for burial for some time."

"Quite. Quite."

"Don't you want to know who is responsible for her murder?"

"Of course, dear boy. Was just about to enquire."

"In fact, we're not yet ready to make any arrests. Tammy has identified one very possible suspect, but I'm not at liberty to say whom at this stage."

"Anyone I might know? Or just some random stranger." There was a moment's silence, then, "Or someone she met on one of her jaunts?"

"Sorry, Oscar, still can't say."

"I don't like her, you know."

"Who don't you like, Oscar?"

"This black private eye."

"She has a name, Oscar."

"Pierre, then. I do know. She's bloody rude."

"I'd be willing to bet she rubbed you up the wrong way. Not too difficult, I'd wager. She's a feisty woman. Not easily intimidated."

"A Jew as well. Not like us."

"For heaven's sake, man. You're beginning to sound like some sort of ultra-right extremist. Next, you'll be trying to persuade me of the concept of white supremacy."

"Well? Aren't we?"

"Please, Oscar. You're in line for a top government post. Even if you think like that, you can't be talking like that. The days of Mosley's anti-Semitic rants in the East End are history. The world's grown up a bit since then. Racism is the province of a vociferous extremist minority mob."

"They used to lynch blacks in the US. And not all that long ago."

"I know. In the force we're well aware the last lynching took place as recently as 1981. A lad, nineteen-year-old Michael Donald, was beaten to death by Ku Klux Klan members, his body hung from a tree."

"Any idea what happened to his killers?"

"As a matter of fact I do. Henry Hays was executed in the chair, James Knowles gave evidence against Hays and got life. A third was convicted as an accomplice and the fourth died before his trial was completed."

"We used to have public hangings in England."

"Pretty barbaric, don't you think?"

"Damn good deterrent though."

"Against what? Don't you know, when there was hanging for the stealing of a loaf of bread, men still stole. When you're hungry…"

"The public wants to see a return of the death penalty."

"That's debatable. And execution is no deterrent."

"In whose opinion?"

"As a matter of fact, Albert Pierrepoint."

"Albert Pierrepoint? You are joking, of course. Pierrepoint was Great Britain's official executioner from 1931 to 1956. It was he who officiated at the Nuremberg executions, which took a number of good men who'd made Germany into the power it was."

"A power that lost the War. As for Pierrepoint's credentials, you should know he is on record as having said, and here I'll quote, 'I do not now believe that any of the hundreds of executions I carried out has in any way acted as a deterrent against future murder.'"

"You seem to know a lot about it."

"Of course I do, Oscar, I'm a policeman. And I'd add," he went on to say, "and I'm quoting Pierrepoint again, 'Capital punishment, in my view, achieved nothing except revenge.'"

"Isn't that enough, then? Revenge? Isn't justice and the scales all about revenge?"

"No, my friend. The scales are all about fairness in the judicial process."

"Well, we'll see about that when I'm in a position of real influence. Meanwhile, I don't need to kowtow to this black Jew any more. Mosley would have known how to deal with her and her type."

"Oscar, you're beginning to alarm me. You'll be threatening Tammy with death next."

"No comment," replied Mountford, and hung up.

CHAPTER 56 DAY 15

A T JUST ELEVEN YEARS OF AGE the boy had already been around six feet tall, a man in all but years and maturity. His father had disappeared months ago, completely losing touch with the wife and son, leaving them to fend for themselves. He'd stormed out after a fight with the lad he'd spent years abusing, that had left him with a bloodied, broken nose, swearing never to return. He'd kept his promise.

In order to make ends meet the mother had resorted to casual prostitution, frequently arriving home in the early hours, drunk and ranting. A cadaverous individual in her mid-fifties, she was tall and angular, with sunken cheeks and an ash-grey complexion, flat-chested and with jutting hips and thinning, curly, dyed blond hair. She eagerly took over the practice of abuse where the father had left off, holding her son utterly within her sway.

The youngster was twelve years old the first time he'd had sex. It was with his mother, and it became an increasingly required activity.

She'd ride him like a horse. "You're a big lad, ain't you, for twelve years old. I seen ya jerkin' off. Well, you come before me and I'll have your hide, my boy," she said, eyeing a baseball bat that decorated one wall. He had no doubt she'd use it, having administered it at least once while his father still lived at home. More afraid of her than he ever was of his father, the boy had done as she'd insisted, coming copiously when she'd finally let out a long drawn-out sigh of satisfaction and indicated, grudgingly, it was his turn now. "Get on with it, then," she muttered. "And be bloody quick, 'aven't got all day."

The sight of her stringy, blue-veined arms and legs revolted him, at the same time fascinating him. She left her smell on him, a sour stench like rotting seaweed. It appalled him that he couldn't hold back, even began dreaming of the sex he had with her. Found himself staring at tall, slender women wantonly. If they had any disability, he would find himself aroused immediately. The greater the disability, the greater his arousal. Unable to contain himself, he'd choked one woman he'd met on an online dating site to death, while they were having sex. He imagined it was his mother, and realised he'd needed more.

Moving around the country he found he was able to kill almost at will. Always meticulous, it never failed to amaze him how gullible women could be when he insisted on wearing surgical gloves during sex, on the pretext that until he got to know them better, it was safer for them both this way. Some of them found it and him intriguing, wondering what made him tick, determined to find out. None survived long enough. He had no police record and there was no DNA left at any murder scene to enable any authority to track him down.

He resembled his mother, being extremely tall and gangling, with overlarge hands and feet and floppy dark hair. Equally cadaverous, women seemed drawn to him, like moths to a flame. He presented a danger, something to pursue and tame. Many of his victims cried out in pleasure during sex, in the moments before they died.

Searching the dark web, Ephraim Loughty, after the American actor Ephraim Zimbalist Jr, popular around the late 1950s early '60s, whom his mother idolised, deduced there was a market for his services and started hiring himself out. Online sites coaching the use of guns, knives and skills in martial arts equipped the man for his chosen profession. He looked more like a computer geek than a hired killer, and it all helped him mask his identity. Other than women of a certain leaning, he attracted little interest or attention from the general population of females.

And now, the man ran his hand up and down the length of her. A sensuous caress. It was almost as though he could hear her respond softly in his ear; feel her react so she might nudge up closer to him. They fitted together like two pieces of a jigsaw puzzle. She was his. All of her. She'd been with him as long as he could remember, she as part of the family that had preceded her, and he loved her. He knew they'd never be parted. In the general scheme of things, that's just how it was. With her close at hand he could handle any situation, no matter how challenging, no matter how dangerous. She made him feel safe, in control, untouchable, a mighty, mighty man. He sighed, smiled and went on polishing her till she shone. Then he screwed her suppressor into place, and the gun was ready to fire.

Dusk, a clear evening and Queen's Park was chill and empty, save for the solitary woman who had been proceeding swiftly around the one-mile perimeter. She looked tired, and had a lameness that became more pronounced the further she paced. He'd been following her from as far as he might, observing her every movement. Long and lean, with close-cropped hair and a smallish bust visible through her flimsy tight-fitting T-shirt, the scar high up on her thigh, the cause of the stumble, apparent just below the hem of her ultra-brief running shorts.

Sensing familiar moments of arousal, he wished he had more time. He'd make her squeal. He made them all squeal, he grinned, moistening his dry lips. Mama wouldn't have been best pleased. But then, Mama wasn't here to complain, or to take the baseball bat to him. Forcing himself to concentrate on the task he was being paid for, Loughty made to edge as near to her as he could, without being detected. The gun was cocked and he was ready.

* * * * *

Tammy froze the moment she heard the familiar click of a Heckler & Koch USP 45 being readied to shoot. From innumerable visits to shooting ranges she'd come to recognise the sounds of a variety of semi-automatics. With an effective firing range of fifty metres, the assailant would want to get as close to his target as possible.

The scream of a gaggle of geese flying in V-formation directly overhead held the world in momentary stasis.

Then she heard the double thump of a silenced gun, and as she dropped to the ground, witnessed two shells from three shots take lumps of metal from one of the support columns of the Queen's Park bandstand, close to where her head had been a moment earlier.

Tiring after her evening's gentle jog, she'd elected to curtail her exercise routine, opting to short cut across the park, passing by the east side of the bandstand, which supported six steps leading to the stage, on her way home. Completed in 1887, the octagonal Grade II listed building was an elegant Victorian structure, occupying pride of place in the centre of the park.

The jolt as she hit the turf disturbed the stitches in her most recent wound, causing her to groan involuntarily as they pulled and tore at her flesh, still in no way weakening her vigilance. Quickly twisting to one side, she sought any cover she could find, for the moment only the steps on her side of the bandstand offering some, albeit scant, protection.

Climbing onto the stage wouldn't be an option, so, hopelessly exposed out here, she rolled and scrabbled her way around the structure as fast as her pain-wracked body would allow, putting it between herself and her antagonist. Hearing the repeated crack of the semi-automatic, she found herself counting the shots, as lumps of turf and bits of brick from the bandstand plinth flew around her.

The evenly spaced firing, crack, crack, crack, suggested she was dealing with an experienced cold-hearted killer as the shooting went on unabated. An individual who knew exactly what they were doing and who wouldn't stop until they'd achieved their objective, which was the murder of one Tammy Pierre. Abruptly, it all stopped, leaving a hollow echo in her head. In that moment she reckoned he'd have four, possibly five, shots left in the magazine which carried fifteen at most. Then what? she wondered. If she survived, would he be armed with a knife? Would he seek to grapple with her hand to hand?

* * * * *

He'd seen her drop to the ground a nano-second before he started loosing off shots at her. God, she was sharp. He'd been told she was good, but this was exceptional.

Despite the injury, she was graceful as a panther. All arms and legs flailing madly, but somehow still in control.

"Mama," he muttered as a wave of mixed desire and nausea threatened to swamp him.

The park was empty. He had to have her. Hear her squeal with pleasure like the others, before she died. He'd indulge himself, just this once. Too good an opportunity to miss. So tall, with that tiny bust, the muscled thighs with the obvious scar. He was already swelling with want and he hadn't even touched her yet.

"Mama, oh Mama." She'd told him he was a big boy when he was just twelve. He was a bigger boy now.

* * * * *

She could hear him panting, getting closer, though the firing had stopped. Out of bullets? Unlikely. He'd have loaded the magazine to the maximum, or else in the moments from the last shots, had time to slot in a fresh magazine. Looking around her she merely confirmed in her own mind there was nowhere she could go, nowhere she could hide, and nowhere she could run, even were she able in her present state.

"Okay, mon brave," she murmured under her breath, clambering slowly to her feet, ignoring the now lancing pain in her side, the weight of her pregnancy making her leaden. "Let's wait this out and see what you're made of."

He appeared almost skeletal, a worn baggy suit hanging from his spare frame. A thin tie, knotted at the neck, added a note of the bizarre. He'd looked smarter the last time she'd seen him. She spied the rising flush against his grey pallor, perceiving a man in the throes of an urgently mounting need.

"Mr Loughty," she said. "I seem to recall we've met."

"You remembered," he responded, in that strangely effeminate voice she remembered. "How kind."

Confronting this ungainly, towering freak of an individual, a familiar sense of the rearing of sex in the most dangerous of situations sent an unwelcome frisson of desire up the inside of her legs.

She faced him now, ankles slightly spread, arms folded defiantly across her chest. He'd holstered the gun and smirked at her. "I'll have you first, dear. Make it nice before you go."

In her weakened state she was slow, too slow to stop him pouncing and grappling her to the ground. Hands on her breasts, he swiftly changed tack, holding her tight with one deceptively powerful arm, while he groped her shorts with the free hand, seeking access.

For an instant she visualised Dov, how it was with him, and as a groan escaped her she heard the man say, "That's right, darling. Soon be there."

She didn't wear the belt with the shuriken when she was out jogging. It was too heavy. But in a sheath on her belt she carried her Gerber 06 automatic knife. Trouble was, it was at her back and she was lying on it unable to grasp it.

He opened his trousers, lying on her spread legs, his breathing becoming erratic.

Hauling her hips up off the ground, she was aware he might take her at any moment. Incongruously, where she lay pinned, she could smell grass at her cheek, feel pebbles scratching the back of her head. The bile now rose in her throat, rough and bitter at the prospect of the man, as she struggled against his strength, twisting and turning, becoming frantic.

"Ready for me, my lovely. Don't squeal, not yet. Just enjoy; while you can," he said, drawing back and pausing a moment before resolutely pursuing his goal.

Her fingers finally grasped the knife handle and she slid it from the sheath, at the same time pressing the button in the shaft as the barely legal 3.7-inch blade snapped open.

He heard the muffled snap, glancing down in the same moment as he sought to roll away from her, swearing, "What the fuck?"

Her chance to escape, but he was on her again before she could move, a hand tearing at the shorts. "You don't know how to use that thing. Stupid tart," he sneered, pinning her weapon arm down so that it was useless.

The stresses she'd been recently subjected to were smothering her and as she quickly weakened, her muscles turning to jelly, this was one fight she was losing. Contorting herself in an attempt to finally escape the man's grip, she heard him laugh.

Then something clicked in her brain, switching her into survival mode. She could assess with immediacy her prospects, poor, and his, uncertain. It produced a rush of adrenalin in her, enough to focus on the blade and the hand grasping it, which she twisted out of his grip, leaving her a bare moment, as he laughed at her again, to plunge the point deep into his thigh.

He screamed, his lips drawn back into the rictus of a smile, revealing the tiny shark's teeth, his eyes opening wide, uncomprehendingly as Tammy stumbled to her feet.

She stood over the man for a moment, rearranging her shorts as he grasped his thigh in agony. This was a win, but with an individual like Loughty it wouldn't be the last she'd hear from him. There'd be a reckoning.

She was panting, heaving, but muted her elation, speaking softly, "You better get that seen to, Mr Loughty. It's bleeding copiously. I'd suggest A&E at St John & St Elizabeth private hospital in Grove End Road, St John's Wood. Shall I call you a cab?"

"You fucking bitch."

Gazing down at her attacker she said, "I suppose I'd better report this to the local nick. They should know. I'll send them round to pick you up, help you to the hospital. I'll remain anonymous, of course. Unless, that is," she added, suppressing a smile, "you feel the overwhelming urge to enlighten them."

"I'll have you," he muttered predictably.

"Who sent you?" she asked, still making sure to control her breathing so he wouldn't hear her exhausted gasps. "No, let me guess. Our Chancellor-in-waiting, I'll be bound. Hmm? Mr Loughty?"

"We're not done yet, lady. My turn next time."

"As you wish," she responded, walking away from the man. "À bientôt, monsieur."

CHAPTER 57 DAY 16

THE CLUB WAS APPROACHED through a pair of magnificent Regency fan-lit glossy black double doors. Its decorative, antique-form brass door furniture was polished to a glittering shine. The building itself was Regency red brick with bay windows framed in grey stone.

The interior was equally impressive, all marble pillars and flooring, with a collection of Hepplewhite and Sheraton sofas, some Chesterfields and a number of easy chairs. It all smelled of furniture polish, leather and disinfectant. The reception area which greeted the visitor boasted a vast antique mahogany desk behind which sat a suntanned, white-haired individual probably in his mid-fifties wearing a navy blue open-neck shirt, with sleeves rolled to the elbow, revealing forearms like fresh hams.

Standing up to greet her as she entered, the man introduced himself. "Walter Gibbons. I don't think we've met."

"Would you remember if we had?" asked Tammy.

"Oh yes." He smiled. "This club hosts up to five hundred members at a time, all of whom I know, with room for a further two hundred guests, more or less. It's my club, and I own the freehold, so I make it my business to know."

She was immediately at ease with the man. After the events of yesterday evening she'd taken herself for a further short walk to unwind, then home to a hot shower, a self-indulgent vodka and bed, where she lay restlessly cuddled up some of the time with Risky, when the cat didn't chase off in frustration at her mistress's constant twisting and turning.

It had been close. Too damn close, she thought, while reviewing what and why it had happened and how to ensure there would never be a repeat. Going over it in her mind, there was no way to predict what appeared to be

346 • THE POLITICIAN'S WIFE

a random attack. The man couldn't have known the park would be empty, and must have decided to take a chance. So, not entirely random, but then, hardly meticulously planned. Her sixth sense, instinct, or simply recognition of the sound of a semi-automatic being cocked had saved her. There was nothing to beat herself up over. Unlikely anyone else in her position could have done better.

That left Oscar Mountford. The assailant had to be Oscar's man. He'd chosen the park because of the apparent lack of cameras. She'd jog in the streets for now. The man would think twice before a return match, one that wouldn't be required if enough evidence could be gathered to see Mountford put away. Meanwhile, the hole she'd left in his thigh would occupy the man's time and thoughts for a while. Pondering it all, she tentatively examined the wound in her side. Fortunately the sutures had held, although there had been some bleeding, and were now dry. And the pregnancy, thank God, was still intact.

Despite her lack of sleep she'd woken reasonably refreshed, and now faced with the benevolent features of Walter Gibbons she became optimistic there'd be something of value he might add.

Explaining who she was and what she was seeking to find out, she asked candidly if Walter had a club member or guest called Letitia Mountford, or Philips. He pondered for a moment, then said, "Name doesn't mean anything to me. Do you have anything else to give me?"

"Description? Above middle height, age mid to late forties, but could pass for thirties, or less. Stylish specs. Shoulder-length auburn hair. Usually fashionably turned out. But sometimes wears flamboyant clothing."

"How flamboyant is flamboyant, Ms Pierre?"

"Well," she returned. "Drum majorette's costume for a start. Or, Bohemian, Middle Eastern balloon trousers—"

Walter held up one hand. "Stop."

"Stop?" she asked, puzzled.

"Larissa Filipek."

"Yes?" she asked eagerly.

"She fits the description you've given perfectly."

"Well, well. Larissa Filipek, now Letitia Mountford. Our mystery missing lady. A useful alias to have when out clubbing, away from hubby's inquisitive eye."

"Missing lady?"

"I've been charged with the task of locating her, and any help from anyone who's come across her would be welcome."

"Happy to oblige. Look, why don't I get you a tea or coffee while we chat?"

"Coffee would be perfect. Black please, without."

"On its way," said Walter, as he made his way to a coffee machine sitting on a magnificent credenza, that was probably Regency, by a wall of the reception area.

A few moments later, now seated on sofas facing each other, they sipped their drinks while exploring what could be deduced about Letitia and her movements.

"She is quite a character, this Letitia woman."

"Tell me," said Tammy.

"She came here with a variety of men and, though we don't encourage it, on a number of occasions on her own. We let her in as she's well known to us. But on those occasions it was my impression she'd go off with the first man she came across. Some strange specimens, usually guests rather than members."

"Strange, in what way?"

"Hard to be definite, but you know, one gets a feeling about some people. Intense, distracted, shifty. Nothing you could pinpoint about any of them."

"Anything else?"

"Yes, sometimes she'd waltz off happily arm in arm with another woman. I suppose she might have been gay, bisexual, or just off for a drink somewhere else. Who knows?"

"Did she have any regular partners here?"

"Now you mention it, yes. She was here several times with the hedge fund manager."

"One Mr Caspar da Silva, by any chance?" Tammy asked.

"Occasionally. But no. Matter of fact it was his partner she was with."

"Theo Cranfield?"

"That's right."

"That's a surprise, I thought he was in fact dating Letitia's daughter Juliet."

"I only ever saw Theo with Letitia. Now there is a really strange one."

"Who, Theo?"

"Yes. I should have mentioned it before. But Theo has served time, you know."

"Good heavens. What for, financial crime, as he put it?"

"No. I found out by chance he'd been away, and actually asked him about it. And yes, he said it was for a financial misdemeanour. But what puzzled me was that when I enquired, I found out he hadn't been in any of the usual open prisons. He looked respectable enough to me, so I let it go. As a matter of fact I later found, to my astonishment, he'd served five years in a closed prison for manslaughter."

"Good heavens. Do you know any more? I mean, who was killed? How and why?"

"No, but the whole thing left me mystified."

She drank some of the coffee while turning over alternatives in her head. What about Caspar, then? she wondered. Are we barking up the wrong tree? Does Juliet know this? "Let me guess, Walter. A sex game that went wrong?"

"Very possible. It would certainly fit the mould."

"Still no further." She sighed. "Is there anyone else you think might be able to shed light on what's happened to Letitia? Anyone who might have stood out among the oddities you mentioned?"

Walter scratched the back of his head. "Yes, there is one strange character."

"Tell me what you know of him. Can you describe him to me?"

"Okay. Well, he was very tall, gaunt features to the point of being skeletal. Clothes hung off him like washing on a line, like he was really thin, except that under that loose-fitting jacket I saw the build of a wrestler, or maybe a weightlifter. Not a man I'd fancy tangling with, and I can cope with most situations."

As Walter described the man Tammy's pulse increased exponentially. "I know this man," she breathed. "You don't happen to remember his name, do you?"

"As a matter of fact I do. I did say I remember the names of all my members and guests. His was an odd name, Ephraim Loughty."

"I know him," said Tammy.

"You do?" Walter sounded surprised.

"Yes, we had a little contretemps only yesterday evening."

"Really!" Walter asked, intrigued, the hint of a smile playing at the corner of his lips. "As you appear in fine fettle, am I to understand you acquitted yourself with aplomb, Ms Pierre?"

"Well, let's say Mr Loughty may need the use of a stick for a while."

"You know something of martial arts?"

"I do, but when someone takes pot shots at you with a Heckler & Koch USP 45, martial arts don't help a great deal. However, despite some recent setbacks, I am reasonably fit and strong. You might say I gave him a run for his money. He, of course, won't be running anywhere for a while."

Walter laughed out loud. "I can see if I ever need a bouncer at the club, I know where to look."

Tammy smiled. "I'd be interested to know if Letitia ever met this man. Come to think of it, do you know who introduced him to the club? I'm assuming he was a guest, and not a member?"

"You're right."

"And I can tell you, counting on your discretion, that Letitia Mountford is the wife of junior minister Oscar Mountford."

"Well now, I would never have made the connection with her being signed in as Filipek. So here's something you'll find interesting, the man who introduced her, tall, distinguished, greying, a bit older than most of my patrons, was Oscar Mountford. I'd no idea they were husband and wife."

"I wonder why he brought her here?"

"I got the odd feeling he wanted her to go off with someone. It was he, in fact, who first introduced her to Theo Cranfield whom she accompanied, as I've said, on a number of occasions, but then without her husband. The strangest thing, though, she took a shine to the Loughty character whom her husband also introduced her to. Once she'd met them both, her husband stopped coming. Almost as though he'd achieved his desired objective."

"Walter," she said, getting up. "You've been a real help."

At that moment, Tammy's mobile rang. "Tammy Pierre," she answered. Then, concerned, "Rose? Is everything okay?"

"Tammy." The voice a whisper.

"Talk to me."

"The DNA results are in."

"We've got a match?"

"It's Letitia?"

"Right. The headless corpse is Letitia. As we surmised. Now all we need to do is find her killer."

CHAPTER 58 DAY 16

"DARLING, I'M TERRIFIED. Absolutely terrified. Beside myself. I don't think I can take much more."

"Tell me all about it, dearest. Remember, you're not alone. I'm here for you. Always. Ever and for always."

"You have no idea what I've done. What I've been involved in."

"Do you want to tell me later, when we're in bed?"

"No, dear. I think I need to talk a bit now, before I go completely insane."

"Go on, then. I'm listening." The reassuring interest.

"You remember the Kevin Anderton thing?"

"He was murdered? Killed by a hit and run. But, sweetheart, you didn't kill him, did you? So what's the problem?"

"No. I didn't kill him. But a Jamaican called Ainsley Borrell did."

"And just who is this ghastly Borrell character you seem so frightened of?" The feminine voice was raised questioningly.

"The instruction to do the killing was supposed to come from me."

"And did it?"

"In an oblique sort of way."

"But not directly?"

There was a moment's pause, then, "No. Not directly."

"Darling, in that case, stop fussing. You'll only smudge your mascara."

"You always say that when I'm worried about something."

"Of course I do. But truly, I can't wait to have you in my arms. To feel your lips on mine, you gorgeous creature."

"Oh, do be serious for once." The voice betrayed growing irritation.

"Very well. I'm listening. Since you're clearly not going to stop worrying, why not get it off your chest. Once and for all."

"The woman, Georgia Keith."

"Yes. What about her? Who is she anyway?"

"She's the PA of Oscar Mountford."

"The MP?"

"Yes."

"The one rumour has it may be our next Chancellor?"

"That's correct."

"She was involved in an accident, or something. There was a bit in that freebie, The Evening News. Not on the TV bulletins though. So presumably nothing too serious."

"She's dead."

"Well, accidents, darling. Accidents."

"Ainsley Borrell."

"The man does seem to crop up, doesn't he? What did he do, shoot her?"

"Of course not. She was run down. You said you'd read the newspaper article."

"Only the headline. But, how terribly calamitous. Well, one has to admit, that to run someone down once in questionable circumstances may be regarded as unfortunate, but to be involved in two similar fatalities is positively careless."

"Please, for God's sake, don't start quoting Oscar Wilde to me at a time like this."

"Very well, sweetheart." The other sighed. "But you do seem to be getting yourself into an awful tizz. Is that all, then? Any other suspicious deaths?"

"You read about the MP's son."

"That Oscar Mountford again. Some lunatic flying accident. Widely reported. Of course I did. Don't tell me you were the pilot who flew off and was never seen again?"

"Don't be absurd."

"Have we been terribly naughty, then, darling. Such fun."

"The pilot's dead."

"How do you know? Did you kill him?"

"Well…"

"What do you mean, well? Don't be ridiculous. You could never kill anyone."

"If any of this got out. You know how rumour and innuendo get exaggerated. The practice would fold. Do you know how long it took my father to establish Smollett Davis Carleton. If there were even a whisper of scandal—"

"Mac, just stop it. Do you hear me? Stop it. You're getting hysterical. There is going to be no scandal. You're not a murderer. There are no rumours doing the rounds. I insist you come round immediately. Do you hear me? Immediately."

"Yes. Yes, of course. You always make me feel so much better. A burden lifted. On my way. I can't wait to have you make love to me, Edward my darling."

CHAPTER 59 DAY 16

"TAMMY, ROSE HAS ALREADY told me, we have a match." There was a note of relief in Detective Chief Superintendent Bob Walker's voice.

"That's right, Bob. We finally know who we're looking at. Letitia Mountford. The problem now, is to find whom we're looking for."

"Have you said anything yet to Oscar?"

"No. I think we should leave that on hold a little longer. I was going to say, let him stew. But frankly, I don't think he's the least bit concerned. I spoke with Caspar da Silva, the hedge fund manager, and he seems to think that Oscar did his best to palm her off on him. Or possibly his partner Theo Cranfield, whom I'm seeing this morning. In either case, with Oscar's contacts, even if he'd not been aware of his wife's past political activities, he must by now have brought himself fully up to date. Obviously, he'd want her out of the way until he'd gained that promotion."

"Right," agreed Bob. "And the PM is ever more urgently awaiting Oscar's Budget. The economy, as we've acknowledged, is in a parlous condition. Whatever the nature of Oscar's financial criminality, thus-far undetected or proven, we can't deny his commercial skills and how badly the country is in need of some of his vision."

"Strange, isn't it," offered Tammy, "the financial genius of some criminals. You can go right back to Roman times with the attempted sale of the Roman Empire, where the plotters were all executed. Then there was Charles Ponzi who advised Mussolini to disastrous effect. Enron, Jordan Belfort, The Wolf of Wall Street, Edgar Lustig who sold the Eiffel Tower. Bernie Madoff's fifty-billion-dollar Ponzi scam. They mostly ended up in poverty or in jail.

"Mostly men, it seems," she went on. "But not to be outdone, the stunningly beautiful Elizabeth Holmes with her

Theranos tech scam which took in such luminaries as Rupert Murdoch. Her worth once reckoned by Forbes magazine at over nine billion dollars is now quoted at zero, and she's awaiting sentence. Many, many more, probably with the talent to be rich by legitimate means, if only they'd had the patience."

"You're right, of course," agreed Bob. "But then, there's also a criminal type, I believe, who whatever their talents will always seek the thrill of breaking the rules. Just for its own sake, I suppose."

"Oscar Mountford. A case in point. Although, as psychopaths go, his extreme right wing activities are based on a sincere belief in the benefits his approach might bring the country. It's just that he's prepared to kill, or have killed, anyone who impedes his progress towards that goal."

"Let me know how you get on with Cranfield. You said you thought his partner da Silva might be a suspect?"

"Just a throwaway comment he made. Sometimes it's those little asides, the moments of indiscretion that give away the criminal. Da Silva's reputation as a woman beater makes me wonder about the inevitable sex game going too far. I'll keep that idea on the back burner for now. Meanwhile, I've asked Rosemary to check out the ANPR for sightings of any of the known vehicles of our potentials in the vicinity of the Mountford home at about the time she got back from the States.

"Then, I'm going to take a close look at the van that mowed down Kevin Anderton. See if there's anything at all to link it to Oscar. I know forensics have been over it thoroughly, but sometimes an independent view will produce something missed."

"How about you, Tammy? I know I keep enquiring, and I wouldn't have asked you to undertake or continue this investigation if I didn't have faith you're one of the few I could trust to reach a solution."

"I'm okay, Bob. Pacing myself as best I can. I had a little set-to with one I assume had been sent to entertain me by Oscar, in Queen's Park the other night."

"A set-to? If I know you, Tammy, and your genius for understatement I'd say the event was more than a mere set-to."

"Oscar wants a lot of people out of the way. Not least me. There's no CCTV that I'm aware of in the park."

"What happened?"

"Man took a couple of pots at me."

"My God, Tammy." He sounded horrified. "You've said nothing... You were shot at? Didn't anyone see? Hear?"

"It was late afternoon, Bob. The park was empty. He must have followed me around then simply acted on impulse. The gun was suppressed. A moment seized."

"But really, if I hadn't asked... Were you hurt?"

"No. But my assailant may be shuffling around on a stick for a while."

"I don't know how you can be so casual, my dear. You amaze me. Incidentally, did you report this to the local police? You know that..."

"Bob, of course I reported it. And yes, I was discreet. I know what we're up against with Mr Mountford and that it wouldn't do right now to risk my name being linked to the man or any of his possible associates."

Mrs Gilchrist waving caught Tammy's attention.

"Bob, it seems Theo Cranfield has arrived. We'll see what he has to say for himself."

"Tammy," said Bob quietly. "Please don't take any unnecessary risks. You're too, too important to all of us."

She flushed with pleasure, realising that when Bob had embarrassed himself with that kiss on her cheek, if he were here right now, she'd be embarrassing them both by hugging him.

As soon as she'd hung up on Bob, her phone went again. "Rose?" she exclaimed, seeing the caller ID on the screen.

"Hi, Tammy."

"Is everything okay?"

There followed a bout of coughing. Tammy chose to say nothing. Rose would give up smoking when she was ready.

"Rose?" she asked, as soon as the hacking cough abated.

"Hi." She sighed. "I've been leaning on our forensics team, letting them know we need results now. Right now."

"What have you found? I imagine it's more than the news you've given me about Letitia's corpse. No. Let me guess. You've been looking in Caspar da Silva's Ferrari."

"Right. Very careless, or just forgetful is our Mr da Silva."

"Letitia's DNA in the front of the car?"

"Not surprising, of course."

"You're going to tell me you've found something in the boot."

"Absolutely."

"Go on. I can hardly wait."

"Under the flat floor panel. A gentleman's denim jacket. But hear this, we found a receipt from a firm of cleaners in the pocket."

"And you followed it up?"

"And it wasn't Caspar's jacket, as we presumed it would be."

"It was Theo's?"

"It was Theo's." She let the revelation sink in. "Caspar must have forgotten it was there. Or not known it was."

"I've a feeling you're going to tell me something more."

"Too right. On the outside of the jacket we found Letitia's DNA."

"Nothing of her identified on the inside?"

"Nope."

"So she couldn't have been wearing it. But very possibly lying on it if and when her body was crammed into the boot before being disposed of."

"Yes. But we found her DNA in other parts of the boot. That could have come from the jacket, of course. It's all circumstantial at this stage."

"It is, Rose. But I'm seeing Theo. I'll wait and see what sort of reaction I get when I give him the news."

CHAPTER 60 DAY 16

LIKE HIS PARTNER, the man was about middle height, although of significantly slimmer build, with a habit of grinning a lot whenever he spoke. Good-looking in a vague sort of way, with a weak chin and slightly receding hairline, he wore blue chinos and a denim jacket with open-neck shirt.

Sitting opposite Tammy in the proffered chair, he asked, "You wanted to have a word?"

"Mr Cranfield; thank you for agreeing to see me."

"Theo, please," he suggested in an echo of his partner's invitation.

He had a little boy lost look about him, that gave the lie to his maturity in his dealings in the hedge fund market. She'd learned the hard lesson that first appearances counted for little. The oft quoted American dictum, that you never get a second chance to make a first impression, was in her opinion, entirely misconceived. It was what you learned about the individual as you got to know them that counted for everything. She wasn't about to be seduced into being the dupe of this apparently harmless individual.

Without asking, Mrs Gilchrist brought in a tray with tea and coffee pots, bone china crockery and a selection of shortbread and garibaldi biscuits.

"Help yourself, Theo," offered Tammy, seeing him eyeing the teapot, pouring herself a coffee and taking several garibaldis.

"You're well aware the whereabouts of Letitia Mountford are being investigated," she said.

"I know," he replied. "Any joy so far? Caspar told me you'd said you thought you had something definite."

"We're working on a number of leads," she replied, not yet disclosing anything of the case. "What do you know of Letitia Mountford? Your partner says you were frequently seen accompanying her to Rags nightclub."

"That's right. She was bored at home. Caspar and I met her through her husband, by whom we were engaged to handle some of his investments. We both were of the opinion that Oscar wanted her off his hands. So we obliged him."

"Just taking her to the club? Nothing more?"

"Oh, come on, Tammy." He grinned mischievously, sipping from his cup of tea and dipping in a shortbread. "We were both screwing her. Everyone was screwing her. She often went to the club alone, picked up the first bloke she looked at and went off with them."

"Just like that?"

"Just like that. She was very sexy. Caspar said he couldn't keep up."

"And did you keep up, Theo?"

"Matter of fact, I did. Caspar's good when it comes to picking up weights. I'm good," he grinned again, "when it comes to picking up girls."

"I thought you were seeing Letitia's daughter Juliet?"

"I am. Was," he corrected himself. "She wasn't too pleased when she learned I'd been seeing her mother at the same time as I was seeing her."

Tammy sat for several moments, chewing biscuits and drinking from her coffee cup. "What do you know of Caspar's relationship with Letitia?"

"Not a lot. He can be a brutal bastard when it comes to the ladies, adds to what he needs to add; what he lacks, I suppose, when it comes to bed. I've not heard he suffers too many complaints."

"And what about you, Theo? Do you like to push the ladies around as well?"

"Who me?"

"Yes, you, Theo."

"You must be joking."

"I'm being serious. I don't know what you two get up to."

"Not my scene at all. Gentle as a lamb. That's me."

"Caspar puzzles me. He suggested that if anything had happened to Letitia, in his words, she'd have got all she deserved.

"You know about her left wing tendencies?" she added.

"Yes. Word gets around. Also, she blabbed a lot."

"Did she have any contacts with any overseas agencies that you know of?"

"You tell me."

Remembering the man with the NHS type spectacles and the written warning she'd received to cease the investigation, she asked, "I'll be frank, Theo. Did she, to your knowledge, have any dealings with any Communist spy agencies?"

"Well," he pondered. "I don't know about that. But Caspar did say he was being harassed by someone who he said was blackmailing him. He wouldn't say any more."

Theo didn't seem to be smiling so much now as he talked, having become rather more circumspect. "He was in trouble. Said someone was leaning on him."

"In what way, leaning on him, Theo?"

Theo sat saying nothing for several moments, as though debating with himself whether to add anything further. Finally, he said, "Caspar told me that someone had something on him."

"Really, Theo? You two do seem to leave yourselves somewhat open to blackmail. What was it this time? More financial irregularity?"

"He told me the man had a mid-European accent. Maybe Czech or Russian. He practically forced Caspar to admit to killing Letitia, that's without Caspar even knowing for sure that she's dead."

It was time to gauge a reaction, so Tammy revealed, "Letitia is dead, Theo."

"But I thought you said…"

"I know what you thought, Theo. But before you came in this morning I was given definite proof from forensics, we have her DNA. It was the corpse found on the Heath."

"I see," he said.

"Caspar said Letitia was a kickster. His term. She liked innovative sex, he told me. Threesomes, Theo."

"If you say so. She was pretty promiscuous."

"Did you and Caspar indulge in threesomes with Letitia Mountford, Theo?"

"What?" He shifted about in the chair uncomfortably.

"Did the three of you engage in a sex game that went wrong. We both know Caspar likes violence and from what you tell me, Letitia didn't discourage it."

"No. No," he protested. "I never did. We never did."

"We found your denim jacket in the boot of the Ferrari. It was yours, wasn't it, Theo? Easily identified by the cleaners ticket left in the pocket."

"Nonsense," he said, getting to his feet.

"Very careless of you both. No?"

"Rubbish. What's that supposed to prove?"

"You had a threesome with Caspar and Letitia. Things went dramatically wrong. She died, didn't she, Theo? So you and Caspar shoved her body into the boot of the Ferrari, and dumped it on the Heath? Your jacket, Theo. Letitia's DNA. When did you cut her up? Hmm? Not much in the way of blood in the boot, so presumably you chopped her up when you got to where you dumped her."

"You can't prove a fucking thing," he yelled and stormed out of the office.

"Well," said Mrs Gilchrist. "What a rude young man."

"Rude is the least of it," said Tammy. "Two nasty pieces of work."

CHAPTER 61 DAY 16

"IT'S ALL STILL UNDER WRAPS, but I'm delivering the Budget speech very shortly." Oscar's voice was calm and considered.

"There'll be a Cabinet reshuffle and my promotion to Chancellor of the Exchequer will be announced. PM's a bloody fool. Wouldn't recognise Herr Hitler if they were introduced at a cocktail party. He's going to find that my ascendancy to the role is a poisoned chalice. Yes, I'll deliver the Budget he wants, that this country under his pathetic stewardship needs, but then I'm going to start angling for his job."

"How long is that gonna take, Oscar?" The voice was distinctly American. "We need proper direction. Our Mr President is a busted flush. The Special Relationship needs a shot on the arm, my friend. A lot of my colleagues in the Senate are with me on this."

"That's precisely what I shall be aiming to re-establish, Carl. I've got friends in France, Germany, Hungary, Italy. When the time is right, the right will rise." There was a smile of triumph in the voice. "All over Europe the far right, our people, are gaining in power and influence."

"How about inside your own backdoor, Oscar."

"Soon to become a well-publicised front door, Carl. I've dozens in the House on all sides who want what I want. After my speech they will all feel able to show open support for me and my ambitions for this country and for the world. Be aware, the Labour Party has much in common with ourselves. For one thing, they believe in traditional female roles in the home and society; the attacks on their female candidates who stood for the leadership were labelled misogynistic. An entirely misconceived notion. They, like us, believe that women should only take a back seat, a supporting role to the men in politics. The primary role of women has always been, and will always be, in the home, that's both historically and still holding good today.

"Then again, with one or two notable exceptions, Labour has been described as being more racist than the Tories at our worst. That's nonsense of course. They merely acknowledge the superiority of the Caucasian people. And they, too, wish to see an end to the financial influence of the Hebrews. The so-called conspiracy theory of world domination. Look at how the leadership of the Labour Party has paid homage to Middle Eastern terrorist groups."

"Erm, Oscar, you're losing me a bit here. We want a strong right wing government, but no-one in their right mind believes in any conspiracy among Jews to dominate the world. Christ, they're less than a half a percent of the world's population. And, man, look at the contribution they've made to the arts, science, business. You name it."

"Best not to name it. We need scapegoats, Carl. Hitler realised that and had the perfect foil among the Jews."

"Oscar, I kinda think maybe you're taking this all a bit too far?" Carl sounded increasingly doubtful.

"No, Carl. I'm not. If we're going to have influence, real influence, we've got to go all the way. No half measures. Look," he said in a placatory tone, "wait and see what happens after my speech."

"Not sure if I want to wait that long," Carl muttered, almost inaudibly under his breath.

"What's that, Carl? What was that, old boy?"

"Nothing, Oscar. Nothing. Just keep me in the loop. I can't help wondering, does your PM know what he's letting himself in for with you?"

"Not yet, he doesn't. But he will soon," said Oscar with a chuckle.

"Give him my best wishes, Oscar. And my sympathies," he added softly. "Boy, is he going to need them."

"Sorry, old boy. Say again? Didn't quite catch your drift."

But the line had gone dead.

CHAPTER 62 DAY 16

"**N**OT DOING TOO WELL are we Nikki."

The voice was instantly recognisable, and Nicolai felt hot and uncomfortable. It was a sunny day and he'd taken a walk in Hyde Park to try to clear his head. Get his brain around events which were apparently outside his control. The call, which was unexpected, threw him.

He gazed over the Serpentine. Park-goers and tourists rowed this way and that on the glinting surface. Swans moved gracefully among the boats. It was tranquillity for all, except one man, whose feeling was of simple dread. "She dead. What else you want? I do as you say."

"I'm not so sure. Tell me, how did you kill her? By what method? And how did you dispose of the body?"

"I say she dead."

"You haven't answered my question, Nicolai. And my friends back in the Party are not amused. You were given a job to do. And you failed. Try answering my question."

"I cut her throat, yesterday, right across. Then I take the body —"

"Yesterday? Hah! The day after we last spoke? I thought you said she was in America."

"She back now. We speak."

"Really? That was quick work. And then you forgot to tell us? Enough, man. Signs are she was drowned then battered to a pulp. We've just heard a body, probably hers, was found on Hampstead Heath, more than just a few days ago. She probably died a day or two after that disastrous right wing rally in Trafalgar Square. That's more than three weeks ago."

"But…"

"No buts. She's dead, and you're a liar who can't be trusted."

"Is not true. I kill her, I kill her."

"You really haven't a clue, have you. God knows why you were picked to be her handler. We'd have done better to keep Anatoly alive."

"What?"

"Never mind."

"What happen to me now?" The voice was a whine. Pleading.

"We haven't decided yet." There was long pause, then, "One way you might redeem yourself."

He took off the wire-rimmed spectacles agitatedly, then just as quickly, replaced them. "Anything. Just say me."

"It seems Filipek had an associate. A double. Possibly a half-sister, our sources suggest."

"You want I should deal?"

"We want you should deal. And don't get it wrong this time. I'll text you where we think she can be found. I'll give you a number as well. Do it before the authorities pick her up. Understood? Why not arrange to meet her at that Soho club you always went to when you spoke with Filipek."

"Yes. Yes." The relief in Nicolai's voice was almost palpable.

Two days later the news reported the murder of a man found close to a well-known Soho bar. There was no ID and no distinguishing features on the corpse, save for a pair of snapped wire-rimmed spectacles by the body.

It was noted, however, that the leather jacket he wore bore a Russian manufacturer's label inside the collar.

CHAPTER 63 DAY 17

SHE'D SLEPT WELL and had agreed to meet Rose-mary for a morning coffee and update at Gail's.

In a simple navy blue tracksuit, she strode towards the bakery a shade more purposefully than she'd been feeling of late. Some small progress was being made. But, if Caspar and Theo were the killers of Letitia, there was still insufficient evidence to charge them. And what of Oscar's involvement? Apparently, none. He could hardly have put the two boys up to it. There was still a long way to go. Nothing like any sort of evidence to pin on Oscar, their prime target.

She'd opted for a latte, just for a change. That and one of the bakery's traditional pain aux raisins, which she'd sliced into halves then quarters in order to pop the bite-size pieces into her mouth without getting her fingers too sticky. Grinning at Tammy's performance, Rose poured herself a tea from the pot. For once, she too looked rested.

"How're you doing, love," Rose asked.

"I'm okay. Mending, anyway," she said, taking one of the pieces of crusty cake and chewing on it contentedly.

"How about the palms," she said, reaching for Tammy's hands and turning them over, holding them almost tenderly in her own. She said nothing, merely glancing up at Tammy sadly.

"Don't be down, Rose. If I can put up with it… They'll heal. Doc said to be patient, that's all."

Catching Tammy's eye, Rose, changing the subject, said, "Bob told me about the incident."

Tammy shrugged. "Seems I'm a target at the moment."

"How can you be so casual about it, Tammy?"

"Ours is a hazardous job, Rose. Yours and mine."

"I suppose. Yours more so. It invites danger. And you're mostly on your own."

"To work, then," said Tammy, moving on. "Any joy with tracing that unusual name, Polonia Filipek? Did you take a look on the NCA computer to see if there was anything recorded?"

"I did. And we found the name with a recorded speeding incident. I've an address in North Wales."

"Excellent. We really need to speak with her ASAP. Like now. We should probably go together."

"Agreed. We're looking at more than just who might have killed Letitia, there're all those killings in America, clearly linked to the St James's Hotel murder. The two women look so alike. Coincidence? Or might they be related?"

"How soon could you have a car ready? We should go with a couple of uniforms. Nothing here too confidential."

"I could have a car here within the hour. I'll bring Sergeant Powell and PC Chaudry."

"Best if we go in an unmarked vehicle."

"Sure. We can stick a magnetised blue light on top," agreed Rose, who tapped out a number on her mobile.

The car, a magnificent new black Land Rover Defender, equipped with every possible item of modern technology, arrived within twenty minutes, pulling up outside Gail's. Boasting an infinite number of seating configurations, the layout was arranged to accommodate six.

With a choice of dashboard gear shifter or paddle-shift, this top-of-the-range model 400 could manage a top speed of around one hundred and fifty miles an hour, reaching sixty miles an hour in under six seconds.

PC Chaudry, a burly, cheerful individual, was at the wheel, clearly eager to demonstrate his advanced driving skills when advised they needed to get to North Wales quickly.

Next to him in the front passenger seat, Sergeant Powell, a man in his forties with a pale, worried demeanour, quietly expressed the hope they'd all survive the journey in one piece.

With both women safely strapped in the back, they moved quietly out of the area, until they hit the A5, Kilburn High Road, when Powell affixed a blue light onto the roof and PC Chaudry was able to demonstrate the vehicle's capability. The M1 was about four miles away and Chaudry hit the motorway, averaging an insane sixty miles an hour with the siren screaming, in just four minutes.

From there they had approximately a one-hundred-and-eighty-mile trip to North Wales to complete. A police vehicle may legally exceed the speed limit by twenty miles an hour. In short, PC Chaudry might race along at ninety miles an hour and expect to get to their destination in about three hours. But this was not what PC Chaudry had in mind when he took the police advanced motoring course, and again when he put in for his advanced driving test. It was a skilled drive, but not one that any of the occupants of the car would wish to repeat. Often touching one hundred and forty miles an hour, they completed the journey in two and a quarter hours. For Rosemary it was white-knuckle ride. For Tammy, it was to witness a sublime bit of motoring skill.

Leaving the M6 motorway, they'd picked up close to the Rugby Road, finally reaching the outskirts of Llanfyllin, a thriving market town of fewer than eighteen hundred people. The siren was turned off and the blue light retrieved from the roof of the vehicle.

Dating back to medieval times, the town is best known for its holy well dedicated to Saint Myllin, who baptised people there in the sixth century. The Lonely Tree, a large Scots pine, some two hundred years old, and said to bring good fortune if hugged, was felled in a storm in 2014. An attempt to rescue it involving the packing of sixty tonnes of soil at its roots, failed. Most of Llanfyllin's buildings, including churches and chapels, are built of locally made brick. The place is a popular tourist spot.

The Land Rover attracted a few glances from locals, not used to seeing something quite as extravagant on their village roads.

The Filipeks lived in a modest red-brick detached house not far from the High Street. Flower beds and a patch of lawn made for an immaculate front garden. Pulling up outside, Tammy offered, "Let's hope they're in after all that."

"We might have called ahead," said Powell. "It could be a wasted journey."

"We might have," agreed Tammy. "And we could have made all sorts of excuses, saying we were any number of people wishing to examine the property, from the Gas Board to the local council concerned about reports of subsidence in the area. Frankly, I prefer not alerting them to our visit, at least, the first time around. If they are out, then plan B is simply to advise them next time of our proposed visit and trust no-one decides to abscond."

The four people exited the vehicle and stretched their legs. One or two sets of curtains among the neighbours could be seen moving as the two uniformed officers were spotted.

The front door to the little house was tucked behind an open-sided porch with a pitched roof. Some movement was apparent behind one of the two long windows flanking the entrance. But it could have been a trick of the light.

Apart from a couple of parked cars, the street itself was deserted. A small black and white mongrel ran across the road, seeming to glance with interest at the unfamiliar four. Voices of children playing in one of the back gardens floated over. A few cumulus clouds shuffled overhead, not interrupting the otherwise glorious sunny day. It was all very peaceful and civilised.

"I'll go first," said Rosemary. "Uniform behind me and, Tammy, you make up the rear."

When confronting, without warning, individuals who might have been involved in some form of questionable activity, the trick was to be prepared for anything.

Nobody was prepared for what followed.

Reaching forward to ring the bell, Rose was knocked back with shock as the door was flung open to plainly reveal a gaunt-faced and hysterically screaming Letitia Mountford.

"BOB, TELL ME, how is this young lady, this private detective, progressing with the investigation?"

The PM, a white-haired avuncular man in his late sixties, sat back in his leather button-back swivel chair in the oak-panelled office facing Bob Walker across a wide leather-topped desk. Seven years in office had taken its toll, with the man showing signs of the endless stresses he'd been subjected to. The once ebullient features now hung loose. He appeared more like a bulldog than the ageless, if somewhat thinning, cherub he'd been when first elected.

"Well, Prime Minister, she is making progress," offered Bob. "But the case is complicated. We've killings in America, seemingly linked to at least one murder in the UK."

"And what of Mountford's wife? Has she been located?"

"The private investigator, Tammy Pierre, spotted something on the mutilated corpse found on the Heath when she examined the body at the mortuary, and as she correctly surmised, it turned out to be the body of Oscar Mountford's missing wife Letitia."

"Does Oscar know this?"

"Yes, Prime Minister, he does now."

"Anything more? What about your contact in America? The man who calls himself Felix, isn't it? Has he been able to help?"

"It's not really within the province of the CIA. They're understandably less interested in Letitia's activities, regarding it as essentially our domestic problem, than they are the issues with Oscar's international far right activities."

Bob could hear the PM drawing breath. He sounded worried. "We need to get this Budget speech organised."

"Yes, Prime Minister. But if we don't have enough to indict Mountford, a strong Budget speech will simply entrench his position. I firmly believe Oscar Mountford will

372 • THE POLITICIAN'S WIFE

seek to unseat you if his speech gains him sufficient popularity in the Party. He already has a cabal of cronies eager to increase their numbers."

"On the other hand, if we get his Budget proposals, and they're what we and the country need, if you have the evidence you require, he can be arrested in the House, right after delivering his speech."

"Exactly. We're on a tightrope here as far as timing is concerned."

"At least he won't be able to claim the Parliamentary privilege of immunity from arrest in the House."

"I'm aware it only applies in civil cases."

"Correct. Of course, precedent will require the sanction of the Speaker, but that will just be a formality."

"Everything possible to close this case is being carried out. As we're considering more than just the disappearance and now murder of Letitia Mountford, DCI Rosemary Sharpe is leading the investigations from the point of view of the police. She knows Tammy Pierre from a recent case they collaborated on, and they work well as a team, exchanging ideas and opinions. Tammy is also concentrating on Oscar Mountford and his activities, and how he might be linked to other killings that have taken place in the recent past."

"Good. I'm glad to hear that, Bob." The PM appeared to have finished whatever it was he'd planned to say, when his phone rang. Putting the receiver to his ear, Bob could hear a commotion and rising voices from where he sat.

"Is everything alright, sir?" Bob enquired.

The PM's voice was withdrawn and sombre. "Bob, you're quite right in your assessment of the situation. I've just been told there's a faction, practically outside my door, already seeking to oust me, and planning to move within the next few days. Do what you can, Bob. Any coterie supporting Oscar Mountford is going to spell disaster for the country."

"We're doing everything we can, Prime Minister."

CHAPTER 65 DAY 17

"AAAAAAAARGGGHHH!!!! I knew it. I knew you'd find me. I knew it. I knew it."

Running her fingers frantically through her long auburn air, scraping it back frantically, manically, she sank to the ground sobbing, her face in her hands, tears staining the front of her blue smock top.

"Letitia?" asked Rosemary. "It's really you, is it? Isn't it?" Turning to face Tammy standing behind the others, she asked, "What do you make of this? I thought DNA never lied."

"Wait," Tammy counselled. "A minute or two."

A couple of moments later a grey-haired woman in her late sixties, wearing an old-fashioned floral dress partly covered by an apron, her hands red from washing, or else cleaning, came to the door to stand over the younger woman. "What is it, darling?" Then seeing the uniforms, she demanded, "What is all this? Why are you here? What do you want, and why have you upset my daughter?"

"My name is Detective Chief Inspector Rosemary Sharpe," Rose announced. Then turning to the others, she introduced Sergeant Powell, PC Chaudry and finally, private investigator assisting with enquiries, Tammy Pierre. The young lady now sobbing quietly on the ground still said nothing.

"May we know if you are Sarah Filipek?" Rose addressed the older woman.

"That's right," she replied, sounding both suspicious, yet irritated at the same time.

"Ms Filipek, we are looking for Polonia Filipek, your daughter. We never expected to find Letitia Mountford here. We thought we had identified Letitia Mountford's body as that found murdered on Hampstead Heath in North London some weeks ago. But clearly we were mistaken."

"Yes, and you're still mistaken," she said, bending down to comfort and then help the distraught woman to her feet. "This is not Letitia Mountford, as you seem to think. It's my daughter Polonia. Polonia Filipek."

"Do you think we might come in, Ms Filipek? It's really not necessary to have your neighbours viewing proceedings," said Rose.

The living room was small and furnished with neat, tidy, but shabby easy chairs ranged around a 1950s style brown-tiled fireplace. Some scenic prints adorned the walls, with Vladimir Tretchikoff's green-faced Chinese Girl, taking pride of place. Sarah looking doubtfully at the visitors, clearly uncertain whether to extend hospitality or not, finally opted for the courteous approach. "Can I offer anyone teas? Coffees? Soft drinks?"

The offer was politely declined.

Tammy and Rose had sat down next to each other on the sofa, with Sarah and her daughter occupying the two armchairs opposite. The PC and sergeant stood behind the sofa, with notebooks ready to record the exchanges.

Opening the proceedings and addressing the younger woman, Rose asked, "May I first confirm, you are Polonia Filipek?"

The woman nodded, holding a handkerchief to her face, but otherwise remaining mute.

"Polonia? May I call you Polonia?" Rose asked gently.

The woman merely shrugged.

"You must surely be aware of why we're here?"

Speaking for the first time, she replied, "I've got nothing to say."

"You have been observed on CCTV travelling to the United States accompanied by the woman we now realise was Letitia Mountford."

"So what," she said, sounding belligerent.

"Polonia, darling, what is this all about?" asked Sarah, staring uncomprehendingly at her daughter.

"It seems Letitia Mountford's maiden name was Fili-pek," Rose interrupted. "For reasons I shan't go into at the moment, she changed her name to Philips. Now, of course, her married name is Mountford."

"Pyotr?" gasped Sarah.

"Exactly," offered Rose. "Would I be right in thinking you had a brief relationship with one Pyotr Filipek about forty years ago, Sarah?"

In an astonished reply Sarah said, "They're half-sisters, then, my daughter and this Letitia woman?"

"We think that that is almost certainly the case."

"Polonia? What is this all about." Sarah addressed her daughter. "Tell me, who is this woman, this Letitia Mount-ford, and what is she to you? Do you know her? You've never said anything to me about having a half-sister." She looked over at her daughter, who still said nothing.

"We have reason to believe, Sarah, that your daughter has in some way been involved in the killings of a number of people, both in this country and in the United States."

"What?" said Sarah, aghast.

"I'm sorry to have to break it to you so brutally, Sarah."

"Killings? A number of people? Am I going insane?" Then addressing her daughter, Sarah begged, "For God's sake, Polonia. Say something."

Getting to her feet, in an abrupt change of attitude Polo-nia, gazing at her distraught mother, snarled, "That's right. Killings. Forty years of living in this dump, with a fucking neurotic for a mother."

"My God, Polonia. My God," exclaimed Sarah, starting to weep, her face in her hands. "I don't know what to say. What to think. I can't believe this is happening."

"You'd better believe it. You kept him from me, didn't you? Never told me exactly who he was. My father. Only once you let slip his name, by mistake. You thought I hadn't heard. But I had. A year or two ago. I started making my own enquiries. It took a while. Then I found her. I found my half-sister. She told me about my father Pyotr. He was a Ukrainian carpenter, with Communist sympathies. Came to this country about half a century ago. Married a girl from back home he'd met in London. Had a daughter, Larissa, who changed her name when it suited her to Letitia."

Once started it was as though the flood gates had opened and years of pent-up resentment were released.

"They were killed in a car crash when Letitia was five years old. She was brought up by an aunt. Went to the LSE, where she teamed up with a Communist group, then met her future husband while still at university, so had to pretend she'd never really been left wing. Or else that it was a temporary blip."

"But, but… Killings? What killings?" Sarah turned a tear-stained face up at her daughter.

"You never wondered why I stayed single? Time and again you told me some rubbish about illegitimate girls never finding a mate. Really? What part of the fifteenth century were you born in, mother dear. You even scotched the few relationships I tried to make. Why? I'll tell you why. Because you had some cockeyed idea about what the local community would say or do if they found out I was a bastard. Even changed your name to Filipek, a man you were never married to and hardly even knew."

"Please, Polonia. Please stop now. I can't bear it," her mother begged.

"How would my staying here with you stop the gossip? And what gossip? Nothing ever filtered through to me. Spent my life wrapped in tissue paper and cotton wool. That riding accident. You'd have thought I'd been attacked the way you went on. Don't do this. Don't do that. A slight limp was what remained. That's all. So bloody what. I'd have gone back to riding if you'd let me.

"I'll tell you what it was all about. You were lonely. Frightened of life on your own. Bloody helpless. So you did all you could to tie me down."

"That's not true. Polonia. It's simply not true."

While this was going on the two uniformed police officers were writing frantically in their notebooks. Neither Tammy nor Rose said or did anything to interrupt what they were listening to.

"I traced her. Letitia. And we hit it off immediately. It was only when I met her, I realised for the first time in my life, at age fucking forty, that men could fancy me. Living in this Godforsaken shithole where the youngest man is over sixty, I found things rather different once I'd met my sister."

"Polonia, I can't bear it," said her mother, now sobbing. "I only ever wanted the best for you."

"Oh, please spare me the drama. I'll tell you what, mater dear, once I'd met Letitia, on one of my many trips to London you thought were sightseeing trips, I started having a life. A sex life. She was beautiful. That meant I was beautiful. You never twigged I was beautiful, did you. Old cow," she spat.

"Then Letitia and I started an affair. It was heaven. I never knew it could be that way. So when she said she was going to the States to have a bit of fun, I readily agreed to go with her. It was like being released from prison.

"Then she said she was a Communist, like her father. Our father. My Christ, she made me buzz. Told me she'd been working for Russia for years, undetected. They'd made her into a killing foil. One who got rid of dissidents. But she was bored. Like me, disillusioned. A rebel, with a cause, supposed to deal with dissidents discreetly. Discreet, hell. She did everything she could to draw attention to herself. And when she asked me if I'd like to have a go, I thought, yeah. Why the hell not. If she could get her rocks off that way, so could I."

"The St James's Hotel?" Tammy quietly prompted.

"That's right. The very same."

"So, you. Not Letitia?" asked Rose.

"Letitia planned to come back from the States a day or two after me, but I didn't see her again. I don't know where she got to in that time or what she was doing. Trafalgar Square was scheduled for about three weeks after that, say, three or four weeks ago. She was fully aware I'd be on CCTV in the UK. Let's really confuse the buggers, she'd said. Boy, was she a bandit? Never do as you're told, she added. Always do as you want. That's the only way to live."

"Where did you stay after you got back from the States?" asked Rosemary.

"Here," said Polonia. "With mother dear."

Her mother looked down at the floor, but said nothing.

"Was that the only killing you did?" Tammy asked.

"That's right. All the others were carried out by my sister, more's the pity. Wouldn't have minded adding to my own toll, of just one."

Turning around to face the two taking notes, Rose asked, "Have you got all this?"

"Yes, Guv," they replied in unison.

"In that case," announced Rose, getting stiffly to her feet, "Polonia Filipek, I am arresting you for the murder of one Toby Trimble. You do not have to say anything. But it may harm your defence if you do not mention when questioned, something which you later rely on in court. Anything you do say may be given in evidence."

"Go fuck yourself. Couldn't believe it when you came to the door. I've worried about this since the day. What the hell for, I ask myself? It was just a bit of fun. I loved her. Now she's gone, what's left for me? I'll tell you what's left for me. Nothing," said Polonia, and burst into tears again.

CHAPTER 66 DAY 17

THE RETURN JOURNEY had taken nigh on three hours, PC Chaudry having regained a sense of sanity and proportion. By the time they got to New Scotland Yard, they were, all five of them, thoroughly weary. Polonia had refused to allow her mother to accompany her, leaving her on the doorstep wringing her hands as they all departed for London.

Once Rose and Tammy were facing Polonia across a table in an interview room, the woman was offered the chance to be represented by a lawyer, or else to retract the statement she'd made earlier recorded by the two in uniform. When she declined a solicitor and further insisted her statement would hold, a version was presented to her in due course to read and sign, if she agreed its contents.

From there Polonia was advised she'd be held in custody overnight at the facility in Charing Cross police station, then presented to a magistrate's court in the morning by video link, after which there would be a first hearing in a Crown Court within four weeks.

The two uniforms were dismissed and Tammy and Rose exited the building to look for a pub, and deciding on The Blackfriar, a traditional pub a short walk from the Yard, made their way to it. The interior, all reds, golds and faux marble presented an astonishing sight to the unfamiliar. Built in 1875 on the site of a Dominican friary and redesigned by free-thinking architect H. Fuller-Clark and designer Henry Poole, around 1905, the original sculptures, mosaics and reliefs still adorn the place.

What's more, they did an excellent pint of Guinness, which is just what a thirsty Tammy craved. Rose settled for a lager, and the two found themselves a table.

"Long day," said Rose with a sigh, settling down with her drink.

"Hang on," said Tammy, throwing her head back and downing most of her pint in one. "Needed that." She smiled, then proceeded to finish off the drink in a second draught, winked at Rose and went off to get another.

"Better?" Rose asked when Tammy returned.

"Improving by the minute."

"You know what'll happen when it gets to the Crown Court?"

"Of course. She'll be asked how she pleads, then if, as we expect, it's guilty, she'll be remanded for psychiatric reports."

"Exactly," said Rose. "What an extraordinary set of events. Seems the two sisters have or had a lot in common."

"Apart from just looks," added Tammy. "The inconsistent behaviours, characters, suggest they might be bipolar?"

"That's as good a guess as any, at least till we see the reports."

"I wonder what ever attracted Letitia to a man with views as right wing as Oscar's? Could be she was having second thoughts about her left wing affiliations when she met him. Charismatic individual. Good-looking. Sexy. Ambitious."

"Didn't seem to prevent her killing to order, though," Rose pointed out.

"True. That'll remain unanswered, I'm afraid." Downing half of her second pint in one, Tammy noticed Rose smiling to herself. "Thirsty," she said, grinning.

"So I see," said Rose.

"People are so totally unpredictable," said Tammy. "For all Letitia's insane life, everyone has pointed out how she adored her autistic son David. The curious thing though, is that although Oscar regarded the boy with disdain, Jayne, knowing that, nevertheless worshipped her father. They just connected, those two, despite Jayne being the sort of timid individual you'd expect her father to regard with contempt."

"Might be worth having another chat with Jayne, Tammy. See if she can give us anything further on either of her parents."

"I was proposing to do just that, Rose. But before I do, I'd like to take a look at the Ford Transit you've got tucked away. The one used to run down Kevin Anderton. See if there's anything might have been missed."

"SOCO and then forensics have given it the full treatment. They're pretty thorough, you know."

"Still, even if I don't find anything suspicious or helpful in terms of bits of evidence, occasionally an inspection can reveal other things."

"What did you have in mind?"

"Oh, I don't know. Wear on tyres may indicate particular driving habits. Ditto brake pad wear. I've seen a partially caved-in driver's seat where the perp was a particularly heavy individual. Also, when I examined a motor with damaged rack and pinion steering it transpired our driver was a muscleman, too heavy on the steering wheel. It may be a wasted day, but worth a look. This murder of Letitia may not bother Oscar, but it sure as hell concentrates my mind."

"Okay, love. I'll set up the appointment for you. Mind if I come along. After that mortuary discovery, anything is on the cards."

"Sure. Come along," said Tammy, finishing her second pint and getting up, with a nod from Rose to replenish their glasses.

CHAPTER 67 DAY 18

IT WAS CLOUDY, with hoped-for rain promising to clear the muggy atmosphere.

She recognised the voice immediately, the feminine pitch was unmistakeable, the menace insistent. "One nil to you, bitch. But I'll be back. On your way to Perivale, are you? They found nothing and neither will you."

"Why good morning, Mr Loughty," said Tammy. "Following me around, are you? Evidently you got home, or to a hospital in good time. Nasty cut that, on your leg. You need to be careful who you accost, good sir. Never know what you might be up against. Really should have let me call you a cab when I offered."

"You won't be laughing much longer, butch lady."

"I've handled better than you before breakfast, madam."

"Madam? Who the fuck are you calling madam?"

"If the cap fits," Tammy replied.

"We'll see, lady. We'll see," he muttered.

"You know, I may be in touch sooner than you anticipate, Mr Loughty. Now do forgive me; must dash." And with that she rang off.

Rose asked Tammy enquiringly, "Someone you know?"

"We weren't formally introduced, Rose. He's the gentleman I met in the park a couple of nights ago. The one I mentioned to you. I think I must have made quite an impression on him."

Rose said nothing, just shook her head and smiled.

"Here we are," said Tammy, steering the Lexus into the entrance of the car pound.

The Vehicle Recovery and Examination Service (VRES) had organised the recovery and holding of the vehicle used to run down and kill Kevin Anderton.

The VRES presently processes some forty-six thousand vehicles a year, using the services of seven private contractors spread around eleven sites in the UK. There is a procedure involving the Metropolitan Police Service (MPS), whose central call centre, termed the Garage Desk, will contact the VRES with a request to recover a given vehicle.

The Perivale car pound, where the Ford Transit had been taken for examination, presented a pretty forbidding aspect, with high wire fences around it. A series of low, white prefabricated structures within the perimeter comprised offices and dry storage facilities for vehicles recovered. One building in particular appeared to be about the size of an aircraft hangar.

Holding around one thousand vehicles in all, the place is open 24/7, 365 days a year, albeit opening hours to the public are between 11.30 am and 7.30 pm, seven days a week.

It was to this venue that Tammy repaired, accompanied by Rosemary with the object of examining said Ford, now entering the place through the sole access in Walmgate Road, off Aintree Road, near the Hoover building on the A40.

Presenting the relevant forms to the office, the two women were then taken to one of the smaller sheds close to the perimeter of the lot to look at the Ford Transit Custom. A mid-size vehicle with a wide range of options and extras to choose from. Rear storage capacity, depending on whether one opted for the short or long wheelbase vehicle, was from 6 to 6.8 cubic feet. The interior boasted an impressive range of technical driver assist features. Including Blind Spot Information System, Traffic Sign Recognition System, Cross Traffic Alert System to alert the driver of approaching traffic when reversing, and more besides.

Still parked over the capacious steel inspection pit, it must have been an impressive vehicle before the crash. Painted in silver grey, the front was comprehensively crumpled like crushed tissue. Clearly, without the requisite airbag the driver too would have been unlikely to survive the impact. Easy to see why Kevin Anderton hadn't made it.

The vehicle had, of course, already been examined in detail by a forensic collision investigator and a forensic vehicle examiner and an extensive report prepared, covering mechanical damage and forensic findings, all of which Tammy and Rose had access to prior to their visit.

Having accompanied the two women to the relevant bay, the young constable excused himself, leaving Rose and Tammy to spend time going over the vehicle themselves.

She'd opted for jeans and a sweatshirt, while Rose was in a less practical working suit. Both women donned blue nitrile hygienic gloves, although at this stage there was little they'd likely contaminate.

The report gave details of the onsite examination of skid marks, which were minimal, suggesting that only at the last moment in an apparent attempt to preserve his own life had the driver applied the brakes.

The dried blood, now comprising extensive brown marks over the radiator, indicated that Kevin Anderton must have suffered a catastrophic loss of blood. He'd been crushed up against the brick wall of a building in Hornsey, North London, and a residue of brick dust was visible on the front of the motor.

While Rose climbed inside the cabin, Tammy crawled into the storage space at the back of the Ford, pulling out the floor panelling, searching around for anything that might have been missed, however small and however unlikely. But the team had done their work with meticulous care, as would be expected. They'd gone so far as to remove the tyres from the wheels, examine the airbag for any information that could be gleaned and even to reconstruct from skid lines on the road and pavement the likely trajectory of the Ford in the lead-up to the atrocity.

After an hour and a half, they both agreed there'd be little chance of finding anything missed by forensics.

Tammy stood back with her hands on her hips, then, watched by Rose, walked around the vehicle like a caged lion. "Something missing," she muttered. "Anything in the driver's cabin, Rose?"

"Nothing at all. You know we got DNA from the airbag. But we don't know who to match it with. CCTV in the area shows a man, well, very likely a man, in a hoodie, running from the Ford right after the crash."

"You inspected the glove compartment, side pockets, under the seats, in the crease between the seats and the backrests?"

"All that, and more."

"I think we'll call it a day, then," said Tammy. Then, as an afterthought, "What about the rubber floor mats? Anything under, or on?"

"No, I checked."

"Okay," she said, stroking her chin pensively. Then, peering in the driver's door, Tammy leaned down and pulled out the two mats, dropping one onto the concrete floor while she examined the other. "Nothing," she said with a sigh, then picked up the other mat. Examining it closely, she pulled at a tiny bit of muddy paper stuck to the underside, and was about to discard it, when, taking a further look, she said, "I wonder what this?"

"Looks like a bit of grubby tissue to me," said Rose.

"There's a faint line here, as though this is a bit of page from a notebook."

Turning on the torch facility in her mobile, Tammy trained it at the scrap. "Mm! No," she said, shaking her head. Then, "There's some numbers written here, a bit faded, smudged. Hardly surprising if it was under the mat for a while."

"Numbers?" Rose asked. "How many?"

"Eight," said Tammy. "One end of the paper is clean, as though it's an edge, the other is torn."

"What do you think? Code for something?"

"I wonder," she mused. "I've got a better idea. This could be eight digits of a mobile. UK mobile numbers are normally eleven digits in all. In which case what we have here has three digits missing, the first two of which would almost certainly be 07. If I'm right, we've only to try 07 followed by 1 then 2 and so on up to 9, added to the eight we have, to see where it takes us."

"Worth a try," Rose agreed. "Then depending on what happens I'll take away the scrap of paper for DNA examination and see if I can get a make on the airbag too. I'll cut out a sample before we go."

It was when Tammy got to 07 7, followed by the eight digits on the scrap that she hit paydirt. "It's ringing," she practically gasped.

On the fifth ring, a voice said hesitantly, "Hello. Who is that?" Tammy said nothing. The voice went on, nervously now. "Smollett here, MacDonald Smollett. Who's there? Is that you, Oscar?"

"I think I must have the wrong number," said Tammy. "Sorry to have troubled you."

There was a long silent pause while Tammy held her breath. Then a voice erupted, "Who is this? Who is this? My God. Oscar? What have I done? Who are you? Are you French? Where are you calling from? How did you get this number?"

But Tammy hung up.

"THAT WAS NICE."

Sounding half asleep, he said, "Hmm?"

"I'm glad you approve." She was walking around his place, unselfconsciously naked.

He was sitting back on the double bed in his flat off the Edgware Road in his boxers, heavily muscled arms folded across his chest.

In the light of day, she watched him surveying the scars. "Thank you, Dov," she said.

"What for?" he asked, puzzled.

"For taking care last night."

"Oh, that." He smiled. "Don't I always take care?"

"You do, my love. But with the stitches still in…" She left the rest unsaid.

"I think you need taking care of."

"By whom?" she asked.

"Why, me, of course."

She grinned. "If there's one thing I don't need, it's being taken care of. Not by you. Nor by anyone else." She paused for a moment, then went on, "Apart, that is, from the occasional armed response unit."

It was his turn to burst out laughing.

"I love this place, you know," she said, spinning around. "It's an absolute treasure trove of fun."

"It's a business, Tammy, not a toy shop."

"I know. I know," she teased.

But he couldn't deny the place was pretty overladen with wall-to-wall bookshelves, and towers of books all over the floor. Added to that Dov, as always, had flowers everywhere, providing a lovely splash of colour. Then there was the memorabilia from his time in the army, and porcelain of every type gracing antique occasional tables and shelves not already filled with books. It was all a melee of business and pleasure.

Dov had met Tammy some six years ago, she recalled, when she'd turned up at one of his Krav Maga sessions. They hadn't immediately become an item, as it were. Indeed, Dov still wasn't sure where he stood as far as his staccato relationship with Tammy was concerned.

Dov's mother, a children's author, lived on her own, close to his fiercely independent eighty-four-year-old grandfather, following the death of Dov's father in the Yom Kippur War of 1973. She'd never remarried. Being brought up without the benefit of a father, he'd learned to be independent and to defend himself at a very early age. It had stood him in good stead on innumerable occasions.

"I'm showering," she announced, and ambled towards the bathroom where she stood for an age under a hot shower, letting it ease away some of the aches and pains and recent bruising. Would he bring up the question of her pregnancy? she wondered. And if he did, how would she respond? Presumably, as the mood took her. She'd never want to see him hurt. But how do you justify rape to a man who knows you've the morals of an alley cat.

Wrapped in a snug white towelling robe, Tammy came back into the bedroom and flopped onto an easy chair.

Looking over at her fondly, Dov said, "We've not talked much about the case since America. It looks as though the Letitia and Polonia murder cases are all but dealt with. But that still leaves Pierce? Kevin Anderton? William Davenport and, of course, Letitia herself. A mountain of unanswered questions. What do you think?"

"As you know, I've had a meeting with Oscar's daughters, and after a fair amount of debate, they all agreed their father isn't a murderer. So the death of Pierce remains an open question.

"Kevin Anderton, I may have made a breakthrough. I found a muddied scrap of paper in the vehicle used to mow him down and guessed it might be a mobile number. Or at least, part of one. I took a stab at a few alternatives, and then miracle of miracles, found an answer when Mr MacDonald Smollett, senior partner at solicitors, Smollett Davis Carleton, picked up the call."

"Wow!" said Dov, sitting up. "That looks like some progress."

"It is, particularly when gauging the response I got when he answered."

"Go on."

"He panicked. Wondered if he was being called by Oscar. You should have heard it. Anyway, I shall be giving the eminent Smollett, partner of a firm turning over around fifty million, a visit in the imminent future."

"Well done, Tammy. Tell me, what about the two hedge fund partners you spoke to. Anything further there?"

"Not yet. It's still a work in progress. Two singularly unpleasant characters, one with a particular penchant for violence."

"William Davenport?"

"Nothing, as yet. I'm hoping Smollett will open up a number of new avenues of investigation for us. We're still trying to be as discreet as possible. Don't want the press alerted before we get Chancellor Mountford's Budget speech, which has been delayed several times already because of the need to wrap up as much as is possible now. If the media get hold of anything at this stage, they'll call for his resignation and there's no way a discredited minister could speak in Parliament with any degree of authority."

"Bit of a tightrope you're walking, aren't you."

"You could say that." Then getting up and making for the kitchen, she said, "Fancy a coffee?"

"That'd be very welcome. Hey, before you disappear, I hadn't realised how far gone you were."

So there it was. It had to be mentioned. Only surprising it had taken this long. "You noticed." She smiled, hoping he'd leave it there.

"Our baby." He sounded wonderfully happy.

"Our baby," she agreed, sounding as happy as she could.

Something in her tone must have alerted him to the suggestion of a change in her attitude.

"Tammy," he asked intently, swinging his legs off the bed, "we are talking about my baby, aren't we? That is, our baby?"

"Who else's might it be, Dov?" she said, trying to appear as indignant as possible.

"Tammy, can you please answer the question? Is this our baby? I need to know. You must realise that, for God's sake. Please don't play games with me."

"Dov, what an absurd question. Who did you imagine I was seeing in war-torn Syria? Hmm? A freedom fighter? It's enough now. Just stop it."

He shrugged, unconvinced and thoroughly discomfited, but said no more.

On hold for now, she prayed, hoping he couldn't see her shaking. But for how long? And who might the baby resemble?

CHAPTER 69 DAY 19

SHE'D GOT TO WORK that morning feeling elated and at the same time troubled with the way the conversation with Dov had gone.

Mrs Gilchrist, as always anticipating Tammy's moods, had a hot coffee and a plate of garibaldis on her desk almost as soon as Tammy had sat down.

"Emails are mounting, Miss Pierre," she said. "A lot of matters requiring your attention, some quite urgent."

"I know, Mrs Gilchrist. But Bob Walker is seriously anxious to tie up things on the Letitia Mountford matter before anything else."

"I understand," Mrs Gilchrist replied. "I'll make the appropriate excuses where I can."

"Thank you, it's really appreciated. Sorry you're so often in the firing line these days."

Leaving Tammy's room, Mrs Gilchrist nodded and smiled in understanding.

Then Tammy's phone rang.

"Tammy." The voice was exultant. "We've got a result with the DNA."

"From the Ford?"

"That's right."

"Already? How'd forensics manage that? It must be a first ever."

"I put a rocket under them. They put in the overtime."

"Do you know who?"

"We think so. And the paper and the airbag both match."

"Tell me."

394 • THE POLITICIAN'S WIFE

"Nasty piece of work called Ainsley Borrell."

"Known, then?"

"Very much so. Robbery with violence. Money with menaces. Record of beating up women. You name it."

"Odd name. Where's the man from?"

"He's Caribbean. Jamaican. What little we have suggests his father was the minister of a church back home, a good man from what accounts we have, but couldn't interest his son in pursuing the Ministry. Young Ainsley came to the UK and immediately embarked on a life of crime. Judging by his prison record, a none too successful one at that."

"You know, Rose; I may have met him. After one of my late evening Embankment meetings with Bob I was accosted by a tall man, Caribbean appearance and accent, who warned me off. We think he may have been attempting to listen in to our conversation. He seemed to have the gear for it in his car."

"Interesting. We've been reviewing some of the CCTV images we have on file. Among those we picked up from the Hornsey killing of Kevin Anderton, we can see a man run from the vehicle after it hits Kevin. Tall, similar sort of build to Borrell. Sporting a hoodie, but unmistakably Caribbean from the small glimpse we have from the side view."

"Any idea where Borrell might hang out?"

"We know some of his haunts from previous meetings we've had with him."

"Rose, if it's okay with you, I'll chase up da Silva, rather than leaving him to you as I planned, and maybe chase up Cranfield at the same time if I can get them in their offices together, give them a grilling, as neither has a criminal record. Seems a practical way to go about things, if you care to go for Borrell, whom it appears you all know quite well."

"Suits me."

"If I get past da Silva and partner before you collar Borrell, perhaps I could sit in?"

"Sure, why not."

"While I think of it, there's also the little man with wire-rimmed spectacles and the Russian accent who tried warning me off. Not sure if I ever mentioned him?"

"Don't think so."

"If Letitia was offing Russian dissidents, it makes sense if, as we believe, she was going rogue to have a handler dealing with her himself, if that's what he was. We could be barking up the wrong tree entirely. We know the Russians' reputation for dealing with dissidents. After all, that's exactly what Letitia was employed for."

"True. But if it was him, or one of his associates, we're not likely to ever find him. Of course, he may seek me out again." Rose sighed. "We'll see."

At that moment Tammy's mobile rang and, excusing herself, she finished her call with Rose and answered Bob Walker.

"Hi, Bob. Is everything okay?"

"No, Tammy," he said, clearly concerned and speaking as softly as one afraid of being overheard. "Being discreet as you're not on a burner, the PM is increasingly worried about the level of extremist support our mutual friend is gaining, both within the Party and without.

"He's desperately worried that if the man isn't swiftly discredited his progress may become unstoppable. With the very real possibility he could unseat the PM, then with the support of other European extremist factions we could be faced with an entirely new and unpredictable situation here and on the Continent.

"Trouble is the Budget. There's been far more time than we anticipated to prepare it and I gather it's all ready to go. The reshuffle needs to be announced imminently. How near are you and Rose to a result?"

"Give me forty-eight hours, Bob. Then the PM can make his announcements."

"Alright, Tammy. Forty-eight hours. That will have to be our limit."

CHAPTER 70 DAY 19

SHE TURNED UP AT the offices of Maerland da Silva without announcement. She didn't have time to make appointments, which they'd probably try to delay anyway.

In a sober two-piece with low heels, Tammy presented herself at the elegant reception and asked to see the two men. As chance would have it they were both in, but they kept her waiting over an hour before doing her the courtesy of appearing. She was in no mood to play games, and there was no way she was leaving without first seeing them. So she hung on, and would have hung on if it took all day.

Eventually the two men appeared, both impatient and annoyed at the same time.

Da Silva wore a similar outfit to that she'd seen him in last time, with black chinos and silk white shirt. Cranfield was again very casual with navy chinos, expensive trainers and a denim open-neck shirt.

"You'd better come into my room," muttered da Silva, leading the way.

As they sat down in the man's office, she wasn't offered hospitality, and neither partner spoke, waiting for her to break the ice.

"Well, gentlemen," she opened. "You'll be delighted to learn we're not looking for anyone else, other than your-selves in the matter of the murder of Letitia Mountford."

"And just what the fuck is that supposed to mean," spat da Silva.

"Exactly what it says. As you well know, we have Leti-tia's DNA on Theo's jacket hidden in the boot of your Fer-rari, Caspar, with no plausible explanation from either of you as to how it came to be there. And we have her DNA around the boot space as well. So you tell me. Sex game? Unfortunate accident? Quick disposal? Body rendered unidentifiable in the most horrible way. Nasty. Where are her other bits?"

"What?" Theo's voice was insistent, but hushed by an indication from Caspar's raised hand.

"You know. Her bits. Head. Arms. Legs. Where did you hide them?"

"We didn't hide them because we didn't kill her."

"Not on purpose, perhaps. So, maybe not murder. But manslaughter? Awful lot of damning evidence in the car, isn't there? Lots for a jury to get their teeth into."

Both men shifted about, increasingly uncomfortable.

"Should we say something, Cas?" Theo asked.

"Suit yourself, mate." Caspar shrugged.

Facing Tammy full on, Theo said hesitantly, "Okay. So we did have the occasional sex game, the three of us. But that was all. Nothing more. And nothing went wrong."

"Progress at last," said Tammy. "And of course, nothing went wrong, as you said."

"And what the hell are you talking about?" asked Caspar.

"Just that the story keeps changing, a bit like the weather. I guess if we go on talking for long enough you'll be admitting to manslaughter and pleading extenuating circumstances."

"We've killed no-one," growled Caspar.

Getting to her feet, Tammy said, "Well, thank you for your time, gentlemen. I'll leave you to ponder our little chat. Remember, a guilty plea to the crime of manslaughter would carry a greatly reduced sentence when compared with murder. You'd probably both be out within about seven years."

Surveying their ashen faces, she added, "No need to see me out."

Really Rose's province now, she decided, as she exited the building. Time to bring them both in and question them under caution.

CHAPTER 71 DAY 19

SHE'D GRABBED A PREFERRED black cab after leaving Maerland da Silva, since they could use the faster bus lanes, aiming to get to New Scotland Yard on the Victoria Embankment in time to sit in on the interview between Rose and Ainsley Borrell, whom they'd quickly located at a bar in Notting Hill.

She was tired, should really ease up. The wound to her side was pulling, the stitches biting deep. It was time they were removed anyway, and if she couldn't make the time to get the job done by a medic she'd do it herself. A busy time, hence her state, but with the minutes ticking away, she'd no real choice but to push herself. Would Ainsley Borrell provide anything to link his likely involvement in the murder of Kevin Anderton to Oscar Mountford?

Also, she'd been getting some odd twinges in her lower abdomen. She dreaded losing the baby, but was almost equally concerned at the reproof she'd face if she went for a consultation with her GP, Doctor Aziz. It would wait, and hopefully she wouldn't regret the decision to do nothing. Probably the worst of all options.

Waving her in, the doorman, who by now knew Tammy without the need for her to produce ID, smiled in her direction.

She reached the appropriate floor and designated interview room with no time to spare. Rose, looking up as Tammy hurried along the corridor, angled her head towards the interview room door and whispered, "Glad you could make it. They're inside."

Seated facing the pair as they entered was Ainsley Borrell in a crumpled suit, as if he'd been dragged out of bed, collar not properly fastened, tie askew, and with him a bespectacled young black woman in a dark business suit, a notepad on her lap, whom Borrell presented as his lawyer Grace Timoni.

Once seated, Rose introduced Tammy, explaining that she was a private investigator assisting her in her enquiries, and present, contrary to established precedent, at the express requirement of Detective Chief Superintendent Robert Walker, and asked if there were any objections to her sitting in.

Grace turned to Borrell for comment, and was met by a noncommittal shrug. Taking that to be an approval, Grace said, "We have no objections." She glanced at Tammy, inspecting her with obvious interest.

Rose went on to run through the protocol, explaining to Borrell that he was not under arrest, but was being interviewed under caution, and that he could leave at any time, further confirming with him and his lawyer there were no objections to the interview being recorded on video.

"Mr Borrell," Rose opened. "You will be aware of the purpose of this interview?"

He shrugged again but said nothing.

"Mr Borrell? Would you favour us with an answer?"

His lawyer nodded once, and Borrell said, "De accident, y'all have say."

"The accident, as you put it, that resulted in the death of Mr Kevin Anderton."

"Ent nuttin' tuh do wid me."

"Let me show you a recording of the unfortunate incident, Mr Borrell."

Rose picked up a remote lying on the table and pointed it at a large wall-mounted screen whereupon a picture sparked into focus. On view was an apparently empty street in early morning Hornsey with a single individual in short-sleeve shirt and navy chinos walking away from the CCTV camera.

"That's Kevin Anderton," said Rose, by way of explanation. "May I warn you, Ms Timoni, this isn't pleasant to watch."

Borrell shifted uneasily in his seat, obviously knowing full well what was coming.

Rose said nothing more at this stage.

A moment later the Ford hove into view, driving full pelt at Anderton who was thrown forward, crushed against the brick wall of a building fronting onto the pavement.

"He never stood a chance," said Rosemary quietly.

As they all watched, the driver's door of the Ford opened and a man could be seen struggling to get out from behind the inflated airbag. Eventually freeing himself, the individual, wearing a black tracksuit and hoodie, was filmed running from the scene.

Grace Timoni looked horrified, but made no comment.

"I'll get straight to the point, Mr Borrell, that's you running from the vehicle isn't it."

"Dat ent me, lady. Me have never see dis ting afore."

"You drove into Kevin Anderton, killing him in cold blood."

"Nah me."

"Very well, let's try something else. We have your DNA on samples cut from the Ford's airbag."

"Nah me," he protested again.

"We also have a DNA match on a scrap of paper found stuck under one of the floor mats in the van."

"You have Mr Borrell's DNA on file?" asked Grace Timoni.

"Of course, as a known felon his DNA was taken some time ago."

"Yes, I do realise," she responded, slightly flustered at the sickening scene they'd just witnessed.

"The scrap of paper had what turned out to be a mobile telephone number on it." Rose studied Borrell's face for some sort of reaction but seeing none carried on. "Would you like me to tell you whose number we were dialling?"

"Yuh gwan tell me anyways." Borrell twisted in his seat, gazing intently at the back of his hands.

"We found we were talking to the eminent Mr MacDonald Smollett, managing partner at solicitors Smollett Davis Carleton. Do you know the gentleman at all, Mr Borrell?"

"Neva hear a him," he replied.

"We're proposing to interview Mr Smollett, Mr Borrell. Do you think he may claim to know you, when we question him?"

"Me neva hear a him," he repeated.

Rose, checking her notes, caught Borrell's attention, and quoting the precise date of the killing asked Borrell where he was on that date and at that time.

He had no response for her.

"Mr Borrell," Rose went on, "I suspect you may be aware that MacDonald Smollett, with whom you've clearly been in touch, is a colleague of the MP Mr Oscar Mountford, whose wife has recently been found murdered. Insofar as you appear to be involved in the death of Kevin Anderton, might it not be reasonable to conclude you may have been involved in the killing of the MP's wife, Ms Letitia Mountford?"

"Wass da man talk about. Me ain't know nobody call Letitia." Borrell gazed at his lawyer as though for inspiration or support, but she merely carried on taking notes.

"Then again," added Rose, "Mr Oscar Mountford's PA, Georgia Keith, was killed in a similar fashion to Kevin Anderton. The vehicle in her case has gone missing. No surprises there. But the CCTV images show an individual bearing the same description as the gentleman seen exiting the Ford in the Anderton matter, this time a white van, and apparently inspecting the damage to it, and then looking over a further red vehicle involved whose occupants escaped relatively unscathed, and finally, it would seem, the injuries to Georgia, who survived the incident briefly. You took care this time, didn't you, Mr Borrell, not to hit the subject too hard. The airbag didn't inflate, making it easy for you to drive away, and presumably dump the vehicle."

"Nah comment," said Borrell.

"Have you been to Geneva recently, sir?"

"Wha?"

"Geneva. It's in Switzerland, you know."

"Nah. Neva go dere afore."

"A man called Davenport was recently found murdered at his private house there."

"Nah me, lady."

"So, to conclude," Rose adopted her most officious tone, "we have three possible murders which might be attributable to you, Mr Borrell. You're what might be called a mass murderer."

"Rubbish nah, man."

"Rubbish?"

"Me ent no mass murderer. Gotta kill lotta folks one time."

"Would serial killer be more appropriate, do you think?"

"Serial. Na, man. For serial, gotta kill tree parsons."

"And you haven't killed three, then, Mr Borrell?"

"No way."

"Just two, then?"

Borrell without thinking nodded, muttered, "Jus two." Then immediately retracted, "What de fock?" He now behaved like a cornered rat, gazing this way and that, as though there might be a way out.

But Rose now continued, "Mr Borrell, I have to conclude that in the absence of any alibi, or any explanation for how yours is the sole DNA found in the vehicle, that you are responsible for the killing of Kevin Anderton. I appreciate that a court might take the view that this was a hit and run, and eventually return a verdict of manslaughter, but for now I am arresting you for the murder of Kevin Anderton…"

At that Borrell rose to his feet. A tall man, towering over those seated, he pointed an accusing finger first at Rose then at Tammy, who met his gaze, eyeball to eyeball.

"Ain't no-one tekkin' me in for no killin'. No-one, lady. No way."

Rising to her feet, Tammy eyeballed Borrell. "Mr Borrell," she said in her most placatory tone, "don't you think you might best serve your own interests by co-operating with the police?"

"Keep outa dis. Fockin' coconut."

With that comment, Borrell's lawyer raised an eyebrow in astonishment.

Borrell then made as if to leave the interview room, making for the door, until Tammy, quickly stepped over and barred his exit. "Now, Mr Borrell, we're not going to do anything silly, are we?"

"Outa my way, lady, afore someone get hart."

"Quite right, sir. You wouldn't want to get hurt now, would you."

"Me? Fock off, lady. Who gonna hart me?"

"As a matter of fact, me. If you force me to."

It stopped Borrell in his tracks. His eyes travelled up and down, taking in Tammy as though sizing up his prospects, then thinking better of it, stood back and folded his arms defiantly.

But before anything else could transpire two burly police officers entered the interview room, and taking Borrell by the arms, marched him off still protesting to the cells.

"TAMMY. WE NEED TO TALK."

"Hi, Bob. You sound as though you're under the cosh. PM leaning on you?"

"'Fraid so. MI6 have identified far right groups from Austria, Hungary, Poland, Italy, to name but a few, coming to the UK, ostensibly to see Oscar. I can't and don't believe he's been foolish enough to forewarn them of his imminent promotion. But there are any number of other ways he might have put things in order to encourage a visit from them. And it seems there's also a contingent on its way from the States. Felix has been in touch. He's very worried. A lot of these groups are more than just far right, they're really neo-Nazi."

"I'm keeping an open mind, Bob, but chasing up as many avenues as possible."

"That leads me to another issue, Tammy." He sounded even more apprehensive.

"I'm listening."

"Top brass are leaning on me for a result, else they're considering removing you from the case. They're arguing it should never have been given to a private investigator to do police work."

"Come on, Bob, you said yourself that the only way to keep this thing watertight and away from the press was to employ a PI outside the force."

"I know. And I haven't changed my mind one iota. MI5 and 6 also think you're doing a fantastic job."

"So? Where's the problem?"

"The problem, Tammy, is Oscar Mountford."

"I might have guessed. I presume he has contacts in high places."

"That's about the size of it. He knows my Commander, and the Met Commissioner, Tom Wallace. Mountford's been complaining you're harassing him. Insisting they take you off the job."

"What do the Met know of his far right activities?"

"Not a lot. MI5 and 6 have both chosen to play this very close to their chests. Mountford is a respected MP, whatever we think we know of him. The security services, whom I know well, have taken me into their confidence and have absolute belief in my choice of you in this matter. Trouble is, if we don't get a result soon, I'm going to find myself overruled."

"I don't need much more time for what I have in mind, Bob. Has Oscar got his Budget in place?"

"Yes. And he's ready to go. Has been for days."

"Word doesn't seem to have got out. So far."

"No, Carstairs suspects. But he's too wise to try putting his foot in it. And," Bob paused before continuing, "he knows his stewardship of the economy has been weak, lacking in vision. He'll probably be glad to cede the problems to someone else."

"One problem less, then. Oscar must have been burning the midnight oil."

"Yes. He's been working effectively out of hours with a small team from the Treasury to get this all together. It'll be unprecedented. Cabinet reshuffle in the afternoon and Budget from the new Chancellor within twenty-four hours."

"Then you want an arrest right after the Leader of the Opposition has given his response to Oscar's presentation?"

"Correct. If at all possible."

"That means the PM is going to have to appoint another new Chancellor the day after."

"Right, Tammy. I know. Three Chancellors in as many days."

"Press won't know what to make of it."

"Neither will the public."

"But it has to be done?"

"Economy's in a dire condition. We need someone with the authority of Oscar Mountford to deliver the thing."

"Even though he's going to be up on a murder charge?"

"Don't remind me. But in the history of Parliament stranger things have taken place. And the PM already has a successor lined up. Someone who will willingly pursue Oscar's policies."

"May I know who?" she asked.

"Woman called Janet Beening."

"A back bencher?"

"Fast up and coming. Qualified actuary. Gets on with people. Will support the PM absolutely, for as long as she's needed. Personally, I think she'll shine. Make the job her own."

"Our first ever female Chancellor." Tammy sounded impressed.

"Long overdue, if you ask me."

"What if, after all, there's panic in the markets."

"There won't be."

"How can you be sure?"

"Initially no-one will believe Oscar could be a murderer. The new Chancellor will be introduced as a caretaker until Oscar is ostensibly proven to be innocent, which will allow the markets to settle."

"I hope you're right."

"The PM knows what he's doing."

"No comment."

"I understand, Tammy. But it's easy to be cynical."

"I just hope he does know what he's about. What is it you think that'll re-inspire the markets?"

"It'll be the overweening scope of the Budget. The sheer audacity. It's utterly confidential, even between ourselves. But it'll make people sit up."

"In that case I hope I can deliver in time, Bob."

"We can't wait any longer. If we don't act immediately the markets will go into free fall. We need that Budget speech now. What's your schedule going on?"

"I saw Ainsley Borrell earlier today. Rose will have told you…"

"That's right. We've got to find out who he's working for."

"Has to be Oscar."

"Okay. While we're on, do you have any other possible leads in mind?"

"I've been approached, warned off if you will, on a couple of occasions by a man with what sounds like a mid-European, or possibly Russian accent. There's no way I know of to contact him. And he's not likely to be in touch with me, is he. Also, I don't know what his involvement is. It's possible he was Letitia's handler. In which case, with her going rogue, he'd have probably had instructions to deal with her. But in such a brutal way? Still, as we know, Russia doesn't waste time with its own dissidents, even if they are generally rather more subtle. Anyway, he's high on my list of suspects."

"Anything more?"

"I've spoken with the two at Maerland da Silva. They're also very much in the frame. Rose will spend some time with them. See what she can elicit. If anything," said Tammy dubiously.

"Rose had mentioned it to me already."

"The thing is, Bob, if it can be proven that those two are the killers, we're left without a reason to arrest and control Oscar."

"That's right. And so…?"

"There may be other factors putting Oscar at the front of the queue."

"Can they be found in time?"

"I don't know. Everything is very touch and go. We're on a knife-edge here in terms of the time available."

"But then, Oscar had both motive and opportunity." Bob was sounding more hopeful.

"Of course he did. A left wing psychopath for a wife. She has to be congratulated for keeping it from him for the number of years she did. Assuming she did? That is, before going completely off the edge."

"I wonder what the catalyst was that finally got her going?"

"God knows. I'm seeing Oscar in the morning. Mrs Gilchrist, my PA, set it up for me. She said he had to be persuaded. I'm not surprised after our last little chat. There's that Cabinet reshuffle tomorrow afternoon. And then I'm seeing someone the day after. That is the morning of the Budget. That'll be my last throw of the dice. If that doesn't work we may find ourselves saddled with a right wing fanatic for a Prime Minister before we know it."

"May I know who you're seeing?"

"Let's not tempt providence, Bob. I'll let you know soon enough if I get a result."

"And how optimistic are you, Tammy?"

There was a long moment of silence while Tammy weighed the odds. Finally she spoke, expressing her thoughts carefully.

"Bob, I have to say, this isn't going to happen. I don't believe we'll have enough evidence to arrest Oscar and charge him with murder in time. We have to be realistic."

"I see. So we'll have his Budget for consolation. Win on the swings. Lose on the roundabouts. MI6 and 5, come to think of it, will need to do all in their power to contain the man."

"Do you think they'll be able to?"

"I don't know," he said quietly. "The alternative hardly bears thinking about."

CHAPTER 73 DAY 20

OSCAR MOUNTFORD'S NEW PA greeted Tammy as she entered the man's office with what amounted to undisguised hostility.

Pippa Southon, a tall, distinguished young woman with blond hair tied back in a pony tail, bright red lipstick, blue horn-rimmed spectacles and an expensive if somewhat incongruous knitted bat-wing sweater, showed Tammy to a chair to wait for Oscar. "Pretty insistent, isn't she?"

"I beg your pardon," said Tammy, noting the woman's aristocratic accent as she settled herself in the proffered seat.

"Your PA. I told her Oscar was busy, didn't have time for interviews. But she wouldn't let it alone. Insisted it was a matter of some urgency. Oscar was even less keen to meet when I told him it was you who wanted this appointment."

She was kept waiting for some forty minutes before she heard Oscar's curt voice over the intercom. "Show her in, Pippa."

Without being invited to, Tammy sat down, Oscar having ignored the offer to shake hands. She was wearing a grey herringbone suit with a black silk scarf. An outfit chosen for what she judged to be the necessary combination of the striking and the business-like. She carried a small clutch bag, but no notepad. This was to be, for all appearances, an informal chat.

As immaculate as ever, Oscar Mountford glanced up from behind his wide desk, the surface totally devoid of any clutter, save a couple of landlines and a pair of mobile phones, as Tammy entered his office. He appeared angry, his shoulders hunched belligerently, hands making fists on the leather top.

"Thank you for agreeing to see me again, Mr Mountford."

"Thank me, nothing," he said aggressively. "I'm busy. I can give you five minutes, no more."

"That's appreciated. I'll try to be brief." She smiled, in what she hoped wasn't too patronising an attitude. "As you are aware, Bob Walker called me in some three weeks ago, at your behest, for someone to investigate the disappearance of your wife."

"Is that it, then? Are you here to tell me what I already know? I don't require a verbal in-person report when an email would suffice. And anyway, my friend Bob has kept me up to date. So, if there's nothing further." He started to get up from his seat.

Continuing as though he hadn't moved, Tammy said, "Your wife seems to have led a somewhat colourful existence, Mr Mountford. Did you know about her patronisation of a club called Rags?"

"What?"

"It's in Sloane Street, near to Sloane Square."

"Never heard of the place. What's it got to do with me anyway? Rags? Sounds none too wholesome."

"It seems when she wasn't being escorted there by either one of your two hedge fund managers…"

"D'you mean Theo? Or Caspar?"

"That's right."

"What were they doing with Letitia?"

"What indeed, Mr Mountford?"

"Don't get clever with me, missy. I can have you —"

"Eliminated, Mr Mountford?"

"That's not what I was going to say. Don't be ridiculous."

"I understand Letitia enjoyed the company of those two gentlemen, often for days at a time."

"So what. She was a free agent."

"Yours was an open marriage."

"You might call it that. I'd call it a failed marriage."

"You could have divorced?"

"It wouldn't have done my political ambitions any favours."

"Neither would the public knowledge that your wife was in the habit of meeting up with total strangers at the club and going off with them for days at a time."

"I had her followed on occasions but wasn't prepared to pay to have her under constant surveillance."

"You could have afforded it."

"I lost interest. As soon as I realised she was a shallow-minded scrubber. She was of no importance to me and no threat to the Party."

"But then that all changed."

"All this Communist crap at university. She had me believing it was a brief flirtation with all sorts of exciting and glamourous people whom she'd dropped as soon as she discovered they were as shallow as she."

"But she didn't drop them, did she?"

"No. Pity the security services let it go. She could be pretty convincing. Fooled me, at any rate. For years. Still, her handlers would have been top-class professionals. Known their stuff and how to keep things covered up."

"She got away with murder."

"In the States, maybe. Not here."

"I'm sorry to have to disabuse you, sir. But she was almost certainly one retained by the Russian Secret Service to discreetly eliminate any troublesome opposition to the Party in the UK, as well as anywhere else deemed necessary."

"You mean she was employed to kill dissidents?" He sounded disbelieving.

"Precisely."

"How long had this been going on?" Oscar had gone white.

"For some years, it seems. But I'm presuming you only got wind of the recent slayings in America?"

"Bob told me. And it was in the press. They didn't link it to me, though."

"You thought it might all be contained abroad, that is, until the rally you helped finance in Trafalgar Square was followed by a further murder by Letitia. Or perhaps someone closely resembling her. This time, not only in the UK, but near to where the rally had taken place." There was no need to tell Mountford of the arrest of Polonia Filipek for the St James's murder. He'd find out in due course.

Oscar remained mute, staring at Tammy as though daring her to go on. So she continued, "That meant now your political career was very much on the line, wasn't it?"

"Nothing I couldn't handle," he grunted. Then picking up the intercom he barked,

"Pippa, bring me a coffee will you?"

Resisting the temptation to make a facetious remark, Tammy said, "And how were you proposing to 'handle it', as you put it? If you felt you might need to?"

"That's my business. Not yours. And now if you don't mind..."

Once more he moved to get up, and again Tammy forestalled him. "Did you kill your wife, Mr Mountford?"

"Don't be bloody ridiculous," he replied. "But I can tell you, I take my hat off to whoever did."

"How about your son Pierce? Did you have him killed?"

"My own son? Are you mad? What father kills his own son?"

"You tell me, Mr Mountford. How about Kevin Anderton?"

"Well, what about him?"

"A member of our security forces. Getting too close to identifying some of your far right friends and activities, was he?"

"Rubbish," he snarled.

"Mr Davenport? Pilot of the plane that let your son fall to his death? He's also been murdered. Seems there's a sort of pattern here, wouldn't you say?"

"This is getting beyond a joke."

"I don't see anything remotely funny here." She sat unmoving for a few moments, then asked, "What about your PA, Georgia Keith?"

"Well, what about her?" He glowered. "She was run down by some hit and run maniac. Presumably the police haven't traced anyone yet?" This time he smiled.

"She will have been privy to a lot of your dealings, wouldn't she? Did she perhaps know too much?"

"Keep trying." He smirked. "Anymore for the Brighton Belle?"

"Do you know someone called Loughty?"

"Who's Loughty? Friend of yours?"

"He and I met a few days ago. Had a minor disagreement. He should be up and about in no time."

"Enough!" he barked.

"Precisely, Mr Mountford. With what the police have, expect to be entertained by them shortly." At this Tammy got up to leave.

Then Mountford, as though persuaded into action, stood up and whispered, "You've got nothing on me, young lady. The police have nothing on me. Not a shred of evidence of any wrongdoing. The PM is my friend. Bob Walker is my friend, and his superior and then his superior. All the way up to the top. I've known the Met Commissioner for more than twenty years. We occasionally meet for a pre-prandial. Police are in my pocket. You see, this country, and most of Europe, is run by the likes of me. Not by the likes of you. Mongrel nobodies."

The hair on the back of Tammy's neck rose. It would be easy, and so tempting, to teach this arrogant bastard a lesson. But there was no way she'd let him goad her into a response she'd later regret.

He still hadn't finished though, seeing she wouldn't be provoked. He went on, "I'm producing the Budget tomorrow. As I've no doubt Bob has let you know. A Budget this country is desperate for. That fool Carstairs hasn't a clue. We'll be well shot of him. When I've delivered my speech, and you see the extent of the international support it'll garner for me—"

"For you? What about the country, Mr Mountford? Or is it all about you?"

"I'm untouchable. Absolutely untouchable," he announced in a note of triumph. "And don't forget what can happen to dissidents, Ms Pierre. Just take a look at what my wife got up to."

It was only when she got outside the building that Tammy fully appreciated the strength of Oscar Mountford's position. With no evidence, beyond the circumstantial, added to which the need for the PM to generate some confidence in both the government and the economy, there was every reason to keep the man in power.

Her hoped-for ace in the hole, MacDonald Smollett, might come up trumps, eventually, with some sort of admission. Even some sort of confession. But they needed that tomorrow morning. At the latest. She'd told Bob she didn't think the evidence could be found in time. She hadn't altered her opinion. Morosely she acknowledged they could be facing the prospect of an extreme right wing PM in days. Right wing? Hell! Bob had talked about neo-Nazis. It couldn't happen.

But then, hadn't the same thing been said about the Second World War?

CHAPTER 74 DAY 21

SHE'D LET HIM STEW since the day before. But it was time to start a last-minute, last-ditch attempt at drawing some of the threads together.

Dialling the number she'd found on that scrap of paper once more, she waited until the line clicked open and there followed a whispered, "Hello? Who are you? Is it you again?"

"Mr Smollett?" Tammy enquired.

The voice was trembling. "How did you get this number? No-one is supposed to know this number."

"Mr MacDonald Smollett, of solicitors Smollett Davis Carleton?"

"What is this all about, and why are you harassing me? If you don't answer I'm going to hang up and complain to the police that I'm being targeted for abuse." The voice was verging on the hysterical.

Time to ease up, she said, "My name is Tammy Pierre, and I'm a private investigator."

"Ohhh nooo!!"

Ignoring the impassioned outburst Tammy went on, "Looking initially into the disappearance of Minister Oscar Mountford's wife. Letitia Mountford."

The voice now recovered some of its composure. "I, I heard her body has been found?"

"That's right. We're trying to ascertain how she died, and of course, who was responsible."

"And you think I might have had something to do with her killing?"

"Good heavens no, Mr Smollett. It's not that at all," she said, gradually reeling him in.

"We just thought that as you're familiar with her husband, any assistance you could give might help us in our investigations."

"Well," he said, sounding more in control of himself, if still a tad uncertain of what was going on. "Anything I can do to help."

Then, as an afterthought, "Shouldn't the police be involved in this rather than a private investigator?"

"Well, of course they are now, but in the interests of absolute discretion I was brought in in the first instance to avoid word getting out. We couldn't afford to risk any leaks, you understand."

"Of course," he added, now on firmer ground. "I do understand. I do."

"I was wondering if we might have a brief chat, Mr Smollett? Somewhere to suit you? Your office?"

"No, no! Not that. Not that!" The voice was losing some of its calm.

"Your home?"

"No. Not there either."

"The New Scotland Yard building on the Embankment is pretty new and quite magnificent inside. Visitors are welcome to come along and take a look around. Would that suit?"

"Scotland Yard? Would that involve my being brought in a police car?"

"No, of course not. Just come under your own steam. Westminster station is about four minutes' walk away."

"Very well, then." The voice was sounding doubtful again. "Might I perhaps bring a friend? You know, for moral support?"

"Yes. I don't see why not. Could you come along today, do you think?"

"Today? Really? So soon? I'm, I'm not sure."

"Of course. I'm being too precipitate. How about to-morrow morning?"

Afraid of frightening him away, she'd allowed Smollett the luxury of thinking he could come in when it suited him. If he refused, however, he'd be brought in, whether under protest or not. She held her breath.

"Ah," he said. "Budget day."

"That's right. If you could make the morning then we'd all be free to watch the Budget speech in the afternoon. Promises to be a corker."

All spoken in as chatty and reassuring a manner as possible. Tammy didn't ask how Smollett knew that the next day was to be Budget day, when the Cabinet reshuffle wasn't due to be announced until that very afternoon.

"Yes, well I suppose the office can spare me for a morning." The voice now was very much more in control. "Could we perhaps make it around mid-morning? Say 11.00 am?"

"Of course we can, Mac. May I call you Mac?"

"Oh please, of course."

"And do call me Tammy."

"I shall, my dear. And where shall we meet?"

"Come into the ground floor reception. I'll brief our delightful doorman. And we'll take you up to the fifth. Lovely views of the Thames from the penthouse floor. Extra comfortable Eames chairs to lounge on. You'll love it. Decent coffee too."

"I shall look forward to it, Tammy. Jusqu'à demain." Then he added, "You sound French, Tammy?"

"Part French, Mac. Jusqu'à demain. Until tomorrow," she returned. "Incidentally, best to be discreet about all this. No need to broadcast it from the hilltops."

"Mum's the word," he said, appearing relieved.

After hanging up she mused, to have brought Smollett in right away, and then possibly arrested him, would have got back to Mountford and spiked their guns, giving him time to address the issue of avoiding arrest himself.

If Mountford was that friendly with all those police sources, there was always a chance he might be able to anticipate Tammy's next move. Equally, leaving the interview until the morning might give a nervous Smollett time to talk to and warn Mountford during this evening.

She just had to hope that either Smollett would heed her advice, or with a Budget to check over Mountford would be too busy to take a call from the man.

CHAPTER 75 DAY 22

THE SUN BLAZED into the reception area of the magnificent riverside New Scotland Yard building.

The architects, Allford Hall Monaghan Morris, had done the Met proud with this building, a mix of the neo-classical and Art Deco styles. The curved glass entrance pavilion on the Victoria Embankment frontage providing light and an impressive welcome to staff and visitors alike.

"Morning, Rose." Tammy had dressed deliberately in casual flared, high-waisted trousers, with a round-neck blouse and bolero jacket. Apart from the pendant, concealed beneath the blouse, she wore no jewellery. The object was to look as informal as possible for the interview with Smollett to, hopefully, give him a false sense of security.

Rose was sensibly turned out, as would be expected from a senior police officer, in her usual working suit. "Hi, Tammy. How goes it?"

"I've slept better."

"You look gorgeous. I've told you, you should be knocking 'em dead on a catwalk not risking your life with a bunch of ne'er-do-wells."

"Sweet of you, darling."

She sighed, taking Rose's arm as they moved towards the lifts. "I could murder a coffee. How much time do we have before Smollett's due?" she asked, glancing at the watch.

"He's here already, Tammy."

She frowned. "Already? He's very early. I thought we'd have half an hour at least before he arrived."

"He's with a friend. I'd guess boyfriend, judging by the way they are together."

"Okay, then," she said, coming to a halt. "Before we go up, where are we?"

Facing Tammy, Rose said, "To recap. We've got Ainsley Borrell placed in a vehicle that ran down Kevin Anderton. He can't deny the presence of his DNA. We have Smollett's mobile number in the same motor, making Smollett and Borrell a pair, I should think. So, was Borrell instructed by Smollett? Highly likely, I'd say. Was Smollett instructed by Mountford? Again, probably. None of it too far-fetched."

"Then Ainsley himself," said Tammy.

"If he's a general fixer, an assassin factotum, if you will, could he be responsible for the murder of Letitia?"

Slipping her hands in her trouser pockets, Tammy added, "Then we've got the Geneva killing. The Pierce connection. Again, it all points to Oscar. But now, what about the little Russian man? Was Letitia getting too out of hand? Was he her handler? He warned me off twice. And there's also this man Loughty. Ephraim Loughty, who attacked me. We need to try to find out where he fits in with all this."

"But, with everything we've got so far, we still have no clear line of enquiry into Letitia's murder."

"We've not yet explored the possibility that Oscar murdered her. I asked him, and of course he denied it. He's an ambitious man with what was a dangerous and unpredictable spouse, but even his daughters think it unlikely he killed her. More likely got someone else to among those we've been talking about."

"Or someone else, not yet in the picture," offered Rose.

"Heaven forfend." Tammy sighed.

"How do you want to deal with this interview, Tammy? Will you go first?"

"I think so. As I've spoken to Smollett already, and come to think of it, persuaded him to come in. If I seem to be floundering, then I'll nod in your direction, and you can take over. If I'm coping and we're making progress we'll not interrupt the flow."

"That's fine by me."

As they stepped into the lift, Tammy said, "Bob tells me the Commissioner's not pleased at the lack of progress. Thinks this whole thing should have been handled by the force, not by someone approved of by the intelligence services. He's not best pleased with Bob, is my impression."

"Worrying," said Rose.

"I don't know what we'll get from Smollett today, if anything. I couldn't judge his mood when I spoke with him yesterday. One moment calm, the next appearing to panic. He'll not lie down and die. That's for sure. Loss of professional status would crucify him, more so than the loss of income. As for the possibility of prison…"

"How much time have you got left, Tammy?" Rose sounded tired, almost beaten.

"I haven't," said Tammy. "This is the last throw. Budget speech today. We need to be in position before Oscar starts to talk. After this, it's goodbye. While I think of it, Rose, I need to thank you for all the help. It's been a pleasure and a privilege."

"Oh, Tammy," she whispered.

But they'd arrived at the fifth floor.

As they exited the lift, Smollett lumbered out of the recliner and, smiling broadly, approached Tammy. A big man, around sixty, with bushy hair and eyebrows, lumpy porridge complexion, he wasn't as Tammy had imagined him. On a warm day, as it was, the three-piece suit appeared a little overdressed.

Extending a large fleshy hand, he said, "Ms Pierre, I assume."

"That's right." She smiled back. "So glad you could make it, Mac."

She turned to face Rosemary and said, "Mac, I've asked Rosemary Sharpe to kindly sit in. She's a DCI," then seeing Smollett pale, Tammy quickly added, "I thought her input might allow us to put this whole thing to bed once and for all this morning. Then we can all go off and watch the Budget speech. If that's acceptable to you?"

"Very well, then," Smollett said, staring warily at Rose, who smiled back at him encouragingly.

"Shall we sit down? And I see you've come accompanied, Mr Smollett."

As they went back to the recliners, which they all unconsciously shifted to the upright position, Smollett indicated his colleague. "This is Freddie. Freddie Harper whom I've asked to keep me company today. You know," he grinned, "moral support and all that."

He was a small man, with what looked like base make-up and eyeshadow applied to enhance his appearance. The relationship didn't require to be spelt out.

Just before Tammy sat down, she enquired, "Coffee, anyone?"

And with requests from Smollett and Harper, Tammy, joining them, was able to maintain the friendly atmosphere in the room.

Finally all seated, Rose, who'd eschewed the offer spoke up. "Okay," she said, trying not to sound too concerned, "we'll make a start. To repeat, I am DCI Rosemary Sharpe, the Senior Investigating officer in the matter of the disappearance and now murder of Letitia Mountford, former wife of the MP Oscar Mountford. Seated next to me is my colleague Tamsin Pierre, a private investigator brought in to assist. May I first thank you for coming in today, Mr Smollett—"

"Oh, please," he interrupted expansively. "Do call me Mac."

"Yes, of course, Mac." Rose sounded a trifle nonplussed but carried on. "You have kindly agreed to come in voluntarily for this interview, which is, as you will be aware, conducted under caution."

At that, Freddie Harper spoke up, clearly alarmed. "Does that mean Mac is under arrest?"

"Quite the opposite, Mr Harper. If you'll let me continue. A voluntary interview under caution simply means the individual will lend what assistance they can to a police investigation. For the sake of completeness and without the need to take extensive notes, the interview is always recorded."

"Rose pressed the record button before we sat down, Freddie," Smollett explained.

"Alright, love," said Harper, apparently reassured.

"As I've explained, the purpose of the interview is to seek any information that will assist us in our investigation into the circumstances surrounding the death of Letitia Mountford. Mr Smollett, I am required to enquire whether you would wish to have legal representation?"

"You will not need reminding, I am a lawyer of some repute."

"Of course. I am required to enquire anyway, but assume you are happy to represent yourself?"

"Absolutely." Smollett beamed.

"As Ms Pierre has been involved in all aspects to this case, I've asked her not just to sit in, but to have the floor for a while. If that is agreeable to you, Mr Smollett?"

"Fire away, Ms Pierre."

Impossible to know what to make of the man, Tammy mused. He's perfectly aware we know of the link between himself and Ainsley Borrell, yet he's willingly agreed to be questioned today. He's also linked to Oscar Mountford as his lawyer.

Difficult to know where to start.

Has Smollett been coerced by Oscar into instructing Borrell to commit murder? If so, what does Oscar have on

Smollett. Further, is Borrell Smollett's only recruited assassin? Again, has Borrell killed others? Are the various other suspects we have simply not involved?

One thing, the only way Smollett could be as relaxed as he appears would be if Oscar had reassured him they were both untouchable.

"Mr Smollett. Mac," Tammy opened. "My thanks to you too for agreeing to come in today to assist. I assume you kept this all confidential, as I requested yesterday?"

"Well, I called Oscar last night, actually. Thought I should keep him informed, as it were."

"You did what?" said Tammy aghast. The realisation that they'd make no further progress if Smollett had appraised Oscar of what was happening made for a lead lining in her stomach.

"I specifically asked you not to, Mac." Small wonder he was so pleased with himself.

"I know, I know. But I just felt he should know."

"And what was his reaction, Mac?" she asked, dreading the reply.

"As a matter of fact, I couldn't get through. I tried all the numbers I had for him, and when I eventually got through to someone, I was told he was busy working on his Budget speech."

Silently heaving a sigh of relief, Tammy went on, picking her way carefully, going for the least contentious questions. "Mac, how would you describe your relationship with Oscar Mountford?"

"We're solicitor and client."

"Mac, did you know a man called Kevin Anderton?"

"The security man who was killed in a hit and run?"

"That's right. Did you know him?"

"No, I read about the incident in the press, but that's all."

"Nothing more?"

"I don't think so. No, nothing more."

"How about Georgia Keith?"

Smollett paused fractionally as he moved the coffee cup to place it on the occasional table next to where he was sitting. "Oscar's PA."

"That's right."

"Pretty girl."

"Nothing more?"

"I believe she was also killed in a hit and run."

"You believe? It was in all the newspapers. MP's assistant mowed down."

"Well, alright, then, I did read something." Smollett beamed, sounding confident. Too confident.

"A similar incident to that which took Kevin Anderton's life."

"Quite."

"Have you nothing to add, Mac?"

"What is there to add, my dear?" Smollett held his hands out as though testing for rain.

"Why the connection with Ainsley Borrell? The similarity in the two manners of death."

"Ah, I see. A problem. But not of my making. And not one I can assist with."

He waited a beat. "I appreciate your line of enquiry, Tammy. But I am the managing partner of a one hundred-partner, fifty-million-pound turnover partnership. You can't possibly suggest I would be in any way able to supply information concerning these two incidents.

"Why," he laughed, "someone will be accusing me of murder before we know it."

Tammy was tempted to make an observation about the cap fitting but demurred. The man was laughing at her.

Still, it was her job to plough on. "Mac, what was your opinion of Oscar's son Pierce?"

"Lovely lad. Bit of a hothead. You know, a risk-taker. Out for thrills wherever he could find them."

"He's also dead."

"Oscar's really having a bad time right now. Don't know how he's bearing up at all."

"Did you know Pierce was investigating his father's apparent far right activities?"

For the first time Smollett appeared a bit uncomfortable, but soon recovering, he asked, "Far right? Never. Not Oscar. You'll be claiming next he is a racist."

"That was the distinct impression he gave me when we met up."

"All news to me, my dear."

Time was pressing and she was making no progress at all. Hopes of an arrest? Pie in the sky. She glanced at her watch. "How about William Davenport?"

"Never heard of him."

"He was the pilot of the plane that left Oscar's son Pierce to fall to his death. Do you remember that?"

Smollett had gone grey. He looked distinctly ill. But she was out of time. The man wasn't going to buckle, no matter how guilty he came across. Oscar had made sure he was safe.

Rose looked at Tammy anxiously. No cause here to make an arrest. Oscar Mountford would be supping a celebratory wine with his Nazi colleagues before the day was out.

"Yes, I do remember," he whispered.

So that was it. Effectively all over. William Davenport, reckoned to be her last shot, had not produced what she wanted. An admission of involvement. Of guilt? The man was disgusting. Beyond the pale.

An idea occurred to Tammy. A last throw of the dice, perhaps? Worth a shot.

"Tell me, Mac, your father. A most respected man in the community. Am I not right?"

Smollett's eyes opened wide with fear for the first time. Tammy seeing Rose glance at her watch, shook her head imperceptibly.

But Tammy went on, "How do you think your father, a religious man, by all accounts; how do you think he'd react if he knew you were homosexual?" It was meant to sound brutal. Gay would have been too gentle. Tammy was in no mood for gentle.

There was a prolonged silence during which Harper looked as though he might be about to come to the rescue. Upon first seeing Harper, Tammy had made the obvious assumption about the relationship between the two men, and pushed the envelope.

But she didn't get the response she'd expected. In fact, there was no response at all. At least, not immediately. Shrugging inwardly, she accepted she'd probably now be pursued for harassment.

Rose checked her watch yet again, and worriedly glanced towards the lifts. But still, Tammy held fire.

There was still no comment forthcoming from either of the two men.

At last Smollett frowned, seemed enraged, as though at any moment he might explode with anger. She'd have to accept she'd badly misjudged the situation. Should have kept quiet.

A single tear coursed down Smollett's face. Tammy stared, fascinated.

The tear became a flood. The man put his face in his hands and sobbed uncontrollably. His whole body shook with his anguish.

"Oscar told me it would all be alright. Everything had been taken care of."

Harper now got up from his seat, and putting an arm around Smollett's shoulder, hissed, "We've heard enough. This is out and out bullying. Come on, Mac. Let's get out of here."

"No, love. You go. I need to talk. I can't live with this any more."

Turning to Tammy, he said, "I'll tell you all you want to know. Starting off, Oscar Mountford is the incarnation of evil. He's got to be stopped. My father would be ashamed. For my own safety, I'd be better off in custody. You don't know what the man is capable of."

CHAPTER 76 DAY 22

BOB WALKER WAS WAITING for her in the public gallery when she arrived at the House of Commons.

She'd entered the Commons via Black Rod's Garden entrance at Number 1 Parliament Street and Derby Gate, rather than using the main public entrance at Cromwell Green in order to avoid any attention. Bob was accompanied by a dozen plain clothes police officers. On the way in, and clearly after Mountford had entered the chamber himself, another two dozen uniformed police officers had planted themselves strategically.

If MPs wondered at the activity, they weren't about to be enlightened. Apart from anything else there was a hum of expectancy over the new Chancellor's awaited Budget which effectively obviated the need for questions over the increased police presence.

On her way into the House of Commons Tammy had witnessed growing numbers of demonstrators clustering around Parliament Square, some with what appeared to be hastily prepared banners proclaiming extreme right wing sentiments. The US contingent had the gall to parade banners announcing white supremacy. If they were hoping to celebrate the triumph of their hero, Oscar Mountford, they were shortly to be disappointed. In side streets she glimpsed a number of parked riot vehicles. Bob had prepared well.

The press in the public gallery gazed with interest at Bob and Tammy. Whatever it was that was going on, they'd learn soon enough. The media had been full of the reshuffle and speculation about why and how the new Chancellor was able to present a Budget within twenty-four hours of his appointment. And further, what the Budget would comprise in the face of a desperate economic downturn.

The long green House of Commons leather benches were spread out like manicured strips of lawn, the place smelling of hide and polish.

As Tammy slipped into the seat next to Bob, he beamed over at her. "Well done, Tammy. Superb work."

"Thanks, Bob, couldn't have cut it any finer. I wasn't sure we'd get a result at all till practically the end, when Smollett finally caved in. It was when I introduced the issue of his father, with whom Smollett clearly has a complicated relationship, that the fortress walls eventually crumbled. But it wasn't just me. The way Rose opened the proceedings was perfectly balanced. Just the right degree of formality and informality to draw Smollett into the web."

"I presume Rose is taking a statement from Smollett now?"

"That's right. And I think we're going to have a goldmine of information. She's going to be busy for some hours."

"Your text said there'd be more than enough from Smollett to warrant our arresting Mountford?"

"More than enough. He's been carrying the burden of Mountford's hold over him for years. It looked as though he wanted to unload everything, whatever the consequences to himself. He knows he's finished as a lawyer. I'm guessing he'll want to square his conscience before he goes to prison. He'll gain the doubtful satisfaction of seeing Mountford, his partnered nemesis, going to prison too."

"You've seen we're ready to deal with Oscar."

"Oh yes, I have. Mountford's not aware of what's happening?"

"No. We brought in uniform after he'd gone into the chamber so he wouldn't be put on notice of anything planned. Just as well we have the numbers. Judging by what's brewing outside I'd say we're ready to nip in the bud any uncalled-for or aggressive demos."

The packed chamber appeared to be settling down, with MPs taking their seats.

Bob said, "You're familiar with procedure, Tammy?"

"Up to a point," she said. But watching Jennifer North taking the Speaker's chair, she asked, "Not the usual speaker, then?"

"No," Bob explained. "The Speaker for the Budget is the Chair of the Committee of Ways and Means. That's the Deputy Speaker of the House of Commons." Facing the Speaker's Chair, Bob whispered, "They're about to start."

In her sixties and highly respected, Jennifer North, a large, bespectacled woman wearing the Speaker's black gown over her white-collared navy dress, entered the chamber and stood in front of the Speaker's chair. Then to roars of approval, she announced, "Members of the House; the Chancellor of the Exchequer."

Bob surveyed the scene intently, gazing this way and that with an experienced police-trained eye, for any signs of disturbance, or otherwise infiltration from undesirables. But seeing nothing untoward, he settled back.

Following Bob's gaze, her eyes fell first on Oscar Mountford, as debonair as usual. Then something unexpected happened. Two members of the Party flanking Mountford, seemingly acting in unison, glanced over at the public gallery, their focus settling on Tammy, where their slate-cold faces told their own story. Then, to Tammy's astonishment, one of them made his fingers into a gun which he pointed straight at her, before mouthing, 'Bang. Bang.'

If anyone else saw it, it attracted no attention or apparent comment. Clearly a devoted Mountford supporter. An extremist like his Chancellor. She wondered what, if anything, Mountford had been saying about her to his colleagues. Infantile. She'd dealt with his type over tea and cakes at Fortnum's.

More pertinently, after the race of the last three weeks to complete the planned operation, Tammy found herself experiencing butterflies in her stomach. The Budget would be unexpected, what followed even more so. Any undue activity would require to be contained. She leaned forward, looking closely at Mountford, who appeared supremely confident. One might almost have concluded, smug. On the despatch box, waiting for the Chancellor's attention, a full tumbler of what looked like whisky.

This occasion was the only time alcohol was permitted in the House, tobacco having been banned completely since 1693. William Gladstone in the nineteenth century drank beaten egg and sherry cocktails. Disraeli favoured brandy with water. More recently, Chancellors Kenneth Clarke and Norman Lamont preferred whisky. While George Osborne and Gordon Brown both stuck to mineral water, as did Rishi Sunak.

The House came to order as Mountford, carrying his file of notes, stood up at the despatch box and arranged his paperwork. Glancing momentarily in all directions as though to ensure he had the attention of everybody present, he began.

"Madam Deputy Speaker, Honourable Members, I suspect many of you will be as astonished as I to find me delivering a Budget speech within just twenty-four hours of having the honour of being appointed to the post of Chancellor.

"Let me begin by thanking my friend the Right Honourable Member for Hampstead South for his stewardship of the economy in these most challenging of times."

Murmurs of "Hear, Hear" throughout the House.

"However, our PM has decided that what the country needs is a fresh approach, a new direction, a difference in emphasis, not that that in any way denigrates the work carried out by my Right Honourable predecessor.

"There are, however, major concerns among the people of this country at what are perceived elements of drift, undermining all efforts to regenerate business and enterprise.

"Accordingly, I am proposing a raft of measures designed to regenerate demand, boost output and increase confidence. In that regard I shall be planning to reduce the burden of many of the current crop of taxes, with details to follow in a moment. But in general, Stamp Duty, which I believe is clogging up the property market; Inheritance Tax, which in my opinion fulfils no realistic purpose beyond robbing already taxed individuals of the right to bequeath their wealth where they choose, and top rate Income Tax, which I propose to reduce to thirty-five percent. Value Added Tax will be reduced to fifteen percent and Corporation Tax, with the example of industry attracted to Southern Ireland, to a level of twelve and a half percent."

At this juncture Mountford paused to let what he'd just said sink in, and take a long pull on his whisky. After a few moments of shocked silence, the government benches rose in a cheer of approval, while the Opposition gazed back in bewilderment.

Standing up, the Speaker announced, "Order. Order. The Chancellor must be allowed to continue uninterrupted." Quiet was unevenly restored.

Tammy, turning to Bob, said, "Well! To use an old music hall expression, 'That should knock 'em in the aisles'."

"I think it's probably done just that, Tammy. Still, if the PM wanted something bold from Oscar, it seems he's got just what he hoped for."

The longest Budget speech in UK history was that delivered by William Gladstone in 1853. It lasted four hours and forty-five minutes. The shortest was given by Benjamin Disraeli in 1867, lasting just forty-five minutes.

Oscar Mountford's speech beat Disraeli's by five minutes, taking no more than forty minutes to complete. There had been some odd references to 'Our friends in Europe', which Bob and Tammy surmised was an oblique allusion to some of the representatives of the extremist groups in Europe that Oscar was confidently expecting to celebrate with that very evening. Those beginning to congregate outside the Houses of Parliament who were starting to whoop and cheer in line with the cheering taking place in the Commons.

Knocking back the last of his whisky, Oscar gazed around him, an expression of triumph on his face, and rounded off his Budget speech with the words, "This is a Budget aimed at improving the lot of all classes and all sectors of our community, and I commend it to the House."

The cheers of approval from the government benches continued for fully three minutes, until Madam Deputy Speaker called the House to order once more.

"How're we doing," asked Tammy, feeling the first flutterings of adrenalin pumping through her system. There'd be the reply from the Leader of the Opposition, after which the plan was to have Oscar arrested and spirited away as soon as possible, and with as little fuss as could be managed. No guarantees it would all go smoothly.

"I think we'd better go down into the lobby ahead of the Opposition leader's response, Tammy. We'll need to be ready. Uniform have instructions to keep the lobby as clear as possible. We plan to arrest Oscar and keep him in one of the offices in the House, until we're sure Parliament Square is quiet, not an easy thing; then we'll move him to the Yard for questioning and if appropriate charging."

"Where do you want me to be, Bob."

"Might be an idea if you stick with me. It would probably be a tacit message to Oscar that his arrest is not mere speculation on our part. He'll link your presence to his apprehension."

"Very well. How will he be escorted to the Yard?"

"To prevent the indignity of a police car or, indeed, a Black Maria, he'll be transported in an unmarked car, which is more than he ever allowed his victims. As long as he cooperates, that is."

They'd made their way down into the lobby where uniform were strategically placed, having moved as many as possible of those congregating there out of harm's way. There was no immediate sense of something about to happen, as Oscar's speech had been fully expected to encourage crowds to turn up.

If Oscar's delivery was brief, the Leader of the Opposition's was even briefer. He spoke for just half an hour, deriding Oscar's appointment and Budget proposals as the half-baked policies of an effete and irrelevant government seeking to recover some plausibility in a rapidly deteriorating economic situation. Nobody, he said, least of all the public, would be taken in by this catalogue of gimmicks. He was met by loud boos from the government side of the House and cheers from his own Party.

Then the debate was over and members started making their way towards the Commons lobby.

Tammy's stomach shimmered again as she approached Oscar, close behind Bob.

The crowds in the lobby, many of whom were his supporters from within the Party, many others from his extremist friends, surged towards him, only to have a mix of uniformed and plain clothes police officers surround him, keeping his admirers at bay. There were murmurs and protests of, "What goes on?" and "What's happening here?"

Oscar, puzzled by the intervention, spotted Bob followed by Tammy, and his eyes narrowed as though in comprehension of what was developing. Tammy could see the man's mind working. His obvious dilemma, to either force his way out of the Commons to the waiting adulation outside and risk the embarrassment of public arrest, or the less controversial option of going quietly with the police.

He opted for the latter, exclaiming, "Bob, old man. To what do I owe the pleasure? And what did you think of my Budget? Pretty damned good, if I say so myself. Hmm?"

"Oscar, you need to come with me," said Bob, affecting a friendly hand on Oscar's shoulder.

"Oh really? And where are we going?"

"We're going for a quiet chat in one of the small conference rooms. If you'd like to follow me?"

Oscar, expression darkening into one of malevolence, muttered, "Something to do with the black you employed, at my expense, to look for my wife? Then didn't find her till she was dead?"

"This is not the time or place, Oscar. Will you please walk with me to where we can be more private? I assume you don't want to attract undue attention out here?"

Stony-faced and without saying another word, Oscar accompanied Bob Walker and Tammy into a nearby small office. Nobody sat down. But Bob now spoke. "Oscar, we have reason to believe you may have been involved in an indictable offence, or a number of offences."

"You can't arrest me here," he stormed, gradually losing some of his composure.

"Actually, I can, Oscar. Arrests are permissible within the House of Commons where it is believed a serious crime has been committed. As a serving MP, and presently Chancellor of the Exchequer, you should know that."

"And so what is it precisely you are proposing to arrest me for?"

"Oscar, at this stage we merely want to interview you, albeit under caution."

"Where?" he fulminated. "Scotland bloody Yard?"

"That's right. As soon as uniform tell us the square is quiet we'll move to the Yard in an unmarked car."

"I'm a lawyer, you know."

"Yes I do know," said Bob.

"Not been in practice since the early post-degree days. I'll want my own man to represent me?"

"Of course. Who did you have in mind?"

"Don't be bloody stupid, Bob. You know who my lawyer is. Do I need to spell it out?"

"If you would please, Oscar."

"God in heaven. I want MacDonald Smollett of solicitors Smollett Davis Carleton. And I mean at the bloody double, man. Do I make myself clear?"

"You do, Oscar." Bob paused for several beats.

Tammy watched as Oscar Mountford directed his hate-filled attention at her. "Fucking mongrel," he spat. Then turning to Bob Walker, said, "Knew she'd be a mistake. Never should have taken your advice. Should have used my own man. Man being the operative word here."

"Oscar, I'm sorry to have to tell you, you won't be able to instruct MacDonald Smollett."

"Why the hell not? It's my choice who I use not yours. Or hers," he railed, making as though to approach Tammy.

"I think not, Mr Mountford," said Tammy softly. "Why don't we try to keep this all civilised?"

"Civilised? Civilised? What the hell do you Afros know about civilisation?"

"You know you're not doing yourself any favours, Mr Mountford," replied Tammy.

Turning to Bob Walker, Mountford said, "My friend Commissioner Wallace won't be best pleased when he hears about this. Your career may be in the skids, Bob. Have you thought of that?"

"Oscar, Commissioner Tom Wallace already knows about this. I informed him before coming to the House this afternoon. And you're right. He's not best pleased. Particularly not at the idea a long-time associate of his might have been involved in a murder. Or murders."

"Murders? Murders? You're talking through your backside. I'll deal with both of you in due course. Meanwhile what's this crap about my not having Mac represent me. He's my choice. He's who I want. And I bloody well insist on him. So, you tell me why I can't have him speak for me? And it better be good."

"Because, Oscar, MacDonald Smollett was arrested this morning on multiple charges of murder and being an accessory to murder. He's presently in custody, having given us an extensive statement involving your recent and past activities, as well as his own."

Oscar Mountford had turned deathly white. He looked as though he might throw up, shrinking visibly as Bob and Tammy watched. Then, gradually recovering himself and standing erect, he said, "We'll see about that. We'll just bloody see about that."

Bob Walker had turned away for an instant, and in that moment Oscar Mountford, in an echo of his colleague's recent gesture, made his hand into a gun and sneering, pointed it at Tammy's head.

CHAPTER 77 DAY 23

"TAMMY, YOU'VE DONE brilliantly, but do be cautious. It's not in the bag yet." The smile in his voice could be heard down the phone. "You still need convictions. As you well know, they could be problematic."

She was seated at the breakfast bar at home, a steaming coffee planted next to an enormous bowl of muesli, the wholewheat toast already quartered with its various Marmite, peanut butter, cheese and honey awaiting her attention, together with Risky contentedly munching down a breakfast of chopped chicken and ham. In the background Alexa was playing Stravinsky's *The Firebird*.

Beams of sunshine slanted into the kitchen echoing her mood, motes of dust floating around randomly.

"I know," said Tammy.

"In fact, being realistic, the evidence against Mountford is either circumstantial or from a questionable source, namely Smollett, and or, frankly, inconclusive."

"Okay," Dov added. "So, you're not being over-optimistic. That's good. Of course, there is a chance he could walk free. Not a happy prospect."

"I am aware of that possibility too," Tammy responded, feeling a little of her upbeat start to the day begin to flag slightly.

"We've only got Smollett's word to go on, and is anyone going to place much credulity in that? What would a jury make of a respected lawyer claiming his client coerced him into organising a number of murders? Scarcely credible."

"And there is one more thing, Tammy. I don't have to remind you, there's still been no resolution to the murder of Mountford's wife."

"The continuing mystery." She sighed, idly moving the muesli around the bowl with her spoon.

"Has to be Oscar, though. Who else? He had motive and opportunity."

"We both know that won't be enough to convict. He'll put on a sad face for the jury, and without any concrete evidence he'll walk free there too."

"So, where to from here, then?"

"I'm talking to Rose this morning. She'll have taken statements from both Mountford and Smollett. She is very thorough and extremely competent. Whatever she manages to get from those two will hopefully give us something to work on."

"Isn't it all supposed to be down to the police now?"

"I suppose. But Bob hasn't taken me off the case, although the original brief to find Letitia has been fulfilled. I might as well carry on as I've been so involved up to now."

"But basically, Tammy, there don't seem to be any other avenues to explore."

"Well actually there are. I've got names like Ephraim Loughty, if he could ever be located. The two hedge fund managers, Caspar and Theo. They definitely need to be questioned further. I think Rose may have some info there.

"Then we've got the man with the Russian accent. There's no way I could find him. But the police? Although, nothing from them on that front so far. Bob did say he'd look into that avenue.

"Then we've got Ainsley Borrell. A real possibility. There's even a chance, with what he's been up to, that Smollett might be directly involved. Although, with him unloading to Rose, if he'd admitted to the murder of Letitia, Rose would have called me. No matter what the time."

"Plenty to keep you busy," Dov said, a note of doubt creeping into his voice. "Where will you start?"

"I want to know more about Oscar. What makes him tick."

"Money makes him tick, Tammy. That's the beginning the middle and the end of it."

"If his wife's Socialist commitment had become public... You see, they'd have accepted her as a Labour supporter. But for a minister of the government, a would-be Chancellor to be exposed as being married to a Communist? That would have ended his political career."

"Absolutely," Dov agreed.

"Before I start examining the obvious suspects, I want to find out about the man himself."

"Why not talk to his daughters again? No-one's been closer to him than they. See what they can provide in the way of information."

"My thoughts too, Dov. I'll chat to all three. Up to now they may have been protecting him, saying little. Once they know he's in custody, if they want him out and truly believe he's innocent of his wife's murder, they should really be willing to open up."

"Are you going to try and catch up with them today?"

"I don't see why not."

"Keep me in the loop?"

"Of course."

Then, sounding somewhat hesitant, he asked, "Dinner tonight?"

She let him wait several beats, before saying archly, "Okay, Dov! I don't see why not."

"You're a bloody monster, Tammy," he breathed. "One of these days..."

It was his turn to pause.

"Yes, Dov? One of these days?"

This time he let her wait.

A count of ten, then, "I might ask you to marry me."

Her immediate response was, "No you won't."

"I won't?" He sounded surprised.

"That'd make you a bigamist, darling boy."

CHAPTER 78 DAY 23

"MACDONALD SMOLLETT is one of life's victims," said Rose, comfortable on one of the recliners on the fifth floor with her notes spread on her lap.

Unexpectedly, she went into a prolonged bout of coughing before taking several heaving breaths, settling herself and then continuing. "He attracts the world's bullies."

The bright start to the day had been sustained with a blaze of sunlight illuminating the penthouse floor of the New Scotland Yard premises.

Wearing casual denims and a coral sweatshirt, Tammy paced the floor chin in palm, listening to Rose's resumé of the statements she'd secured from the two men in custody. It made for startling listening.

Starting with Smollett, a man in awe of his father's achievement in building Smollett Davis Carleton into the massive enterprise it now was, Tammy's inspired question about the father's likely reaction to definite knowledge of his son's homosexuality, was the catalyst that broke open the dam of Smollett's pent-up conscience.

From there the information poured out in a Niagara of revelations. There was his father's disappointment his son never married. An acknowledgement to himself that Smollett for all his competence as a lawyer, had none of his father's drive, ambition or vision.

Then there was the bullying. One of Smollett's partners had some years ago guessed at his proclivities, and deciding to capitalise on it, began blackmailing him. At first small sums, then in time growing bolder, the demands becoming more and more outrageous.

Finally, Smollett was forced to borrow. And for that he turned to his firm's client's account for funds, something that was on the Law Society's list of the absolutely forbidden.

Despite trying to hide the transactions, things were being noticed and questions were being asked, word began to get around between the partners, and Smollett, desperate to correct the perceived 'book-keeping errors', turned to his client, the mega wealthy MP Oscar Mountford. Mountford lent Smollett what was required. Monies were discreetly repaid. Questions stopped, and Oscar let the blackmailing partner know by various means that if he played any more of his games, to be sure his and his family's life assurance was all in order.

From Smollett's point of view he was out of the frying pan and into the fire. He would now be for ever and a day at Oscar Mountford's bidding. And didn't Oscar make hay? Of course, Smollett didn't carry out Oscar's dirty work himself. At least he hadn't in the past. The running down of both Kevin Anderton, the security man, and the PA, Georgia Keith, were, as had already been established, the handywork of Ainsley Borrell.

Oscar never enquired how or where Smollett had found Borrell, he merely made the cash available, which he was delighted to learn would be surprisingly little. The man was clearly underselling himself.

Arranging the killing of Pierce through the pilot, William Davenport, involved Smollett in more detailed planning. Oscar had become apoplectic when he'd discovered what his son was up to, and had no hesitation in planning the young man's demise.

That left the loose end, namely, Davenport himself. This was the only murder committed personally and specifically on Oscar's orders, and by Smollett himself. This more than any of the other killings, showed Smollett how far he, a respected lawyer, had sunk.

He'd been unable to work for some time after the killing, and went so far as to contemplate taking his own life. But accepted, ruefully, that he didn't even have the courage to do that.

Finally, Smollett was unable to shed any light on the killing of Oscar's wife, Letitia. He agreed, Oscar had every reason to want her dead. He loathed her, her politics, her lifestyle, her obsession with the lad David. But nothing he'd come across in any way suggested an involvement in her death. And there the statement, signed and witnessed, concluded.

Although not part of the statement, and not relevant to present proceedings, Smollett did offer to provide a wealth of detail on some of Mountford's other, much earlier 'business' activities which he'd kept under cover, either through ingenuity or bribes to the police. Apparently the headings included money laundering on an industrial scale, people trafficking, arms deals and drug running.

"Wow!" said Tammy. She'd quit pacing the room, and looked admiringly at the DCI. "Quite a mouthful. Well done, Rose. Another coffee? Let's take five, shall we?"

The penthouse floor had a pleasant ambiance lending itself to a casual intimacy. Thinking back once more to the sticky start they'd made to their relationship, Tammy concluded it was now one of mutual respect.

"So," Tammy broke the silence, "Oscar Mountford."

"Oscar Mountford indeed," Rose responded. "After raging on about not being able to have MacDonald Smollett represent him, he brought in at short notice James Heathcote, the eminent QC, to sit in on the interview.

Frankly, he's admitting to nothing. He knows we can't keep him in custody for more than twenty-four hours without further court sanction. We could apply for an extension, as you're aware, for up to thirty-six, or even ninety-six hours, but his QC is calling for his immediate release on the grounds that we haven't a shred of real evidence, beyond what he calls the spiteful testimonial of Smollett."

"You are going to have to let him go. That is before he starts suing for wrongful arrest."

"He'll be lucky," said Rose, adding, "this is not wrongful arrest, and he's not the wrong person. No, we'll have to let him go later today. But for now, we'll let him stew and rage for the maximum time we're allowed."

"You got nothing further from Theo or Caspar?"

"Nothing. And again, we've not enough there to charge them. What about you?"

"I'm going to go back to the girls," said Tammy.

"To see if there's any further light they can shed on their father's personality, behaviour, contacts. They seem to have a mixed attitude towards him. Davina is very fond. Jayne is somewhat in awe. Juliet appears to hover between love and hate. Best if I can have a chat before Oscar gets out and starts muddying the water."

"Will you try to see them all today?" asked Rose.

"Absolutely. If I can. I'm not sure what their work schedules are."

As they both sat back on the recliners sipping their coffees, Rose, studying Tammy, asked, "Tammy, do you mind if I ask you a personal question?"

There was only one question Tammy imagined Rose might want to put, and she wasn't to be disappointed. "Sure," she said. "Go ahead."

"Are you...? Are you...?"

Deciding to help her out, Tammy said, "Yes, Rose, I am."

"Pregnant?"

"Pregnant."

There followed several moments of silence, then Rose asked tentatively, "Is it Dov?"

"Rose, it's complicated."

"I'm listening."

"Okay. I hope it's Dov. We were together just before Syria."

"Okay. Understood."

"And then in Syria, as you know, I got shot. I'm not sure what happened while I was drugged. Asleep.

"But the man that saved my life might have helped himself to a reward when I wasn't aware of what was happening."

"You mean, rape?"

"I suppose. Technically, perhaps. I'm confused about the whole thing....

"He saved my life, then got killed. I find it hard to classify what happened with the brutality I've always assumed accompanied rape."

"Do you want the baby?"

"More than anything."

"Will you tell Dov?"

"Only if I have to."

"Your father?"

"Papa is fantastic. He knows, and just wants me and the baby to be okay. Even pointed out that Islam reads the Old Testament like we do."

"You're lucky. I'd have liked kids. Still," she sighed, "some things aren't meant to be."

"I'm keeping my fingers crossed it'll all work out." She paused for a beat, then as if struck by an idea, asked, "Hey, Rose?"

"I'm here."

"I've had a thought. Would you like to be my child's godparent?"

"Oh, Tammy." Rose burst into tears, unable to speak for several moments. "I'd be so honoured."

Then, thinking about it, she timidly asked, "Do you have godparents in Judaism?"

"No. But Papa would be so pleased. And I'm sure the Lord won't mind."

CHAPTER 79 DAY 23

TAKING THE MOBILE from her ear and ending the third call she'd just made, Tammy said, "You probably heard, Davina is finishing up with clients and will see me at the family home shortly. Juliet will take time out of work to assist and Jayne's already at home. Got a day off work. That'll be a start. Anything they've got that can help."

"Say, Rose," she asked, the notion suddenly occurring to her, "would you like to come along with me? See if you can think of anything I might have forgotten when we talk to the girls? You know, two heads et cetera."

"Sure. I've no immediate commitments," Rose agreed.

"I've just got this nagging feeling something is being held back. I want to follow a train of thought. It may lead nowhere, but worth a punt if we're going to get anywhere near finding Letitia's killer.

"Juliet is the biggest puzzle. She talks with contempt about her father in one breath, then gives the impression she likes and admires him in the next. I want to know more about Theo and Caspar. Juliet can fill in some gaps on that front.

"And hang on a minute." Tammy, who'd been pacing again, stopped abruptly. "I've just had another idea. I wonder if William Davenport was involved in any way. He dealt with Pierce. Killed him, after all. Smollett never mentioned him specifically in connection with Letitia's murder, and there was no reason why he shouldn't have. I suppose Oscar could have got Davenport to deal with Letitia. Trouble is, we've little chance of proving anything against him now he's no longer around."

She glanced down at Rose, shrugging that they'd got no further. Then said, "Rose, if you're fit, we'll take my car if you like?"

"I'm fit. Let's go, then."

Oscar lived in a magnificent eight-bedroom red-brick 1930s property on Hampstead Garden suburb's Winnington Road. Close to Hampstead Golf Course, Hampstead Heath, the Spaniard's Inn pub and Kenwood, famous for, among other things, its summer open air concerts. The house, in its dream location, would be worth several million. Where Bishop's Avenue that ran parallel, the original millionaires' row, now sported an array of, some would say, ghastly oversized and overblown kitsch edifices, Winnington Road retained its elegant reserved charm.

Entering the carriage drive, Tammy noted two other cars parked and guessed that Davina and Juliet were there ahead of her.

"To be honest, I'm not sure what the girls can contribute," said Tammy. "But we're somewhat scratching around for ideas right now, and insofar as they're willing to help…"

"Absolutely," agreed Rose.

The interior was every bit as sumptuously appointed as the exterior was understated. Tammy gained an impression of bookcases, Art Deco and Renaissance art, bronze and marble statues and, as in his office, Persian rugs and antique furniture. It all had the smell of furniture polish and potpourris, several of which were dotted around the place, together with vases of fresh cut flowers.

Having been shown into the main living room, apparently there were several, Tammy and Rose settled back into comfortable modern sofas, the other three girls arrayed in easy chairs opposite them. Jayne had, in the short time available, thoughtfully prepared bowls of mixed heated nuts, cocktail sausages and Japanese snacks, including gyoza dumplings with an assortment of fillings.

"You've gone to far too much trouble, Jayne." Tammy smiled as her mouth watered.

"It's no trouble, really," said Jayne, handing round the selection, together with tiny plates and napkins.

"We're only here for a few minutes. Still, I won't say no."

"Me neither," added Rose.

Excusing herself for a few moments, Jayne returned with a trolly bearing a large pot of tea, a cafetière of coffee and a selection of soft drinks.

Before Tammy could remonstrate, Jayne said again, "It really is no trouble at all."

In between mouthfuls of food and drink, Tammy started to explore what further information the girls might be able to provide. What she managed to add to her present knowledge was pretty minimal.

"Girls, you don't mind me bringing Rose, do you? I confess I'm casting around for ideas and inspiration. I thought Rose might be able to add her two penn'orth."

No-one objected.

"Fine, thanks. So, Davina," Tammy enquired. "Did you ever meet Theo Cranfield, or Caspar da Silva?"

"Nope," she replied. "Theo was Juliet's muse, and apparently Ma's as well. I saw neither him, nor his partner."

"Juliet? What do you think? The two have admitted they were involved with Letitia, occasionally in threesomes. They're both noted in the area at about the time of Letitia's death. A sex game gone wrong?"

Juliet shrugged, stretched her long legs, then drew them back and crossed them. The same provocative display. "Theo always was a greedy shit where sex was involved. I wouldn't have been enough for him. I don't know. I suppose anything's possible."

"Jayne? Anything to add?" Tammy asked hopefully.

"Nothing," said Jayne, shaking her head in the girlish way she had.

"Any thoughts, Rose?" Tammy asked.

"Not really," she replied. Then addressing Davina, Rose enquired tentatively, "How's business, then? Are you still designing jewellery for wealthy Middle Eastern clients?"

"Yes," said Davina, brushing some stray crumbs from her jeans. "Very much so. I certainly couldn't rely on my macho breadwinner at home to earn enough to buy a single white sliced bloomer. Let alone pay the mortgage."

"You busy at work, Juliet?" Tammy asked.

"Always. Whether it's regular trade or sale time, we're always rushed off our feet. My boss is a stickler for detail. But as I am too, it suits me fine."

"But you like it, don't you?"

"I love it," said Juliet.

"How about you, Jayne? You teach at the College for Autistic Children in Chelsea, don't you?"

"That's right."

"You must find it very rewarding."

"Oh I do. I really like it. Although the Head there doesn't seem to understand very much about the children and their special needs."

"And you do?"

"Of course. Read a book called *The Spark* by Kristine Barnett. It tells how, by encouraging her autistic son Jake and other youngsters to do what they wanted, rather than what they were told, she could gradually bring them out of their isolation."

Tammy could sense the fervour and was surprised at the maturity in one who looked and sounded so young, despite the impression the girl generally conveyed of withdrawn timidity. She might almost have been one of her own students, were it not for the passion she displayed in promoting her ideas.

"You looked after David a lot of the time, didn't you, Jayne?"

"He was lovely."

"You and your mother spent most time with him."

"I did," she said shortly.

Tammy wondered what more there was. Jayne seemed unsettled. Unhappy. So she gently pressed on, hoping to probe a bit deeper. Ask, and let matters take their own course.

"Was there something I need to know, darling? Was your mother less committed than you, Jayne? Did she take the credit for your efforts? Was that it?"

Jayne looked down at her hands in her lap. Tammy watched the girl's expression, so frail and vulnerable. Still, Tammy was working a hunch Jayne might be able to help with. No more than a gut feeling. An instinct. It just needed patience, a chance to draw the girl out. Find out what she could offer.

Jayne said nothing for a full minute. Tammy, catching Rose's eye, shook her head almost imperceptibly; a hint to say nothing. The other two girls seeing the gesture, glanced at each other puzzled, but also kept silent.

Then Jayne spoke hesitantly. Softly. She might have been a fawn lost in thick woodland, groping for a way out. But she was on her own, no-one was going to interrupt the young girl's chain of recollections.

"Mama didn't really like Davie," she murmured. Everyone in the room exchanged surprised glances. Jayne carried on undeterred. "She pretended to love him. But I knew better. He was hard work. A heavy burden. But Mama had other things on her mind. She was always away, having fun, I suppose." Jayne paused before continuing, hesitantly, like one groping in the dark.

"And when she was away, that's when David did best. Came out of his shell. More and more. I saw Mama with him when she didn't know I was peeping. She was always short-tempered with Davie. She used to pinch him on the inside of his thighs where it hurts most. She'd get angry with him, over nothing and slap his head, so there'd be no bruises. He'd run to me crying. He'd say, 'Why? Why?' and I'd hug him. Hold him. She made him cry, and it made her laugh." Jayne's voice was beginning to rise.

"She didn't love him. She hated him. Mama hated Davie. I was the one who loved him, I was the one he loved. Dada didn't want him around but accepted him because he knew I loved him. Knew I loved David."

Her eyes still trained on the hands in her lap, Jayne composed herself before going on. Tammy still said nothing. No prompting. There was that sense of something important about to be revealed. Something that would help unlock some of those closely hugged family secrets.

"It was just before she disappeared," Jayne went on cautiously. "As we now know to America, and she was in a funny frame of mind. She was tetchy. Irritable. Tired. Acting as though someone had lit her blue touch paper and she was about to go up. No-one wanted to risk upsetting her. Being the trigger that allowed her to let rip.

"David was being difficult, fractious. He had been all day. Mama was getting ratty, as though a nuclear explosion was about to happen. She poured him a bath, and practically dumped him in it. He squealed because it was too hot. That was the thing that finally set her off. I was coming to the bathroom. Stopped outside. David was quiet. I didn't know what was happening. I peeped around the door. She had his feet in her hands, pulled up, his head under the water." Jayne was weeping by now, tears coursing down her cheeks.

She went on, "I just screamed. Then fainted. No-one was home when it happened. When I came round, Mama was standing over me. 'David had an accident,' she said. 'Darling, he slipped in the bath.' She was sobbing. 'He's gone, darling. Gone.' She acted as though distraught. *Am I going mad?* I thought. I know what I saw. The doctor pronounced him dead. I was given sedatives and spent the next few days in bed. I couldn't believe it. Couldn't believe what I'd seen. She'd killed him.

"Either that or I was going insane. Having hallucinations. But no, I thought, I wasn't having psychotic illusions. I knew what I'd seen, and I was going to confront her. Then, before I could, she'd gone. Gone off to America, we now know. Just like that.

"About seven or eight weeks after she first disappeared, she reappeared. Without warning. No idea where she'd got to, until you told us about the States, and later, what had been going on there.

"She'd been back a very short time. Another day? The house, empty, apart from Mama at home. Juliet at work. Pierce away somewhere. Dada in the office. Mama in the bath, humming to herself. Happy. Just weeks after David had died. No time at all since she'd killed him. Humming as though nothing had ever happened. I pushed open the bathroom door. Overcame my doubts and fears. I knew what I'd seen," she repeated.

A ripple of unease in her belly, Tammy's throat constricted, like hands pressing in. She barely breathed, as though the merest whisper might block Jayne's narrative.

"You killed him, I said. YOU FUCKING BITCH. YOU FUCKING KILLED HIM. She laughed at me. The cunt actually laughed at me. 'So, what are you going to do about it, honey? Hmm? Tell your Dada?'

"I'll tell you what I'm going to do about it, I screamed, and I rushed forward. She was still laughing when I grabbed her ankles, the same way she'd grabbed David's, and I pulled her feet up out of the water. Her head went under, just like David's, and the water rushed up her nose. She went unconscious almost immediately, died quickly after that. I stood staring at her body for, I don't know how long. I was in shock. It had been so easy. Too easy. I'd needed more, much more. Wanted to see the bitch suffer."

Juliet and Davina gazed at each other uncomprehendingly. Both women were weeping. Still Tammy counselled silence. Jayne hadn't finished.

"Then I got the hammer from the tool box in the kitchen. She was dead," said Jayne, now speaking quietly. "But I was going to punish her for all she'd done to David. I hit her with the hammer." She waited for several seconds before looking down yet again at the backs of her hands. "So I made her pay," she said with a determined deliberation. "I bashed her with the hammer. Over and over. It still wasn't enough. So I went on. I don't know how long. There was a lot of blood. Gristle, bone. It felt good. Really good. I wasn't sorry.

"Then Dada came home, and I told him. I knew he'd be angry. Dada has a terrible temper. He scares people with it. I'd overheard Dada on the phone to people. A few times.

"I knew he was involved with killings. It gave me migraines. But who could I tell? I wondered what he'd do. What he'd do to me. I was frightened. I wanted to run. There was so much mess. So much blood everywhere.

"But he wasn't angry. Not at all. He said, 'Leave this with me, darling. I'll deal with it all.' He cleaned up everywhere. Bleached everything in the bathroom. The floor, the walls, the bath. There was blood everywhere. It looked like what it was, a slaughter house.

"Then he dressed Mama in a white blouse and those ridiculous harem pants they found her in, which he got from her wardrobe, and he took her body away. I never saw it again.

"Dada's funny. He hates disability, like David's. But he'll sometimes go out of his way to help people he sees as weak. Like me, I suppose.

"I love Dada. Is he coming home later?"

EPILOGUE

MULLING OVER the individual outcomes, Tammy, in her nightdress, feet up on the sofa, sips from her tumbler of vodka, a rare indulgence these days. A hard-won success, she muses. But a success, nonetheless.

Oscar Mountford –

At his trial, as expected, Oscar Mountford had pleaded not guilty to all charges of murder, including those of his son Pierce; Kevin Anderton, the security man; his PA Georgia Keith and William Davenport, the pilot of the plane his son Pierce had leapt from. His defence that he knew nothing of the murders and that MacDonald Smollett's testimony was pure fabrication failed to impress the judge or jury. He was duly convicted of conspiracy to murder and sentenced to life imprisonment with a recommendation he serve not less than thirty years. On the separate charge of conspiring to prevent a proper burial taking place, he was convicted of the lesser crime of perverting the course of justice and sentenced to a further five years in prison, sentence to run concurrent with the life tariff. He was taken down raging at the judge and jury, claiming a vast injustice had been enacted, and declaring his intention to appeal. The search for Letitia's missing body parts is ongoing.

Jayne Mountford –

Jayne had pleaded guilty to the murder of her mother, but her counsel pleaded loss of control, previously known as extreme provocation. The judge took a sympathetic view, bearing in mind the crimes of both the parents may well have had a bearing on Jayne's state of mind, notwithstanding her not relying on a plea of murder while the balance of her mind was affected. Also, he took into account her guilty plea. She was sentenced to the minimum, three years imprisonment, suspended for two years. Breaking down in tears when sentence was declared, she was free to leave the court. Her overjoyed sisters were there to accompany her home.

MacDonald Smollett –

Agreeing to turn Queen's evidence, he entered pleas of guilty on all counts of murder, together with conspiracy to murder, laid at the door of the blackmailing, Oscar Mountford and a further conspiracy to murder with the involvement of Ainsley Borrell. Furthermore, it was his spectacles found at the scene of William Davenport's killing in Geneva, damning in itself, whatever his plea might otherwise have been. Notwithstanding his cooperation with the Crown, MacDonald Smollett was sentenced to life imprisonment, with a recommendation he serve not less than thirty years. He is well aware he will die in prison. Curiously, when sentence was announced, Smollett appeared calm, almost relieved. And that odd cryptic call on Tammy's home line? Of course, the accent, MacDonald Smollett, fruitlessly warning her off.

Ainsley Borrell –

Also turning Queen's evidence, Ainsley Borrell pleaded guilty to the murders of Kevin Anderton and Georgia Keith and was duly given a twenty-two year sentence. He claimed that at no time did he know anything about the involvement of Oscar Mountford.

Polonia Filipek –

Had entered a not guilty plea to murder claiming diminished responsibility, in that the powerful influence of Letitia Mountford impeded her ability to make a rational judgement. The jury were shown CCTV of Polonia at the Trafalgar Square demo and at the hotel she took Toby Trimble to. She was found guilty of murder with sentence deferred pending psychiatric reports. In due course she was sentenced to sixteen years in prison. Her mother, in the public gallery, broke down sobbing when sentence was announced. Polonia just appeared white-faced and confused.

DCI Rosemary Sharpe –

The detective and Tammy, after a shaky start, had both found friendship and mutual esteem for each other. Tammy has been saddened to learn Rose is undergoing tests for suspected lung cancer.

Davina and Juliet –

The girls are having to come to terms with the knowledge of Jayne's occasional unpredictable bouts of rage. Jayne has become withdrawn. Working at the College for Autistic Children is a challenge that helps her come to terms with how she sees herself. The principal seems to have a new-found respect for her and her methods. Not altogether surprising.

Dov Jordan –

Dov is embroiled in a nasty divorce from his wife Esther. He still doesn't know for certain the child she is carrying isn't his, although, sadly, he suspects as much. He consoles himself with the hope that tests may eventually confirm otherwise.

Tammy –

With the assistance of the capable Mrs Gilchrist, her PA, Tammy is finally catching up on the masses of accrued correspondence and emails and using the aftermath of this investigation to enjoy some early nights as her wounds continue to knit and heal. Sadly, she has had to accept her hands will never be as beautiful as they once were. She is pragmatic about that.

Detective Chief Superintendent Bob Walker has reported fully to the PM and Home Secretary. The outcome is all that could have been hoped for. Tammy will dine with all three as their guest in the House of Commons restaurant in the near future.

Aspects of the case continue to run through Tammy's mind. The US pathologist talked of traces of detergent on Letitia's body. It puzzled her till the penny dropped. In

America, unlike the UK, the terms detergent and soap are used interchangeably. It was soap, not detergent, on Letitia's body and in her lungs. From the bath she'd been drowned in.

And then, what of the purple harem pants Letitia's corpse was dressed in? The same as Polonia was wearing when she attended the Trafalgar Square demo. But Oscar couldn't have known what the double would be wearing before he dumped Letitia's body, any more than he could have predicted Jayne would kill her mother in a random attack. So, coincidence, then? Or had it been the intention of the two women to confuse even more, retaining a pair each, one of which had been found at home by Oscar after Letitia's return, then pulled on to his dead wife's body, maybe as a sick joke?

Though no longer important, the issue of the date of Letitia's return to the UK had been pinpointed by Incognita as four days before her corpse was reckoned to have been dumped, that is five days before its discovery. It seems she returned on a hitherto unknown Russian passport under the name Larissa Filipek. Dates of her use of her credit card in the UK have assisted. Polonia, not on the same flight, had presumably followed on.

The pregnancy continues and the anticipation of motherhood gives Tammy much joy. The vodka remains in the drinks cabinet, untouched; most of the time. Unlike today, the temptation for a celebratory drink, a bit too much to ignore. The panatellas are discarded. The stash flushed away. She wants a strong healthy baby. If it's a boy, she will call him Matty, after her adored father. If she has a daughter, she will be Pascale, after her beloved maman.

The thought of Georgia makes her wince as she's pierced with guilt. She's overcome with the knowledge she pushed Georgia too hard, too far. There is no saving grace. It was an unforgiveable error of judgement. It will remain for ever a ghost drifting behind her eyes.

What of Jayne? A timid teenager, until roused to fury. Always the quiet ones that hold out the biggest surprises.

Tammy was right in that instinct Jayne might be involved, though she'd be the first to admit in no way could she have predicted the outcome.

She visualises Dov, it makes her happy. He would like to live with her, to marry her. Maybe it could work, she thinks. But could he put up with her philandering? She seeks variety. Like a drug. All the time. Even now she recalls her reaction to Juliet's blatant display. The micro-mini, edging ever higher. The challenge represented and her pulse quickens.

Her only real issue is what and whether to tell Dov, if it ever becomes necessary, that the child she's carrying isn't his. He'll be greatly saddened, and she balks at the prospect. It will wait for now.

Ephraim Loughty –

He hasn't been seen again. Tammy will keep an eye out for him, the man was humiliated by her and may seek to redress the balance.

The little man with the NHS type glasses who attempted to warn her off –

He's out of radar view at present. Was the Soho murder of an unidentified little man her stalker? Or were the broken spectacles a plant? She's probably not seen the last of him.

*　*　*　*　*

She yawns, comfortable in the plush armchair, the tranquilliser she swallowed earlier beginning to kick in powerfully, bolstered by the vodka. Not a good idea to mix the two. But she is so deliciously relaxed. Once can't hurt. She strokes Risky behind the ears and anticipates sleep as she ponders the case and those involved, only vaguely becoming aware of an unexpected, thundered hammering at the door of her flat.

It's not Dov, she decides. He now has a key. The person, whoever it is, has somehow got past the security of the front door to the block. Her own door has a Banham lock and two security chains. She senses problems. Big ones. Glancing up at the CCTV screen, one of several in the home, she sees a tall cadaverous presence in the hall immediately outside her apartment, the grey face, with its sunken cheeks, she recognises immediately, despite its being largely obscured by a hoodie. And is that a shadow she sees behind the figure? Or could it be a second smaller individual?

She knows she should try to clear her brain, but the usual adrenalin punch that sustains her at times like this is missing. The sedative isn't helping either. Her eyelids are drooping, leaden, and her injuries are throbbing in time with the beating of her heart, exacerbated by the recent stabbing in America and the older bullet wounds at her neck and thigh, suffered in Syria. The hypnotic ticking of the lovely French ormolu antique clock on her sideboard lulls her further. Now her head sags forward till her chin touches her chest. Fatigue turns her bones to rubber, her muscles to sponge. She should be on alert she knows, but can't summon the energy. Leave me alone, she thinks. The cat is attentive, ears pricked up, sensing her mistress's disquiet; she hisses softly. But it's late and her owner is weary, longing for sleep.

In the flat, by her bedside, she keeps a Desert Eagle Mark XIX semi-automatic pistol made by Magnum Research. Recently given to her by Dov, it fires the largest centrefire handgun cartridge of any magazine-fed, self-loading semi-automatic firearm in the world. It would stop an elephant. If the man can gain entry to the block that quickly she'll not have time to retrieve the weapon. And why has he bothered to knock at all? Not to warn her, that's for certain. To give her time to consider what is about to occur? To prolong the agony, perhaps.

The pulsing of the clock is louder now, more insistent. A thrumming of disjointed sound behind her eyes.

She feels quite alone. An island in a hostile sea. She is seated in her living room, the door to her own hallway is shut. The empty apartment is closing in on her, stifling her. A steel band around her chest makes it difficult to breathe. The residence feels cold. Fingers of ice trail up and down her back, and she shivers uncontrollably.

The situation has already evolved beyond her command; she is powerless to do anything about it. Glancing distractedly this way and that, she stares at blank nothingness. This time Dov will not be there for her. Her charmed existence has, at least in part, been due to him and his cool assessment of situations where she's been inclined to charge in blind. That all too close call in New York.

Now she hears soft laughter, "Heh, heh, heh," and her heart rattles in her ribcage. A shuffling of feet. The man's already gained silent entry to her haven. Her sanctuary. Of course, idiot, she forgot the security chains at the entrance to her property. A fine PI, she. He, or they, are now on the other side of the living-room door. A heartbeat away. There'll be no time for offers of hospitality, none of the usual pleasantries. Even in her semi-befuddled state she hasn't entirely lost her sense of irony.

Realising, all too clearly, how this is going to play out, and her apparent powerlessness to do anything about it, produces a muttered observation. "Loughty." Of course, who else could it be? Here to level the score. She'd hurt him that time in Queen's Park when he'd shot at her. Hurt and humiliated the man. Challenged his masculinity. The knife she'd plunged into his thigh. He's picked an opportune moment. She needs to focus, focus, focus, but is finding it impossible.

The insistent tapping of the clock reverberates inside her skull like ricocheting lead shot. Still, she sits motionless, as though paralysed. Blessed sleep is what she craves. If only she could…

The muffled laugh, again. Manic. Jubilant. But this time not Loughty's. There are two of them. She was right.

And so she waits on. But for what? The end? A witness to her own demise? Papa will be devastated. And Dov won't be impressed. Darling, darling Dov. The one man she'd always hoped to affect with her cool competence and ability. "Where are you, my love," she murmurs. "When I need you so much. My God!"

The cat is agitated now, senses impending danger, her fur bristles and she emits a low growl, with ears flat back she scratches her mistress's hand drawing a bead of blood, provoking a response.

A belated prickle of adrenalin. Like pins and needles in the tips of her fingers. Eyes wide open, she's emerging from the fog, at bloody long last, willing herself to become clear-headed and functioning. But this time it'll be too late.

A surge of enquiry occupies her mind, brows knit in concentration.

The clock is silent. It no longer beats its whispered rhythm.

In moments it will all be over. "Heh, heh, heh." The laugh is familiar. She's heard it before. The wire-rimmed spectacles. Not dead after all. She readies herself for the endgame, knowing it is the finish for her.

A plane rumbles overhead, the sound reverberating around the room.

The cat settles at last, as though she too is resigned to the inevitable.

Her mistress looks bleak, but a faint smile plays at the corners of her mouth. Finally. Alert. She looks around, as though stirring from a dream. This might be interesting after all. She sets the cat down. Survival may not be an option, but she'll give the bastards a run they'll remember. Then sighing grimly as the room tilts before her, she lurches unsteadily out of the chair, ready to greet her visitors.

END

ABOUT THE AUTHOR

IN HIS "DAY JOB" PROFESSIONAL CAREER, handling bankrutpcy and corporate liquidation matters in London's business environment, Andrew Segal gained extensive experience with people and organizations pushed to the limits, including financial ruin and threats of violence.

In his personal life, he learned much about Caribbean culture from his ex-wife's mixed heritage.

He brings that knowledge to bear in creating his main character in this series, private detective Tammy Pierre. She's an ex-police detective, whose work now includes both criminal and "forensic accounting" cases. Skills and experience from both realms, combined with Tammy's imposing physical attributes and specialized martial arts training, helped unravel devious schemes and deal with dangerous villains in *The Lyme Regis Murders* and *The Black Candle Killings*.

He raised the stakes for Tammy and the world in this book, adding eerily familiar political extremism to the criminals' motivations. Now turn the page for a preview from his next Tammy Pierre thriller:

The Clubhouse Slaughters

Little boy blue, explosions at dawn
As ye sew so ye'll reap,
It's not you that they'll mourn?

But where is he now, who treats life so cheap?
Why, he's setting those timers to wipe out more sheep.

— R.A.

PROLOGUE

3 AM. THE SCREAM OF TWO monster motors bellowed their challenge to duel, a pair of night-time predators.

A freezing night of deserted roads in Oxford's town centre. A white faced, full moon reflecting eerily on the shining surface of icy puddles in the city's many potholes; spectral, blind eyes, making motoring treacherous. A sparkle of hoarfrost, sugar coating parked vehicles in streets too narrow for the two racing supercars to squeeze through unscathed. Insane driving, inviting catastrophe.

Empty pavements, apart from a few late-night wandering pedestrians, partygoers, nightshift workers, breathing vapour, staring speechless as the two vehicles raged past them.

The two-seater, 6.5 litre, 789 bhp, Ferrari 812 Superfast, a flash of elegant red, weighing 3362 lbs, swooped past. Emerging from a side street, Private Investigator Tammy Pierre's brand new, supercharged, 621bhp, Porsche Panamera Turbo S in a typhoon hail of gravel.

With a top speed of 211 mph or more, the Ferrari could climb from nought to sixty in 3.0 seconds. She'd seen this car before. Only recently, she'd duelled with it. The same car? Had to be. Not too many of these super cars around.

Tammy's more practical, 4.8 litre, heavier at 5290 lbs, four door, four seater, silver car would reach sixty, unofficially in about 2.6 – 2.9 seconds, but it's top speed, at 196 mph would fall short of the Ferrari's by some 15 miles per hour, her car's smaller engine carrying the greater kerb weight.

Overtaking the Ferrari would require all of Tammy's skills. Accompanied on this chase by long term colleague, her ex Met boss and mentor, Detective Chief Superintendent, Bob Walker, her vehicle's heavier payload might yet prove useful.

On Israeli Secret Service Mossad's discreet advice, having kept a low profile throughout the investigation which was not their brief, they'd tracked the Superfast through ANPR and CCTV images over a number of weeks, never getting anything other than blurred images of the man they were trailing. Even when he was out of the car, he was still too far distant to secure a clear picture.

All they knew was that he was probably Middle Eastern, as evidenced, if nothing else, by the company he kept and the clothes he wore. Sort of loose, cropped harem trousers with collarless placket cotton tops, usually in khaki, but sometimes in plain white. And always with a black taqiyah, or skull cap. His only other distinguishing feature was his height, which was slightly greater than those with whom he mixed, so that he usually stood out in a group.

Also, worth noting, a man answering Eckstein's description, had been seen looking into the Ferrari, talking to the driver. Again, the positions had occasionally been reversed with the Eckstein lookalike being the driver. Impossible to know by whom the luxury car was owned. Unsurprisingly it carried false number plates.

Today, neither Tammy nor Bob could clearly discern who the passenger might be; at a guess, the tall Middle Eastern gentleman spotted by Mossad?

But both Bob and Tammy knew full well who the other man was, the driver. After all, hadn't he recently fled their presence? The balloon white of hair distinctive. Dexie. But if this was his car, how could he possibly afford it on his presumed wage?

Swerving at breakneck speed through the town centre, the red car, slamming into a power glide, ignoring the 40mph limit, roared on to the A34 outer ring road heading north, from where they'd almost certainly be aiming for the M40 at junction 9, the Wendlebury interchange. A distance of no more than 8 miles. They'd be there in bare minutes, that is, if Tammy's instinct still held good. At 68 miles to their next main junction off the M40, the M42 would lead them to the M6 thence into Birmingham, barring accidents. At the speeds they were travelling, they'd cover the distance to Birmingham in about 30 minutes. Another 110 miles to Blackburn would take no more than 45 minutes.

Eckstein, who lived in Blackburn, had mentioned he had a lock-up in Birmingham, but Eckstein wasn't in the car in front. And while the driver might be seeking to shake them in Birmingham, if he didn't succeed, Blackburn was, she felt sure, his only final option. But then, if she was wrong, did this pair even know where Eckstein might be right now? Or was this all a blind alley?

"They will be making for Blackburn," Tammy observed quietly. "Sure of it. Somehow Eckstein is involved and these two will be looking to him for help."

"It's a long way to their destination, Tammy." Bob sounded doubtful.

"Yep," she shrugged. And with their speed they'll ultimately be leaving us behind."

"Do you think you can catch them before they hit the M40? You've hardly got the time."

"We'll have a problem if I don't."

She didn't sound optimistic, neither did she feel it. But she was geared up for the hunt. Taut as a bowstring. Despite her earlier failing exhaustion, she felt a renewed adrenalin rush and smiled to herself as she urged the engine towards its capacity, her palms clasping the wheel light as a lover's caress. Realistically it was unlikely they'd overhaul the Ferrari, but for her, not entirely profession-ally, it was all about accepting the challenge. Too exciting to ignore. She felt the back of her neck prickle; onward, she decided, whatever the consequences.

The Ferrari taking a bend too quickly, crashed its nearside flank into a row of illegally parked cars producing a hollow crackle. Tammy took the same corner using better judgement and gained on the car ahead. There was still ground to make up. Bob breathed a sigh and reached forward, a hand on the dash to brace himself as Tammy squeezed through the mercifully thin, slow local traffic, slaloming left and right like a speeding skier, trying not to lose sight of her prey.

She flicked on the wipers as a thin smattering of rain spattered the windscreen. "That's all we need," she said. "It'll make the roads treacherous."

Bob remained mute, his fists clenched.

The direction of the pursuit had been based on no more than a hunch. A hunch the driver would be making for what he considered to be safe ground. Bob Walker had agreed with her. Blackburn, the city. Eckstein, the man. She'd been positive she'd been right, and they were on a trail now, the right one, the individual motoring at a rate suggesting something close to panic. They'd lost him when he'd first raced from them but had made up time with her driving and his ignorance of how close she was to him. He was no longer ignorant, as reflected in his lunatic manoeuvring.

One thing was certain, however; he was their target, Eckstein's plant. The driver. Had to be, or else they were back to square one.

"You know you'll never overtake him Tammy," Bob advised quietly.

"I don't intend to. He's got the speed. I've got the acceleration. Anyway, I've got something else in mind." Bob looked perplexed but made no further comment.

"M40 junction ahead," said Bob. "What next?"

"I'm thinking," she muttered, watching the red car gain distance, the gap between them widening as the two made the M40.

"We are going to be outrun," Bob muttered. "He's too fleet."

The wipers smeared the screen as they settled into their rhythm, and Bob asked tentatively, "Should we, maybe ease up a bit?"

Pressing her foot harder on the gas, she said, "We need traffic now. There's not enough here for us," she added, pushing the Porsche to 140 mph, the howling of wind in the vehicle's slipstream more pronounced, in response to the Ferrari's burst of speed.

"Traffic?" Bob glanced at Tammy, alarmed.

"If there's nothing in front of him, there's nothing to slow him down. That's how he'll escape us."

"Wow!" breathed Bob as the car ahead made for the tightest of channels between two cars, practically straddling the middle and overtaking lane, getting it wrong again.

"He's mad," murmured Bob, as the Ferrari was hammered on both its sides, sustaining further damage as the carbon fibre bodywork showed fine but visible cracks. But it was through the gap, barely slowed and now surging to 170 mph.

"Not good," said Tammy, her heavier car momentarily matching the lighter Ferrari's speed, like a lion chasing gazelle. The chase would be limited if the bigger beast failed to quickly capitalise its short-term advantage.

"A single car in front of us now, Tammy, then it's all open road ahead." Bob, agitated.

"Don't panic," she said quietly.

The car immediately ahead of them, a lumbering black SUV, seeing the menacing red motor in its rear-view mirrors shifted from the centre lane to the nearside gifting the Ferrari access to a clear and uncluttered road.

"Damn! We're losing him," said Bob, shaking his head in frustration, as Tammy floored the accelerator pushing the silver car to 180mph.

"Maybe," she said, her palms dry, focus sharp.

The two cars were past the black SUV, engines roaring, exhausts billowing, the red car having barely slowed, but still, allowing Tammy the briefest instant when her greater acceleration brought her briefly alongside it, her nose actually in front.

Then, "You're easing up, Tammy? Why?" Bob stared at her. "Empty road in front. We might have had him."

She saw the flashing image of a crumpled wreck, an explosion and ball of flame. Her car? A premonition? The truth, seconds away. Then she'd know.

"You could be right," she sounded angry. "We just needed a moment, that was all."

"Do you think…?" Bob started but was cut off as the red car, using its greater speed, eased forward, its nearside rear wheel dangerously levelling with the Porsche's offside front, rim to rim, the two vehicles practically touching.

What happened next happened very fast.

"Last chance. No! We're gonna be too late. Dammit. You were right, Bob," she breathed, the wheel gripped hard. Knuckles white. Glancing to left and right, a final futile check. All clear.

"NOW!" she shouted, as Bob looked on aghast while she deliberately rammed the Porsche's offside front end into the Ferrari's nearside rear, wheels crunching against wheels, the ominous sound of carbon fibre breaking up, coupled with a metallic screeching of her own car's aluminium, titanium bodywork as it was torn into.

"Christ!" called, Bob, sounding alarmed for the first time. "You'll destroy us all."

The two cars were momentarily trapped together, rearing like stampeding horses that might topple at any moment, before scraping untidily apart.

"Watch what's going down now," she said, softly, slowing the silver car further, while the red, its rear end forced to the right, its nose to the left by Tammy's gambit, careered forward, out of control, heading straight for the safety barrier on the hard shoulder, unimpeded by any stray motors.

The shriek was jagged, terrified. Sounded clear. But, a woman? A man? Someone beyond the edge of reason?

"They're going to crash. My Christ, Tammy they're going to crash. What've you done? They'll be killed at their speed," Bob cried out, anguished. "Madness! Madness!"

"Not necessarily," she replied softly, continuing to brake, the Porsche now completely under her control. "Although no great loss if they were," this last under her breath.

A second of silence. A lull. Unnatural. Endgame beckoning.

They both heard the thunderclap, as the Ferrari hit the barricade, collapsed and broke up, with bits of eggshell bodywork flying off in all directions, the vehicle still retaining something of its overall integrity. Moments later the silver car skidding in a cloud of dust and pebbles, was brought to a stop by Tammy on the hard shoulder, 300 yards further on.

"Where the hell did you learn how to do that?" Bob whispered, clearly shaken.

"US cops. It's safer than trying to overhaul a car ahead. Our weight gave us a slight advantage." She sounded as though she did this sort of thing on a regular basis.

"Their car looks like bits of jagged Bakelite. How can you sound so relaxed? Do you think they've survived the crash? Not possible, surely." He was registering confusion. Unusual for someone generally as cool as Bob Walker. But then, it wasn't every day he enjoyed the benefits of Tammy's reckless risk taking.

"Let's take a look," replied Tammy, as if it were of little consequence either way, leaning back to see through the rear-view window, reversing the Porsche, until they were parked in front of the ruined Ferrari. Parallel black skid marks traced the vehicle's path from the motorway impact to the safety barrier. The red car's doors had burst open, whether at the behest of the pair inside or a result of the collision, couldn't be clear. Otherwise, there were splinters of red carbon fibre all over the hard shoulder looking like sprays of blood. Maybe it was blood.

Bob frowned, distinctly uneasy, as he heaved himself out of the Porsche, and made for the red car, "I dread to think what we've got here, Tammy. God willing, no corpses."

She was close behind him, a considered expression on her face. Time to assess the damage.

Two bodies. Both men. That scream? A conversation with death.

The passenger was slumped forward, his head sideways against the steering wheel, his eyes wide open. Something about the man struck a chord. Couldn't put a finger on it. It would come back to her. But still, alive, just. He caught Tammy's gaze and spat, "Infidel!"

On the other side of the car, Bob gazing in, had gone deathly white, "Oh no! My God, Tammy. My God. It's horrific. It looks as though the man is decapitated."

"What?" she replied.

"Decapitated. Decapitated. Do you not hear me, Tammy?"

CHAPTER 1

THE PERMANENT UNDER SECRETARY to the Minister of Defence, Norman Cutler, a dynamic, pink-cheeked, besuited little man, who seldom seemed to sit still, faced his auburn-haired wife, Phoebe, in the dining car of the Northern Region Train as it sped towards Edinburgh for the family's first holiday together in five years. Phoebe wearing her usual travel outfit of, grey two-piece suit and white blouse, looked happy. Happy and contented, as well she might, having finally persuaded her workaholic husband through a cocktail of bullying, cajoling and the promise of an excess of sexual favours, to take the break he so badly needed.

The vacation had been further encouraged by his friend and parliamentary colleague, the erstwhile MP and 'Chancellor for a day,' now, astonishingly, convicted murderer, Oscar Mountford.

They say, still waters run deep. But who would have believed it of a fabulously wealthy highflyer like Oscar? He'd even been tipped as a future PM, but at the trial, had been revealed as a mover and shaker involved in a number of extremist far right groups, characterised by the term, alt.right. It would be some time before Oscar would be able to enjoy a furlough with such of his friends, if any, that still existed.

Next to Cutler was his five-year-old daughter, curly haired, Milly, in her new birthday pink frilly dress, giggling with every opportunity at anything and everything. On the table in front of her, thoughtfully prepared by an accommodating rail company, a small cake with five candles just waiting to be lit.

The train rumbled on, it's rhythm gently accompanying the family's festive mood.

Opposite Cutler and next to his wife sat their older daughter, Poppy, in her Paddington party dress. At seven years of age, she'd largely taken over responsibility for Milly, berating the little one when she didn't use her knife and fork properly, and generally finding every possible excuse to otherwise boss her adored younger sister.

Reaching forward with the gold Dunhill lighter his wife wished he'd ditch, along with the twenty a day habit, Cutler applied the flame to each wick till the circle of five candles flickered together like a group of medieval country dancers.

"Norman," said Phoebe, suddenly fretful, "I've just thought. Did I pack my sponge bag?"

"Check your case after we've eaten, my dear. All up there on the rack. I'm sure I saw you pack it, though."

"Okay, darling," she smiled, reassured.

A family of three, that is parents and a young son no older than Milly, at the table on the opposite side of the gangway, looked over and smiled indulgently. They had that, 'going on holiday' look about them too. Casually dressed and relaxed. The boy, a tousle haired lad in shorts, a check shirt and a cowboy hat, whispered, "Can I talk to the little girl, mum?"

"Yes, Jimmy," replied his mother, softly. "As soon as they've finished with their birthday song, coming up about now, I should think."

As if on cue, and turning his attention to his youngest, Cutler said, "Why don't we all sing Happy Birthday to our Millicins,"

"I've got my case, daddy," interrupted Milly, looking up at her father. "See here," she said, eagerly pointing down with a chubby pink finger, to her khaki rucksack on the floor in the gangway.

"So you have, little one." Then glancing over his daughter's head, he added, looking interested, "Are you sure that's yours Millicins? It looks a bit big to me. I wonder if you picked up the wrong one when we were getting our tickets."

"It was heavy," said Poppy. "I know, 'cos I picked it up for Milly."

The Cutlers had married late, and at age forty-five doubted they'd ever have children. Norman's commitment to what was amounting to a highly successful Civil Service career meant there was little time or energy to think about family. So, they'd been overjoyed when Phoebe conceived and Poppy was born, and were, they knew, now doubly blessed with the arrival of the talkative and cuddly little Milly.

An undemonstrative man, Cutler nonetheless viewed his family with enormous pride and affection. Sitting in that train carriage with the three women in his life he felt his heart being squeezed with love for them.

Winking at his wife, and taking her soft, extended hand in his own, Cutler said to his youngest, "I wonder what could possibly be in it, Mills. Not birthday presents. Surely?" Milly was squealing with delight. 'Come on now,' he grinned. "About time. All of us, let's sing Happy Birthday before the candles burn down and set the place ablaze."

Still the train rumbled on, it's rhythmic pounding lulling the family into a delicious state of soporific apathy.

But Milly couldn't wait for the song to end, and, unzipping the bag, went, 'Weeeee!!! All for me?'

"All for you darling, Millicins."

Then, "Phoebe," Cutler added, peeping into the bag, before turning to his wife. "My dear, weren't you looking for your travelling clock?"

"No, I found it before we left," she replied, relaxed and smiling, as the sun blazed through the windows of the carriage, accompanied by a volcanic explosion and the white heat of a blast that blew the carriage and two families to shreds.

Printed in Great Britain
by Amazon

57549435R00280